AMERICAN BETIYA

ANURADHA D. RAJURKAR

ALFRED A. KNOPF
NEW YORK

For Piyush,

for a love that feels like freedom.

And for Ajay and Avi,

for revealing how deep love can go.

THIS IS A BORZOI BOOK PUBLISHED BY ALFRED A. KNOPF

All rights reserved. Published in the United States by Alfred A. Knopf, an imprint of Random House Children's Books, a division of Penguin Random House LLC, New York.

Knopf, Borzoi Books, and the colophon are registered trademarks of Penguin Random House LLC.

Visit us on the Web! GetUnderlined.com

Educators and librarians, for a variety of teaching tools, visit us at RHTeachersLibrarians.com

Library of Congress Cataloging-in-Publication Data
Names: Rajurkar, Anuradha D., author.
Title: American betiya / Anuradha D. Rajurkar.
Description: First edition. | New York : Alfred A. Knopf, [2021] | Audience: Ages 12 & up. |
Audience: Grades 7–9. | Summary: Eighteen-year-old Rani, a budding photographer, grapples with first love, family boundaries, and the complications of a cross-cultural relationship.
Identifiers: LCCN 2020025033 | ISBN 978-1-9848-9715-2 (hardcover) |
ISBN 978-1-9848-9716-9 (library binding) | ISBN 978-1-9848-9717-6 (ebook)
Subjects: CYAC: Dating (Social customs)—Fiction. | East Indian Americans—Fiction. |
Family life—Illinois—Fiction. | Illinois—Fiction. | India—Fiction.
Classification: LCC PZ7.1.R346 Ame 2021 | DDC [Fic]—dc23

The text of this book is set in 11-point Berling MT.
Interior design by Ken Crossland

Printed in Canada
March 2021
10 9 8 7 6 5 4 3 2 1

First Edition

CHAPTER ONE

He's my mother's worst nightmare. His intricate tattoos and the way he's been covertly studying me from across the gallery would give her palpitations for sure. *Dude does need some manners,* I think as he stashes away several damaged portfolio sleeves before glancing over again. Avoiding his gaze, I turn to arrange my glossy artist's statement cards. Seriously. Who is this guy? I take a long swig from my water bottle and attempt to refocus.

It's my first-ever Gallery Night opening, and I'm still in shock that I was invited. My photographs—the ones I took with my grandfather in India last summer—pop against the burgundy walls. Artwork is hung floor to ceiling, and modern sculptures on pedestals are strategically placed and uplit like deities. I submitted my photos to this student art show on a whim, and amazingly, they were chosen. Framed, polished, and practically art, they're gleaming images of India that I can't stop looking at, despite having seen them a thousand times before.

Across the room, the guy's eyes flicker to me again, and I flush when he catches me looking. I pretend to study a nearby sculpture. If only I could lurk behind my camera lens, I'd avoid all this nonsense. I need to recenter: *I am calm. I am confident. I am legit.* A fresh stream of gallerygoers comes pouring through the double doors, and I brace myself, flashing my brightest smile: some of them I know a little too well.

Close family friends I call my auntie-uncles spill in like a wedding baraat minus the horse. A sight in the prim atmosphere—a crowd blinged out in jewel-toned saris and yellow gold—they're Indian Standard Time late but quickly make themselves at home. Calling my name, they come barreling into my corner, the aunties shrieking as they kiss and hug me, the uncles raising their glasses in a toast, having already somehow descended upon the nearby refreshments. Eyes flicker to us, some shining in wonder, drinking in the scene, and others bemused, like we're a comedy.

I love these guys, but God.

"Proud you're showcasing our India with these photos, Rani," Veena Auntie says, chucking me under the chin while making a smooching sound. "Goodness knows we need more representation in the arts." Veena Auntie is my artsy auntie— she's a potter when she's off dental duty—and probably the only one who gets the magnitude of my being here. I squeeze her hand.

A dozen auntie-uncles now cluster around me, chatting and ignoring the artwork. And then—as if there's not enough of a scene—my parents bustle in. Baba shuffles across the gallery floor, hands in his pockets, while peering at the pomp and circumstance of an event devoted to something as self-indulgent as art. Beside him marches Ma in a blazing coral sari—one of the favorites she wears for Indian parties. She scans the gallery critically, a Mumbai mama bear ready to take out anyone who messes with her family.

God.

They arrive at my exhibit, and my mother's hands butterfly about, finally settling on my hair. As she twists a wild lock behind my ear, I glance in the guy's direction. Despite a significant crowd by his exhibit across the gallery, he's doing what he does best—staring, like we're rare birds.

"Did you get enough to eat earlier, betiya?" my mother says.

Baba makes a quick sweep of my photographs, jingling change in his pocket. "Nice photos, Rani." He jabs a finger at the one of my grandfather grinning from the rust-colored steps of a crumbling temple. "Ay, I thought *I* took this one." He winks at me.

The next hour's a full-on visual and noise extravaganza—an Indian party in my tiny nook. Pratap Uncle tells an admittedly funny joke at top volume, and Baba throws his head back and belly-laughs. Indu Auntie is wearing too much rose oil, the floral scent gripping us in the fist of its power. A couple of aunties knot and arrange my scarf while launching into a barrage of questions: Would I be willing to convince their kid to apply for an internship at the hospital, or consider Hindi lessons, or take AP bio next year? Mira Auntie whips out a bright pink lipstick and begins dotting it on my lower lip, saying to the others, "Ay-yo! She's now our very own Amrita Sher-Gil!" When I ask who that is, she looks at me in surprise. "The famous Indian painter? Like the Indian Frida Kahlo, no?" She scans my face, and I shrug deeply, a bratty

3

American. She turns to the others and announces, "We are failing our youth, yah! Even Rani here knows nothing of our India—shame on us."

My mother asks me a couple of times about my homework situation, all the while keeping every human within her vicinity under close surveillance. Her gaze settles on the guy across the room, and her face fills with concern as she takes in the stark branches etched along his arms.

God.

If only my grandfather, my aajoba, could appear. He'd find a way to distract my mother, saving me as always.

But my best friend, Kate, appears instead. She waves cheerily to the auntie-uncles before touching my mother's arm. "Mrs. Kelkar, hi!" She hugs my mom tight, then appraises her, holding her by the shoulders. "You look gorgeous," she says, fingering the cluster of tiny seed pearls that clings to my mother's earlobe. "You know I'm giving Rani a ride home, right?"

My mother's eyes light up. No adult on earth can resist Kate's charms. "Thank you, betiya," she says, beaming. (Case in point: non-Indians are never addressed as "betiya," a term of endearment reserved for those you consider daughters—my mother would gladly adopt Kate if possible.) "Auntie-uncles are coming for dinner at our place tonight. You come, too, yah," my mother demands in her special way.

"You guys head back and party," Kate says, grinning. "When this is over, we're so there. I literally cannot wait to taste your parathas."

They are magic words. As Kate flits off to talk to Mimi and her grandmother the next exhibit over, my parents and the auntie-uncles finally line up and file out, hugging me again and telling me congratulations and how much they enjoyed my "sweet little pastime." I thank them, smiling and waving at the receding chaos before slumping onto my stool in silent relief.

"Quite an entourage." It's him, leaning against my wall like freaking James Dean. He tugs on his silver-studded earlobe and gazes at me with that weird-but-weirdly-flattering intensity. I've totally seen him before.

"That's a generous way of putting it," I say, and immediately feel guilty. Why am I slamming my family and friends to this random stalker guy?

He grins, raising a silver-hooped brow, and holds out his hand. "Oliver Jensen."

"Rani," I say, grasping it. It's dawning on me who he is. His hand is big and warm. Not that I notice.

"Rani," he says, trying it out. "Dang. Great name." Slipping a hand into the frayed pocket of his jeans, he returns to his James Dean lean against the wall. A faint blush rises in his face, undercutting his veneer of cool.

"I think I've seen you in the Arts Wing. You—you're a senior, too, right?" I say, as though I don't already know the answer.

Oliver nods. "Yeah. And if I could live in the Arts Wing, I would." He rubs his head, his hair sticking up in dark tufts. He looks at me straight on and smiles, and despite myself, I see something in that smile, something deep and wide and real.

You will not fall for this clown. I twist my mess of silver rings.

"I love your work," Oliver says, studying my photos. He

steps closer to the one of my aunt swinging from the hanging roots of a banyan tree. "Where was this taken?"

"Near my grandparents' place. Pune, India."

"Amazing that you've been to *India*," he murmurs, scrutinizing my other shots. "Immersion in a culture like that . . ."

Pushing my hair from my face, I tug at the scarf the aunties knotted tight at my throat.

"Man. This one," he says, peering at the photo of my grandmother standing before a string of shanty shops. "The light's refracted in a way that highlights the irony here."

I nod like he's onto something, but really I have no flipping idea what he's just said.

"Those women sweeping garbage behind your—is it your grandma? Their colorful saris create this, like, brilliant juxtaposition . . ." He trails off, studying the shot.

"Yeah, I was really angling for all that when I took it."

He scans my face, and whatever he sees there breaks him into an embarrassed grin. "Sorry, that came out super pretentious." Heat flushes his face again. "Anyway. You must know these kick ass."

"Right," I laugh, heading toward his crowded gallery wall. "Why do I have a feeling that there's no comparison here?"

Oliver trails me to his exhibit, and we stand before a collection of his paintings, suddenly enfolded in the lush fantasy of a Hobbit world, beasts and beings live and thriving upon linen canvases. There are at least fifteen frameless pieces, hung as if by happenstance. They look lit from within, like the loose, uncut rubies I once raked through at a Mumbai jeweler's—precious and raw.

"Yeah," I say, "these are not terrible."

Rocking on his heels, he stares down a group of nymphs in a flowering forest. I think about my meager snapshots and flush. But he mutters, "Whatever. Demons, gargoyles . . . mundane shit."

"Wait, what? But these colors, your technique—"

"Rani. Anyone can learn that." He leans in like he's sharing a secret. "But what you've got there?" He smells like fresh herbs and soap. "It's so relevant and, like, *of the moment.*"

A couple of beats and then . . . I can't help myself. I grab the pencil from behind my ear—when getting ready at home, I decided it made me look "artsy"—and air-scrawl in my palm. "My . . . culture's . . . 'relevant . . . and . . . of . . . the . . . moment.' Got it."

His eyes trail over my hair, down to the hollow of my throat, where the sterling amulet from my cousin Shalini rests. They flicker to my hands—my bitten, bare nails. I fidget, twisting my rings as I glance toward the exit.

Is he mad that I mocked his compliment? Possibly that was too much. The truth is, I have no experience with guys, for the following reasons:

1. I've been too busy studying, working like a dog toward my goal of one day becoming a pediatrician like my aunt Lalita Mami.

2. My strict-ass parents—whom I love and adore but who obviously drive me crazy—don't allow me to date. They're even uncomfortable with the notion of guy friends. Seriously.

3. I've had zero opportunity. No guy's ever really seen me *in that way* before. I've always chalked it up to the fact that I'm not athletic enough or hipster enough, political enough or chill enough, theater enough or edgy enough, Black, white,

Latina, or even Asian enough. ("What . . . are you?" is the banal but offensive question of the decade, the inquirer's eyes examining my too-long nose, my brown skin, and the heavy brows that I refuse to have threaded, out of sheer laziness. . . .) The point is, at a school like Frances Willard High School, despite the student body being super diverse, there's still only a tiny minority of South Asians. I'm not enough of anything to be seen or assigned, and I've half accepted that.

4. I am a fan of self-preservation and have built spiky walls around my heart.

Despite how badly things seem to be going, Oliver says, "I'd totally get it if you say no, but would you maybe want to hang out sometime?" The gallerygoers have wandered off. He does an ear tug before shoving both hands deep into his pockets. "I mean, I'd love to know more about your photography. We could talk art, like nerds. Or I could bore you with all my obvious and myriad flaws. Um. Or we could just hang while you regale me with . . . whatever *you* wish to regale me with?"

Maybe it's the hidden layers he's unearthed in my photography, or it's his smile, hesitation and earnestness and a tinge of desperation all captured in this moment's portrait. Maybe it's that his pickup lines are spectacularly bad, or that for the first time ever, someone is actually fascinated by the things that make me different. Maybe it's because he used the word *regale*. Twice.

"Mr. Larson lets me eat lunch in his art room," he continues uncertainly, rubbing at his dark stubble.

Maybe it's the fact that there's this tension between us, like the kind of renegade art that demands you sit up and take notice. The kind that teeters precariously between light and dark and makes you uncomfortable in the very best ways.

Some kids I recognize from school come sauntering toward Oliver's exhibit. "Oll! Hoooooly shit! Your collection is shrooming!" Oliver actively ignores them, eyes fixed to my face.

Ma and Baba will disown me just for maintaining eye contact this long.

"Would you maybe want to meet me there Monday?" he asks. He stands, helpless, rumpled but elegant somehow in his Velvet Underground tee, his face blooming pink.

Maybe it's the fact that for once, I am visible.

I have to say something, and soon. I think of Ma, who glanced over her shoulder while exiting the gallery behind the Sobti family. I thought I saw her eyes lock on Oliver before shooting me a look.

I stare evenly into his face. This is a challenge. "Sure." I blink. "That'd be great."

Relief and joy remake his features, and my insides leap. Maybe this is what you'd call a gut decision. Is it delusional to think that the gut might be our smartest organ?

CHAPTER TWO

As I arrive at the dinner table the next night, Ma intercepts me with her nightly blessing. Steadying a flickering oil lamp on a sterling silver dish, she circles it before my face like I'm a goddess. A refracted oval of light hangs in the air, and I wonder if I could capture that magical trace on film. Dipping the tip of her ring finger into a pot of powdery haldi, also known as turmeric, she touches the space between my brows before going through the whole deal again on Baba. As hungry as I am, there's something comforting in Ma's daily blessing. We finally sit, my mouth watering from the fragrance of her steaming food. I rip off a piece of roti, drag it through the soupy tarka dal studded with black mustard seeds, and stuff my face.

"Rani. Who was that boy at the gallery last night?"

My heart implodes. I swallow. Just as I'd feared: the woman misses nothing. "What boy?"

Ma chews slowly, studying me. "The boy watching you. He looked . . . troubled."

On cue, Baba coughs. A rigid left-brained industrial engineer by training, he can't handle anything even remotely alluding to opposite-sex interaction. He fumbles with his napkin, then pretend-coughs into it. The movement causes some of the haldi on his forehead to flake onto his nose.

"I don't know who you mean," I say, as bored and evenly as I can manage. "I was with Kate pretty much the whole night." My eye twitches. Point-blank lying to my parents is a new and unpleasant experience.

Ma looks at me for a beat before blessedly changing the subject. "Betiya, what is happening with your college applications? Did you decide to apply early decision to Northwestern?" She tosses a warm roti drenched in ghee, the clarified butter she makes fresh, onto my already overfilled plate.

"No. No early decision anywhere." I move the roti to my napkin in silent protest at receiving food I didn't request. My heartbeat's returning to normal now that we're not talking about Oliver. "I'm not in love with any one school enough to commit to early decision, Ma."

They're both regarding me with surprise. I almost always go along with my parents' suggestions—why fight when they're usually right? But something has me wondering if a little pushback could be a good thing. She blinks rapidly. "What does being in love have to do with anything?"

That alone could be my practical mother's mantra. A chemistry analyst at a quality control center, she's tough, discerning, and takes no shit.

"Applying early," she continues, pouring a small silver bowl of dal over her vegetable pulao, "tells the school you are serious. Indu Auntie—who, as you know, works at

UIC—said being willing to commit looks impressive in this flaky-bikky era."

"But what if I *am* a flaky-bikky American? Isn't it important to be true to yourself?" I hate to admit it, but contradicting my parents is giving me the kind of rush I remember from when I ran cross-country. Dopamine?

Ma's lips twitch in annoyance, while Baba works to hide a full-on grin. "Betiya?" he pleads with an open palm. "Please, consider what your mother is saying."

"Rani?" Ma says in her reasoning voice. "We are telling you this for your own good. Early decision gives you one small advantage. One must find ways to be different."

We eat in silence, me smoldering in my wrongness. I tip my chair back, balancing on its spindly legs while gazing at the reds and purples of the stained-glass pendant hanging above our small dining table. The interior of our house is all pastels except for this vibrant lampshade. *Be different.*

"Betiya, you will fall back and get hurt." My mother tries to pile more zucchini masala onto my plate, which I shield with my palms. "Do the early decision, uh? Think: you will already be accepted into college in December, and then you can relax and spend more time with Aaji. She will be visiting from India soon for several months."

"Wait. Aaji *and* Aajoba, right?" Aaji and Aajoba are my grandparents—my two favorite people and my biggest fans.

"Just Aaji. Aajoba's not in good enough health to make the journey."

I put down my spoon. "But how will he manage in India without Aaji for so long?"

"Aaji's visa allows her to visit up to a year on account of a

12

new rheumatoid arthritis treatment she qualifies to receive. You know how practical your grandfather is. He wants her to make full use of her treatment—and visa."

I do know. Aajoba would totally insist on her maxing out every last minute of that visa.

"Your aunt and uncle have moved into their place and will care for him while Aaji's here," Ma goes on. "Plus, Shalini will have a job transfer to Pune soon enough. Between her, Lalita, and Ramesh, he will manage fine, despite the diabetes."

"But Lalita Mami and Ramesh Mama are both super-busy doctors, and Shal works intense hours. He'll be lonely during the day." My grandfather is my ultimate defender, especially against his daughter—my mother—so the least I can do is advocate for him. If my mother chastised me for having my feet up on the couch, my grandfather would say something like: "Rani is nimble, sitting like a cat in a yoga pose. Leave her to her self-actualization!" If she harped about me wasting food, he'd say, "Rani has learned restraint—if only the rest of us heavyweights could acquire such a skill." If Ma criticized me for not helping to set up the bed's mosquito netting because I was buried in a book instead, my grandfather would paw at my head with rough affection and say, "Rani is too busy enriching her mind to be bothered by such menial tasks. Excellent." We've been intergenerational twins for as long as I can remember.

"Aajoba will be okay. Besides, when he learned of this experimental treatment program, he insisted that Aaji receive it, so it's done. He is too stubborn to argue with."

I grin, sweeping a shred of roti through the shrikhand. It's true—no one can win an argument against Aajoba. "Mmm,"

I say involuntarily, a shock of saffron-cardamom creaminess melting on my tongue. Despite worrying about my grandfather, I do a happy dance in my chair.

Ma rolls her eyes. "Speaking of diabetes, you're still bewitched by sweets," she says. "I must remember to relay important messages after dessert only."

They're both smirking at me now, and I chair-dance with an extra flourish.

The fact is, I'm secretly rejoicing.

Apparently, my newfound acting skills are stronger than expected. My hypervigilant mother seems to have forgotten all about "that boy."

This is definitely dopamine. And I do not hate it.

CHAPTER THREE

After third-period photography, I head down the Arts Wing to Mr. Larson's room with my bagged lunch, catching my reflection in the plate glass of a hallway showcase: hair flat at the crown but frizzing at the ends, gray jeans, open-weave sweater . . . bland at best. I shake my hair out. I told Kate everything as we drove home from Gallery Night, and she launched into my "first date" clothing possibilities.

"It's not a date," I insisted.

"Of course it's a date. He asked you out, without having to leave school grounds and risk freaking out your parents, I might add. Brilliant, this one."

"Well, Ma did give him the hairy eye. Not hard to connect the dots."

"Ah. Ma's hairy eye *is* a force," she said, turning onto my street. "But I'm curious: How did he break through your 'Don't fuck with me' force field?"

"I reject the notion that I have a 'Don't fuck with me' force field."

"You can reject it," she said, grinning, "but the boy must've been seriously persuasive to get a yes out of you, darlin'."

I pause now outside the art room door, suppressing the urge to fix my hair for the eleventh time. My camera is slung cross-body, lending me the look of a (quasi) working artist. I shift focus from my hazy outline to a painting propped inside.

Window to the World
Oliver Jensen

A painted windowpane, and beyond that a picnic scene of families by a lake surrounded by dense trees, canoes and sailboats dotting the water in lush impressionist style. Beside it hangs a newspaper article from the *Evanstonian*. I scan it quickly. Oliver is hailed as some kind of rising maverick artist from our ginormous high school.

Holy crap.

I hesitate, suddenly feeling out of my depth. The National Honor Society is my main high school activity. I'm a science nerd who knows a modest bit about art and even less about dating. I stare at the grainy photo of Oliver gazing into the camera lens in that signature intense way of his. My eyes follow the letters of his name. . . . This could be a mistake. Then again, it could also be the best mistake I ever make.

I open the door.

Hunched over a battered wooden table, Oliver is absorbed in a sketch. I move closer: it's an elderly man's face, deeply shaded and lifelike. Oliver sees me and pops up, knocking over his chair. "Rani! Hi. I— Hi," he says, picking up the chair. He points to the corner. "Mr. Larson, Rani."

I wave to the cute, young Mr. Larson eating a salad at his

desk and settle across from Oliver, removing my camera and placing it on the table between us. I make a quick sweep of the luminous art everywhere, the room saturated in color and light.

I try to smile breezily, like meeting guys for lunch is something I do on the regular. "Hi."

"Hi, hey. Glad you made it," Oliver says, grinning widely.

"Me too."

We take each other in for a moment. His eyes are a grayer blue than I remember, his skin scrubbed, rosy, and clean-shaven. He cleaned up for me . . . ?

"Um. Where's your lunch?" I ask.

"Okay. This is embarrassing." His face gets rosier. "I *had* a well-rounded, nutrient-rich bag of chips, but I ate them third period."

"Ah." I sigh in mock exasperation. "Guess I have no choice but to share." I pull out the contents of my bag, suddenly a little self-conscious. A green chutney and cheese sandwich, extra-spicy barbecue potato chips, a pickle, an apple, and three kaju barfi—sweet, soft, diamond-shaped cashew-and-butter bars, covered in silver leaf.

"Dang, mamacita." His eyes dance. "You've got enough for an army."

"I—well, my mom packed all this." *Stupid!* "She's worried I may starve, apparently."

"Your mom packs your lunch?"

I hold my hand up like I'm taking an oath before a judge. "Guilty. I'm a complete, pampered baby." My scalp blazes.

But he laughs in appreciation. "Lucky baby. A homemade

17

sandwich and spicy barbecue potato chips! How'd she know this is my dream come true?"

"You two must have some kind of psychic connection. Perhaps you're her long-lost son and she can intuit your every dream," I say, handing him a sandwich half.

"Man, I've always wanted to be someone's long-lost son. But maybe not if it means we'd be brother and sister." He takes a bite of the sandwich, fiddling with the edge of his sketchbook.

"What are you working on?" I nod at it.

"Just— Nothing. Everything I'm doing at the moment is super-conventional crap." He shrugs like he doesn't care but a shadow crosses his face.

"Mundane shit?" I say, grinning, compensating. It works.

"Why, yes," he says. "Mundane shit. Who coined that? He sounds so good-looking."

I smile, handing him a kaju barfi.

"Whoa. What're these?" He scrapes at the thin layer of silver. "Can I ingest this stuff?"

"Yeah. It's edible silver. They're cashew . . . cookies, I guess you could say. But I'll warn you: they're heavy."

He takes a careful bite. "Mmm. I could live on these, Rani. Not your ordinary cookies, these. What's in them, other than live silver?"

My heart pulses double time every time he says my name. "Uhhh . . . cashews?"

He chews happily. "Now you," he says. "Tell me *your* latest thing."

"Other than college applications and trying to survive BC calc? Nah—nothing really."

"But—your work's so cool. Keep putting it out there, you know? Keep your power going." He swallows, gazing with such sincerity that I'm suddenly flustered.

I twist my rings. "Um . . . My grandma's visiting soon from India, and I'm hoping to do some portraiture of her . . . ?" I split a kaju barfi diamond into two shimmering triangles. "She'll be amazing on film, I'm pretty sure."

"Hell yeah." He reaches for my camera, a sly smile on his lips. "Like I'm pretty sure *you'd* be." He takes the camera out of its case and raises it to his eye.

"No." I try to take it back, but he leans away, out of my reach.

"No?" He moves it aside to grin at me, a brow cocked.

"Uh, no." I lunge and grab it from his hands. I arrange its strap back around my neck and across my body. Territorial as hell, but somehow, I can't help it.

"I can't take a picture of a gorgeous Indian girl?" he says, palms up, before folding his hands on the table. His nails are wide and flecked with gray paint. Color has risen in his face, though he grins through it.

"You are not taking my photo while I'm in this state." I snap a photo of him to make my point, though my hands are trembling. Um. Did he just call me a gorgeous Indian girl? I wrestle with feeling flattered and also, well . . . something else I'm too flipped to figure out.

His eyebrows waggle. "And what state would that be?"

My traitorous cheeks are now on fire. He's charming, and I'm stupid. I'm flustered and falling for him, just like I told myself I wouldn't. "Uhh . . ."

He laughs. "Want to meet up tomorrow? Maybe outside

19

by the soccer field?" He gestures toward the outdoors. "I'm bringing the grub," he says, lightly double-punching my shoulder.

He's asking me out again! "Really?"

"Dang, girl. Don't look so shocked. I'm genuinely failing if you already have such low expectations. Did you plan on feeding me every day, like I'm some man-child?"

An outdoor date. Increasing the chances I'll be found out. "Okay," I say. "But only if you provide lunch *and* a photo of your family."

"Shit, now there are conditions. What have I started?"

"And it has to be a real photograph, not a phone photo." I shrug, like my weirdness is out of my control.

He smiles wide. "A real-life, non-phone photo. Sure, Princess Jasmine. Your wish is my command. Speaking of phones, wanna input each other's number?" As we pull out our cells, our hands brush and my breath hitches. Princess freaking Jasmine? But dragonflies are swooping inside my chest—I'm already afflicted. He leans in and gives me a swift kiss on the side of my face, near my jaw. "See you then."

———

I first met Kate in the fourth-floor bathroom of our middle school, the one that was usually out of order. I'd been seeking refuge there for months, hiding in humiliation, gazing at the graffiti on the inside of a stall: *Angie loves Kenny. Sarah sucks cock! K.B.+N.S. 4ever. If you are reading this you are a looser!*

She rushed in one day, red-eyed, splashing her face with cold water and sucking postnasal drip down her throat. I touched her shoulder, asking if she was okay, and out tumbled a quintessential middle school mean-girl story: Her friends had dumped her, saying she was "dragging down their social status." That was two weeks earlier, and things had gotten so gruesome that she was seriously considering homeschool.

In commiseration, I found myself spilling my guts about why *I* hid out in that crappy vintage bathroom: In a momentary lapse of judgment, I'd invited one of the school's starting basketball players, Jason Hittlemeyer, to the Sadie Hawkins dance, despite the fact that he had no idea I existed. He'd reluctantly agreed, but then his friends wouldn't shut up about it: apparently going with me was a hysterical joke. Packs of them taunted me in the hallways and cafeteria in the days leading up to the event, elbowing each other and grinning wolfishly. I found fake love notes in my locker, and the final straw was in PE, when I was bestowed an esteemed new nickname by a couple of his Neanderthal friends: "Little Gandhi Girl." A few days before the dance, I broke down: I called him to rescind my offer—an oily new layer of abject humiliation.

"But wait—wasn't Gandhi the guy who led India to freedom? *And* inspired Dr. Martin Luther King Jr.?" Kate said. "Those dumbasses don't even know that Gandhi was, like, *amazing.*" She swept her hair into a messy bun and looked at me, her green eyes bright and full of humor. "Dumb. Asses!" she said, emphasizing each word with jazz hands.

I burst into snort-giggles, which quickly escalated into a full-on belly-laugh attack, the kind I hadn't experienced in months.

"I'm serious!" she yelled, wide-eyed with mock gravity.

Connecting with a human my age was a shining, wondrous thing. After Alice, my best friend since nursery school, had moved away in fifth grade, I'd become an introverted, unknowable nobody, retreating into the safe predictability of academics. Making new friends was a mystery I hadn't cracked—I'd found myself suddenly self-conscious, awkward, pained. As others got invites to birthday parties and confirmations and bat mitzvahs, I'd watched silently from the sidelines, privy only to hallway gossip: *Can you believe what he was wearing? Oh my God, her hair was so greasy! But Colin said yes, so he's obvs into grease.* . . . I had quietly built a spiky, protective gate around my heart.

On a summer visit to India after seventh grade, while following my aunt Lalita Mami on her hospital rounds, I was struck with a lightning bolt of purpose: I would be a doctor. I didn't need people or parties because *I had goals!* To hell with the code-encrypted trials of befriending middle school girls—girls who, when brought home, glanced with concern at the large photograph of Ganesh, the elephant god, gazing peacefully from our kitchen counter; girls who wrinkled their cute, freckled noses at the pungent aromas of incense, cooking oil, and spices . . . girls who didn't seem to value me or what I stood for, whatever that even was. I was done enduring Ma's detective-style questions about these girls' families, grades, and ambitions. I'd no longer have to suffer through watching them pick at Indian dinners or twitch-smile uncertainly at Baba's awkward dad jokes. Retreating into family life and our small Indian community—which praised me for babysitting at parties and for my unwavering aspiration to become a doctor—was uncomplicated. Pain-free. But it didn't equate to saving face around boys.

Kate smirked at me. "Want me to hunt these imbeciles down?"

In that moment, Kate became my advocate, my kindred spirit, my best friend. When I brought her home, she chatted with Ma effortlessly, devouring her food and announcing that Indian was her new favorite cuisine. She giggled with genuine glee at Baba's jokes. She even dance-stepped a Bollywood dance number, eyes tracking the blaring YuppTV as Ma made dinner. Her funness was infectious, and Ma and Baba loved her. Nowadays, life events aren't real until I pore over their details with her.

So as Kate drives me home Monday in her old Corolla, Cyndi Lauper hollering from the speakers, I give her the rundown on my lunch with Oliver, knowing she'll have down-and-dirty insight.

"Oh my God. The *gazing gallery guy* asked you out again?" she shrieks softly.

"I know. Despite the fact that I bitch-slapped him over that 'relevant and of the moment' comment the day we met."

"But way to shut that shit down."

"He asked to meet up tomorrow. Outside, in public! At this rate, how am I going to keep all this from my mother?"

"I'll keep Ma off the case."

"She'd literally disown me."

"We won't let that happen, I promise," she says, waving a hand like she's swatting gnats.

"He's maybe a tiny bit . . . problematic." Even Kate wouldn't understand how ruinous it'd be to one day tell my parents that

I'm choosing the very thing they live to dread: high school me dating a white American artist who's tattooed and pierced and has a possible "difficult life"—a living, fire-breathing goal distractor whose dysfunction could impact our survival. Drops of rain dot the windshield.

"What's his family like?"

"Not sure. But I did kind of ask him to bring a family photograph tomorrow, so maybe I'll know more then."

She laughs. "You would." She swerves west onto Grant, where the trees are majestic, leafy umbrellas, canopying dense and low. "Whatever happens, *you* call the shots."

After Kate's dad left her mom, she vowed—upon observing her mother unravel—to never allow a guy to treat her like her dad did her mom. She became obsessed with feminist icons, from Beyoncé to Simone de Beauvoir to Roxane Gay, and started dating a wide variety of people to reaffirm her sexuality and freedom as a modern woman. I get a front-row seat to this exploration, which always includes a reflection on why the guy of the moment is ultimately not worth her time—an entertainment and an education.

"Just remember," she goes on, "your life belongs to you and you alone. Not some man."

"Let me guess: Chimamanda Ngozi Adichie?"

"Her aunt, actually, but yes."

———

That night, a text zaps in from Oliver while I'm helping clean up from dinner. At the sight of his name, I tuck the phone swiftly into my back pocket.

"Who's that?" my mother asks, her soapy hands frozen in midair over the sink, holding two plates.

"Just someone asking about an assignment," I mumble, shrugging. *Must tell Oliver to text only after ten p.m.—parental bedtime.*

I feel her studying my face. I keep it immobile as I dry a pot, like I'm a bust at Gallery Night. She returns to washing dishes as I exhale. God. This ruse could ruin me.

"Betiya?"

"What?" My heart's thrumming wildly.

"Veena Auntie called today, wondering if you might be willing to babysit Salil on Tuesdays after school while she attends her pottery class," she says. "She trusts only you."

Salil is the kid I fussed over at family parties from the time he was born. Salil, always Nilesh's "right-hand little man." My chest suddenly feels tight, bound by burning memories of Nilesh, the brother I never had. I try to focus: Salil. Now ten. Hyperactive. Hilarious.

"When would I start?"

"Tomorrow."

I turn to look at her. Her eyelids are fluttering fast, a thing she does when she knows she's requesting something unreasonable of me. "She just learned of the class and sounded desperate for the break." Ma cups my chin and makes a kissy sound. "Please, betiya."

I raise an eyebrow. "Does this mean I'll be allowed to drive the car there?"

She clucks. Her irrational fear of driving—any of us driving—means I basically have no car privileges. To top it off, she insists we only travel city streets, no highways. (This

25

means socializing with only those Indian families who live in close proximity—families whose kids happen to be mostly younger boys.) "Please, betiya," she pleads again, code words for *I will drive you there myself.*

"Fine, I'll do it," I say, rolling my eyes at the immediate wash of relief on Ma's face. Maybe this will absolve me of guilt for sneaking around to see Oliver. "Can Kate drop me there, at least?"

She hesitates, then nods curtly. Somehow, Kate is fully trusted behind the wheel.

I mean.

When the dishes are done, I scamper to my room and whip out my phone:

OLIVER: Thx for sharing your lunch ☺
Great to see you today
Can't wait for tmrw.

A guy unafraid to text feelings. Hmm.

CHAPTER FOUR

Stepping outside for lunch the next day, I spot Oliver sketching beneath a giant, flaming-red tree near the soccer field. He glances up, closes his sketchbook, and gets to his feet, flagging me down like an air traffic controller and grinning. I glance around, worried about the public display. He doesn't know any better. As I approach, he curtsies, one arm out.

"Chivalry with a feminine flair," I say, laughing. "Very progressive." A PE class is gathering on the soccer field, led by an overenthusiastic Coach Hendrickson blowing his whistle and jogging in place. Will Oliver kiss me out here?

"Just what I was going for," he says, with another, lower curtsy. "I'm comfortable with my feminine side."

I laugh. "Baby girl, you've picked a cozy spot." He's not going to kiss me now, I realize. I settle into the grass, both relieved and disappointed.

"Yeah. Thought we could mix things up—meet in a place where we're not surrounded by art for once."

"You wild thing." I notice a pink Solar Subs bag and two soda cups.

His face reddens as he smiles. "I, uh . . ." He fiddles with his straw. His discomfort blasts a voltaic surge of joy through my veins: I have the power to provoke this level of blushing. A whistle blows.

"Solar Subs!" I say, grabbing at the pink bag between us, peeking inside. Subs and a huge cookie. I'm suddenly ravenous.

"I know. I'm sorry. Not exactly gourmet. And this is water, not soda. I had something else in mind, but we had no— I, uh, decided to spend my life's savings at Solar Subs instead."

"I love Solar Subs, so excellent use of your life's savings." I pull out the subs—Venus Veggie and Mercury Meatball.

"Does—is that okay?" He looks worried.

"Very okay." I hand him the meatball sub, then tap my sandwich against his like I'm making a toast. "The Venus is my favorite. I mean, I'm a vegetarian, so."

"Are you serious?"

"I'm serious. It's Venus Veggie every time."

"Dang." He unwraps his sandwich. "Got lucky."

I chew happily. We watch Coach Hendrickson try to form fair teams, while the Beautiful People switch behind his back so they can remain in their Beautiful People pack. The sun emerges from behind a dense cloud, backlighting the fall leaves like stained glass. "So. Did you bring your assignment?" I ask.

He digs into his backpack. "Yes, ma'am." He pulls out a square photograph printed on something like cardstock and hands it to me. Our hands touch, and a little zing shoots through me. I blink, trying to focus: it's a glossy Polaroid of a family in front of a Christmas tree.

"I love Polaroids," I murmur, studying the photo. "Do you still have the camera that took this?"

"Do I look like I'd have anything cool at my house?"

The photo: A teenage brunette has her arm around the neck of a tween boy, grinning wickedly. A blond woman's face tilts toward them, her mouth a puckered O, a twinkling tree in the background. I gaze at the boy—the shiny dark hair, the sullen, distinctive eyes, the rosy lips.

"Little you?"

He nods, taking a long suck through his straw.

"Who's taking the picture?" I ask.

"My dad, I assume. Shortly before he bailed. They both were—are—alcoholics . . . um, and that . . . let's just say there were a very limited number of photo ops."

The air stills as the weight of his words settles between us. "Crap," I say finally. "I'm sorry."

"Nah, it's cool. The great side effect is that I can't even stand the smell of alcohol, so there's no chance of perpetuating that lifestyle at least. Anyway, it's better with him gone."

I nod. I should clearly steer away from the topic of family, but I apparently can't help myself. "What's your sister like?" I say quietly.

He swallows the last bite of sandwich, then squints, thinking. "She's kind of—I don't know. Fragile, but also wild? Plus, smart as shit, though you wouldn't know it based on her choices."

"Maybe she needs new challenges in her life."

"New challenges." He wipes his mouth with a napkin and laughs. "Yes, she probably needs new challenges."

"What?" I mock-yell. "People make poor choices when they're not being challenged!"

He stretches out onto his back, hands behind his head, and grins up at me. "Proceed. You know you want to."

Looking into his face and the casual way he's lying there, his T-shirt hiked up a little on one side . . . the effect is making me jittery. The lighting is so luminous; he'd make a great photo if I dared. Which I don't. Twisting my rings, I turn toward the struggling soccer players and let their obvious misery ground me. "The research shows that kids tend to make questionable decisions if their energy's not properly channeled."

He scans my face, then rolls onto his side, propping his chin in his palm. "You really are such a teacher. A teacher-doctor. A teacher of doctors?"

"I know. Sorry. I, um, read geeky articles about child development—for fun." He raises his eyebrows, lips parted slightly. My cheeks burn, but I plow onward. "My aunt in India is a pediatrician, and she recommended it so that I can get a taste for the field before committing to it."

"I— Wow. I mean, I love teachers and doctors. I mean, I probably wouldn't be here, as in *on this planet*, had it not been for teachers and doctors."

I eat in silence, and my toes curl inside my shoes; I wonder how to respond to that. Maybe Oliver's troubles run deeper than I thought. A ball sails through the air and bounces off the goalpost. Creatively, I settle on: "Um. What's your mom like now?"

"Crazy."

"She's pretty, though," I think aloud. I shift. "Because, you know, it's all about how you look."

"Yeah, who cares how you treat people so long as you look

good doing it?" He smiles, scanning the Polaroid. "Pretty? Huh. She—she'd appreciate that. Or she'd bite your head off. Hard to say which." He sits up, stuffs his sandwich wrapper into a side pocket of his backpack, and pulls out the giant chocolate chip cookie. "I hope you don't mind sharing the cookie?"

"Big-ass cookie, so no."

He splits it and hands me a half—our fingertips graze, and another little thrill moves through me. Is this what they mean by chemistry? Holy crap. . . . "So did *you* bring a photo?" he asks. "I mean, I know I sort of already saw your family. . . ."

"Well, you've seen my parents. The others at Gallery Night were family friends, though they're basically family stand-ins. And then there're my grandparents, cousins . . . my actual family—but most live in India."

He sets down his cookie half on the plastic sleeve that's serving as our plate. "What—what are they like?"

The wind has picked up, and he squints against it, watching my face. His fine hair blows across his forehead, dark with tints of gold in the sun. I fight the urge to reach out and touch it.

I pull at the grass, telling him about the days with my grandparents in Pune—arising early to a crowing wild rooster, shelling peas on the covered back porch, watching the monsoon rain fall in silvery sheets, collecting flowers from the garden for the morning puja ritual, the daily breakfast toast and Amul butter and jam and milky sweet chai. I tell him about the scooter rides with my uncle through the choked-up city, the quiet, tree-lined streets of Koregaon Park, and beyond that, the villages dotting the rural outskirts of town.

Selecting ripe vegetables and fruits from the street vendors along the roadside. The nights playing rummy on the veranda, the garden, the glow of so much family, all together, all in one place. . . . He listens intently, like I'm revealing the secrets of the universe.

And then the bell rings.

He shakes his head as if awakening from a trance. "Wow. Uh, okay," he mumbles. He clears his throat, and we gather our things before heading toward the main building. "So . . . um, tomorrow? Unless you're sick of me, which I'd completely understand."

We're standing in an alcove beneath the eaves of the West Wing. In the distance, the PE kids move toward the far entrance, looking dejected—the soccer match was clearly demoralizing to many. We're suddenly so close to each other, and before I know it, his arms are around me, holding me in a tight hug. My blood streaks through my veins—his scent of soap and herbs and pepper is heady up close. He pulls back and I look into his eyes. Something that I see there keeps me steady.

"Is this . . . ?" His voice is a rasp, and my knees morph into hot lava. I close my eyes, lean in; and despite ten million thoughts ping-ponging about my tortured brain, I bring my lips to his: warm, soft, and surprising.

Something rises within me—happiness? heartburn? My skin tingles as his arms draw me closer, my pulse quickening like I'm sprinting a marathon. Pressing up against him and kissing him is like spinning out onto an undiscovered forest terrain of bramble and jagged cliffs and wildflowers, spanning miles, leaving everything I know behind. . . .

32

Just as his tongue touches my lower lip, he pulls away. "Okay, the bell . . . Another tardy would not be good. . . ." He steps back, straightens his T-shirt, his jeans, and his hair before mildly striking a guy-model pose, blushing furiously. "How do I look?"

I'm trembling. I lean back against the wall, cross my arms, and pretend my soul has not just been turned inside out and struck with starlight. You hear things about first-ever kisses, but that . . . I force a grin, checking him out. "Good. Baseline rumpled, not kissing-a-girl rumpled."

"Yeah?" He looks down at me and smiles as my insides landslide into molten goo. "Cool. What I'm going for. And hey, um, tomorrow night? I'm going to Open Mic with some friends—it's held in the school's Upper Theatre. Wanna join me?"

Wednesday evening. Kate and I usually do homework together then. I'm sure she'd understand, and would cover for me. . . . I swallow. "Um, sure." I'll have to come up with a story to tell my parents. And read up on what Open Mic even is.

He squeezes my hand. "Great. See you then."

CHAPTER FIVE

"Wait—what?" Kate turns off the ignition and faces me, her green eyes wide. We're about to head toward Salil's as I dish about my lunch date with Oliver.

"I know. It was intense." Students stream to their cars in the school's vast parking lot, teasing, texting, whooping.

"Okay, back the hell up. Last I knew, he'd only pecked your jaw, of all places."

"I know."

"So how—?"

"I don't know, Kate. There was this . . . like, *electricity* between us. Literally. I kept getting shocked by his hands whenever we'd accidentally touch." A girl sprints by; three guys are chasing her. They catch up and tickle-attack her as she squeals, sprawled across the hood of the neighboring car. Head hanging off the edge, she laughs soundlessly, her shining black braids twitching. I wonder briefly if she needs rescuing.

"That's kind of amazing."

"Yeah . . . but weird. He'd brought us Solar Subs—"

"Wait, he brought you guys lunch?"

"And he somehow knew to get the Venus Veggie."

"Okay, so two major points: one, he's feeding you, and two, he intuitively knew to get the Venus. It's a sign."

"I don't believe in signs, but yeah."

"But that's like the cutest sign I've ever heard of. So cute that excuse me while I ponder the state of the patriarchy. And puke."

"Sorry. Anyway, yeah. I don't know how it led to the kiss. I heard myself tell him all about India, and then his arms were around me, and he kind of tried asking if it was okay."

"Okay, someone's taught the guy feminist make-out etiquette."

"I know. So I decided to just kiss him so he didn't have to stress."

"*You* kissed *him?*" She turns on the ignition, which breaks up the next-door tickle fight. The girl gets up and walks away limply with one of the ticklers, shrieking happily at the others: "I hate you!"

Kate sets the car into reverse and trails other cars in the slow crawl toward Dodge Avenue. "You are my hero."

"And it was actually *good*. Not that I'd know the difference, since it was my first real kiss. Because I don't count that weird spin-the-bottle mouth plant from Eli Oerter in Casey Jones's basement in eighth grade."

"Totally. You'd *know* a good kiss from a bad one. What'd he taste like?"

"Nothing, I don't know."

"Really? After subs?"

"Well, we'd both just had water. He tasted good, I think. Okay, this is getting into sort of gross territory."

She clicks on her turn signal. "Please. No such thing.

Goodness, you two. Doin' it like movie stars. I mean, who on our tragic planet earth has a great first kiss like that?"

"I just— What if I'm not actually a good kisser?"

"Impossible."

"What? How is that impossible?"

"Because you're a thinker. And thinkers are always excellent lovers."

"What?"

"Yeah. Read it in the *Times*," she says, pulling in front of Salil's house.

I snort, getting out of the car. Kate asked for an online subscription to the *New York Times* for her birthday, and all she ever does now is quote from it.

"Okay," I say. "Good luck with your scrimmage. Call you later."

———

I stand on Veena Auntie's doorstep bearing colored pencils, tissue paper, and an old atlas I found this past summer at a garage sale.

"Rani!" Veena Auntie practically cheers, palms in the air like I'm a celebrity. She's wearing a mirrored banjara scarf over a navy jersey dress—my artsy auntie has completely mastered an East-West aesthetic. "Salil is so excited to see you. And I am forever indebted to you." She places both hands over her heart and hangs her head in gratitude.

"I'm excited, too," I say, stepping in to give her a hug.

Salil rushes to the door. "Rani Tai!" My heart swells at

hearing him address me as "tai," an honorific that means older sister. He smacks my palm several times in a high five, leaping and doing a booty dance. He spots the materials in my arms and stops short. "Wait. Is that an atlas?"

"Sure is. Wanna check it out?"

"I love maps," he yells. He beams at me like I've come bearing the most resplendent gift in the land. We settle at the table, I spread out the colored pencils, and he begins carefully paging through the atlas.

Veena Auntie watches, wide-eyed. "I don't know how you do it," she says. "He sits." She gathers her purse and keys. "Rani. You are a doll. Thank you so much. Anything from the fridge or pantry is fair game. I'll be back in two. Hours, that is." She kisses Salil gently atop the head, murmuring, "Be good," and hurries to her car.

After twenty minutes of map tracing, Salil bounds to the backyard, dribbling a soccer ball toward a net. I try to keep up with him, but he's actually schooling me. Upon failing to block about seven goals in a row, I head into the house to grab some snacks for us. Soon I hear voices by the back fence.

I poke my head outside. "Salil?"

"Rani Tai! It's Henry!"

The next house over, a blond guy is unloading bags of groceries from his car. I recognize him immediately.

"Hello," I call. "I'm Rani, Salil's—"

"I'm Rani Tai's Right. Hand. Little Man!" hollers Salil, hopping to his words. He strikes the ball into the net and checks to see if Henry saw the shot. My stomach clenches at those words—Nilesh's words. *Right-hand little man . . .*

"Whoa, Salil! Good hustle." Henry grins at me. "Hi, Rani. I'm Henry. I just moved here from Connecticut. And apparently, we have English together."

"It's great to meet you, Henry," I say. "Sorry, I didn't know you were new to Frances Willard—the school's so huge I actually don't recognize half the people in our class."

"Henry told me the other day that I'm his only friend," Salil tells me matter-of-factly, sending another shot into the goal and just missing Henry's head.

Color rises in Henry's face. "Careful, buddy," he calls good-naturedly, heading to his back door. "You're gonna clock me one of these days with that power shot of yours." Salil bursts into giggles and watches with rapt attention as Henry waves to us, disappearing into the house with his groceries.

"Henry. Is. Awesome," Salil says to me with sudden seriousness as he plops himself down at the picnic table, ready for snacks. "He's like Nilesh. He'll always play."

———

When I was a kid, Nilesh embodied the perfect big brother.

The oldest boy in our tight group of Indian families and three years older than me, Nilesh was the one we all worshipped: the longish hair streaked with bronze highlights, the white, slightly overlapping teeth, the teasing eyes, the tennis physique . . . The overall effect had us all giggling, unable to disguise our collective crush; the younger boys each perfected their saunter, their chuckle, took up the guitar, and made Adidas their shoe of choice.

As long as Nilesh was there, the family party was guaranteed to be thrilling. While the parents would be upstairs eating and drinking and yelling over each other, we kids would be in the basement, mesmerized by Nilesh. He was a Pied Piper of our Indian community—with an edge. He'd tell inappropriate jokes, organize games, and call us "child," or "kid," or "dumbass"—all affectionate nicknames we quietly accepted. He'd smuggle in teen-rated video games long before we were teens, pulling them from beneath his hoodie and holding them above his head, *Lion King*–style. He taught us poker and blackjack, and when some of us got pouty and threatened to quit the game, he'd say evenly: "Try again, peeps. Two times a charm." We'd yell, "It's three, you goof! *Three* times a charm!" Looking at us like we were nuts, he'd say, "Uh, no . . . ? It's *two*, dummies. Try it." We'd inevitably succeed the second time, dissolving into giggles while he'd shout, "*See?!* You stick with *me*, fools." Nilesh was everyone's favorite, but *his* favorite was tiny, hyperactive Salil—his "right-hand little man." The crushes and favoritism should have been a source of competition, but somehow, everything existed in perfect balance with Nilesh around.

Until the year everything came undone.

During his junior year in high school, Nilesh quit the tennis team and, unbeknownst to us at the time, began hanging with a group of hard-core partyers. He rarely came to our weekly family gatherings anymore, and when he did, he'd spend most of his time silent, hunched over his phone or staring at a ball game in a brooding fog. He went from being the person the auntie-uncles held up as the gold standard to the guy who filled them with quiet terror—he was a disappointment, a cautionary tale, a blemish. Eventually, his parents stopped attending the parties—rumor had it they had kicked Nilesh out of the house. We pieced together snippets overheard through bedroom doors—skipping classes, failing grades, acid, Molly, a DUI—and endured our parents' threats: *If you ever try . . . Don't think that we will tolerate . . . Why bring shame on us only to . . . ?* I'd simmer when I'd overhear a few of the auntie-uncles using Nilesh's struggles as a threat, a fear tactic with their kids. How could they turn their backs on him?

But over the next few months, fury soaked my heart like poison. What was he doing to himself, and why? Didn't he care about us anymore? Couldn't he think about anyone other than himself? As time passed, I became repulsed by drugs: They'd changed Nilesh in some fundamental way. They'd stolen him.

Then again, maybe blaming the drugs and community are just excuses, a delusion to help me believe that what happened his senior year was not my fault. . . .

Oliver doesn't drink—because of his parents—and I can't help but feel that here's one more alliance between us. One more connection that's lit with meaning. One more *sign*, as Kate would say, that we should be together.

That afternoon, a text swooshes in:

So we on for tomorrow? 7?

I blink. Meeting in yet another public space. If someone sees us and it filters back to my parents, extreme and terrifying things will happen.

I absentmindedly pluck at some stray mustache hairs. I've

got to pull myself together, for chrissakes. No one's going to see us and then tell my parents or the Indian community. *Stop being a weirdo.* I've already been with him at the field—we kissed in public!—and the universe is still intact. I stare at his words, letting them seep into me.

This. Is. Happening.

I dwell on my reply for fifteen minutes before texting the most original response in history:

Sounds good

CHAPTER SIX

"Are you sure you're okay, betiya?" My mother stands beside me at our kitchen counter, her brow furrowed.

"Of course. Why wouldn't I be?" I roll out the samosa dough with special aggression.

"I'm just not accustomed to you helping with dinner, that's all," she says, shrugging deeply.

I stop and look at her. "Can't I help with dinner without the third degree?"

"Of course you can. Such dramatics, Rani."

We work in silence side by side. It's Tuesday evening, and I've decided to bring a snack to Open Mic Wednesday that Oliver and I can share. It has to be something memorable, and luckily, Ma had samosa dough all ready and waiting. What could be more perfect?

"We've got the filling, right?" I blink, all business.

"Yes. Here." She rolls out a small piece of dough, arranges some aloo masala inside, adds a dribble of water, and seals the edges. "Hah. Make a few, then we'll fry them."

I create several questionable-looking ones, then slip the savory pastries into a shallow pan of hot oil. I watch them sizzle into browning islands. "What—what's the dough made of?" I'm not exactly comfortable in the kitchen, but I should probably know the basics of samosa making, for chrissakes.

"The usual. Flour, oil, water, salt." She slices a head of cauliflower into tiny pale trees. She looks up. "Why?"

"I'd just like to know a thing or two about my favorite dishes. What goes into them." What if Oliver wants details?

"Smart betiya. Of course. You'll need those skills when you head off to college. And for when you meet a suitable boy." She winks, waggling her head.

I freeze. Does she somehow know about Oliver *already*?

But she's grinning. "When I first married Baba, I was a horrible cook," she says dreamily over the din of the stove vent. "I learned nothing from your aaji about cooking. I like that you're thinking."

I seal up a raw samosa. "I'm a million years from marriage, and I'm not *thinking*. I'd just like to learn to cook a little, that's all."

"Of course." She looks at me sharply, her hands in mid-air, an oily lump of dough shining between her palms. "You're focused on your studies and your future only."

"Right. That's what I'm *saying*."

"Haaah," she says stubbornly, for effect.

Irritated, I remove the browned batch of samosas, place them on a plate lined with paper towels, and slip new ones into the pot of oil. The embarrassing irony is, I *am* kind of doing this for Oliver, "unsuitable" as he may be. As Ma throws chiles, cilantro, and coconut into the blender for the chutney, I roll out a new piece of dough. But instead of a smooth, even triangle, it's turning into a worthless, lumpy trapezoid. I grunt, scrape it off the counter, and reroll it in my palm. Why does my mother have to interlope, anyway? Can I not have this one great thing happen without worrying about what my parents will do?

I knead the oily chunk into a perfect flattened ball. Oliver is going to flip. I try to focus on that.

"Okay," I say, wiping my hands on a dishrag. "What's next?"

———

That night, I text Oliver.

> Eating allowed at Open Mic?
> Thought I'd bring a special snack ☺

He texts back:

> Interest officially piqued.
> Anything's allowed . . . ;)

And now I'm amped, bursting with anticipation. My first evening "date" with Oliver is tomorrow. How on earth will I get to sleep tonight? I root around in a drawer and dig out the jump rope Aajoba gave me when I was little, the one with the yellow-painted handles. He believes that "unproductive thoughts are the demons of the human psyche," and that it's our duty to "conquer them with vigorous exercise." He'd coach me on the rooftop terrace overlooking the garden, shouting, "Faster—no dithering! Skipping is critical for the well-being."

I hit my favorite playlist and hold my arms out, the rope at my ankles. I hop it a few times, annoyed and bored, the rope whipping the ceiling. Before long, I fall into a rhythm. I jump for twenty minutes straight, Janelle, Beyoncé, and Selena leading the way, before my mind eventually empties.

As I'm drifting off, a vision of Aajoba himself jumping rope appears at the edges of my consciousness. He's grinning that toothy grin of his, and I feel myself loosening.

Finally, I'm out.

CHAPTER SEVEN

Giant posters of legendary films hang in the entryway of the Upper Theatre: *Vertigo*, *Breakfast at Tiffany's*, and *King Kong*, all framed in burnished gold. Baba and I, renouncing the Bollywood films that my mother adores, used to watch these classics together instead. Peeking into the softly lit theater, I see students sprawled in clusters over the cushy red seats: hipsters, artists, punks, and activists are poetry-slamming about world issues. . . . I gulp.

I spot Oliver and his friends at the far right of the stage as a performer takes the podium, her mermaid-pink tresses aglow beneath the spotlight. She clears her throat. "I wrote this poem for my cousin Alejandro," she says, her voice low. "He was an activist against gun violence. Y'all know he died last year after a battle with cancer." She blinks, pauses. A hush settles over the theater. She leans into the mic. "It's called 'Voice.'"

Oliver turns, sees me, and salutes me with a grin. Others turn to look while I move toward him, the performer's voice staccato and clear as rain.

As I approach, Oliver leans over a row of empty seats

and pulls me in for a tight hug, his chest crushing against mine. He turns to his group and gestures toward me like I'm a queen, mouthing *Rani* at them in this way that sets bees swarming in my rib cage. His friends tip their chins or wave.

And there amid Oliver's crowd is Tonio, my study buddy from physics sophomore year. He waves, and I breathe a silent sigh of relief. Tonio was down-to-earth and generous with his notes, and his murmured quips always made me laugh. I remember that back then he was transitioning. Seeing him now as a part of Oliver's friend group instantly calms me. *I know someone here, and he's awesome.*

Settling between Oliver and Tonio, I gaze at the poetry slammer's dark lips, heavily lined, her heartbreaking story of Alejandro exploding across the theater, the audience engaged, enraptured. . . .

When two minutes are up and she steps away from the podium to wild applause, I sit, stunned. I'm a senior—how have I never once attended something as powerful as Open Mic?

As confusion stirs over who will take the mic next, in the row in front of us are Oliver's best friend, Saul, a big guy with a blue-tipped mohawk; Fiona, Saul's girlfriend; and Jared, who's wearing a hipster beret and has an impressive brown beard.

"Saul and I were beginning to wonder if Oliver hallucinated you," Fiona says. Beneath her undead makeup, her features are striking and as pretty as a pixie's. "Oh, and that's Trick beside you."

I turn to Tonio, aka Trick, wide-eyed. "Tonio, it's so good to see you. Uh . . . Trick?"

Tonio smiles sheepishly. "Hi, Rani. It's great seeing you, too—it's been basically a lifetime. Trick's a, uh, nickname that these fools came up with."

"*You're* a fool," Jared says, possibly only half joking.

"No," Saul says to Jared, "*you* are the fool." He swipes the beret off Jared's head and slips it to Fiona.

Tonio and I exchange a glance. His face is all sharp planes offset by soft curls falling over one eye. He looks fabulous.

"So . . . how do you know these guys?" I ask.

"Oliver and I had graphic art together last year. Brought me into the fold, as they say."

"Do you make art, too?"

He smiles, watching as a reluctant girl with striped palazzo pants is encouraged onto the stage. "I mean, if you consider what I do 'art'—I assemble weird things and call them installations."

"Weird things like garbage," teases Jared, carefully replacing his beret.

"I believe the appropriate term is *mixed media*, but yeah, garbage," Tonio says, grinning.

"So the garbage represents . . . ?" I'm out of my element, and I hope it's not obvious.

But he smiles. "The shit people dish out." He lowers his voice. "You can imagine."

"I can." I've read articles about doctors' lack of training on how to support their trans patients. "Makes me wanna get up there and slam about it, to be honest."

Tonio turns to Oliver. "Um, by the way, this girl here is the best."

"Well, you can't have her," Oliver says. He glances at me.

48

"What I mean is . . . no one can have her. She's not a *possession* to have," he says deliberately, mock-solemn.

I smile. "Nice save."

"Thanks." Oliver's eyes shine. "Trick's work is—" He makes the mind-blown gesture at his temples.

"Must be cathartic to make great art out of people's . . . stupidity," I tell Tonio. "It's brilliant, actually."

"Thanks, yeah. My latest piece explores intersectionality. Between being Filipino, Latino, and trans . . ."

"You've got a trifecta," I finish.

Tonio nods slowly, then hangs his head forward toward Oliver. "You do know she's too good for you, right?"

"Yeah, I know," Oliver says in all seriousness. "But extra thanks for that publicity."

We watch as the girl in the palazzo pants, despite her initial reluctance, transforms onstage, her voice growing stronger, her stance loosening as she slams about her strength as a woman in the face of misogyny.

Jared is whisper-arguing with Fiona—I catch a snippet. "You're seriously complaining to *me* that she's *whining?*" Fiona mutters, tilting her head at the performer. "You're disgusting."

"Alls I'm saying is that there are two sides to every story," Jared says. "And the male side is the side no one wants to hear."

"As usual, you miss every point," Fiona hisses. "I'm done with this conversation."

When the performance ends, Jared turns, grinning wickedly. "Poll: Who believes that *everyone's* voice should be heard? That we all have a perspective worth two shits? Oliver? Trick? Princess Jasmine, what's your vote?"

Whoa.

"Seriously, Jared? Stop." Tonio manages to sound good-natured. "And also, Rani's not a Disney princess."

Saul proceeds to play-pummel Jared, and Tonio widens his eyes at me in commiseration.

As Fiona launches into an impressively articulate lecture on male privilege, something turns over in my head—a smooth rock with a slimy underside. . . .

I, like Tonio, have a questionable nickname already. And Oliver is probably the one that started it.

As I ponder this, Dante Tangier lopes toward center stage, black braids swinging. Dante is one of those insanely brilliant kids you just know things about, somehow. He's currently writing a novel inspired by his Black family history in the antebellum South.

He clears his throat, ducking toward the mic. "Hey, y'all. This one's called 'Little.'"

Suddenly, I remember the samosas. I reach into my bag and offer one to Oliver. His eyes light up; he bows deeply, hands clasped around my samosa, reverent namaskar pose. My heart skips a beat.

Maybe the Princess Jasmine thing is just a coincidence. . . .

And then—Dante begins, his tone as urgent and powerful as a pastor's, slamming about his little brother, born when Dante was twelve:

> *His little is power,*
> *His little is potential,*
> *Forgiving my fallibilities,*

50

Honing my sensibilities—
He is my hope, my strength,
My heart.

Oliver bites into his samosa, shoots me a look of appreciation, and gently takes my hand. I glance around, but nobody's looking at us, and for God's sake: no one cares and no one is going to squeal to my parents and omg Oliver is holding my hand.

> *I know*
>> *I gotta grow*
>>> *Gotta show him all he can be,*
>>> *All the gold that gleams inside of him*
>> *Despite history.*
>>> *Too loud to stay quiet*
>>> *Too bright to stay dim*
>>>> *Too vast to hold in . . .*

A gristly lump's in my throat as I sit, enthralled by the cadence of Dante's voice and the buzzing electricity of Oliver's hand in mine. Oliver quietly inhales the samosa as I sneak a look at him: he's in real-life portrait mode—stubbly jaw and humor-lit eyes and shining hair and wide, full lips, all in luminous focus. . . .

A text swooshes in on my phone:

MA: Don't forget to apply for those senior awards! Deadline is upcoming!

I stuff my phone into my bag. Dante moves about the stage, slamming with pitch-perfect delivery about guiding his little brother to behave respectfully, preparing him for a battle he seems destined to lose. . . .

I think of Salil, which makes me think, inevitably, of Nilesh. Swiping at a tear, I watch Dante make his way back to his seat amid roaring applause. The notion of children suffering . . . I probably have no business being a pediatrician—one poem about a kid and I'm a wreck. The poetry-slam hour now over, I wave at Tonio as he squeezes my shoulder before heading out. "It can be intense, your first time here," observes Saul, nodding at me appreciatively.

"Yup. If you don't cry your first time," says Fiona, hoisting a backpack onto her tiny frame, "you're essentially a sociopath." Oliver's friends begin to wander away, saying *sayonara, Princess J; later, love-doves; hasta luego, Ollie* . . .

Then Dante himself ambles over. He and Oliver share an elaborate handshake before hugging, chest to chest. I hear Oliver say, "That was something . . . thank you, my brother."

The theater is close to empty as Oliver and I wander toward the exit.

"Uh, *that* was freaking amazing," I say.

"And your dough-pocket thingies?"

"Samosas," I say.

"Your *samosaaas*," he says, "also freaking amazing. One day you're gonna show me how to make those." He laces his fingers through mine.

That would mean uninterrupted hours together, plus access to a kitchen stocked with Indian spices—both of which will never happen, but I just smile.

"Hey. Want to meet somewhere Friday after school?" At least I can promise him another date. Friday is my usual hang-out time with Kate, but probably she'd support me using the opportunity for Oliver time; the logistics of seeing him on a Friday straight after school are simpler. . . . He pulls me close, leans down, and brushes my lips lightly. With his body tight against me, the strength and heat and bulk of him, a weakness oozes thickly from my core. He kisses me again, deep but quick.

"I would fucking love that," he says.

CHAPTER EIGHT

"Who knew you were so passionate about whether children today are given too many trophies?" I say. It's the Friday after we finished performing our dreaded debates in English, and Kate and I are now puttering through downtown Evanston before my date with Oliver. We pass boutiques and eateries and Northwestern spiritwear shops before slipping into a parking spot by Unicorn Cafe.

"I already dread the parents who will be helicoptering their way to your future clinic," she says. "How will you convince them to stop giving their kids a cupcake for hanging up their coats? May the force be with future you."

Inside, we order chai before settling at a tiny round table by the window. I note a collection of stuffed animal unicorns on a high shelf, and beneath that a random vintage camera collection packed tight above the busing station.

"Okay, fill me in. Why do I know nothing about the latest?"

"Sorry," I say. "Debate prep. Tests. This school thing."

"Tell me already. How was Open Mic?"

"Here?" I hiss. "*No.* These tables are on top of each other."

"And they're either empty or filled with college kids we don't even know."

I glance around. Several students sit at the rustic counter facing the windows, tapping on computers with earbuds in. A heavily bearded guy in his thirties on the other side of the café is engrossed in a novel, nursing an espresso. Maybe I'm being a little paranoid.

"Okay, Open Mic was intense," I say quietly. "There were some seriously talented people. It was intimidating."

"Well, that's their path. And you're on yours. What did Oliver think of the samosas?"

I smirk. "He loved them."

"I'll bet," she says suggestively.

"What's that supposed to mean?"

"What? I mean, food is love is sex, right? Don't tell me you've never seen *Like Water for Chocolate*." I shake my head, and her eyes widen in disbelief. "Okay, a movie night is in order. We'll invite Mimi and Irene and snarf gourmet goodies as we watch. It'll be so meta."

I smile, sipping my chai. "So . . . he held my hand during the performances."

"Ooh."

"And then he kissed me, twice, after the theater had emptied."

"What? Holy mama. You guys!"

"They were quick kisses, but oh my God. How will I manage this?" I stare into my chai. Louis Armstrong's mournful trumpet pours from the café's speakers.

"Um, a hella hot and talented guy kissed you twice. What's the problem again?"

"Um . . . my parents?"

"Right." She blows on her chai. "Yeah. They will not be cool with or understand this. But, as *Homo sapiens*, we're allowed private lives, don't you think?"

"Yes, but—"

"You're eighteen. I mean, you have the adult American privilege to vote in the next president of the free world, who will obviously be some kick-ass woman."

"I know. It's just that—"

"In like eleven months, you'll be in college, and at that point, there'll be lots of fucking going on that your parents will not be comfortable with." She's clearly enjoying herself.

"*Kate,*" I say, laughing. "I just— Look. I know I'd like to see him more."

"Right. *See him more.* Is that what we're calling it now?"

"I just don't know how I'm going to handle the logistics," I say, ignoring her innuendo. "And the guilt."

"The guilt will fade," she says. "And the logistics we'll figure out. Anyway, your mom loves and trusts me. I've no problem exploiting that in the name of getting it on."

"Oh my God, is being quiet outside the realm of possibility?"

"More or less," she says, standing. "Okay. Let's get you to your booty call on time."

Outside, we climb into her old Corolla, and she turns to me. "Can I ask you something?"

"Sure."

"How did you *know* that first kiss with Oliver was a good kiss?"

I consider. "I dunno. . . . There was this magnetic pull, and like a chemical heat when our lips touched." I strap on my seat belt. "But no, it was more than that. It was—well. The way my whole body reacted. Despite me being a stress case."

"Yeah, if he can break through *your* anxiety . . ." She raises a brow.

"I know. It's like my brain stopped talking, and my body got all . . ."

"Your body got all what?"

"Weak and gooey. Like my legs."

"Okay, gooey legs, a real thing. What else? Details, girl." She starts the engine, slaps her phone into the glove box, and cradles the back of my seat as she backs out of the space.

"And then I got . . . there was something sparky or druggish coursing through my limbs."

"Okay. Druglike sensations. Interesting," she says, moving south along Sherman Avenue.

"And then I got lost in the feeling of him pressed up against me. And everything else kind of faded away."

"Damn!" She hits the brakes, hard, and faces me. "I knew it! A kiss can do all that!" She checks the rearview mirror and moves on slowly, taking a careful right at Davis Street.

"And he— I could feel him get hard through his jeans."

"Mm. Impressive work. That's what I needed to know, thank you."

"So has all this happened to you before?"

"In bits and pieces. But usually the guy's seriously lacking in *something.* As in, he's someone I'd never consider actually *being* with. You know the people in my recent past I'm talking about."

I grin. "Yes, I do. Hey, seeing that you're on a guy rampage, maybe we can get to know some of Oliver's friends better. You'd probably meet some cool people at Open Mic. . . ."

But she's lost in thought. She murmurs, "You and Oliver Jensen? Night and day, but electric together. This is good. You've given me hope. Thanks, babe." We rattle up Ridge Avenue before turning east and into the Noyes Cultural Arts Center lot, where Oliver wanted to meet.

"I'm waiting till he shows," she says, eyeing the clock. She points at me with both index fingers. "And whatever happens, remember the three rules."

I sigh. "Remind me of the rules again?" Kate has created so many tenets for various life events, they're hard to retain.

"Damn, girl. I'm glad I remembered to remind you! Number one: Don't go down on him unless he happily goes down on you first. Two: Don't go falling in love. And three: Don't let him break up with you—meaning always break up with him first."

"Right," I say, laughing. "*Those* three rules. The ones I won't need for, what? Six, eight months?"

"It's never too early to do something stupid, like fall in love. So if you feel like number two is possibly happening, jump to number three and call me to get you the hell out of there."

"And number one?" I say, smirking.

"Like I have to reiterate number one. I mean, I do have faith in your basic instincts."

And right on schedule, he appears, swinging off his bike and locking it to the rack by the playground in one smooth motion. A lightning bolt of joy zaps through me.

58

"Crap, he *is* sexy," she says, watching him. "*I* couldn't have picked better for you."

Oliver ambles over, a black hoodie open over a T-shirt that reads BLINK IF YOU WANT ME, his eyes a pale, shocking gray in the afternoon light. I step out of the car, and he waves at me before ducking toward Kate. "Hey. Hi." He reaches in through her window. "I'm Oliver."

"Kate," she says, taking his hand awkwardly. "Good to meet you. And if that shirt is any indication of some kind of gross caveman philosophy, I need you to know that this is my girl, and she deserves way better." Heat rises up my neck.

God.

"Okay," he says, "so, this shirt was a very stupid gift. My bad." He turns slightly, shrugs out of his hoodie, strips off the shirt, pulls it back on inside out, and faces us, palms open. "Better?" I try to pretend I didn't just glimpse his bare chest.

Oliver and Kate regard each other a moment, then erupt into giggles. They are literally both giggling amid this supremely awkward moment, communicating in their own alien tongue as I go weak with relief. Kate approves.

"Have fun, kids!" Kate says. As her car purrs away, she waves with a cupped hand like a princess in a parade.

"Best friend?" Oliver says.

"The best."

"So it seems."

CHAPTER NINE

We step inside the Noyes Cultural Arts Center, where Oliver tells me he gets open studio time—a perk of an evening class he takes here. Meandering along the old building's wide, barrel-ceilinged hallway, I admire the art commingling on the walls—nude sketches and woodblock prints, paper collages and Technicolor weavings. . . . I pause before a nook that has a couch and a funky bookcase filled with art books and hanging plants, but Oliver tugs on my hand. "Naw, little lady, this way," he says, pulling me toward the open stairwell.

"This place," I breathe, staring at the tissue-paper flower exhibit winding above the handrail like a tropical vine. "How did I not know it existed?"

"Because you're an art baby. And I get to be your art dad, nurturing your growth."

"Okay, cringey." I give him a shove.

He laughs, and the walls of my chest fizz like pop. We reach the second floor, where more exhibits are clustered: a group of glossy 8 x 10 photographs looking like neon negatives, mosaic portraits composed solely of dried beans, and a bulletin board crowded with pamphlets on art classes and upcoming shows. . . . This casual space exists for the sole purpose of self-expression, and there's something so freeing about that idea that I'm in awe. Whole worlds flourish while I painfully chip away at my AP classes, holed up in my room. He stops before a closed classroom door, fumbling with the antique doorknob.

"Welcome," he says, finally forcing open the door, "to my private universe." We step inside: Easels line the perimeter of the airy classroom, whose leaded-glass windows overlook a leafy park. The room smells like paint and turpentine, a smell I've come to associate with Oliver.

"Sweet universe," I say, peering at the works in progress on the easels. Each painting's a variation of the same nude blonde, her creamy back to the viewer, head turned in profile. Oliver's standing before one, arms crossed, appraising. I come up beside him. She is masterfully rendered: high cheekbones, voluptuous, and with a big, round, perfect ass—everything not me. "This one yours? Wow. She's—wow."

"I didn't peg you as a jealous type," he says, grabbing palettes and paint tubes from a cabinet. "It becomes you."

"Thanks. I take pride in my insecurities." I glance around. There are inordinate numbers of nudes in this room—more than I've seen in my lifetime.

He sets the supplies down and wraps his arms around me while I quietly fill my lungs to capacity with his irresistible scent. "Think of it this way," he says. "I'm just a doctor examining a patient. Doctors do not get hot for their patients."

"Actually? That is an amazing analogy. Consider this left brainer impressed."

Oliver squeezes a glob of color onto his palette. "You're

61

no straight left brainer. I mean, look at your photography. Your right brain just needs a little emancipation." He clears a nearby drafting table. "You bring your prints?"

I nod, digging into my bag. He asked me to bring photocopies of my latest shots so we can "experiment" with them, whatever that means. I pull out a few beach landscapes and a couple of Kate in the silky bomber jacket I got her for her birthday, gazing left against the backdrop of a chain-link fence. Oliver studies the photos a moment. "Perfect," he murmurs. He carefully tapes a photo of sand dunes onto the drafting table. "There's something I looked up last night that I thought we could try."

"Does it involve more . . . nudity?" I close my eyes momentarily: *What even?*

He grins. "It does not. We're too new, you and I, for full-on nudity. I think, anyway?" he says, light dancing in his eyes.

I laugh awkwardly, my cheeks burning, and all I can do is whack him in response. "Anyway," he says, pulling out a jar of rubber cement. "Remember what Trick said about using mixed media in his work? It got me thinking about ways you could explore that, using your photos as the foundation." He pulls up some examples on my phone (his being too old and slow), and we scroll through them together. I pause at an image that resembles an abstract urban scene. "I love that one," he says, "and it's perfect for beginners. While I work on layering up my painted lady, you layer up your print, using that photo as a guide." He sets out a tray filled with various materials. "Cool?"

"Sure."

He squeezes more paints onto his palette, then shifts into artist mode; eyes laser-focused, jaw in a slight underbite, brush in hand, he begins working. I stare at my photocopy of the lake up by the Harley Clarke Mansion, semi-stupefied by options. I hover a scrap of metal above my print, but then switch it out with a shred of patterned fabric that reminds me of a man's tie . . . though that doesn't seem right, either. I sneak a look at Oliver's painting. His brush moves rapidly, creating a golden sheen along the left side of the model's body where the sun would hit. An expression of deep concentration has transmuted his features. He's in a zone. He doesn't even notice I'm watching him.

After a few more minutes of me floundering, Oliver looks up, glancing at my barren page. "Hey. How're . . . okay, what's happening here?" He sets his palette down and strolls over, trying not to smile. "Need inspiration?"

I blink. "No. Yes. I mean, maybe? I can't seem to start."

"The beauty of this form," he says, pulling up a chair, "is that you can literally start anywhere. Like, you can actually *close your eyes* and stick something somewhere on the page, and that's where you begin to build. You will not fuck anything up."

I stare at him blankly. Being this close to him, I feel almost dizzy.

"But if that's too open-ended," he continues, "focus on the part of this scene that draws you in, and begin building your layers around it to help highlight it. What section of this piece captures your imagination?"

I point to the strip of water in the distance.

"Great. So place bits that highlight the foreground." He begins clustering nails together within the lines of the trees to represent bark. Looking at me for permission, he douses the section with rubber cement. "Now don't judge—this form is less about perfection and more about flow, free form, letting go . . ."

"Hmm. That sounds . . . not easy."

He smiles widely, eyes twinkling as he lines up some nails. "Why do you think we're doing this exercise?"

I laugh. "An exercise designed for type A's. So I'm a guinea pig for your curriculum."

"Type A's do require special care," he says, grinning with eyebrows raised, and I shove him playfully. "But seriously: To be able to give yourself over to the process is a skill. One we all can develop. It's how meaningful art reveals itself, you know? So play. Let go," he says in a Bob Ross voice as he heads toward his easel. "Believe that things are going to come together, even if it looks jacked at first. Now go, baby bird."

Studying the image on my phone, I coat one side of a metal shard with rubber cement and place it vertically amid the trees. Doubtfully, I continue, gluing more scraps of metal and then strips of fabric to the wood benches overlooking it all.

Oliver peeks over his easel. "Dang. Not bad." He comes closer. "What do you think of adding paint now?"

The way I look at him makes him laugh. "You got this." He sets down tubes of acrylic paint, a palette, and a jar of water. "Fill in the negative spaces with patches of color, and don't be afraid to mix colors."

I squeeze out several acrylics onto the palette, then blotch in the lake. Next I work on the sky, pale and cloudy, and finally begin to patch in the forest areas that flank both edges of the lake. Color seeps onto the page, transforming everything.

I start layering on black seed beads along the shoreline to signify rocks, or maybe algae, the beads impossibly small in my fumbling fingers. My shoulders are stiff and my hips are beginning to ache from sitting.

I lean back and regard the result.

It's a weird, laughable fail.

Oliver glances over. "Keep adding."

Layer after layer of beads and nails and paint and metals, until finally, things are looking not-horrible. It's a landscape with an edge, which (I think?) is what I'd hoped for.

I stretch, move toward Oliver's easel, and gawk in amazement: his blond bombshell has sprung to life.

"There's something off about this one spot here," he murmurs, pointing to her calf. "It just doesn't look natural."

"Maybe you need a hint of shadow to suggest the curve of the muscle there?"

He stares at the painting, nods, then dips into a rich purple brown. He strokes it on so confidently that I cringe . . . it looks immediately screwy. He shouldn't take advice from me.

But before long, he's blended it in a way that looks, well, perfect.

"See, you're already an expert," he says. "My work here is done!" He sets his palette down, and we settle along the ledge against the wall of windows, so close that our hands graze. "Making art is kind of hard," I blurt.

He laughs quietly, hanging his head forward. "Yeah. The general misconception is that art is effortless and fun and farty."

"Totally. That's my parents, all the way," I say. Fleetingly, I wonder if I should keep my family out of things.

He leans back against the windowpane. "Typical. But really, it's a study, like anything else. I mean, it's not like doctors saving lives or anything"—he grins at me—"but there's a lot you can do through art. A lot you can say, and work through. And the result is not always a pretty picture."

"Case in point," I say, nodding at my creation.

He laughs. "I genuinely like the way yours turned out. But really *you* have to be happy with it. There'll always be hype beasts out there, but it's not about an outsider's assessment of what's cool or current. It's about whether you've created something that embodies your beliefs, your values, your message. Or whether it at least allowed you to explore and release some shit."

His eyes are pale against dark brows and lashes—a study in contrast. "It probably forces you to examine things carefully," I mumble, attempting to sound coherent despite his nearness. "So you know what you're trying to say."

My eyes flicker to the windows—the day is overcast, translucent clouds blowing through a silver sky. Aajoba loves when the light is like this—he says that a cloudy day is best for "photo-graphing."

"You're already an artist." He regards me evenly. "You just don't always know it."

I shrug. "If you say so."

He tugs on his ear. "Can we meet up again? I promise I'll remind you to bring your camera." I can't stop staring at his eyes, striated grays and blues, like the lake on a stormy day. "What I mean is—can we, like, start seeing each other, for real?"

My hands are shaking; I clasp them together. Is this really happening? "I'd like that."

A slow smile spreads over his face. "Yeah?"

I lean in and kiss him, like it's something I do on the regular. A thrill pulses through me, and I don't recognize myself, sitting in a strange art room, kissing a guy for the third time this week. He moves in closer, and when the kiss ends, he holds me tight.

"Um. But we do have to keep it under wraps," I murmur into his hoodie.

"Sounds sexy," he says.

"I'm serious," I say, sitting up straight. "I'm forbidden to date."

He shifts into attention mode. "Wh-what?"

"My parents—I'm so sorry, but my parents can't know about . . . anything. If they find out, I'd never be allowed out of the house."

"Really? Wh—so . . . they don't know you're here?"

"No. Dating's not a part of their culture, especially for people of their era. They're not even cool with me being *friends* with guys, much less . . ." I gesture between the two of us. Heat rises in my face. Uuuuggh, too much!

But he's unfazed. He takes my hand, every synapse within it charging to life. What is this radioactive thing happening to my hand? "Okay," he says. "Intense."

It dawns on me that I might be scaring him off. Why would anyone tolerate my parents' archaic rules? "I'm so sorry," I hear myself mutter. "I totally get it if you don't want to—deal."

"What? No. Are you kidding me right now?"

"I don't want you to feel like—"

"Rani. You get me, and I think I get you."

A gust of wind rattles the old windows. "Yeah," I say, squinting out at the waving treetops. I look into his face. "You do." I swallow hard.

"Do you know how freaking rare it is for someone to *get me*?"

I burst out laughing. "I can imagine."

"Yeah. We'll figure it out," he says with comical finality.

"Okay." My heart's oozing between the bars of the iron fortress I've built around it. "But, um, just to recap: I need you to honestly promise that you'll do everything in your power to help keep us a secret from my family. Them knowing would actually be catastrophic, so if you could, like, protect—"

"Rani. Holy shit, I promise." He looks into my eyes. "I'll protect you from their wrath. Like a superhero."

My face is burning, and I start babbling. "It's a huge risk for me to be with you, but I'm also too far out to backpedal now, and in all honesty, you're wo—" I stop.

He leans down and looks playfully straight into my eyes. "I'm what?"

"You're . . . um. I guess I was gonna say . . . you're worth it?" I blink. Why am I still talking?

But he draws me in close. "I'm deeply honored that you think I'm worth it." And then we're kissing.

The touch of his lips, his body crushed against mine, feels somehow both freeing and grounding, the chemicals between us a warm, slow-burn energy. . . . For once, we're alone to-gether, and I'm flying, buzzing, electric, careening through a reckless new dimension where I say something honest and in return, I get kissed like this. . . .

He rests his chin on the top of my head, and I breathe his spicy-soap scent in deep. "I love that you're only dating me because it's too late for you to paddle back to safer waters."

I laugh. "You're nothing but danger."

"True." He shifts. "But one day, I'll just knock on their door, introduce myself, and make them love me."

I stare at him.

"Kidding! I'm kidding." He laughs at my expression, and I glance down at the empty park. Fireworks burst inside me amid mountain peaks of fear. "Although . . . ," he says, "I've already sort of met them, at the gallery. They seemed pretty cool to me. I just need to get in there, work my magic, and . . ."

"Oliver. This is not a joke. You don't know what you're dealing with here."

"I know a thing or two about batshit families, you know."

"Not my kind of batshit."

"Are there really that many different kinds of batshit?"

"Yeah," I say, laughing. "I think most people are a little batshit. Promise you'll take this seriously."

He gives me a mini salute. "Yes, ma'am. Soldier's promise."

I swallow. "And as much as I like your texts, don't send them before ten when my parents are nosing around."

"Got it. After-ten texting only."

"And you better not call me ma'am ever again."

"Yes, ma'—goddess."

"*Goddess* works."

CHAPTER TEN

About two weeks later, on a Wednesday, I'm lying on the floor of my room, laboring through calc, when the door swings open.

My mother stands in the doorway in a cobalt-blue sari, a matching bindi in the shape of a teardrop between her eyebrows. One hand's on a hip and her nose is flaring. She is a formidable Indian sorceress.

I scuttle to a sitting position. "Ma, *you're* decked out. Getting Aaji from the airport?" It's a new habit: when my mother appears without warning, I shift into panic mode while faking cheery interest in her daily doings. It's panic that she knows everything—that I now spend all my free time with the tattooed gallery goonda behind her back.

"Rani, I must speak to you." She blinks.

I lean against the bed frame, like everything is cool. "Sure, Ma. What's up?" My heart pulses in my throat.

"I found *this* in the laundry." She holds up a shred of paper between her thumb and pointer, like it's filthy.

Trembling, I take the scrap from her and glance at it, though I already know what it says.

How could I have been so careless?

Hi, sexy. Meet me at our tree after school.

Instinctively, I laugh. "Ma! This is a joke. It's from Kate. She likes to tease me."

My mother stares, then plucks the scrap from my hand. I catch a whiff of her gardenia scent, infused with fried mustard seeds. She studies the note, squinting, while I remind myself to breathe. "This handwriting looks funny," she says finally. "Cramped and ungraceful. Like a *boy's.*" She says the word as if it's dirty, worthy of revulsion.

I sigh. "No, Ma. I told you. It's Kate. Do you want her to come over right now and prove it?"

My mom peers at me, still mistrustful, her thin lips a crumpled frown. But then, before my eyes, her armor peels away like the prickly layer of a dragon fruit. Her voice is suddenly soft. "You know it's not *you* I don't trust, right, betiya?"

"Yep, I know," I say, shifting. "Boys are the ones you can't trust. Got it."

It's as though I've flipped a switch. My mother's scary mama-bear half rears up, growling. "This is serious, Rani! There will be no hanky-panky." She plucks a photo from my dresser mirror. She holds it up with one hand and points at it with the other. "It is because of *these people* that we are even here! It is *their* support that has gotten us this far in America, and we cannot allow . . . *distractions* to ruin our opportunities."

I gaze at the photo of our family in India, a photo I took myself at my grandfather's eightieth birthday last summer in Pune. Both sets of my grandparents are nestled together on a sofa. My many cousins hang over them like bear cubs, making bunny ears above their parents' heads, laughing into the lens. My youngest cousin, Suraika, sits on my maternal grandmother's lap, her tiny palm planted upon my grandmother's soft face.

I gulp. "Ma. Nothing's going on," I say quietly.

"Rani, I must repeat: your studies are your focus. Education is what allowed your baba and me to succeed here, to have all of this," she says, gesturing toward the window to our beloved neighborhood. "A strong education is what we promised everyone back home that you would receive, too, here in America. Certain kinds of . . . *friends*, they *de*rail that focus."

I gaze into her face, forcing myself to stay trained there. "Yes, Ma."

She tucks the photo back into the mirror's frame. "We are here to support you, betiya. But if you indulge in any foolishness, then you are making a choice. A choice that would ruin your chances at success, and hurt and disappoint our family." She gives me a steely gaze as my heart sinks low. "I'm retrieving Aaji from the airport now," she says, and then she's gone.

The thing is, Oliver has already woven his way into me, frayed hot pink shot through my customary neutrals. We're like a tapestry glinting with uncommon light and contrast. There's no unraveling him from me now.

My heart still pounding, I smile-grimace into the mirror.

"Hanky-panky," I whisper.

CHAPTER ELEVEN

Kate and I have English comp together, and today, Ms. Malley has offered us the rare opportunity to study in class for an upcoming test. As Kate and I compare and fine-tune our notes, I notice Henry, Salil's neighbor, working alone at a table two over from ours. I give him a wave.

"Okay, so what's the latest?" Kate asks, capping her pen. "How's Aaji?"

"She's great. When she arrived at the house yesterday, I did namaskar at her feet, and she spent the next five minutes clutching my shoulders and grinning through tears."

"Aw. I love your grandma. To be honest, though, I'd also cry for five minutes if someone did namaskar at my feet."

I laugh. "And in other news, my mom found a note from Oliver while doing laundry, so not only has her sixth sense been tapped, but I now have three adults to keep off the case."

"Holy shit." Kate stops, mouth open. "What did the note say?"

"Something like 'Hey, sexy, meet at our tree.'"

Kate shrieks softly. "Oooooooooh!" she says, shaking her

hands like they're on fire. "How did you not *open* with this? What did you say?"

"That the note's from you. Naturally."

"You do know that the only way I can cover for you is if you actually *tell me when to cover for you*, right?"

I groan. "I'm sorry, Kate. I meant to tell you yesterday. Things got busy once Aaji arrived. Anyway, any advice on how to manage *three* parental figures now, regarding Oliver?"

"Hey. Your grandma is more like a fairy godmother, based on what I remember. Has she ever gotten mad at you? She could work to your advantage."

"But she's traditional—I can't tell her about him. Plus, she's here for an experimental treatment for rheumatoid arthritis, and I don't want to add stress." We work in silence. "Speaking of traditional, how's your mom?"

When Kate's parents were still together, we'd joke that Kate's mom, Bonnie, embodied a 1950s housewife: She married young, baked daily, was super active in the PTA, and did one hundred percent of the housework in good cheer. She was like a *Mad Men* mom without the angst, outfit-matching earrings, or heels, and Kate's dad took advantage: Ron would come home from his job as an actuary, make a beeline for the liquor cabinet, and with feet up, scotch in hand, peruse the paper or watch a ball game alone most evenings, disengaged from Kate and her brother, Noah. When Bonnie discovered Ron was having an affair with someone from work, she left him and, for the first time, entered the workforce.

"She's managing, kind of. Still shattered, honestly. I have to gently remind her to brush her hair in the morning, but she's kept with the job." Bonnie is now a secretary for a mental health clinic. "I'm super proud of her, but please bludgeon me if my life ever starts to resemble hers. Or Ron's, for that matter."

"How're things with, um . . . Jack?" Kate's latest guy is so new I barely know his name.

"Okay, I guess. But the other day, I overheard him say to somebody: 'Don't be a pussy.' And he actually laughed when I told him just how cringey that is." ,

"Charming."

"Right? Uh, hello, way to uphold your toxic masculinity and raging anti-woman language! Do you not know that the pussy is one of the greatest creations of all time? Calling someone a pussy should be a compliment, dumbass."

Though Henry is sitting two tables over, he is absolutely listening, trying not to smile as he pretends to work. Ms. Malley has stepped out, and the room has gotten louder.

"The days are clearly numbered for Jack," I murmur, leaning in.

"If only he didn't have to *speak*. We could have been so happy, him buying me lunch and then us messing around in his car. But after that comment . . ."

I smile. "Way to single-handedly ruin a good thing, Jack."

"Yeah. I'll probably lay low and swear off dating for a while. Anything to avoid the Bonnie Trap—falling in love with an insufferable teen dude, getting hitched early, and not knowing my ass from my elbow as babies pop out my twenty-two-year-young vagina. . . ."

Ms. Malley strides in, and the room quiets.

Kate scoots close and lowers her voice to a whisper. "On the other hand, I really want . . . *meaningful experiences* before college, you know?"

"You'll have them. But let's find you guys who've got, I don't know . . . heart. And humanity."

"Thank you!" she says, smacking the desk. "Humanity is all I'm asking for, folks!"

"Please keep your voice down, and your thoughts on your work," Ms. Malley says, looking pointedly at Kate.

Kate looks down at her paper, then leans in. "Just promise me you won't let things get intense with Oliver. You risk losing your edge if you fall too hard."

Ms. Malley asks us to rearrange the desks, and in the flurry of activity, Henry's beside me.

"Oh, hey, Henry: this is my best friend, Kate."

He dips his head and does a little wave. "Great to meet you, Kate," he says, settling into a desk beside us.

"Henry is Salil's next-door neighbor," I tell Kate. "He just moved here from, um . . . ?"

"Connecticut."

Kate says, "Wow. Welcome. How do you like it here so far?"

"Honestly, people have been cool. There's an inclusive vibe here."

Kate blinks, her lashes fluttering in honest surprise. "Really?"

"All about perspective," I say quickly. "When you're new, I bet you're more open and less . . . judgy."

"Less judgy," Kate echoes. She turns to me. "Can you imagine what being less judgy would even be like?"

76

I squirm. Do we really need to sully the new guy with our cynicism?

But Henry laughs. "I guess I'm still in the annoyingly up-beat stage. So far, it's pretty easygoing and friendly here compared to my old school."

Ms. Malley passes out a list of research topics, introducing the paper that'll count for thirty percent of our semester grade. We select our topics and the bell rings. Kate and I head toward PE, and Henry's next class is in the same direction, so he walks with us.

"So what did you two pick?" Henry asks.

"I chose the Grosse Point Lighthouse, assuming that a childhood lounging at Lighthouse Beach gives me special insight," I say with a grin.

"I picked the Baha'i temple, 'cause its dome is pretty." Kate bumps my shoulder, then turns to Henry. "You?"

"Evanston Ecology Center. I've worked in outdoor ed, so I figured it's something I'd probably get involved with anyway."

Kate glances at him. "Outdoor ed, huh?"

"Yeah. We lived close to a nature center, and my mom and I used to go there a lot, help with wildlife restoration, weeding invasive plants, that sort of thing. I eventually trained as a counselor, got to work with the kids."

"That's—wow," I say. That explains partly how he's so great with Salil. I can't help but wonder what happened with his mom, seeing that he lives with his grandma now.

"Yeah, and it's how I got into—" He stops.

Kate glances at him. "Got into what?"

Color rises in his face. "Okay. Probably shouldn't mention this the first time meeting . . . people."

We're now both staring at Henry. "Come on, we're not *people*," I say. "And contrary to what you may have gathered: we're not judgy *at all*."

"Right," he laughs. "Well, in that case: it's where I learned to plog," he says, sliding his backpack onto both shoulders.

"Plog."

He hooks his thumbs onto the straps of his backpack and gazes at us patiently. "It's when you run, usually in a group, and pick up garbage as you go."

We stare at him.

"It started in Sweden," he goes on. "And the term is a combo of *jogging* and *plocka upp*—Swedish for 'pick up.' People sort of ridicule you, but I found it weirdly addictive," he says, shrugging. "It's a great way to mobilize groups to keep plastic out of the—"

The passing period bell rings, cutting him off.

"Anyway, it was good meeting you, Kate. Rani, maybe I'll see you at Salil's soon?"

We watch him go; he's not in the least embarrassed. "Plogging," I say, turning to Kate. "Of course."

She laughs. "Unapologetically himself. Admirable."

"Heart. And humanity." I raise my eyebrows at her.

She holds the door for me to the girls' locker room. "The flip side of heart and humanity, though? It can make you feel like a real asshole."

CHAPTER TWELVE

After school, I spot Oliver beneath our blazing maple, one of many giants lining the eastern border of the soccer field (and subject of the ill-fated love note). He's grinning and waving both arms like he's flagging down a jet. I laugh despite myself, my camera banging against my hip as I hurry past the soccer team.

"Okay, *stop*," I say, whacking him. "Way to call attention."

"But embarrassing you is my new favorite thing."

We've been walking halfway home together a few times a week most days after school. Deep in an Indian summer, the sun's been shining fiercely as students sprawl across the East Courtyard. Once, a big group of us hung out on the lawn, Kate getting into an impassioned conversation with Oliver's punk-rock-loving friends about Kathleen Hanna. Another day, Henry joined with Mimi, Irene, and Joren from photography. And one time we had a memorable lunch with Saul, Tonio, Jared, and Fiona, which was basically just live improv comedy. I spent half the time behind my camera, trying not to laugh as I captured shots for class assignments.

But right now, I'm all business. I need to make something crystal.

"Oliver. That little note about meeting under our tree after school?"

"Yeah? Analog, right? *A note.* Like it's the eighties."

"Okay, but my mother found that note *in the laundry.*"

His head snaps up, and he turns to gaze into my face. "Ohhhhh . . ."

"Yeah." I glare at him.

"Um, excuse me, missy," he says, stepping closer. He places his forearms on my shoulders in a way that's somehow ridiculously sexy. "Aren't you the one who put that radioactive shit in your pocket, knowing full well your mom does your laundry?"

"Yes, but—"

"Admit it. I was not the only mistake maker here."

I'm silent.

"Maybe this will bring it forth. . . ." He leans down and drops a kiss on my lips.

"Fine," I groan. "I'm an idiot for keeping it. I just— I didn't want to throw it away." I shrug.

He crooks his arm around my neck as we walk. "God, you're adorable."

I'm suddenly conscious that for once in my life, *I'm* the girl with the cute guy draped over her; a shock of joy shudders through me. "Anyway, I lied and told her it was from Kate."

"What—because having a girlfriend is a lesser offense than having a boyfriend?"

"No—I—I said that Kate likes to tease me by writing silly notes."

"And she bought it?" He looks at me incredulously.

"Well—I don't know. Kate *is* a ham. Plus, mentioning her puts my mom in an instantaneous great mood. The word *Kate* is a natural upper."

We're heading toward my house, walking west on Church toward the arboretum that winds along congested McCormick Boulevard. Periodically, a car horn blares.

"So, theoretically: What would happen if you just—you know." He shrugs deeply. "Told your parents about us."

"They'd kill me. Or disown me. Or, like, move us all back to India."

"Okay. That's a little dramatic."

"Exactly. Something dramatic *would actually happen.*"

"But I mean . . . how do you know? Have you had a boyfriend before?"

I shake my head. "But my mother believes dating is the equivalent of destroying the family. For real."

"I mean, you're eighteen . . ."

"Which, in my world, means exactly nothing. Anyway, my grandma's here now. So I have *three* hyperprotective adults to manage, so can you just—"

"Hey, how *is* your grandma?"

"Cool. Achy from the flight, jet lag, all that. But she's a trouper."

"What's she like?"

"Spunky. Chill. A little goofy."

"Hmm. Sounds like someone I know."

We veer into the arboretum, strolling through crisp, curling leaves. He sits on the pedestal of a steel sculpture shaped like a crude safety pin. It soars into the sky, and a cluster of birches hides us from the road. I arrange myself beside him, and his arms wrap around me.

"So can I come over and meet her?"

I smack his shoulder.

"Ow. Okay, so not today." His eyes settle on mine. "When, though?"

I'm laughing. "Probably never?"

"Rani. Are you embarrassed by me?"

I guffaw, but he looks at me solemnly. "You're kidding, right?" I say. "You—no." A woman jogs by in yoga pants and a Patagonia fleece, pushing two babies in a stroller. I sigh quietly. "Look, they honestly wouldn't understand. They're super traditional. And they're obsessed with my education, including anything that might—I don't know—*obstruct* that. They don't even like me taking photos because it's not 'academic.' My mother basically told me that they'll support me only until I do something 'foolish.' Like be with a dude."

"So—they'll throw you out if you're . . . with me?"

"It's not . . . *you*, exactly. They just don't get the dating thing."

"But—how did *they* end up getting married?"

"Their marriage was arranged."

He blinks. "Wait—that's, like, a real thing? That's so conventional that it's actually *unconventional*."

I stare between the trees at the cars whizzing past. A gray-haired guy with a youngish face strides through the dead leaves in a suit, yelling into his cell: "But I *just* received his portfolio!"

"I mean, how—how do arranged marriages actually work?" Oliver tries again.

"It's all based on family connections—two families know

of each other through social networks, and they arrange for their children to meet. Nowadays, a lot of it's online. In my parents' case, their families set up a meeting, I think. Within two weeks, they were married."

"What? So, like, you and I would be married by now?"

"Sure. If both our families knew each other and were in on it. And if we both lived in India, and you were Indian, and it was one hundred years ago, when people got hitched in their teens. . . ."

"A world of ifs, huh?"

I unscrew my water bottle, take a long swig, and offer it to him. "Nowadays, they wait until your twenties. Then that's all parents talk about, like with my cousin Shalini, who's only twenty-two."

"Whoa. So for us, that'd be in two years." He grins at me.

"Yeah." Does he not realize that a meteorite would have to detonate the universe before my parents would support us dating, much less getting married? The terrifying reality of us actually being together publicly in the world makes my brain shut down. I look at the planes of his face, his wide mouth and strong nose and eyes intent on hijacking my heart. Thoughts of my parents vaporize as my stomach does its now customary flip-and-sizzle, like a fresh fried egg. Powerless as always.

I try to snap a photo of him, but he leans in and kisses me with such tenderness that I forget all about my camera. He pulls me closer, his heat scorching my insides down into igneous gold. I pull away, nervous at the openness, the possibility of invisible prying eyes.

"Okay," he says, straightening up. "If we can't go to your house, want to come to mine?"

CHAPTER THIRTEEN

He unlocks the security door to the apartment building, turns, and says in a demonic voice: "Welcome to the house of horrors."

We crossed McCormick and walked a few blocks into Skokie-Evanston (aka "Skevanston"), past the Middle Eastern grocery stores, the gas stations and dry cleaners and nail salons. My family and I have come to this neighborhood regularly to eat at Pita Inn, our favorite Mediterranean joint, all the while Oliver living right around the corner.

I follow him up the dark stairwell, which smells like old bacon. "Be forewarned," he says, fumbling with his keys. "The witches inside may be casting spells."

"Witches?" I whisper. "I thought you lived here with just your mom."

"I saw Kathy's car parked outside," he whispers. "Around Mom, she can be just as witchy." He kisses me quick on the lips, turns, and unlocks the apartment door.

We enter a carpeted living room. Nestled within the bay window overlooking the street are succulents and cacti in various states of aliveness. The room is sparsely furnished, the carpeting threadbare. A young woman sits on a sagging couch, petting a cat as she reads a book, the television inexplicably blaring. She looks up and mutes the TV as the cat skitters away. I glance at the cover of her book: *The Four Agreements.*

"Hey, Kath."

"Ollie, hey. Hey, hey!" She gets up and moves toward us hesitantly like a stray kitten, delicate-boned, straggly bangs hanging in her eyes. "Hey, you must be Rani," she says with a shy smile. "It's nice to finally meet you." She holds Oliver in a tight hug. "You."

I hear him mumble: "You're alive."

"More or less." She lets him go, then turns to me and gives me a citrus-scented hug, her skinny arms holding me in a surprisingly strong embrace. "Heard a lot about you." She pulls away and we all look at *Judge Judy* on the television. From the corner of my eye, I see Kathy sizing me up. I twist my rings, wondering if I'll pass.

"Where's Mom?" Oliver asks, brushing past her and into a tiny dining room.

"Is that an existential question?" She gives him a sly smile.

"Ha. Seriously, where is Mom?"

"Groceries, I think. She's actually fixing dinner tonight." She smacks both her cheeks, à la Edvard Munch's *The Scream.*

"Really?" He comes back into the room, looking genuinely stunned. "Wish you'd come home more often. I mean . . . dinner."

"I know. Sorry, little brother. Looks like you'll get fed tonight."

Oliver turns to me. "Um. Want to see my room?"

My mind's racing as I follow Oliver past the rickety dining table and into a hallway. I think about Oliver eating only
chips at lunch, about how many nights he probably doesn't
have actual dinner at home. I think about my mother's nightly
feasts, meals I take for granted. . . .

Family photographs hang crooked on the walls, mostly
school photos of Kathy and Oliver in various stages of ado-
lescent awkwardness. I zone in on a black-and-white shot of
a smiling couple sitting on the hood of a classic car. It looks
like an ad, but upon inspection, I see that it's a real photo.
Oliver's parents.

"Welcome to my shit show."

We step into his room. I'm awestruck.

The place is a wreck. Clothes are strewn everywhere:
in corners, under the bed, thrown over a lamp—a lamp!—
balled-up towels. . . . There are dozens of CDs piled and
spilling onto the floor. I can make out names on a few—Big
Audio Dynamite, Siouxsie and the Banshees, Urge Overkill,
the Flaming Lips . . . band names that sound like violence,
obsession, darkness . . . testosterone-ness.

"Sorry it's so messy," he says, picking up a towel and hanging it on the doorknob as he closes the door.

I step around some piles, moving toward his bed, which
for some reason is made. The faded blue comforter is folded
down like in a Pottery Barn catalog. And that's when I notice
his paintings. Everywhere. Different-size canvases suspended,
unframed, and propped along the floors. Forest nymphs, gargoyles, demons, and pixies dance within their thickly textured
landscapes, each a layered story. Stories I could lose myself in.

"Your artwork sure makes up for it."

"God, please don't judge me. I know this place is a war zone." He laughs uncertainly, and he looks so vulnerable my heart leaps into overdrive.

"But your bed's so tidy!" I bounce on it. "Are you secretly enrolled in the army?"

"The sergeant does inspections every morning," he says, scratching his ear and shrugging.

I laugh, inhaling deeply the smell of the room—paint and rain and wet bark and a trace of Oliver's aftershave—the combination sending me into a quiet frenzy. It's like landing in Mumbai for the first time: Your five senses are lured by a luminous, gritty chaos. Left to your own defenses, you eventually adjust to the crowds, the thickness of the air, the rich beauty and mad poverty.

I stand and put my arms around Oliver's neck, kiss him lightly. I hear the faint noises of the television as I move closer, kissing him deeper. He inhales, and with a low, guttural groan he pulls me tight against him. My legs weaken as my pulse races. What am I doing here? Where else would I ever want to be?

A door slams, and we spring apart, adjusting clothes and hair—an intuitive dance. We hear female voices arguing. Oliver turns to me.

"I'm sorry about all this," he whispers. He touches my cheek for a split second. "I probably shouldn't have subjected you, knowing—"

"Nah. I like it here. Your sister—she's great."

He stares at me with an inscrutable look. I scan the room—

the disaster, the beauty of the paintings, the pulled-tight comforter on the single bed—acclimating to this complicated new world. I turn to him, startled by what I see in his eyes.

Fear.

I grab his hand and squeeze it. "Come on. Let's go say hi to Mama."

——

In the kitchen, a woman crouches, rummaging through a grocery bag. She looks up.

"Well, hi?" She stands slowly. She is tiny. "Oliver has told me *nothing* about you." She looks at me like I must have something to say for myself.

"Mom . . . ?" Oliver says, palms open at his sides.

"Um, well then, this must be a shock to the system," I say, grinning. "I'm Rani." I offer my hand. "It's great to meet you, Ms. Jensen."

She studies my face, her gaze traveling slowly down, then up again. She finally takes my hand. "Well, it's nice to . . . *know about* you," she says, looking at Oliver meaningfully. "And please, no Ms. Jensen, though how *respectful*. Call me Tammy. Or how about Miss Tammy? Yeah. That's got a nice ring." She gives me another once-over. "You've already met Kathy?"

"I have." The TV murmurs low from the living room. She nods. Tendrils of fine blond hair escape her ponytail as she moves about the kitchen, stashing items away. I pull a squishy package from a bag. Ground chuck. Something I've never seen in my mother's vegetarian kitchen. "Um, fridge, right?"

She stops in her tracks. Her eyes are a piercing blue, her

cheekbones high in a leathery face. "You're . . . ? Oh. Sorry, I'm not used to *helpers* around here." She rolls her eyes, glancing at Oliver. With her leanness and summer tan, she looks like a teenager in a tank and cutoffs, now shoving a case of Diet Coke into the fridge. "Yeah, just leave it on the counter. I'll cook it up for tonight's tacos." Holding a gallon of milk, she turns to me. "You're staying for dinner, right?"

I glance at Oliver, who's gazing at us, slack-jawed.

"I, uh . . ."

"We'd love you to stay," she says definitively.

Mother and son stare at each other, having some kind of silent brawl. He turns to me, suddenly cool and even.

"Yeah, Rani. Stay. We don't bite. Right, Mom?" He glances at his mother, and for a split second, I see a flicker of that same apprehension in his eyes.

"Right," she says, stone cold. "It'd be nice to have some polite company for once."

Oliver turns and stalks out of the kitchen, muttering, "Where's Kathy?" I turn to his mother, who grabs a bottle of liquor from beneath the sink and pours some into a glass before splashing in a little Diet Coke. I look into her eyes and smile. "What can I do to help?"

———

Thirty minutes later, we settle around a table loaded with taco fixings. Kathy has emerged from a bedroom, looking disheveled, like she's just arisen from a dead sleep. Something about her reminds me of Nilesh, a jolting pulse of memory. Oliver looks at her, then away, filling up a plate.

89

"Dig in, everybody," Oliver's mother says with forced cheer.

Oliver hands me a plate with two tacos brimming with beef.

"Um, I'll fill up my own," I say, declining the plate. "I actually don't eat beef."

"Shit, that's right," Oliver says, his face suddenly flushed. I smile at him reassuringly.

"So, you're a vegetarian." Tammy says this like she always sensed there was something off about me.

I clear my throat. "Yes." I place two empty taco shells on a fresh plate.

"Are you one of those crazy vegans?" she says.

"No. Though actually, my grandparents are vegan."

"What exactly is the point of being a vegetarian? Or a *vegan*, for chrissakes?" she says with a little head shake, her brows arched in disbelief.

"It's, well, it's part of my culture," I say, stuffing lettuce and cheese into my taco shells. "In Hinduism, cows, and animals in general, are considered sacred. . . ."

She barks a sharp laugh. "But how do you manage to get enough protein in your diet? We *all* need protein." Her gaze is piercing.

"Lots of people are vegetarians, Mom," Oliver mumbles. He shoots me a look—a mixture of sympathy and rage.

"We eat a lot of lentils?" I offer. "And leafy greens actually have a lot of protein, too, which people don't always realize. . . ."

"Well, of course I realize that. But there's nothing quite like animal protein to keep you going, is all I'm saying."

I take a delicate bite of my taco. Okay then.

"Here are some chopped tomatoes, in case you want them, Rani," Kathy murmurs, passing a bowl to me.

"So, Rani," Tammy says, taco in midair, "where are you from?"

"Mom?" says Oliver, setting down his taco and staring at her.

"What? I'd just like to know a little about her *background*, that's all," she says, taking a deep swig of her drink.

Oliver chews silently.

"Um." I twist my rings. The dreaded "Where are you from?" question—the question that makes me want to retort, *From outer space.* "I'm Indian American. Born and raised here, in Evanston."

"So your parents are immigrants from India?" Oliver's mother asks, her blue eyes sharp.

I nod, taking another tiny bite of my cheese-and-veggie taco.

She places a hand over her heart and says mock-confessionally: "I, for one, admire immigrants! There's an Indian lady at my work—*Meera*. Brings only Indian vegetarian for her lunches, now that I think about it. Huh. Anyway, family-oriented, works hard, never complains. I'll bet your family raises you with those kinds of values, too, am I right?" She looks at me expectantly. I wonder if she's drunk or if this is what she's usually like. I smile at my plate. "You kids could really learn from these people," she says, eyeing her children like they're guilty of something.

These people. My face burns. Oliver gazes at her hard, crunching tacos the only sound in the room.

Kathy clears her throat, but when she speaks, her voice is gravelly. "Are you into sports or clubs at the high school, Rani?"

"I ran cross-country my first couple years, for JV," I say, pushing at some guacamole with a chip. "But I knew I wouldn't make varsity this year, so I joined the photography club instead."

"Easier on the quads," Kathy says with a smile.

"Rani, I didn't know you ran cross-country," Oliver says. "No wonder you whupped me the other day at the field after school."

"Okay if I take the last one?" says Kathy, reaching for the last taco shell.

"For chrissakes, Kathy, I didn't raise you to be a hog," Tammy says irritably. "Fine, take it, but at least *consider* the rest of us. Go get more from the oven."

The blood drains from Kathy's face. Wordlessly, she goes to the kitchen.

"Jesus," Tammy mutters. With her flushed skin and the lavender half-moons beneath her eyes, she looks weary, and for a moment, I inexplicably feel sorry for her. She chugs her drink, draining it.

Kathy returns, dumping the taco shells onto the table with a clatter.

"What the hell, Kathy?" Oliver's mother half stands, her eyes flashing. "After I make you this nice dinner—"

"Oooh, yeah, dinner. Hear that, little brother? We owe Mom our undying respect now."

Oliver blinks. "Rani, do you want more?"

I shake my head no, smiling weakly. I breathe and think: *You've got this!*

Tammy has just asked Kathy about someone named Vince. Kathy's eyes narrow. "You know we broke up last month," she says.

Oliver puts down his taco to stare at Kathy. She notices, and color rises in her face. "What?" she says defensively. "Anyway, now is really not the time—"

"Well, *I* think this is as good a time as ever," Tammy says. For being so petite and pretty, she is terrifying. "Why don't you tell Oliver?"

"Mom, *no*. We have a guest," Kathy says quietly, chewing at a hangnail.

"Kathy. Before you leave, Oliver deserves to know what's going on in your life."

Kathy stares at her Diet Coke. "I'm back with Richard, okay?"

"Richard? You mean *married* Richard? What the hell, Tiny?" Oliver says. "Is he at least separated now?"

"No," she says quietly. "He's—sorry, Rani, this is a lot."

"No worries," I say. No longer in the hot seat for being vegetarian and answering questions of my origins, I toss my paper napkin over my half-nibbled tacos and witness Kathy get skewered.

———

We're standing outside Oliver's apartment, waiting for Kate to pick me up.

"Um, so that was fun?" I say.

Oliver's face is pinched. He takes my hand in his—it's big and warm, like that first time at Gallery Night. "I'm sorry. I told you she's completely out there."

"It didn't help that I kicked things off by refusing the tacos she'd just prepared," I joke.

"No, it did not."

I glance up at him—is he deadpanning? But his face is set, steely and impassive.

"I'm sorry if I instigated that . . . scene . . . ," I say cautiously.

He turns to me. "So eating beef is something you can, like, never do? Under any circumstance?"

I blink. "No. I've never eaten beef in my life. I was brought up vegetarian."

He's silent, staring unseeingly down the street. "But, like, in the end, it's just *meat*. . . ."

I stare at him. "In Hinduism, animals are considered incarnates of the gods. So killing them for food is not considered okay."

"Oh."

I sigh. Now I seem super religious, which I'm just not. "Look. Vegetarian food is my comfort food, and it makes me feel . . . connected to my roots in a way that's hard to explain. It's just a part of me."

He glances at my face, and whatever he sees there makes him square his shoulders. "Sure. Eating meat's against your culture and beliefs. Mom is super passive-aggressive and loves to pounce where there's—I don't know—vulnerability. But I wonder, if you'd explained that bit to her . . ." He trails off.

"That bit is personal, and plus, I didn't feel like I should have to justify being a vegetarian."

"I'm just . . . I wish that went better. So that we'd have a place to meet outside of school, you know?"

I nod. It's five-thirty, and the sky is a violent purple, the streets a shadowed premonition of the brutal wintry days to come.

"I'm sorry," he says. "It's against your religion, and that's totally cool. Look, I'm an idiot." He steps in close. "Forgive me."

I close my eyes, and he kisses me gently, a kiss that feels like a hundred thousand apologies, heartfelt and honest.

"Not your fault," I murmur. "It's okay."

He picks me up off the ground in a huge bear hug and laughs.

"I can't believe we just had our first fight," he says, setting me down. Headlights shine as Kate's car turns off Dempster and slowly pulls up to the curb. "And that it was about meat."

There was kind of more to it than that, but I kiss Oliver and duck into Kate's cozy car.

CHAPTER FOURTEEN

"Rani," Aaji says. "Come."

I startle at the sound of my name. It's the following Saturday, and I've been skulking around the house, silently planning a getaway for my first late-night date with Oliver. Considering that both Oliver's and my family are, well . . . challenging, Kate and I decided that sneaking out was my only option. "It's a weird counterintuitive thing," I mused on the way home from Lover's Lane, the lingerie store where we shopped for Kate's upcoming date with a guy named Javier. "It'll be stressful to sneak out, but that's better than barely ever seeing him, somehow."

She agreed. "Coach Morris says relationships are like wild weeds—they scramble and run their course and there's not much you can do to control them. Maybe that's an excuse for having a gross affair with her friend's boyfriend—which she doesn't think we know about—but it actually makes sense in your case."

Aaji sits on the sofa, knitting. She glances at me over her reading glasses and gestures to the space beside her. Despite my nerves being on the verge of short-circuiting, I slump down next to her, and she pats my hand, grunting in approval. Her thickly veined fingers fly amid golden yarn.

"The doctor here recommends I knit to help with my arthritis. You know, I was your age when I first learned to knit." She glances at me. "My brother and I were living with my uncle and aunt—my mama-mami—in Kashmir one summer. My mami was ashamed that I had not yet learned this skill." She chuckles quietly.

"And you think *we* are unreasonable, Rani!" Ma calls from the kitchen. She seems to hear everything, no matter where she is in the house.

I grin. "Why exactly would your aunt have been ashamed?"

She shrugs. "Girls were taught the skills that would help them find good husbands."

I stare at her.

Aaji peers at me over her glasses. "I know it sounds foolish to you American girls. But skills like cooking and sewing and knitting gave a girl better prospects."

"Yes. Tell her, Mummy," my mother says, walking into the room, wiping her hands on a dish towel. "See, betiya? We could be demanding that you knit—or else!" She swats me with the towel before settling on the chair nearest Aaji. Around Aaji, my mother is a tiny bit less intense.

I turn to Aaji. "Is that why Aajoba wanted to marry you? Because you made a mean cup of chai and could knit him a sweater?"

Her needles are a flurry. "Actually, no. Your grandfather is an impractical man. He liked me for my singing voice. Singing! A dreamer, your aajoba."

"But that's what's great about him—he fell in love with you for your *voice*. That's super romantic."

She clucks, her brow furrowing as her fingers work faster, almost blurring. "Romantic, beemantic."

"Mummy does not always see Aajoba's endearing qualities," Ma says teasingly.

Aaji tuts, and I watch her hands, transfixed. "So Aajoba really couldn't come this time?"

"No, betiya. His knees, the diabetes . . . he requires a lot of care now."

"I wish he could have come anyway." I think of him in their house in Pune, and my heart contracts. "Do you miss him?"

"Ramesh Mama and Lalita Mami are living in the house, tending to his needs," she says, ignoring my question. "Though he no longer walks easily, he insisted on me visiting you, your final year before college. Then, once he learned of the treatment . . . well. He would have nothing else. You know how he is."

"I do." I finger the skein of golden yarn. "It's hard to imagine people tending to him." When I was ten, Aajoba and I went on these epic walks. He used his cane to point out specific flowers in the overgrown gardens before the crumbling Anglo-Indian mansions left over from the British rule. We were far from home when it began pouring one day—huge raindrops pounding the pavement like silver jacks. When I realized the bouncing raindrops were actually hundreds of tiny, gleaming frogs leaping from every puddle and ditch in the road, I clutched his arm in fear. He put me on his back, and with one arm supporting me while the other gripped his cane, he carried me home. I can still feel the shaking of his laughter through his damp cotton kurta as I clung to him, wincing at the impossibly tiny frogs leaping about his flip-flops. "He doesn't walk much now?"

"No, but he is quite content watching films and reading the paper. During Diwali, he loves lighting the firecrackers on the gachchi." I can totally see Aajoba impishly lighting firecrackers on the rooftop terrace; the Festival of Lights is his favorite holiday.

"That reminds me," Ma says. "Betiya? Will you lead some crafts for the kids at Mira Auntie's Diwali party again? Salil will be there."

I hesitate. Indian parties always remind me of everything Nilesh, but I've been leading the Diwali crafts since the beginning of time, and anyway, I like doing them with the kids. "Sure. Yes."

Relief and joy remake her features, as if I've just told her I've decided to get an MD/PhD in neuroscience, learn Hindi, and have an arranged marriage with a suitable Indian boy.

"Mira Auntie will be thrilled," she says, chucking me under the chin and grinning like her face is about to burst into a billion shining stars. "She worried you might be too busy with college applications. Thank you, betiya."

One more step toward absolving myself for sneaking out—something I've now become obsessed with. With each act of goodness, the burning flare of my guilt dims, dominated by the thrill and anticipation of a night with Oliver.

——

Creeping past the closed doors in the hallway, I tiptoe to the rhythm of my father's snores. The shadows of the house guide me down the stairs, through the kitchen, and to the back door. I slip on my shoes, lock the door, and steal into the night as blood roars in my ears. I hurry through the yard beneath the whispering canopy of oaks and into the alley, where Oliver's mother's rusted Pontiac idles with its lights off. Breathless, I slam myself into the passenger seat, the muscles in my calves a tingling mush.

"Hey, you," he says. "How's it feel, being an escapee?"

Trembling, I unwrap a piece of gum and stuff it into my mouth. "Well, I've probably lost at least a year of my life, but otherwise, cool."

He grins. "Who wants to live until they're old and crotchety anyway?" We move slowly down the alley, tires crunching on the gravel. I look up one last time at the back of the house as we go.

Darkness.

CHAPTER FIFTEEN

We drive through slumbering streets. I try to breathe, fighting the urge to go back, check if the house is still dark. If it's ablaze in lights, it wouldn't be too late to cobble together an excuse. *I thought I forgot to park my bike in the garage. I left some homework in the car. . . .*

Oliver cranks the music up. I turn to him, forcing a breezy smile. "So, where're we going?" I hug a knee to my chest.

"A surprise." He flashes his toothy grin and squeezes my hand.

"Let me guess." I tap my lip with my index finger. "Coffee shop?"

"Hmm, interesting. That was a close second." He looks at me with fake earnestness. "But, snap, it closed at nine p.m. So that was out."

"Too bad," I mutter. "I really could have used a vanilla latte with extra foam."

He cocks an eyebrow at me. "I would've pegged you as a hardcore dark-roast-rocket-fuel kind of girl. Strong drink for a strong woman."

I fake a yawn. "Lord knows I'll need *something* to keep me up tonight."

Shaking his head, he chuckles under his breath, pulling to the side of the road. Shifting into park, he grins at me, an impish gleam in his eye. "You are so asking for it."

His fingers graze lightly against my neck. I yelp, then giggle as he finds my tickle spots. Encouraged, he climbs over to the passenger seat and hovers above me, his hands digging and wiggling.

"Please . . ." I laugh weakly. Who decided tickling was cute and fun? It is, in fact, torture.

"That mouth of yours," he says, his tickles becoming softer. He leans in, his lips barely brushing mine—a feather of a kiss.

"What's wrong with this mouth?" I say, like I expect a real answer.

"Uh, okay. You got me. Nothing. It's perfect." He kisses me again, lightly, then leans against the headrest, his eyes closed.

I touch his eyelids lightly with my fingertips, and they open, a slushy, unreadable gray.

"You look different," he murmurs, studying my face.

"I'll assume that's not a compliment."

"What? No. You always look great."

"Just thought I'd try something new," I say, my face heating up. I spent a lot of time applying dark eyeliner and dressing in black, like I'm some kind of badass.

"Are you regretting being out like this?" he says in his raspy voice.

"What? No. I like being . . . with you."

"That's not what I asked you. I asked if you're regretting this."

I sigh. "I mean, I've snuck out of the house in the middle of the night. If we get caught, my life will be over."

He smirks in amusement. "Why will it be over?"

"Because. I've snuck out to be with an American goonda who will derail my future, my chances of becoming a highly educated person. And for that, my parents will disown me."

He laughs. "What's a goonda?" When I say nothing, he takes out his phone, taps into it, and reads aloud: "'Goonda: a thug or miscreant.'" He looks at me.

"Don't be mad," I say, laughing.

"Mad? I'm not mad. Of course I'm a goonda. I've got tattoos and piercings. My clothes are shit, I'm poor as fuck, and I'm bad at shaving. I'm basically a serial killer."

"Well, I *like* all that about you. Especially the serial killer part. But yeah, you do play the goonda role rather well."

"Unsavory at first glance."

"But to be clear: unsavory mainly because you're, you know. Male."

"Can't say I blame them." He laughs, shifting beside me in the passenger seat so that our clothed bodies are now interlocking.

"So, um, is *this* the surprise?" I say. "Being cramped and tickled to death in your car?" I poke a finger into his ribs, and to my surprise, he recoils, giggling hoarsely.

Apparently, he's ten times more ticklish than I am.

"Not the cleverest, using this tactic on me, when the slightest touch reduces you to tears," I say calmly, my fingers wiggling, barely grazing his neck. He writhes in helpless agony in the fetal position, his cheek smashed against the passenger window, and shakes with soundless laughter.

Suddenly, he grabs my arm, leans in, and kisses me. It's slow, with a quiet urgency, like the soundless flicker-flash of lightning before rain rages. Our tongues touch, and he grips my sleeve, pulling me closer, my body buzzing.

The kiss ends, our foreheads touching. I keep my eyes closed, not wanting to break the spell, the warm, trembling hulk of his chest against me.

I open my eyes. "You good?"

His eyes are soft in the light of the streetlamp, dark striations fanning like sunrays around each pupil. He lifts an eyebrow and grins sheepishly as he readjusts his jeans. "Yeah." He laughs hoarsely, a sound that makes my stomach flutter. "Um. Ready?"

I nod. He could suggest anything and I'd go with it. He climbs into the driver's seat, and I secretly watch him while pretending to straighten my clothes.

Puttering through the quiet, dark streets, we move east along Lincoln Street. I lean back, watching little patches of the inky sky flash through the dense canopy of trees. My limbs hum helplessly as Oliver pulls over, kills the motor, and looks at me, hands in his lap. His eyes are deep in shadows, his hair the color of steel in the dark of the night.

"This is the venue of 'The Great Surprise'?" I say, my eyebrow cocked, scanning yet another residential street.

"Someone needs a whupping," he says wryly.

"Are these threats part of your surprise?"

"All right, missy. Enough of your smack. Let's go," he says, grabbing a knapsack from the back seat.

We climb out of the car and stroll toward Sheridan Road, veering toward Lighthouse Beach. The evening is cool as we head past the Harley Clarke Mansion east toward the lake. When we approach the steps leading down to the sand, I stop in my tracks. A full moon shines, hanging low above the water.

"Uh. Wow."

"I couldn't believe my luck when I realized a full moon coincided with our first night out." He grins, gazing out with appreciation.

"I've never been here at night. It's . . . kind of amazing."

We step down the concrete stairs to the sand. The beach is deserted. Slipping along the sand toward the water, I'm aware of him next to me: his casual, unhurried steps, the tiny creases at his eyes as he squints out at the lake, his height and dark, floppy hair . . . In the blue light of the moon, waves come barreling at us one by one like they're delivering an urgent message. He's so close to me. I shut my eyes and breathe.

"So, what did you do today?" he asks.

I shrug. "Hung out with my grandma. Had dinner with my family."

"So do you guys have, like, real dinner conversations? Like a sitcom?" He seems genuinely interested.

"I guess. But way more boring. I'm usually getting hassled about something: college apps, summer jobs, my unruly hair. Tonight was my mom asking me what crafts I plan on having the kids do at the annual Diwali party."

"Diwali . . . what's that again?"

"Like Christmas. In terms of how huge it is. In India, anyway."

"What's it all about?" He picks up a rock and tries to skip it across the water. It's devoured by the waves instead.

"Hmm . . . God, I really don't know how to explain."

After a beat, he says, "Come on, Jaz. Give me something I can use." He pulls me close and kisses me. "I'm good with secrets," he murmurs.

We start strolling along the water's edge, the waves crashing upon the sand. I've always kept my cultural stuff on the down low, wary of sharing unless it's with someone I trust completely, like Kate. There's something about his persistence with knowing details of my heritage that makes me sweat—*Give me something I can use . . . ?*

But he watches me now, waiting, his eyes patient, earnest. "Okay. Diwali," I say. "It's about how light triumphs over dark, its origins based in the *Ramayana*, which is a Sanskrit epic."

"The *Ramayana*," he says, trying it out.

"Yes. It's the story of how Prince Rama—an incarnation of the god Vishnu—and his wife, Sita, are exiled into the forest for fourteen years by Rama's father and stepmother. Then Ravana—this demon with ten heads—captures Sita, so Rama must defeat him. . . ." I stop. Oliver's eyes are dancing, filled with humor.

"Ah, the demon with the ten heads." He laughs, and I give him the side-eye. "Sorry. Proceed."

I twist my rings. I take pride in my culture, but somehow, articulating it now to Oliver feels weirdly sensationalist. On top of that, I've always been uneasy about religion—any and all religions. Even as a young child, I was a skeptical science girl: *Ma? No actual living thing has ten heads, right? So does that mean that demons are fake, like figments of a person's imagination?* Oliver is watching my face, waiting for me to continue. How must all this sound to him—freaking amazing?

freaking weird? Both possibilities make my skin burn. Then again, maybe I'm being too sensitive.

"So Rama," I say carefully, "defeats Ravana in the forest and returns to his city as its beloved ruler, his path lit with all these little candles as the citizens welcome him back home. That's where the significance of the lights comes in—Diwali is the Festival of Lights."

A slow, megawatt smile transforms his features.

"What?" I demand. "What's funny?"

"You don't usually talk about this, do you?"

I shrug.

"I have a feeling there are more details that we could probably—you know, unearth, what with the internet and all."

"I *know* the details." I sniff. I instinctively left out the part where Rama and Sita were sent into the forest along with Rama's brother—a possible lewd comment was something I didn't feel like fielding. . . . "I'm just not a huge subscriber to religion or mythology. The stories are based in beliefs predating scientific knowledge."

"So you're an atheist?"

"I wouldn't say that." The truth is, the stories are such an integral part of my culture and childhood that talking about them like this feels . . . reductive. Sacrilegious, almost. "I do like doing pujas with my grandma," I offer.

"Pujas?"

I twist my rings. "Pujas are prayers. Most Hindu households have mini altars where you place small sculptures or pictures of gods and goddesses. During pujas, you clean them and make offerings of flowers and sweets, in exchange for their blessings."

He blinks. "That is fucking beautiful. Go on."

I pull one of my rings off, roll it in my hand. "Um. I'd wash and polish them—Ganesh, Lakshmi, Hanuman. And with my grandma, I'd place flowers before each one, along with the diyas—little oil lamps that get lit for Diwali. Though I'm not exactly religious, the firelight shining on the silver gods feels kind of . . . calming."

He stares at me, enraptured. "Huh. So then—you pray?"

I nod. "We sing certain chants and songs . . ."

"Like hymns?"

"Sure. They're all in Sanskrit, so I don't actually know their meanings, but I recite them by heart. . . ."

"Like incantations," he says reverently. "Would you sing one for me?"

"Uh, no."

"Come on! Your version could be jacked, like your Diwali story, and I wouldn't even know the difference."

The way he's smiling down at me—open, good-naturedly—loosens something in my chest, and despite everything, I laugh. "*Apologies* for not having a graduate-level lecture prepared for you on Diwali and its, you know, religious and cultural and . . . mythological roots."

"I would totally take that class! Especially if you were the teacher. Have I ever told you about my professor fantasy?"

I shove him. "Sick!"

He shrugs, chuckling quietly. "Anyway. I'd kill to watch you in puja action sometime."

———

We've reached the northernmost point of the beach, where giant boulders line the water's edge. Oliver climbs onto one and helps me up like I'm the actual Princess Jasmine. Rummaging through his knapsack, he produces two cans. LaCroix.

"To toast our first midnight date. Because getting caught by the police with anything harder on the one night you break out would not be favorable."

I freeze. I hadn't even considered the police. Is there a police-mandated curfew?

We crack open our cans, and I watch as Oliver fumbles with something in a baggie.

My heart skips a beat.

But he pulls out a wedge of lime and carefully squeezes it into the mouths of our seltzers. "My feeble attempt at being classy," he says, grinning.

But now I can't help imagining the police showing up, throwing us into their car, and driving to my house. They'd ring my doorbell while I'd stand in dark dread on the front stoop. The door would open tentatively, my parents' faces filled with shock. The police wouldn't spare me. They'd tell my family everything, and life as I know it would be over.

"To us"—Oliver clinks his can with mine—"and our first midnight date."

I look into his eyes, trying to shake off my fears. "To us." We take a sip. I practically choke on the seltzer bubbles. "Oliver?"

"Hmm?"

"Thanks for, um, organizing this." I search his face, and then he's kissing me, tasting of fresh lime and seltzer salt, his fingers in my hair, the waves smashing the boulders beneath us. I try to lose myself in it. But the funny thing about a kiss is that the moment you start trying, its magic dissipates like vapor. In the middle of his lips on mine, I open my eyes and stare at the paleness of his skin, glowing blue gray in the moonlight. I think about how his face might photograph, what angle I would use to get the lighting right. I also wonder: What is the biological purpose of lips?

"Rani. You okay?"

"Sorry, I . . ." I trail off, suddenly exhausted.

"Hey. It's cool." He gets to his feet. "Let's walk."

I glance back toward the parking lot. No police. In fact, no cars in sight. We begin walking along the shoreline, waves pounding the sand like they've got something to say.

"Did I ever tell you that I'm responsible for my dad leaving us?" Oliver says. "I know every kid thinks they're to blame for their parents' divorce, but in my case, it's actually true."

I reach for his hand. "What happened?"

"When I was in middle school, Kathy ran away. Dropped out of high school and everything. At that time, Dad was still around but was usually wasted and mean as fuck. He and Mom spent most of their time screaming at each other, and at me when I did something stupid, which was often. I was lonely and desperate for . . . to be seen, I guess? Kids are real assholes that way—demanding any kind of attention they can get."

"Okay, I feel an irrepressible compulsion to jump in and advocate for those assholes, though," I say. "Kids need attention, and seeking it out is smart—it's a form of survival."

He laughs. "Right—future pediatrician of the world. Anyway, I started getting into a lot of trouble at school. Pranks mostly—like pulling the fire alarm, mouthing off at teachers, stupid shit—but also failing classes and hanging around messed-up kids. I spent those years spinning perpetual lies, trying to weasel out of the fixes I kept getting into." He stops, stares at the waves lapping the shoreline. I snuggle into him as he puts his arm around me, and I gaze up at the distant specks of starlight, listening.

"One day, my parents were called to the school because I'd started a fire in the boys' bathroom. I was with my buddy Jonah, who had a lighter on him. . . . That night, my parents had an epic fight about my suspension. Things were smashed around the apartment, and the neighbors called the cops because of the noise. . . . Anyway, Dad finally screamed that he was done with us—'all of you assholes,' to be exact. He was gone by morning."

"Holy shit."

"Yeah. At that point, I decided I had to wean myself off the lying and problem behavior. I missed Kathy, and I thought maybe I could bring her back by being . . . better. I played a little game: I allowed myself exactly one lie a day. If it was just one lie, it didn't really count and I didn't have to feel guilty about it."

"Gotta love that creative justification. Kids are the greatest."

"That's your takeaway?" He grins down at me.

"Yeah. It wasn't your fault. You were a kid, and kids do dumb shit."

He laughs. "I could totally imagine that posted in your future clinic." He moves a palm in the air: "KIDS DO DUMB SHIT."

I laugh, and hold his hand.

111

"Anyway. I *was* an asshole, and so was Mom. And even Kathy . . . a quieter brand, but still. Not that any of it warrants Dad *leaving*, but . . ." He clears his throat. "All that is to say: I get it. One guilt at a time—sneaking out tonight is one thing. Messing around with a scary dude like me is another. See? Our life experiences are more parallel than you think."

Maybe he's right. Our worlds seem so different on the surface, but maybe they're shots of the same complex landscape—one taken at dawn, one at dusk. "How'd you pull yourself out of that cycle, aside from your lie game?" I ask.

"I'd spend most of every class doodling and sketching— 'self-soothing,' the pros called it. Anyway, my science teacher, Mrs. Khan, decided it was real artwork and connected me with the art teacher. Before long, art class was where I felt like a decent version of myself. Mrs. Khan also insisted I start seeing the school counselor, Mr. Brown, who pretty much saved my sorry ass. And then, like magic, Kathy came home."

I squeeze his hand. "I'm sorry you had to go through all of that. But a happy ending, at least." Upon the distant water, the opalescent moon reflects a line of filmy light. We reach the rusted breakwater, and I climb onto it, stepping along the iron plank above the dark, swirling waves.

"Uh, Rani? How far do you plan to go?" I turn around. He's frozen a few steps behind me, gazing at the black water. "I—I can't swim."

"Oh." I blink. "Crap. Let's get off this thing." We hop down, run across the sand to the giant lifeguard chair, climb its rungs to the top, and huddle together against the whipping winds. My teeth chatter as chills ripple through me. Wordlessly, he puts his arms around me and nuzzles his face into my neck.

Amid the heat of his breath and the sandy sensation of his skin scraping up against mine, he kisses softly along the hollows there. . . . I relax against the wooden back of the chair as tension releases, my blood defrosting and rocketing to life.

He pushes aside my clothing layers to stare at my neck and collarbone. "God . . ." He touches my throat lightly with his warm fingertips.

"What—you wanna take a bite? I always wondered why you were so pale."

He smiles faintly, gazing at my skin like I'm some kind of mythical creature. I fidget, suddenly self-conscious. Like my collarbone's worth worshipping. But when his lips touch my neck, my shyness slides away. He kisses his way lower, and before long, I feel his mouth through the sheer lace of my bra. Trembling, my hands move along his body under his jacket, along the muscles of his chest, the smoothness of his stomach, slipping lower . . .

I stop.

He breaks away from me and looks at me searchingly. "You okay?" His lips are red and slick.

"Yeah. Um, it's just that my hands are really cold, and I don't want to shock you."

"It'll be a good kind of shock," he says, his eyes shining.

I feel for his fly, unzipping it and then touching the hardness of him, the heat. I watch his eyes close, his face near mine; I feel like I've just swallowed ten million stars. I fumble along, and just as I'm drumming up the courage to be straightforward and ask him what exactly I should do, his fingers slide along me, back and forth. . . . My body takes charge, my brain shutting down. I grip him hard as nerves and blood whoosh and explode inside me, and I open my eyes in time to see his squeeze shut, his expression and his warmth and wetness telling me that I was okay, that maybe I didn't need to study up after all.

"So," he says after we disentangle ourselves. His voice comes out squeaky and prepubescent. I smile. "Um. That was. You are . . ."

I grin. "So are you."

By the time we retrace our footsteps to the car, I've almost forgotten about my parents. As he drives, I think how different the drive home feels compared with the drive here. It's frigid now, the trees spindly, and the moon's disappeared. But there's a warmth inside my belly, my heart swollen, happy. I don't even check my phone.

Finally, the car turns into the alley, slowing to a crawl. Gravel pops in the stillness of the night. I close my eyes, knowing that in a moment, we'll be in a direct line of sight of my house. The car pulls to a stop.

"It looks okay," he murmurs.

I look for myself.

"Rani."

"Yeah?"

He leans in and kisses me in that slow-burn way that sparks a firestorm inside me. Touching my cheekbone, he looks into my eyes. "I—um, am glad we had this time tonight. I love—being with you."

"Me too. See you Monday." I jump out of the car, steal across the yard to my back door, and let myself into the house. Slipping out of my shoes, I shrug off my coat and float up the stairs, Oliver's voice in my head. I wonder at the hidden magic of this new fabulous planet we call Earth. . . .

And on the middle landing is the rudest of all awakenings.

A figure limping from the bathroom toward the bedrooms.

In her signature pink cotton sleeping sari.

Aaji.

I lie on the spot: "Hi, Aaji. I couldn't sleep, so I thought I'd get some homework done on the downstairs desktop," I say breathlessly. I search out the details of her face in the shadowed hallway.

Is it possible that she knows all my secrets?

"Good night, then, betiya."

CHAPTER SIXTEEN

Tuesday after school, as Ma drives me to Salil's, I tell her that I'm going to Saul's Halloween party on Friday.

"Ah, lovely. A Halloween party is such wholesome fun." Halloween is the one American tradition that my mother seems to embrace. It reminds her of Holi—the Hindu holiday that signifies the welcoming of spring—which triggers all these nostalgic memories from her childhood.

Which works, for all intents and purposes.

I tell her Kate and I will be going to Saul's party, but I leave out the following:

1. The party's a screening for a campy homemade horror flick (directed by Saul, my boyfriend's tattooed and mohawked best friend).
2. Kate isn't technically going (she's just dropping me off).
3. We aren't spending the night at Kate's (her family's out of town and she's using the opportunity to show off her new lingerie for her new guy, Toby—to have a "ho-down," as she calls it).

4. Instead, I'll be sleeping at Saul's, where
   Oliver has been staying since the huge
   argument he had with his mom last week.
   In the room that is technically Oliver's
   bedroom. On the pullout couch that is
   technically Oliver's bed. With Oliver.

These omitted details flit through my mind, blips of bubbling guilt.

"So are you too old to go dressed up for this Halloween party?" my mother asks, tapping her fingers on the steering wheel to the soundtrack to the Bollywood film *Gangs of Wasseypur*, which is kept infinitely on repeat in her car.

"Well, it's a costume party, so I should go as something." Something edgy or wild that would help me fit in.

She turns onto Salil's street, chuckling. "Remember all those years you went as a traditional Indian girl? The pictures of you wearing a tiny sari were so sweet!"

"Oh, I remember."

"You were very proud. You ran around the neighborhood, smiling at all the compliments and candy."

I thank her for the ride, then wander up the walkway, ring the doorbell, and stare at a faint crack in the stucco. Through second grade, I wore a sari every year for Halloween, and my parents encouraged it: "No costume could compare to all your beautiful Indian clothes—clothes you should wear more often!" They were not wrong, and I loved wearing a sari.

The year I turned eight, I was invited to trick-or-treat with Brittany and her friends—a group of impossibly stylish, funny girls who defined third-grade cool. Alice was visiting her aunt and uncle in Michigan, so I was thrilled to have a backup Halloween plan. When I unwittingly showed up at Brittany's doorstep in one of my customary saris, her eyes trailed my body head to toe and back up again. I gazed at her furry hood, short skirt, and painted-on whiskers—a sexy wolf?—and tried to ignore her dubious expression. "Hey," she said flatly. Heart pounding, I followed her and her furry white boots and tail to the den, where the others—a sleek Catwoman, a vampy Carol Danvers from *Captain Marvel*, a Kardashian look-alike—stopped in their tracks, gaping at me. "Oh," Carol Danvers said. "What are those . . . *outfits* called again?"

I fiddled with the fringes of my pink-and-gold dupatta. "It's a sari."

"Sari? Sorry, it's a sari," she joked. Two of them snickered while the heat of shame filled me.

Trick-or-treating was a haze; I couldn't help but feel self-conscious about my clothes. Afterward, upon returning from the bathroom at Brittany's, I heard whispering from the hallway.

"Uh . . . costumes are supposed to be funny or cool, not your own, like, cultural toga thing."

"I don't know . . . I think it's kind of cool," said Janie the Kardashian. "I mean, like, the colors . . . ?" She was trying.

"Sure. But you've got to admit that it's weird. Plus, it smells . . . *spicy*."

Giggles.

"What if I just wrapped myself in a stinky sheet and called it a costume? Hare Krishna, Hare Krishna, Hare Krishna!" More giggles.

I should have just owned it—worn my sari with pride that night, strode back in there with my head held high, maybe even busted them mid–racist joke. But something sharp and brittle crystallized inside me: I turned, grabbed my candy bag, and fled for home. Dead leaves swirled in the dark streets as shame flared in my chest—shame over how I was seen, over everything that made me "different." Shame that I was ashamed.

Weeks later, I broke down and told Ma everything. After listening impassively, she said, "This is not your problem. Those girls are silly." She turned back to chopping vegetables. Her usual black-and-white oversimplification.

Anger burst in my gut. I yelled: "How did you and Baba ever think that a sari is a *costume*? You don't even know what Halloween *is*!" She put down her knife and gazed at me evenly. "Betiya. This happens. Some will not choose to be your friend because of who you are, and that's okay. It doesn't matter. Keep your mind off these girls' nonsense and continue to work hard. Never let others' foolishness distract from your higher purpose." Somehow, her crisp response hurt almost as much as the group's rejection.

Veena Auntie now opens the door, and suddenly, there's no time to sulk—Salil is bouncing off the walls. I proceed to use every known tactic to expend his energy after a day of classroom sitting (long jumping and soccer in the yard, plogging together around the neighborhood with garbage bags— Henry has clearly taught him well—and channeling Aajoba by jumping rope) before finally settling down to make cookies. We find the one and only recipe, and together we measure, pour, and mix before spooning dough onto cookie sheets. And, as always, whenever I bake cookies, Nilesh invades my mind.

119

Late June, after Nilesh's junior year and my eighth-grade year, Nilesh's parents found him in his room, unconscious, empty pill bottles scattered across the bed. He was rushed to the hospital, and his stomach was pumped. He survived the suicide attempt but required weeks of treatment in the local psychiatric ward.

My parents and I visited him after he'd been home a week. We came bearing his favorite—oatmeal chocolate chip cookies we'd made using the recipe beneath the oatmeal lid that he insisted was simply the best. I shivered in their over-air-conditioned white living room—white walls, white furniture, white carpeting—and when he appeared, I tried not to stare. He was pale and pudgy (a result of his meds, I later learned). He hardly conversed, this boy who had once crushed parents with his charisma. After he mumbled some monosyllabic answers to the adults' questions, they wandered into the kitchen for tea, leaving the two of us in that living room, the cruel August light slanting in through the picture window. I offered him a cookie, but he shook his head.

"You've grown," he said.

I shrugged.

"How's Salil?"

"Good. Getting tall. He misses you."

"Yeah. Hey. I've gotta tell you something." His voice was thick and throaty, like he'd just awoken from a leaden slumber. "And, Doc, I need you to tell Salil, too, because, honestly, I'm going to be out of commission for a while."

"Okay. What?" My voice was squeaky, a little girl's. He just called me Doc!

"Don't ever get rolling. Alcohol, pills, even weed . . . it's

120

like entering a black hole that sucks you in so deep you can't ever get out."

I waited for more. Despite everything, I felt pride: I was his confidante.

"Whatever," he muttered. "Like I have to tell you. You're not weak *or* stupid."

I stared at him. I wanted to tell him he wasn't weak or stupid, either. But I didn't want to sound like a bossy know-it-all; I wasn't even in high school yet.

"Doc," he whispered. His eyes were vagued out, glassy.

"Yeah?"

He started shaking then, and I watched, cold fear spreading through my limbs. Beads of pearly sweat sprang across his forehead; he was suddenly gray. He closed his eyes.

"Nilesh? Do you need something?"

"Just . . . go."

And moments later, we did.

——

Salil has already gotten plates and poured glasses of milk for the two of us. Once the cookies have cooled, he takes his first bite.

"Rani Tai?"

"Yeah, buddy?"

"These are really, really good. How did you know which recipe to pick? There were so many online."

I hesitate, brushing crumbs off his face. "It's Nilesh's favorite recipe."

"Oh." He puts down his cookie. "Hey, can we bring some over to Henry? I'm pretty sure he'd love these."

CHAPTER SEVENTEEN

The night of the Halloween party, we troll the streets in Kate's hatchback, avoiding the swarming hordes of ninjas and princesses and Power Rangers who clutch bags of candy and trip on hems. Kate slows before an old bungalow, its porch lined with a dozen lit jack-o'-lanterns. Girls in dramatic makeup lean against the railings as guys in black lean in, trying to make them laugh.

I check the address. This is it.

She stops. "Impressive pumpkin carving." She snaps her gum.

Within each pumpkin is carved a single letter, the string of them spelling:

SEX 4 UR SOUL

"What . . . the . . . ?" I breathe. "What's that about?"

"I don't know, but my interest is officially piqued."

"Um, I don't think I—"

"Here." She reaches into the back seat. "This'll give you powers." She hands me a green-sequined mask.

"Sure, this will solve everything." I take it from her.

"At least you're not in the M&M's bag costume your mom stitched for you that one year."

"Are people dressed up," I say, squinting, "or is that what they always wear?"

"For some folks, there's a blurred line between Halloween and everyday."

I open the car door, and Kate touches my arm.

"Rani?"

I turn.

"Remember this is going to be fun. With Oliver? Alone in his room? All night long? The next twelve hours'll go down in history."

"Right."

"And wish me luck."

"Oh my God. You and Toby." Tonight's the night she planned to mess around with her new find. "Hey, why don't you bring Toby here? You can have your ho-down after."

She glances at the scene. "It does look sort of epic. Would Saul mind, do you think?"

"No, it's a movie screening. He said the more exposure, the better."

"Yeah? Okay, you convinced me. I'll pick up Toby and be back in twenty."

I hug her hard. "Great. I'm so happy. And, um, just to recap: with my mom, remember . . ."

"That if she calls me, you're in the bathroom. I text you, then you call her back when you're somewhere quiet. I got you."

"You're the best."

I climb out, hitch up my backpack, and wave as she putters away. A gust of wind swirls leaves around me, whipping at my hair as I lope toward the house. I make eye contact with no one, though I sense the porch kids watching as I climb the stairs, their conversations a low murmur. I note a witch and a couple of ghouls in the mix. I shove the mask into my backpack and open the screen door.

"Whoa," I mutter.

Kids I vaguely recognize are packed into the crowded living room, white teeth glowing in the black light. Though there's a sexy vampire and a Catwoman, plus Michelle and Barack, most aren't in costume. I glance down at my look: shiny metallic blue jeggings topped by a tweedy vest, courtesy of Kate's closet. Few people can pull off the vintage vest, and in this moment, I'm pretty sure I'm not one of them.

I take out my phone to text Oliver, and it immediately dies—how had I forgotten to charge it? Bodies are jammed wall to wall in the dark-paneled house, and I have to push my way inside. There are polyester cobwebs and creepy jack-o'-lanterns everywhere, their innards lit up like goopy caves. Opposite the fireplace hangs a huge flat-screen. The music thuds through my bones. Amid the sea of unknown faces, I want to disappear.

Palms cover my eyes from behind. I whirl around.

It's Oliver, his eyes shining. He takes off a top hat, bowing deeply. He's wearing a black Jethro Tull tee under a thin gray blazer. I slip my hands beneath the blazer and wrap my arms around him.

"Happy to see you, too," he says. "You didn't text."

"Phone died," I say. "You are really rocking that blazer, by the way."

"All right, everybody!" Saul booms over the thudding music. He fiddles with his phone, and the volume goes low. He's in a sports coat over destroyed black jeans and combats. Dapperly badass.

"Guys. Thanks to all of you for coming out this lovely Halloween," he says, bowing slightly and speaking in his distinctive Saul accent, which I haven't yet placed. "Now is the torture part, where I force-feed you this film."

Shouts rise from the crowd: "Yeah, screw you, Saul!" and "This is bullshit, man."

Just then, Kate and what looks like a medieval knight enter—Kate's wearing a bunny ears headband and has whiskers drawn along her cheeks, with a pink button nose. I laugh waving them over. Oliver gives Toby a fist bump while Kate and I hug.

"I won't even ask how you two scared up costumes in such record time," I say as the lights dim.

"Oh, it was nothing," Toby says, removing his mask, wild curls tumbling around his face. He beams confidently. "I already owned this." Kate gives me a wide-eyed glance before turning toward the screen.

Numbers flicker like at the start of an old black-and-white film before the scene opens with a cute guy, sitting in this very living room. He strums a guitar dolefully, sighs, and runs a hand through his dark hair, and when he rolls his eyes toward the ceiling, I recognize him as a theater kid—Tom Lindholm. He's usually decked out in studded leather and

125

Euro jeans, but on-screen, he's a basic jock with cropped hair and a pastel polo. I scan the audience and find him standing next to Saul, squinting apprehensively at the screen.

On-screen, he paces the room, pulls out his phone, and scrolls through various photos of him posing with a girl; he studies her before deleting them, one by one. He crashes on the sofa, and with hands on his head, he gazes sullenly into space. Back on his phone, he hits the Tinder app and swipes through profiles, looking bored. He studies a few, continues swiping; then the camera stills on the profile of a stunning woman named Sam, with long golden hair and deep cleavage. Her profile is brief. It reads: *sex 4 ur soul.*

He stares at those words, incredulous. He swipes right, then waits.

Moments later, *It's a Match!* flashes on the screen as clapping and hooting rise from the crowd. The screen illuminates Tommy's face as an expression of lascivious desire rearranges his features.

SAM: Can I come now?

TOMMY: Yes. 433 Judson

Within moments, the doorbell rings.

Tommy opens the door to a busty blonde. Dressed in a racy corset and garter belt beneath her trench coat, she leads him through the house and into a back room, somehow knowing exactly where to go. We get a panoramic view of the room, decorated with guitars and vintage record sleeves. She removes her trench and draws her corseted body close to his.

"Hmm, a music man's lair," she whispers in his ear. "The girls were right, Tommy. You *are* perfect." She pushes him onto a couch.

"The girls?" he says between kisses, but she's nuzzling and fawning until he's at her mercy. She strips him down while the camera spins. . . . As his eyes close in ecstasy, the girl multiplies: The camerawork shows six of her encircling him. Long black tentacles sprout from each of them, brushing gently along his body. Eyes still closed, he moans with pleasure.

The audience shrieks with disgust and delight; Oliver watches, prideful, a sly sparkle in his eyes. He stands behind me, hands on my waist. I snuggle in close, my blood buzzing.

The girls grow fangs and claws, their irises glowing red. Tommy opens his eyes, screams, and thrashes, but he's ensnared in a tentacle-arm. "Now, that's no way to treat the girls. *You* swiped *me*. It was pretty clear, wasn't it, girls? You get sex for"—she gestures to the scantily clad sextuplets, who shove their barely concealed boobs in his face, her voice morphing from sex kitten to demon panther—"YOUR SOUL!"

He screams, writhing as spiky tentacles sink and disappear into him, the view shrouded by the bare backs of the demon girls. The scene fades as Tommy flails and shrieks, and the crowd hoots and cheers.

The film cuts to a new scene featuring straitlaced Tommy walking up the front path of a suburban house. He rings the doorbell, and a curvy beauty answers. "You must be Sam," she gushes. "That was fast—it's great to meet you! Come in," she says, stepping aside.

"I've got something for you," he says with a charming smile.

"For me? Sam, what for?"

He steps in closer. "A little something," he says, "for your soul."

The door closes on the camera as he steps inside, and music pumps as the credits roll.

The room explodes in applause. People thump Saul on the back, yelling unintelligibly. People start rehashing awesome parts, and some girls flock around Tommy, the surprisingly skilled main actor, laughing and flirting with him. More people stream in from the kitchen with beers, wearing dazed smiles.

"So, what'd ya think?" Oliver yells over the din, drawing me close.

I watch the credits. "Whoa," I mutter.

"What?" Oliver shouts.

"Impressive!" I yell.

"And empowering," Kate says, leaning in. "Especially the part about women portrayed as conniving sex demons."

I laugh. "It definitely makes me think twice about dating apps. But how amazing that Saul shot and screened a film from scratch. How'd he make this happen?"

Oliver says, "He's got this friend—a junior who interns with a Chicago videographer—who helped him with a lot of the details, and who also happens to be crushing on him."

"Oh—who is it?"

"Trevor Trent." He leans in. "And don't tell Fiona, but I'm pretty sure Saul was wholly flattered."

Though a year younger, Trevor's a known genius videographer. "They *would* make a cute couple."

Oliver and I maneuver our way to the kitchen, where he grabs two Cokes. Threading through the party, we meet up with Jared, Tonio, and Fiona.

"Princess Jasmine!" Jared says, giving me a fist bump.

Kate and Toby wander over, and she introduces Toby to the group.

"What'd you think of the film?" Jared asks, his glazed eyes scanning our faces.

"Loved it," I say.

"I did, too," Kate says, grinning. "Despite the, you know, iffy messages."

"Agreed," Tonio laughs. "Fun, but bro-ey."

"No shit," mutters Fiona. Just then, a guy spills a little beer on her back, and she shoots him a death stare while removing her bomber jacket. "I mean, what does it say about our relationship if Saul's making movies portraying women as monsters?"

"Ladies," croons Jared, putting his arms around us, including Tonio. "Simmer down. It's art. Not everything's social commentary. Chill, little mamas."

Tonio shrugs off Jared's arm, while I give Jared the hairy eye. "Wha?" he slurs. "Whad I do?"

Tonio and I exchange a glance. *I'm sorry*, I mouth. How often do people intentionally address him as a girl, despite knowing that's not how he identifies? I break into a sweat, humiliation for Tonio burning beneath my skin.

"Buddy," says Saul, stepping in and leading Jared away, "let's go find you a water."

Music resumes thudding through the speakers. I watch Kate drag an uncomfortable-looking Toby to the open space that doubles as a dance floor.

Oliver says, "Sorry." He takes my backpack from me. "Jared's a good guy, but just . . . you know. Immature. And drunk. Let's get your stuff to the room I've been crashing in." Slinging my backpack over his shoulder, he pretends to stagger beneath its weight. We weave past dancing bodies to the back of the house, where he opens a door marked DO NOT ENTER. He stops short.

"What the— Get out of here!" he yells. "Can you not read?" Oliver gestures toward the sign.

I peek in around him. Four guys and a couple of girls lounge on a kilim rug, blue-gray smoke hanging in the air.

"You're *smoking up*? Shit, you can't *do* that here. Get the hell out."

The group ambles out, mumbling, "Dude. Chill. . . ." One guy carries a blown-glass pipe. Oliver waves his arms at the air before opening the windows wide.

"I'm sorry it's cold, but I've got to get rid of this smell."

I stand, usefully staring.

"I don't want to lose the privilege of staying here because Saul's old man thinks I'm hotboxing his music room."

He turns on the fan in the corner and plugs my phone into a charger. My parents would keel over if they knew I was at a party with my tattooed boyfriend where people were doing drugs.

Scanning the room, I realize it's the very site of the soul-stealing from Saul's film. "This is where you sleep?"

"Pretty awesome, right?" he says, drawing the curtains and leaning up against the wall. "Saul's dad's a music fiend, obviously. Check out these walls—they're padded beneath this wallpaper, which absorbs sound. Plus, this thick carpeting. No one can hear what happens in here."

I raise my eyebrows.

"You know. So that neighbors are shielded from . . . sonic experimentation?"

"Right," I say, laughing at his sheepish shrug.

We settle on the leather couch where poor Tommy had his soul and dignity stolen, blinking in the quiet of the room. Soon Oliver's lips are blazing a trail along my neck, and my heart pounds helplessly against my ribs. The throbbing energy of the party is a fading memory as I breathe in the warmth and scent of his skin.

"I can't believe I get you all to myself tonight," Oliver murmurs.

"I know. Um." I sit up. "Could you point me to the bathroom?" I unplug my phone—just enough juice for a quick call.

"Oh. Okay." Oliver scratches his cheek. "There's one in the hallway. Otherwise upstairs, just past the bedrooms."

I kiss him. "Be right back."

———

The downstairs bathroom is locked. After weaving through a sea of bodies and stepping around a couple kissing on the stairs, I'm finally in the upstairs bathroom, my heart pounding. Why didn't I just step outdoors? One party shriek and the whole ruse will be blown. I curse myself.

"Hello?"

"Hi, Ma, it's me. We're at Kate's now, and we're going to bed soon."

"Okay, betiya. How was the party?"

"Great—yeah. Lots of, um, funny costumes." I fake a yawn. "Okay. So I'll be home tomorrow around ten."

"Okay. Oh, Rani? Do you need me to pick up anything for your Diwali crafts tomorrow?"

"No . . . I'll do it on the way home. I think I know what Salil would like, so I'll go by that."

"All right, betiya."

"Okay, bye, Ma."

I hang up, staring at myself in the mirror. She isn't a big phone gabber, thank God. I feel a twinge of guilt over her offer to help me with my Diwali lesson while I'm supposedly at Kate's. At least I didn't take her up on it, right?

I open the door and glimpse two guys disappearing into one of the dark bedrooms. I tiptoe around the couple now aggressively making out on the stairs. Once, I would have rolled my eyes at all the rampant PDA, but today, I feel a connection with them, empathy for their plight: They don't have access to a room. And even if they did, they can't wait.

CHAPTER EIGHTEEN

Oliver is where I left him. The lanterns have been dimmed, and lit candles flicker beside the pullout couch. I lace my fingers around his neck. "I've got something for you."

"For me?" He grips my hips, looking up at me. "'Oh, Sam, what for?'" he says, mimicking the movie.

Taking a deep breath, I shrug out of the vest and peel off my shirt, revealing the silver-gray camisole that Kate and I found on sale at Lover's Lane. His eyes travel the length of my arms, where a thousand hairs stand up like a field of dandelion fluff, hairs I probably should have waxed, like a lot of Indian girls do. He makes a quick sweep over my neck and the shaded valley of cleavage that has appeared as if by magic, thanks to the garment engineers at Lover's Lane.

He pulls me onto the couch and kisses me gently. My veins ignite. He slips a spaghetti strap off my shoulder so that the silk string hangs down my triceps, a silver rivulet. "God." He stares at my bare shoulder.

I can't help but smile. "Seriously, that did something for you?" I pull it back up. "Well, you're easy. Do it again."

His eyes are hazy, zapping my stomach with a blistering

jolt of electricity. I swallow, working to keep my cool. He looks at me, smiles a half smile, and slips it off my shoulder again.

Voices rise in the hall, chortling drunkenness crashing against the door, and he bounds up to fasten the hook into the eye, locking it. His back against the door, hair sticking up, jeans low on his hips, and a smeary grin on his face, he says, "Guess I should've done that sooner. . . ." An electroshock strikes low in my belly.

He sits next to me, and I do my best not to jump him. "What're your thoughts on this whole scene?" he asks.

"Love it." I'm grateful for a topic. "Your friends—I really like Saul and Tonio and Fiona. And Saul's movie . . . I mean, all that work—I never knew." He's staring at my mouth like he's lip-reading. "What?" I laugh. "You think I'm a nerd."

"No. I love you—why would you say that?"

I stare at him.

I love you.

My insides crack open, releasing what feels like ten billion butterflies into the stratosphere. I swallow. "Um, do you have a dark ulterior motive here?" I say, glancing down at myself in my cami.

"Yeah," he says. "I said 'I love you' so I could get into your pants. Off with your clothes, woman." He grins, looking down at his hands, then straightens up. "I wasn't sure I was gonna tell you tonight."

"Why?"

"Usual reasons." He looks at me. "Don't feel . . ."

"I love you, too." It comes out a tattered little whisper. To hell with Kate's rules. All month my soul has been working to bust its way out, eager to twine up with his like an invasive weed. Why have I been holding back, anyway?

He holds me close, the warmth of his body seeping through mine, my blood channeling wildly through waterslide veins. I pull off his shirt, and he helps me slip out of my shiny pants.

He hovers over me as I lie across the couch, his lips working their way from the hollow of my throat on down, a fevered slow dance. I touch his biceps, closing my eyes and reveling in this moment.

He loves me.

"Rani." My eyes fly open and there he is, poised just above my belly. He's looking up at me. "Can I try something?"

"Um, I don't know."

"Please."

His face is bleary with longing and lust, the muscles in his arms and chest sculpted in the candlelight. He actually looks like one of those Greek statues, except with wild hair and tattoos.

Holy shit. Kate's first rule.

I nod. He pulls off my underwear—the pair I bought to match my cami—and I squeeze my eyes shut, moving through the delicate layers of my squeamishness before giving myself over to the exquisite sensations surging through me.

Oh. My. God.

My life will never be the same.

I'm still levitating in another dimension as he yanks the sofa into a bed and piles some sheets on it. We climb in, throwing off our remaining clothes. Now, both naked, we're pressed up against each other, skin to skin. It feels like we'll burst into flames from the heat between us. I push some of the bedding away.

"Um, I don't think I'm ready," I say, trying not to pant.

"No, I'm not, either." He looks at me with pseudo-seriousness, and we burst out laughing. "No, but really," he says. "It's all up to you. It's always up to you. Let's just lie here together." He gives me an impish grin.

I breathe, trying to ignore the hardness of him against me as I trail a finger over the black branches stretching along his arms, touching their heart-shaped red leaves. "I love your tattoos."

"Yeah? I got them this past summer. Designed them myself."

"They're amazing. How'd you come up with the design?"

"Trees are like life, and the best kind of love—growing, flourishing without a lot of fuss."

"Wild and free, but also rooted."

"Exactly. I'd wanted one for a while. Spent a lot of time figuring out the design. Kathy took me—served as consenting adult. Mom was pissed, as you can imagine."

"I *can*," I say, grinning.

"'Why would you voluntarily *choose* to look like a loser?'" he says in a mother-mocking tone, mime-smacking an imaginary person upside the head.

"Well, *I* love them."

"Hmm. Maybe you should have one, too."

"Yeah?"

"Yeah. In a spot only I could see." He reaches over me,

grabs a fine black Sharpie from the end table. "Maybe . . . right here?" He touches my hip.

I curl onto my side, and he pushes away the covers, leans over my hip, and begins to sketch.

He works silently, the tip of his pen electric on my skin. I close my eyes, my blood coursing in ecstasy. I peek to watch him work with great concentration, the candlelight glossing his hair and brow, the muscles in his arms and chest as he sketches. . . . I feel myself getting warm again. Everything's a dream, an erotic-as-hell dream. . . .

Ten minutes later, he caps his pen. "There. Something like that."

I stand, pull the sheet around me, and shuffle to the door mirror. I'm trembling as I stare at the detailed design on my hip. Encircled by an irregular pattern is an almond-eyed female in an abstract style, her chin resting on her palm, breasts bare, hair wavy and wild. She gazes out knowingly, exuding strength and confidence.

"Wow." I move closer to the mirror to inspect the design, which is about the size of my fist. My breath fogs up the glass.

"I know. That's how I feel every time I look at you."

"What a line," I laugh, but my face burns with pleasure as I stumble back to him.

———

I awaken to a perimeter of light glowing around the heavy curtains. Oliver's holding me, and the slow realization of last night dawns on me. He's motionless, deep in slumber as I stare at him: the dark eyebrows, the wide, full lips, the jutting cheekbones and dark stubble. *I love him and he loves me,* I think, trailing a finger over my hip tattoo.

I glance down at our semi-naked selves. At some point last night, I pulled on my cami and underwear while he dressed in his boxers—it was beyond distracting otherwise. Thank God we didn't actually have sex. Adding that to the emotional mix might have caused my heart to burst.

His eyes squint open. He stretches, yawns, then props himself up on an elbow.

"Hey."

"Hi."

"So, you think we could swing this overnight thing again sometime?" He twirls a lock of my hair around his finger.

"I don't know . . . maybe."

"When?"

My phone trills from the table where I'd returned it to Oliver's charger. I leap from the bedcovers and lunge for it: my mother. My heart shudders. "Hello?"

CHAPTER NINETEEN

Late that afternoon, I sit before Salil and six other impish faces, their thickly fringed dark eyes wondering what I've got. I'm surprised by how tall some of them are now that they're tweens, compared with my memories of them bear-cubbing with Nilesh.

"Uh, hi, guys," I say. I smooth my kameez over my leggings. "Who can tell me what they know about Diwali?"

Hands shoot up.

"It's the Festival of Lights!"

"It's a harvesttime!"

"It's when people eat lots of dessert!" yells Salil.

"It's when Rama returns to his city after his battle with Ravana. . . ."

"The dude with ten heads!"

"Oh yeah. He's awesome!"

I look at them. Apparently, I've taught them well over the years.

It's strange to think that just this morning, I was lying in Oliver's arms. Ma called only to remind me of today's Diwali gathering—I can't help but marvel that I've actually gotten away with an overnight with Oliver.

"Wow—you guys rock!" I say. "You're all exactly right." I bring out the picture books on Diwali and begin reading aloud while I hold up the illustrations, auntie-uncles poking their heads in the doorway with approving grins.

After the books, I lead them to the dining table, where two example projects are set up: a clay diya decorated with glass beads, and a rangoli project involving glue and colored rice on cardboard. The older boys pump their fists and hiss "Yesssss!" as I show them the materials.

Once I've handed each kid a ball of clay, I instruct the younger ones how to make their diyas and compliment the older ones on their interpretations (Nikhil's looks suspiciously like a machine gun; Mahesh's takes the shape of a pentagon with spiky missiles pointing up around its perimeter). Five-year-old Samir struggles with the first step of forming the clay into a pot, so I pull up a chair and sit with him, sticking my thumbs into the center of the ball and pinching out the sides. He mimics the motions of my fingers with his own. When he's through, his face lights up with pride as he holds it out to me in his small palm. Kids are the best.

And that's when I hear the aunties in the kitchen.

"Rani is so good with the children!"

"Such a wonderful role model for the young ones."

"And lovely. I'll bet the boys at school are chasing after her."

There are titters, and then:

"Rani doesn't hang around boys." My mother pronounces the word *boys* like it revolts her. "She is focused on her studies."

"Of course not, Uma," Veena Auntie says, attempting the

140

dangerous mission of coming to my defense. "But it is natural. American girls and boys do become . . . friends, na?"

Salil peeks into a box I brought, running his fingers through a container of colored rice. I firmly fold down the box's top.

"Okay, Salil, that's for our next project—rangoli," I say.

"Can we start that now, Rani Tai?" Salil looks up at me hopefully.

My mother's voice continues, muttering something unintelligible. Veena Auntie responds: "Of course we know she's a fine girl, Uma. . . ."

"Yes, she has good judgment. Nothing was meant by it. . . ."

The kitchen is strangely quiet, considering how many aunties are in there. I strain to listen but hear nothing more.

I look down at Salil.

"Sure," I say, giving him my cheeriest smile. I take a breath. "Let's move on to the next one, yeah?"

———

It's dark as I create a sparklers station in the backyard, another Diwali tradition. Setting out several matchboxes and bowls of water, I plot my next getaway with Oliver. I'd love to show him the mermaid Baba and I found carved into the giant rocks close to the water's edge along Northwestern University's campus, though finding her at night would be a challenge. . . .

The sliding door opens, and out steps Veena Auntie. She smiles. "Need a hand?"

I nod, embarrassed by everything my mother subjected

her and the other aunties to. "Sorry she shamed you all in there," I say, unwrapping bundles of sparklers. "For kidding around."

She wears her bob short in back, with long razored edges around her face—even her haircut is cool. "You find yourself on a short leash, uh?" she says, following my lead with another bundle.

"That's an understatement."

"I'm sure you'll meet many interesting"—she glances over her shoulder to be sure we're alone—"*people.*" She winks at me, artfully fanning several boxes of sparklers on a picnic table before pulling two sticks out. She hands me one, lights her sparkler, then touches the tip of mine with hers, igniting it. We wave our sticks, the lines of their orange sparks making patterns in the air. Veena Auntie crosses hers with mine. "May you find someone who really sees *you*, not just your looks or money or fame or accomplishments or how fantastic you are in bed." We raise up our flaming, starry sticks, and I burst out laughing. Am I really having this conversation with an auntie? "Someone," she says, circling the hissing sparkler above us, "who will cherish you for who you really are and everything you want to be."

"That is one tall order."

"It is. But stand for nothing less. Be true to yourself—good things follow." Our sparklers flame out as abruptly as they ignited, and we drop them into the water bowl. "Even if for now you are leashed." She winks, puts an arm around me. "Shall we call them out?"

Veena Auntie assists as I light the sparklers for the youngest kids. Some adults are having as much fun as the kids, their faces all aglow. I scan the yard for my family—Baba's laughing with his dad friends, and Aaji is helping Rahul light a new sparkler. Finally, I spot Ma by the sliding door: she's watching the crowd, arms crossed tight over her chest, her mouth set in that grim line I know all too well. . . . Apparently the mention of boys has the power to ruin Diwali.

———

Later that night, after everyone has gone home, I stare at the baby-blue walls of my room, the darkest hue my parents would allow me to choose. The blood in my veins thrums ruinously. My mother can't even handle a joke about the concept of me dating. I wonder desperately if it's always going to be like this with her—if I'll always be expected to be something that maybe I'm not: a perfect betiya with an unwavering focus on her future. I go to my dresser mirror, tug my leggings down my hip, and gaze at the design Oliver etched there. *Be true to yourself.* . . .

I snap a photo of it.

Tomorrow, I go to Belmont. Tomorrow, I get a tattoo.

CHAPTER TWENTY

"So, according to my first rule, you are now licensed to go down on him."

"Kate." I knock her knee with mine. We're riding the L into Chicago, and I just spilled the details on the bedroom scene at Saul's (though I left out the I-love-yous . . .).

Arching her eyebrows, she says, "*What?* It's the most fun rule of the three."

I scan the train: most passengers seem to be wearing earbuds, thank God.

"So are you going to?" she asks. "And if so, we should probably discuss technique."

We're heading toward Belmont Avenue to one of the top tattoo parlors in the city. I never thought Kate would support the idea of me getting a tattoo my boyfriend designed—too sappy and too much of a commitment. She doesn't even like the word *boyfriend*. But once she saw the photo of that wavy-haired goddess sketch, she said she'd accompany me. "I mean, it's not like you're getting his *name* inked on your hip," she said. "The design, I'll admit, reps you nicely."

"Possibly," I say now. "And regarding technique: tell me everything you know. But later, for God's sake."

As the L rumbles along the Purple Line, we watch the buildings and neighborhoods fly rapid-fire across the grimy windows. Every ten minutes, we brake to a jostling stop, people stepping off while new ones get on, an endless stream of humanity. I try not to think about how I'm going to have to hide my new tattoo from my parents. Will it be visible if I wear a swimsuit?

"I asked Michael out over text," she says, watching an elderly Asian couple settle in across the aisle.

"What?" I turn to her. "So Toby is . . . ?"

"Yep. Over. He seemed happier and more comfortable in that knight costume he wore to Saul's party than in real life with me. He also used the term *milady* in all seriousness. I'm pretty sure he wanted to reenact some medieval love scene after Saul's screening. Just . . . no."

"Medieval knights were all about chivalry—might've been swoony. . . ." She gives me a withering look, and I laugh. "Yeah. I didn't exactly see a second-date future for the two of you."

"Michael's hot in a different sort of way," she says. All I know about Michael is that he's stocky, smiley, and extremely competitive in PE. "He's chill until someone drops the ball during volleyball, and then . . ."

"He turns into a tiger that wants to rip your face off," I finish.

"A sexy tiger, though?"

"Sure. I can see that." A scruffy, gray-faced guy with a

Cubs hat shuffles on and sits too close. "I didn't even know you were interested in him."

"I mean, we have AP physics together, and he's in my study group . . ."

I laugh. "Oh! Okay. This is making more sense. AP physics with Michael."

"What? He's smart. I mean, not like *Henry smart*, but he's been helping me. . . ."

"Yup."

"And going to the basketball game together just sort of came up in conversation."

Though she'd never admit to a type, it's clear that Kate is learning to appreciate a guy who is her intellectual equal— a promising direction, in my opinion.

A teen gets on at Howard, political buttons covering every inch of her backpack. The morning light catches the burgundy highlights in her hair. When I ask her if I could take her picture for my class, she beams and nods. I half stand, snap a few shots of her gazing out the window at the city whizzing by. I give her my email in case she'd like to see the finished shots, and settle next to Kate to share some techniques I've been experimenting with. I try to ignore the impending sense of dread in my gut as we travel deeper into the city.

"Wow. Look at that light," Kate says, studying the new shots. She pulls up a photo I took of her a few days ago in front of our school library. "How'd you make such a rock star out of me? I kind of want to use this as my senior picture, if you're cool with it."

I tell her about how I've been using a longer lens, finding

angles that aren't eye level, plus gaining a better understanding of backlight when doing portraiture.

And suddenly, my heart's in my throat: we're at the Belmont stop.

We're heading down the rusty steps to street level, when it really hits me: I'm about to get Oliver's tattoo permanently etched into my skin. I break into a sweat. Have I even thought this through? What would Oliver think of this? Does a tattoo—any tattoo, really—reflect who I am? Will it represent me in five years, fifteen years, fifty? And I can't help but worry if the place is as professional and sanitary as they present online. . . . This whole thing is a whim. Why, exactly, am I doing this?

"And . . . we're here!" Kate announces, checking the storefront's sign after glancing at her map app. PLASMA TATTOOS AND PIERCINGS. My stomach in knots, I follow her in.

Sunlight streams through stained-glass windows, highlighting natural woodwork of what's basically the foyer of a historical home. "Welcome to Plasma," says the receptionist. Her black hair is straight and shiny like a flapper's, and her eye makeup is Cleopatra-flawless. "You can hang your coats on the hooks. Be with you in a sec." She turns to answer the phone.

Ink designs decorate the persimmon walls, from simple symbols to lush scenes and portraits. Past the foyer is an airy salon outfitted with leather tables and chairs. I use my phone to peek at the photo of my hip "tattoo." It *is* a great design. . . .

A guy with swirling arm tattoos whisks by and grabs his coat. His gaze lands on us, and I detect a slight smirk. "Bye,

Marcella," he calls to the receptionist as she hangs up the phone.

"See ya, Terry. Love the new tat."

He touches the shiny cobra slithering up the side of his neck. "Thanks. After this fucking shit year, I've more than earned this baby."

As they're talking, I take Kate aside. "I'm, um, kind of freaking out here."

"I can see inside your head right now: 'Needles! I mean, is anything really regulated?'"

All I can do is look at her.

"Okay—I don't blame you," she says. "You know how I feel about permanent anything. . . ." She pulls me into a tight hug. "God, I love your face. And yes, you're allowed to back out."

"Ladies, do you have an appointment?" The receptionist looks at us expectantly.

"Actually, no, we do not." I hesitate. "I guess I should've called first, but I wasn't totally sure if I was going to . . ." I trail off, feeling deeply idiotic.

She smiles sympathetically, her city-slicker face softening. "Happens all the time." She tells us there's a thirty-minute wait for an artist, so we can check out their body jewelry and clothing while deciding. I'm not a huge fan of shopping, but I follow Kate.

We try on jewelry: sterling silver arm cuffs, leather bracelets, and heavy necklaces studded with lapis or rock crystal. Kate documents the experience with her phone before we hit the clothes section.

"So Bonnie was telling me about how we each have a

'color season,'" she says, studying her phone. "I'm a Warm Autumn, and it looks like you're probably a Cool Winter."

"And this means what now?" I'm surprised at how deep the clothing discounts are here. I riffle through a rack of tops, starting to enjoy myself a little.

"That a particular set of colors works well with your skin tone. So I should be wearing deep greens and burnt orange, while you look best in black, pure white, and brick red," she says, reading off her phone.

"So I just wear those three colors and I'm good?" I grab a few basic skirts and tops.

"I knew this would appeal to your no-frills brain," Kate says, slipping her foot into a green leather platform.

Five minutes later, I step out of the fitting room. Kate whistles low. "You. Yaaaas!"

I regard my reflection: asymmetric cropped black tee with a stretchy jacquard pencil skirt. I feel like a chic Parisian teen.

"Try these on," Kate says, tossing me a pair of leggings and combats.

"I can actually afford some of this," I say, checking the tags. Babysitting Salil has earned me a small sum of spending money. "Why are these Docs so inexpensive?"

"Uh, because they're secondhand, love. They're in your size, too. Which happens once in never."

I pull on the leggings and shoes, and I must admit: I feel sexy. Maybe it's time I finally pay some attention to my look instead of just studying, or mindlessly mashing with Oliver.

"Instant swagger," she says admiringly. "Let's find some white and brick red so you can mix and match."

We trade clothes and snap goofy photos of each other.

I decide on the top, a cropped pleather jacket in a color Kate's calling "oxblood," a few black basics, and a tulle skirt à la Stevie Nicks. At the last minute, I choose the combats, too.

"Okay, this wilder version of you is so working for me," Kate says, appraising me. "I'm practically turned on here."

She decides on some great patterned leggings and a charcoal blouse with puff sleeves that makes her look like a sci-fi princess. As we're about to pay, Marcella clicks over in stiletto boots to tell us that an artist is now available.

"Oh. Um." I put my items on the glass counter. Maybe I should just spring for the tattoo—isn't that what we came for? It feels great to revamp. Why not take the next step in my reinvention?

And that's when I spot them: gleaming silver nose rings beneath the glass.

A woman with stunning tattoos covering her arms and neck appears, introducing herself as Kira. "Know what you'd like to have done today?"

I gaze at the nose rings, then glance at myself in the vanity mirror. A nose ring would blend my Indian culture with everything Oliver. . . .

My heart leaps. "Yes. I do."

———

I get off at the Davis Street stop, hop a bus, and twenty minutes later I'm on Oliver's doorstep, toes squirming in the tough leather of my new-old Docs. He squints down at me through a shock of dark hair and smiles. My heart hiccups.

150

"I feel like I know you from somewhere. . . ." His eyes travel my body dressed in new threads. He turns my face to get a good view at my silver nose ring before drawing me in close. Kissing me, he pulls me inside his apartment, where he is staying again, our private world pared down to lips and tongues and skin and mad, beating hearts. As we stumble down the hallway and into his room, his hands tremble, moving over me, under me, slipping beneath my clothes as his fingers trail lightly along my thighs, which are radiating a weird kind of heat. My hands move along his body as time disappears, my pulse beating wildly, moments sliding away. . . .

An hour and a half later, Oliver grins at me, rumpled and sleepy. "You're amazing," he says. "Loving that sexy nose ring. Now you look like a true Indian woman."

"Huh." I pick lint off my skirt, my heart suddenly pounding. "Not an edgy punk rocker?" I gesture with my black nails (which Kate and I painted while riding back on the L) toward the combats still laced tight against my shins.

He shrugs slowly in mock exaggeration, placing a hand on his chest, eyebrow cocked. "*I* see a gorgeous Indian babe who, for kicks, has dark nails and combats, but that's just one humble man's opinion. Besides," he says, lying back and closing his eyes, "how edgy are punk rockers, anyway?"

"So you think I'm a poseur."

"I didn't say that."

"But you think it."

"Rani." He sits up and takes my hands in his. His nails are flecked with paint, like that first day in the art room. "I love you." He looks at me intently with those eyes. "You don't need to change anything. Though, okay, I admit: that piercing is super-sexy Indian princess."

I consider this. For me, my new piercing links his world with mine. For him . . .

He leans in and kisses me tenderly in that smoldering way he has, the way that ignites something deep in my belly. I groan, pushing myself off him. "Hey, can I borrow your bike? It's decent out, and at this point, it's probably faster than the bus," I say, rolling off the bed. A text dings in; he grabs my phone, glances at the screen, and tosses it to me.

MA: Betiya, where are you?

CHAPTER TWENTY-ONE

I lock Oliver's old Schwinn to a lamppost in the alley and hurry toward my back door, my chest heavy with dread; of course my phone died just as I was leaving Oliver's, my mother's text unanswered. I step inside, the smells of frying garlic and onion sharp as I slowly unlace my boots.

"Hi, Ma," I say, breezing into the kitchen. I grab a salted cucumber slice and pop it into my mouth. "Where's Aaji?"

"Are you not going to explain where you were? It's almost five o'clock!" She glances at me, irritated, as she flips a puffing chapati.

And then she does a double take. Gasps. "What have you done to your nose?"

God.

I roll my eyes, though I'm trembling; Ma's intensity is a little terrifying. "It's not that big a deal. I've been wanting to do it for months, and I didn't ask you because I knew you'd say no."

Just then, the screen door creaks open.

"Arre baap re, look at what Rani has gone and done!" my mother shouts to Aaji. "Rani, go show your aaji."

I amble over to my grandmother, resigned and sheepish, like a dog who's just peed on the floor. "Hi, Aaji." She grips the doorframe, slipping out of her chappals.

She peers at me and smiles, staring at my nostril. "Haaaaah," she says, her trademark sound of appreciation. I gape, not quite comprehending. "Uma," she says to my mother, "I remember when you went and got your nose pierced. Without telling me, even!" She chuckles, wheezing at the memory.

"Wait—*you* had your nose pierced?" I turn to Ma in disbelief. "Without Aaji's permission?"

"Oh yes, she was a badmash, that one," Aaji says. "Very stubborn. Wanted it done early, before her friends had it in their minds, even. I said no, ajibaat nahi, but *that* never stopped her."

I stare at my mother's back, at her shiny, thick braid, shaking with each vigorous stroke of her rolling pin; she keeps her head down and her mouth shut. Amazingly, the case seems closed as Aaji moves to the sofa. I can't believe my big act of rebellion turned out to be identical to my mother's. I slink upstairs, feeling both lucky and wretched.

———

Later that night, lying in bed, my body tingling from a hot shower after a spectacular scalp massage Aaji insisted on giving me using her coconut oil, my mind drifts over the events of the day. I love the way my face looks with a nose ring— bold, strong, feminine—and my new clothes feel somehow like a new lease on life.

As I turn off my light, I get a text from Oliver.

So deep in love with you I don't know what to do with myself.

You don't? ;)

Hm. Guess I do. Night. ;)

Half dozing, I let my mind wander to Oliver's room. I think of his lean, muscular body in the dim light, and as I lie in my bed, inhaling the coconut scent of my hair, images of us together form behind my closed lids. I reimagine the moments, but this time his body meets mine, moving farther, deeper. . . . Will there be pain, like I've read about? Pain mixed with some kind of indescribable pleasure? What if sex changes everything, makes things weird between us? What will happen next year, when we go to separate schools? What if my family finds out . . . ?

But my pulse quickens, blood rushing hot through me. I turn over onto my belly, close my eyes, and imagine that it's Oliver there with me, pushing up and into me. . . .

My heart fills up and my body weakens; all I can think is: *Yes, God, yes.*

And then I'm fast asleep.

CHAPTER TWENTY-TWO

The next two weeks are hijacked by my lighthouse paper. Had I known that this topic would involve multiple trips to the Evanston History Center, digging through musty, dusty blueprints and yellowed typewritten accounts of the lighthouse's construction, I'd have chosen something else. My afternoons are now spent poring over the faded documents, panning through ancient rubble. Kate and Henry clearly knew better when choosing topics.

During these days, after hours of scribbling on index cards, I stare out the History Center's huge windows at the glittering blue lake. Thoughts of Oliver settle over me like warm steam, the pull and promise of him drawing me like a snare. And then . . . I gather my things, and find myself stealing away to his mother's apartment, or his room at Saul's. Sometimes we meet at Northwestern's lakefront rocks, where there is carved a secret, bare-breasted mermaid sunning herself just above the crashing waves of Lake Michigan. My body pressed against his, I lose myself in his voice, his smile, his scent, his lips blazing a trail along my skin.

Intoxicated, I think of all the ways we fit together, all the ways this love reinvents me. . . .

Toward the end of these two weeks, tangled up with him on his bed in black cotton underwear and my new Stevie Nicks skirt, I hear myself whisper, "I think I'm ready." My heart is suddenly hammering in my chest. Did I just say that out loud?

His eyes widen. "Now?"

Omgomgomgomgomg . . . ! "Well, maybe not *now* now." I swallow. "You're not . . . prepared. Right?"

"Right." He looks sheepish.

"This isn't . . . the right moment, anyway." I close my eyes as I feel my body try to fuse with his scent, his skin. "But soon. I think . . . I mean, I know," I manage to say. "That I want to. That it's right."

He kisses me, and my insides unfurl, blooming in response. His hands slide over me, lips burning into my skin as the universe blurs. . . .

Moments later, he wipes at his brow and straightens my skirt.

"I'm glad you're ready," he says, his face rugged, glowing. "But if I had to live with nothing but that for the rest of my life, I could die in peace."

"So, what are you saying?" I smirk. "You don't want to do it?"

"Hell no, that's not what I'm saying. I just mean—"

I beam at him.

"Nice. Way to mess with me at my most vulnerable," he says, ducking and hiding his face in my neck. I close my eyes, and the minutes fade out to black. . . .

When my eyes flutter open, the room is shadowed, the air heavy with the smell of turpentine and his warmth. I sit up, look at the clock.

Five-thirty p.m.

"Holy crap," I mutter. I rearrange my clothes, grab my backpack, kiss Oliver, and haul ass toward the bus stop at full sprint.

When the bus arrives, I weave my way toward the back, digging for my phone. I might preempt a blowout by calling home with a reasonable-sounding excuse.

My phone is dead. Again.

I settle in for the twenty-minute ride, surrendering to the fact that there will again be drama.

Lurching through the Evanston streets, I breathe in the distinct bus odors of exhaust and grime. I watch the houses and trees and apartment buildings rumble past in the fading twilight, catching golden-lit family scenes through people's windows. I think of lying with Oliver across his bed, our limbs entwined like vines. I commented that he seemed okay, considering he's back with his mom. "She's a nightmare," he admitted, gazing at my hair. His eyes shifted to mine. "But knowing I'll see you again soon . . . I can take anything."

Once home, I climb the steps, unlock the door, and walk into a torrent of commotion:

"She's here finally!"

"Have you got your chappals on?"

"You will be late, but by ten minutes only."

"But what will Rani do for dinner?"

"I packed it—she'll have it on the way!"

I stand in the foyer, blinking. "Wh-what's going on?"

My mother looks at me incredulously. "You've forgotten? Tonight you and Aaji are attending the Spirit of Life meditation."

I wince. Aaji asked me to join her on a meditation retreat in Chicago that takes place over three evenings, and I've completely forgotten I agreed to go. Crap.

"What is this, Rani. You're late now, but no driving fast to the retreat!" My mother shoves a sandwich bag filled with a couple of roti rolls at me, then presses the keys into my hand like they're sacred.

And in my world, they are. My mother is actually letting me drive to Chicago without her in the car?

I guide Aaji out to the garage.

"Your mother is very upset," she states cheerfully.

"Is she?" I grin at her. There's something about having been with Oliver that makes me feel breezy, lighter, carefree. I settle her into the car, then jump in and floor it. The tires squeal, and Aaji laughs.

———

We arrive late. The Spirit of Life seminars are held in a community center, sandwiched between a bank and a dive bar whose rowdy clientele spills onto the sidewalk. We add ours to the sea of shoes at the doorway, my clunky Docs standing stark and defiant as I swipe at the heavy black liner beneath my eyes. Pinning on our name tags—the last two on the table—we creep into the brightly lit conference room packed with people sitting cross-legged on the carpeted floor.

Thirty pairs of eyes follow us as we weave our way toward the back. The instructor, an Indian woman with extra-long, wavy hair, is curled in a chair in front. She stops talking and, with the others, watches as we locate a spot to sit. I raise a palm to offer my silent apologies, but the look on the instructor's face is serene.

"Do you need a chair?" she asks in an Indian British accent, looking at my grandmother.

Aaji hesitates before shaking her head no. Together, we settle onto the floor.

"Welcome," the instructor says warmly. "We were speaking about moments of resistance. What are your names?"

"I'm Asha, and this is my granddaughter Rani."

"Asha and Rani, I'm Tanuja. And this"—she gestures to a large framed photograph beside her of an elderly man with soft eyes and a long gray beard—"is the Guruji. Tell us what happened as you made your way here today."

I look at my grandmother, who is the picture of serenity. I say nothing. This thing was her idea, and I've already done my part: I got us here.

The silence stretches longer and longer, until I can't stand it anymore. I blurt: "We were late. So I was . . . rushing."

"Yes. And what happened?"

"Uh . . . I hit every single red light?"

The group laughs, and the instructor beams at me as if I am a revelation.

"Yes. Because, you see, you were resisting." She pauses, letting the brilliance of her words wash over us. "Whatever you resist will persist. So the next time you feel yourself fighting against something, allow yourself to rest in the discomfort of the thing. What is it the teens say? 'Chillax.' "

Some titters.

"And once this acceptance occurs," she goes on, "note the changes that come about. Try this with me: each of you, close your eyes."

I'm acutely uncomfortable. Meditating in close proximity to thirty people is not my idea of peace. Aajoba would have so much to say about this.

"Notice the part of the body that is retaining a lot of tension or pain," she says. "For some, it is the shoulders; for others, the neck or feet. Focus now on that part of your body."

My shoulders are crunched up to my ears. I shimmy to loosen them.

"The human tendency is to attempt to fix what is broken, solve every problem," she says. "The idea in this moment, however, is not to do anything about the tension. Simply observe it."

I focus on my knotty shoulders while trying to tamp down the stream of irritants that rushes my brain.

"Gaze inward through your mind's eye at this part of your body. And remember not to judge or try to change it. . . ."

The silence is deafening. I fidget. I try a neck roll. I listen to the faint whistle through the nose of the person breathing next to me. I wonder how the hell I agreed to this torture. And then . . . my mind drifts to Oliver, the moments in his room, his hands on me, the heft of him against me, his warmth. . . . I breathe in deep.

And before I know it, Tanuja is saying in her rich voice, "When you're ready, please open your eyes. . . ."

I glance around. People's faces are relaxed: some are smiling, Aaji included. Many stretch luxuriatingly, as though they have just awakened from the most restful sleep of their lives. I, on the other hand, am amped.

"Does anyone have observations that they would like to share?"

Hands go up.

"The tension in my upper back slipped away as I focused my attention there."

"At first, I had trouble concentrating, but once I stopped fighting, I was able to focus."

The short meditation seems to have actually worked for people.

Tanuja absorbs the feedback, listening intently.

I watch her, fascinated.

"And what about you, Kanu? How was the exercise for you?" She settles her gaze on a college-aged Indian guy a couple of bodies over from me. He's bleary-eyed in his rumpled flannel and jeans.

"Exercise? Well, I'm definitely tired from it," he says, and giggles rise from the group. The instructor smiles amusedly with one corner of her mouth.

"What, exactly, was tiring about it?"

"Well"—he rubs the back of his head—"all the . . . focusing. On not focusing?"

More laughter. "Yes, it does seem like a trick, na?"

"Well . . . yeah. Honestly?" He cocks an eyebrow doubtfully. "I didn't get it."

"Hmm . . . ," the instructor says appreciatively. "Anyone

else feel as Kanu did?" A few hands go up, and I tentatively raise mine, too.

"Good," says the instructor, seeming pleased by people's confusion. I wonder if she especially enjoys the hopeless souls. She turns and looks directly at me. Does she have special mind-reading powers? I squirm.

The rest of the evening is devoted to what Tanuja calls "trust and teamwork": pulled into small groups, we play mentalist-style games, including an adult version of duck-duck-goose, and are arranged to stand before each other, gazing into one another's eyes, which are "windows into the heart." Meditation and mindfulness are catching on in Western medicine, even pediatrics and schools, but . . . sitting there not doing anything? I'd rather just hash out my problems with Kate.

———

"So what did you think?" Aaji says as we shuffle out of the community center onto the darkened street among the other Spirit of Lifers. "Did you feel God's presence?"

Seeing that both Baba and I are not fans of anything remotely religious, we try to keep our disdain in check around my mother and grandmother. "Uh, maybe? But all that . . . close proximity to strangers while we huff and puff?" I shudder. "A little weird." Kanu, making his way through the crowd of smokers outside the bar, overhears and sends me a mini two-finger salute with a smile.

"There is purpose to it, betiya," she says. "Guruji is

connected to God, and meditation brings you closer to him, creating a sense of peace."

"Okay, I admit I do feel a tiny bit more peaceful now than I did when we stumbled in here, fifteen minutes late," I say, helping Aaji toward the car. "But honestly, for a guy connected to divinity, he has got *a lot* of nose hair. Wouldn't God have been kind enough to fill him in on grooming standards?"

She giggles. "Shi!" She swats at me.

And then I hear it—something guttural, like an engine groan. I turn my head and startle as I realize that the sound is coming from a man, his voice a low growl behind us:

"What were all *you* fuckin' people doing in there—plotting your next bombing?"

I freeze, staring at the hulking man about ten feet away, his pale eyes wide with fury, bloodshot. Our group—mostly immigrants from India—scurry to their cars, heads down. Aaji is pulling on my wrist when I finally tear my eyes away.

"Yeah, *leave*, you fuckin' terrorists!" he says, moving closer. "Go back to your call centers and your curry slums! Go back to wherever the hell you came from!"

I try to help her into the car, but she gestures for me to get in quickly. I scramble around to the driver's side as he approaches, throw myself behind the wheel, and lock the doors. We watch the man's face twist in anger, continuing to shout obscenities. I scan the lot to be sure everyone's safely inside or at least near their cars, then carefully pull out and away from the giant figure, the terrorizing face.

We drive in silence, and I grip the wheel, my breath shallow.

"Aaji, I'm so sorry. I probably should have . . . done something."

Aaji's hands twitch in her lap, but she stares serenely out the windshield. "No, betiya, nothing could have been done."

"Can you believe that guy? What if I hadn't come with you tonight? He could have—"

"Rani Betiya, we were together, all is well, and, most importantly, we are safe, na?"

"It's just—I wasn't expecting it. He—he came out of nowhere. And he was so angry. . . ." A chill shivers up my spine, and I'm flooded by memories, moments when it was unclear how deep and dangerous someone's hate or bigotry might run: *So, what's your people's take on 9/11? . . . Aaand here comes Little Gandhi Girl! . . . You gonna start braiding your mustache there, Curry? . . . Oh, look—it's a whole family of Apus! . . . Red dots, go home!*

"Yes," Aaji says quietly. "But there will always be angry people, betiya, as long as humans exist in the world. We mustn't let them poison our minds. Let us summon the Guruji's teachings and breathe now." Aaji quietly begins counting out the breathing series that Tanuja just taught us, and I do my best to follow, my diaphragm filling and deflating to her steady beats as we make our way home, the trembling terror of the night easing away.

CHAPTER TWENTY-THREE

"Hey, so Henry is spearheading a plogging club at school." It's the following week, and I watch Kate slurp her tom kha gai. Thai, after Indian, is her comfort cuisine, so now that her big chem test is over, we're at the cavernous Thai Palace, bright parasols suspended above like happy spiders.

"Wow. Gotta admire the guy who spreads the plogging love," I say, shifting on my embroidered cushion. "So, studying toward an academic scholarship, working at Trader Joe's, and now launching an Earth-saving Swedish fitness craze as a new student—all while seeming relentlessly happy. How does he do it?"

"Maybe it's the release of endorphins from sprinting while saving said Earth." She takes a bite of spring roll. "I think I'm gonna join. It's so bizarre. Plus, it'll keep me fit for soccer."

"Love it."

"Anyway. Transport me out of my strange, random existence and into your charmed life with Oliver. What's been going on with you two?"

"What has been going on. . . ." I drum my fingers on the

table, trying to figure out where to start. I've been a neglect-ful friend.

"You never even really told me about Oliver's reaction to your new look."

"I—I think he liked it? Um . . . he did say I now look like a 'true Indian woman.'"

"Uh, because only Indian women have silver nose rings? Please."

"I guess me in a nose ring reminds him of . . . I don't know. Others can get a piercing and it's self-expression. But I get one, and I'm the incarnation of some Indian deity."

"An Indian deity . . . what is up with men and their fantasies?"

"I have no idea. It's . . . weird, I guess. Anyway, there's something he wants me to see at Noyes Cultural Arts Center, so we'll meet there in a few."

She chews her spring roll, watching me. Swallowing, she wipes the grease from her lips with her napkin, then leans in, elbows on the table.

"You're not telling me something. Something is happening."

"What? It's nothing."

"I know you, Rani. You are the worst liar. Ever!"

I check the other tables, making sure there are no family friends lurking around. Only college kids, a couple with a kid strapped into a high chair, and strangers in suits slicing at their satays. . . . I look at Kate, my best friend. I owe her in so many ways.

"Oliver and I decided . . ." I lower my voice to a whisper. "We're going to do it."

She blinks. "It?" Her voice lowers. "As in, *it* it? Okay, back up. Back the hell up and tell. Me. Everything."

I sweat as I give her a play-by-play of our time in Oliver's room, sexy thoughts of him during the Spirit of Life meditations, and my nighttime fantasies.

"Wow," she says, heaping some steaming rice onto her plate. "It's like your subconscious is demanding that you just do this."

"Right?"

"I mean, who are we to suppress the brilliant subconscious? Plus, he's proven that he's more than just, like . . . sexy. He has goals. He plans *surprises ahead of time.* . . . I cannot fathom the kind of human you are dating at the present moment. Like, are you sure he's not some perfect avatar from Planet Z?"

I grin. "He could be?"

"I'm not proud of it: I'm jealous," she says.

"But his hair is long and unkempt," I point out. "And his teeth are snaggly."

"Save it," she says, palm in my face. "Those things only make him sexier, so just stop. And despite my belief that having sex in high school with someone you deeply love can lead you down a dangerous, dead-end path, I give permission for this to happen, you and this man."

"Boy," I correct.

"Same thing," she says, pulling a pen out of her bag. "Okay. Let's write a how-to guide. How to know when it's right to do it with a guy." She unfolds a paper napkin.

"What are you doing?"

"'Sex with Boo,'" she says, writing at the top of the napkin.

"'When Y'Know . . . It's . . . Right.'" She looks up at me expectantly.

"What—like I'm some expert?"

"Out of the two of us, yes. I need some help here."

I smile. "Let's begin with examining why you let no one close."

A shadow flits across her face. "Ouch."

"Sorry. That was cold."

"Yeah, it really was, holy crap! Anyway, I enjoy meeting guy after guy, escaping before the inevitable crash and burn, okay? Pretty self-explanatory."

"Fair enough." I stare at the napkin.

"Come on! Lists!" She waves the napkin in the air. "They're fun!"

"All right," I hiss, glancing around. I lean in. "'When you've both said "I love you." And mean it.'"

"You know how I feel about the L-word, but fine." She writes it down. "Next."

I chew on a satay, thinking. Pointing the skewer at her, I say, "'When you've been together for a while, and you feel'— um—'good when you're together'?"

"What's 'a while'? Let's get specific. Gimme something I can use."

"Okay. At least three months?"

"Three months."

"Wait—not long enough. Six months."

"Six months?"

"Okay—make it four months." Oliver and I aren't exactly at four months, but it'll probably be weeks before we get the chance to really be alone.

"Hmmm . . . four months . . . that's still a long time, but okay." She prints it carefully on the napkin. "But damn, that's a long time to wait, especially with that perfect guy."

"Well, it's not like you don't . . . *do* other things during those months. In fact, you *should* get . . . intense. With the messing around, I mean."

"Okay—so, 'Do everything but sex first'?"

"Hmmm . . . not quite right." I'm beginning to relish the specifics now. "It starts with yourself. You've gotta figure out what you like before you can expect someone else to take you there."

Kate stares at me. "Are we seriously talking about what I think we're talking about?"

"I think so," I say, laughing.

"Um, okay. This is rather, um, yeah. We're progressive women writing a sex manual, so okay. I like this. Can I just write *self-love*? *Masturbation* is so . . ."

"Sure. *Self-love.* Like *self-care.*" I giggle.

"Got it." She prints carefully. "Next?"

"How about: 'Explore acts of physical love besides intercourse with your partner, and talk freely about it afterward.' Yup. That's it."

Kate is horrified. "Physical love? And talk about it? This is, like, way too . . . flower child." She shudders.

"Okay, weird choice of words. But communication *is* important."

"You talk all calmly about all the down-and-dirty stuff you did together? Isn't it better just to let it happen and not, you know . . . discuss?"

"Well, it's not like you *discuss* it. But don't you think you should be able to have a conversation about the stuff you do together without being embarrassed?"

"What, like: 'When you did this to me, I—'?" She frowns doubtfully.

" '—loved it,' " I finish.

Her eyes light up. "Oh, okay. I get it. Telling him what you liked. And what you didn't like?"

"I guess so. It's not like I have *that* much experience."

"Ah. I think it's more that you don't have experience with stuff you didn't like."

Our waitress whisks by with a sizzling platter of food, blue smoke rising like a volcano about to spew. I feel my face flushing, something virtually invisible except to those who know me well. Like Kate.

On cue, she giggles. "Oh, you should see yourself right now. Love it!"

"Kate . . ."

"LOVE IT!" she yells at the ceiling. Customers glance at us warily.

"Can we please not make a scene?" I hiss.

"Okay, here's what we've got so far: 'Sex with Boo: When Y'Know It's Right.' "

"Shush, not so damn loud."

She clears her throat and in a low tone reads: " 'One: You've both said "I love you." And mean it. Two: You've been together at least four months. Three: You feel really good when you're together. Four: You practice frequent self-love.' I added the *frequent* for fun. 'Five: You can do other physical things and talk about them afterward without embarrassment.' Ugh, I still don't love that one."

"I know it's weird, but it feels important."

"All right—like I said, you're the expert. Anything else?"

"Yeah. 'Have great chemistry.'"

"That *is* important, isn't it?"

"Don't you think? I mean, why would you want to have sex with someone you don't really . . . want?"

"You're speaking my language, girl." She writes it down, then looks up. "Did you ever notice that Michael kind of pontificates? Like he's a professor—a boring one. It feels . . . *patriarchal*."

"I can kind of see that," I say. The one time I had an extended conversation with Michael in the South Study Café, he asked exactly zero questions of others.

"He also failed to show up for my club game the other day, after he *said* he'd be there. Who even does that? As though I need another person like that in my life."

I know she's referring to her dad. I touch her arm. "You deserve better. You deserve the best, in fact."

"I freaking do, don't I?" She grins and re-caps her pen. "Okay, so according to this list, it's a no-brainer to do it with Oliver."

A baby at a nearby table begins bawling, his T. rex arms paused in midair as he channels all his energy into an ear-splitting howl. The mother lunges for him, tipping over a water glass, while the father curses, dabbing at the mess with paper napkins. My resolve to become a pediatrician wavers slightly.

"Next year," Kate says, "you'll be 'hometown honeys,' like my cousin Amy at Michigan and her high school boyfriend.

They're staying together, even though he's at U of I." She sucks ice from her water glass, glancing at the sobbing baby. "Yeah . . . well, that should be on the list, too, maybe. A plan about what to do when college comes around."

"No sweat—here's the plan. You probably won't go to the same colleges, seeing that he'll probably go to art school while you'll be premed somewhere amazing. But you can stay together long-distance. Makes for steamy reunions, I hear."

Copying Kate, I suck ice from my glass. What if my parents find out about Oliver and how deep I'm in it with him? We've never had "the talk." No physical details, emotional complexities, or musings on contraception. The closest we ever came was after my first period. "Rani, you know you must wait until marriage, na?" my mother asked in a tight voice after she'd introduced me to the cabinet where the pads were kept. "Anything else would put your future at risk." And I muttered, "I know, Ma," before scooting off to my room in abject horror.

The thing is, I've been having trouble imagining the future without Oliver. Being with him is like the world has been cracked open and brimming inside is a weird, holy light. Apparently, it's true: love is a drug. Maybe sharing the air and space with Oliver is enough to fortify me for, well, forever.

Or maybe it will deplete me, like drugs do.

"Hey. You still there?"

"Huh? Yeah. It's just . . . There are times . . ." I lean in. "My parents would die, but . . ."

"Holy crap, what?"

"There are times that I can't imagine life without Oliver.

173

As in, my future isn't really my future if he's not there." Deep dread saturates me. How can I contemplate the future when I can't even tell my parents about Oliver? I look into her eyes, fearful of what I might find there. I'm a bad feminist. . . .

But she's grinning.

"I know, I deserve a mocking," I say. "I'm all 1950s: 'Oh, we're going steady, and then he'll'—what's it called, from those movies?—'pin me, and we'll marry and have a bazillion babies.'"

"No, I can totally see it. Minus the pinning crap. Your babies will come out with tattoos and piercings and shit."

"We could give them badass names," I say.

"Yeah, like Chip and Rock. Or Harley," she says, chewing on a dumpling.

"Maybe Vance."

"Rocco!"

"Stud!" We burst out laughing, patrons politely ignoring us. She silently scans the list. "Okay. Perfect. I say we pitch this to an agent." She sticks it into her backpack and grabs a fortune cookie. "Don't you love how Americans think that fortune cookies are an Asian tradition, but Asians know it's actually an American thing served only in America's Asian restaurants and invented by a Japanese American?"

"And how do *you* know such things?"

"What can I say? I'm worldly." She grins, tearing open the wrapper and plucking out the fortune. "'Your path is lined with the golden bricks of true love.'" She rolls her eyes. "All right, Universe, you mocking bitch. I get that Michael is not my true love. Lay off already." She looks at my cookie. "Yours better be better."

Clearing my throat, I read, "'Your theatrical flair is a true force.'"

"Okay, yours is even stupider than mine."

"Hey! I've got theatrical flair," I say, pouting.

She reads it herself, smiles. "Maybe this one is meant for me. Which helps me not at all." She looks up at the ceiling. "Thanks, Universe."

Zipping my coat, I say, "The Universe might know stuff?"

"Please," Kate says, pulling on her jacket. "She knows nothing."

CHAPTER TWENTY-FOUR

"What do you think?" Oliver says, leading me through a corridor of the Noyes Cultural Arts Center. It's a Sunday morning in December—and being here on a risky weekend day is my way of making it up to Oliver for not inviting him to Spirit of Life with Aaji. He somehow got wind of the program online and seemed so wounded when I shut down his idea of tagging along next time. (I couldn't even bring myself to tell him about the racist incident that occurred after the first session.) He genuinely does not get why I can't just reveal his existence to my grandmother, so I offered him this daytime date, Kate covering for me. I know he's been wanting to show me something here, and my imagination spins out.

The past two weeks, I've been in an alternate, meteoric realm, obsessed with the idea of sex with Oliver. Whenever I see him at school, I'm either a spastic weirdo who can't stop talking or I'm silent—helpless, pheromonal tension swirling between us. Sucking on antacids for my new heartburn problem, I've been spending late nights texting with him, or going through my shots of him in the dark, researching all the creative things I might do with them. . . .

I tell myself that sex with Oliver will be a relief, an emancipation. That's the way the magazines and books make it sound. It's something I'm choosing, with someone I love. So why am I a wreck?

Now, painfully aware of his presence, his body so close to mine, I step inside what looks to be a sunny gallery. I gawk. A life-size mural in progress depicting people of all different ethnicities stretches across the western wall; embedded in the scene is offset, bold lettering: WE ARE ALL AMERICA. Sculptures dot the room—one made up solely of paper clips, another of intertwining forks and spoons, another of what reveals itself, upon inspection, to be laundry lint stitched into quirky children's coats suspended by invisible wire. I touch the pink fluff of a coat collar with tenderness. "Whoa." I turn to him. "Where are we?"

"It's basically a communal art studio—various local artists come here to work. To cover the expenses, we offer art classes for kids. And I'm kind of . . . working here now."

"What? I mean, I knew you took that class here Thursday evenings. . . ."

"Yeah, but this is paid work," he says, grinning. "I met one of the artists—Valentia, who you'd love—here last fall. She's shown me the ropes, telling me about this wing—that's her mural there. The artists show on Studio Nights and also teach workshops. Check this out."

He leads me to a long, narrow room partitioned off by heavy canvas panels. Round tables are covered in Mexican oilcloth and wooden paint palettes caked with delicious colors—ocher, rust, dusty pink, raspberry, indigo blue. . . . I snap a series of photographs on the spot.

"We hold workshops throughout the week," he says, rearranging some paintbrushes. "I help with the kids' classes, demonstrating different techniques."

"Salil would love it here," I breathe. Samples of student work are clipped by clothespins onto a copper wire stretching above our heads. I gaze at intricate etchings in silver foil. "Wait, you're, like, an art teacher?"

"Well, not really. More like an assistant."

"But . . . why'd you never tell me? That you work here, I mean?" I fight the urge to press myself up against him.

"It's not a big deal. Anyway, sometimes all I end up doing is sweeping the floors, which is not as impressive as"—he gestures toward the tables—"this. But I can show you the janitor's closet, since I know it so well."

I laugh. "I'd love to see the janitor's closet."

I follow him through the gallery, past a wheelbarrow filled with sprouting potatoes painted to represent aging faces. I gasp in surprise, and he grins, leading me down a hallway toward a closet door. He unlocks it, and we step inside.

"This"—he pulls on a chain, and a bare bulb flickers on dimly—"is where I spend my free time. Except when I'm sneaking around nocturnally with you."

I inhale the scent of Murphy Oil Soap and ammonia. "From one nocturnal space to another. No wonder you're so pale. You *are* a vampire, aren't you? A sexy art teacher vampire." I circle my arms around his neck and move my body close to his.

"Uhhh, Rani."

I kiss his neck. "Hmm?"

"Um. I don't know. I'm . . . I work here. . . ."

But a force within me hurtles onward of its own volition. My hands slide across his broad shoulders and down the black branches along his arms. . . . Helplessly, he groans. He kisses me gently, then unbuttons my shirt with such fumbling, exquisite care that I want to scream; my skin sizzles beneath his hands. His fingers work through the mechanics of my bra, and when the clasp pops open, it feels like such a surprise victory that I raise my eyebrows at him; he cracks the faintest half smile, pushing the straps off my shoulders so that it drops to our feet. I grab his shirt and strip it off, letting my hands roam across his chest, pale and bluish in the low light.

Instinctively, my fingertips trail along the low waist of his jeans, touching the dark, vertical line of hair descending from his belly button that he once teasingly called his "treasure trail." In the cabinet mirror, I catch a glimpse of my bare back, my tangled curls hanging halfway down it, and I startle: that hardly looks like me. With a strange rush of confidence, I turn back to him; his eyes are liquid and so vulnerable, they look like suffering. The ridges of his cheekbones and the angular lines of his jaw are like those of a statue or science fiction superhero, his lips full and shining and wet. I step close so that our bodies touch, then kiss him deeply, my insides burning.

I back up to a makeshift table, shove away some cleaning supplies, and hoist myself so that I'm sitting facing him, eye level. I hike up my skirt and wrap my legs around his waist.

"I want to," I whisper.

His eyes widen. "Now?"

"I mean, it's maybe not the most romantic spot . . . but it'd be memorable?"

He laughs. "True." He kisses my neck, then settles his gaze onto my face, a mischievous glint in his eyes. "Sooo, you won't bring me to your meditation retreat, but this . . . ?"

I pinch his butt. "Shut up before I change my mind."

"Yeah, forget I said anything."

"So, do you mind?" I draw him in closer. "Do . . . Are you, um, prepared?"

He looks down. "Does it look like I mind? And yes, I am."

He leans in and kisses me slowly, deeply. He tastes of something fresh and spicy, like cloves. His body trembles, and the veins in his arms stand out, crisscrossing and running together like lines on a map.

The next few moments are a trembling flurry of unzipping and shedding; his muscular limbs press against me, turning us into something singular and savage. I close my eyes, absorbing the unfamiliar yet familiar skin, its heat and energy rearing up with mine.

He looks so helpless as we try to make it happen: his whispered *Are you ready?* is followed by tiny failings and mishaps—a bumped nose, an accidental elbow in the side, the logistics of the condom, the clumsiness and nervousness underlying everything. . . . He pulls off all the little indignities with patience and earnestness. I feel like I can see right through his hard chest, past the thrilling, bloody pumping of his heart, and into his life force, as Tanuja calls it.

I know I'll remember this moment as he looks at me after all our awkward work pays off: above me, his muscles taut, beads of sweat like tiny transparent pearls across his forehead, the fullness of him moving inside me while he stares into my eyes with amazement and love and gratitude. . . . In this moment, despite the combo of twisting pain and profound joy, I've never felt so alive. It's everything I could have never imagined, and in this moment, it's mine.

I squeeze my eyes tight as his body jerks a little against me, everything loosening, pulsating within. . . .

And with a sudden crack of lightning, I know: things will never be the same again.

———

"I have something cool to show you." Oliver leads me out into the light of the gallery and into a quirky half room overlooking a mass of bare trees whose branches nearly scrape the windows. A battered leather love seat sits beside a giant easel.

He crashes into the love seat, and I settle beside him. That's when I notice, crowded onto an end table, a bar of dark chocolate, a box of strawberries, and a stack of art photography books.

"Um, am I being punked?" I grin. "What's all this?"

"Well, I was hoping to lure you into sitting for a portrait for me. And to entertain yourself while you sit, you can dine on chocolate and fruit and peruse photography books."

"Am I dreaming right now?"

"Yes. I am your dream."

"You are." Heat rises in my face. "So you just"—I shrug nonchalantly—"stocked up on aphrodisiacs. . . ."

"Yeah," he says, laughing. "Maybe I should have brought you here before the janitor's closet," he jokes. "Then again, we obviously didn't need any aphrodisiacs."

"You do know bribery is not necessary to have me sit for a portrait, right?"

"So you'll do it? You can even work on homework or applications or whatever. . . ."

"It's cool. It's more than cool. I'm honored."

He stands at his giant easel, and with my insides fluttery, he begins sketching. Occasionally, he murmurs things: how he's been using some of Valentia's muralist techniques and spare lines; how the northern light through the branches here emits an ethereal glow despite the trees' density; how my facial structure is perfect for what he's trying to accomplish. . . . Allowing the chocolate to slowly melt on my tongue, I flip through the art books and gaze through the branches scratching at the windows. We are now *lovers*. It's a word Kate and I used to mock, but in this moment, it feels legitimate and perfect. I think about how the pixels of my life are checkering in, complex and bright. How my heart is beating hard and strong, and how I'll always remember this terribly beautiful moment, a filtered snapshot in real time.

CHAPTER TWENTY-FIVE

"How is your life so full of creatives all of a sudden?" Kate asks, admiring Veena Auntie's handmade pottery nestled along her mantel. "I mean, I guess you're one of them now."

It's Tuesday after school, several days before Christmas, and I've brought Kate to Salil's house. Veena Auntie's just left for her pottery class, and I've spread out dozens of photos on their dining table to experiment with some new mixed-media techniques. Salil loves weird art projects; the trick is to get him to settle.

Kate eyes Salil as he zooms around the house, stabbing walls and furniture with a rubber sword while making interminable whooshing sounds. "I kind of feel like racing someone right now," she says, sighing wistfully. Salil stops in his tracks—she's got his attention. "But I bet *no one here* is any good at running."

"Actually . . . *I* am GREAT at running!" Salil says, his face breaking into a sunshine grin.

"Yeah? Prove it!" She shrugs on her coat. "Last one to the goal is a rotten egg!" He lets out a gleeful whoop, staggering into his boots. "I mean, do you really wanna be that egg?"

I manage to stuff him into his coat before the two race into the December afternoon. It's unseasonably mild—the snow that fell last week has already melted. I watch Salil laughingly chase Kate across the gray-green grass, and I use the quiet to set out the art supplies. Biting into an apple, I appraise the photos I laid across the table: sepia-toned school shots taken at the school's Upper Theatre or the East Courtyard, photos of Kate and me at the tattoo parlor, and several shots of Salil playing soccer in the yard. There are a couple of me at the Noyes Cultural Arts Center, a few of Henry, and, finally, a single shot of Oliver with a vibrant tree in the background. His face is at the edge of the frame, and he's wearing the expression that makes my heart leap, establishing, in case I was in denial, that I'm helplessly, indisputably in love with him. His eyebrow's cocked, his mouth crumpled like he's about to burst into laughter. I figured one lone photo of him in the sea of others won't give me away if Veena Auntie spots it when she returns.

I peek outside. Salil and Kate are at the fence, talking to Henry.

Henry is now part of Salil's near-daily scene. Not only does he watch Salil when I can't, but he is beloved by Veena Auntie for his handiness around the house. Kate and I sit with him every day in English, and we often meet up with him at lunch. He's funny, sincere, and a persuasive but respectful debater—a winning combo.

I watch Kate expertly juggle a soccer ball. Henry laughs at something Salil says before sneaking a peek at Kate. He's good at disguising his feelings, but it's clear he's interested in her—who wouldn't be? I laser into Kate's auburn braid, willing her to look at him. Henry says something and Kate laughs, meeting his eyes for a split second before returning to the ball. Tiny victory.

Before long, the three of them trundle in, Salil dragging Henry by the hand. "Rani Tai!" he says, the usual vein standing out along his neck when he yell-talks. "Henry said he's free for a bit!"

"Hey, Rani," Henry calls, sliding the screen door closed behind him and removing his shoes. "Kate said she wanted to practice our speeches later, if you're cool with that."

Salil interjects. "But, Henry, first can you—"

"First," he says to Salil, "I *really* wanna watch you guys do this cool art project."

"Not watch: Take part. Play. Let go," I say, using Oliver's Bob Ross voice as the group gathers around the table. "Okay, artsy-farts. There are several options." I show them examples of mixed-media techniques: overlaying portions of a photo with paper shapes, erasing sections of a photo and drawing them back in, or dripping water directly on a photo to purposely distort it.

I turn on the classical playlist that always relaxes Salil, and before long, we're all deep in the zone, cutting and painting and dripping and sketching to Bach and Beethoven. Henry is using the erase-and-draw method on a photo of Salil, Kate's dribbling water on a selfie of the two of us posing just before I got my nose ring, and Salil is pasting red and green triangles fish-scale-style around a photo of Henry. Nilesh would be so impressed by Salil right now. . . .

When everyone's done, Henry suggests Kate and I watch *Scooby-Doo* with Salil while he, Henry, cleans up. Kate and I

185

exchange a glance—*A guy who offers to clean up? Noted!*—
and then crash into the plush couch with Salil. Before long,
Henry's beside us, his deadpan commentary making everyone
laugh, Salil's in heaven at having three big kids here all to
himself, and I . . . I am filled with hope and joy and longing and a tiny little niggling something, like an overlay image
through a transparency, its shape so heavily filtered that I
can't quite see it yet.

CHAPTER TWENTY-SIX

The next day, while decorating the fake little Christmas tree in our living room with Aaji, I get a text way outside the safe zone Oliver and I agreed upon:

Xmas present for you. Meet?

My mother has just informed me that our distant relatives from Cleveland will be spending Christmas with us. I message back:

Not sure. Family comes tomorrow. Will be hard

I hit send and shove my phone into my back pocket. Aaji's been supervising from the couch as "Walking in a Winter Wonderland" tinkles on the radio; she points out bent branches or empty spots that need an ornament. I distractedly wrap tinsel around the tree's top.

"What is this?" she asks. I look over at her holding a plastic angel, its halo covered in silver glitter.

"Oh, that," I say, taking it from her. "An angel for the top of the tree. She lights up when you plug her in."

I work the treetop's bristles into the back of the angel's wings to affix it in place, drape the cord down the back side of the tree, and plug it in.

"Haaaah," Aaji grunts as she gazes up at the glowing angel.

"You don't think it's ugly, all that orange plastic?" I take out my phone and glance at it.

Mom making a rare visit to see her sister in MI...
So... please?

My breath catches.

"But you chose it, na?" she says. Tearing my eyes away from my phone, I see her looking up at me quizzically.

"Yeah, I guess I did pick out the angel," I say. "When I was, like, five." How can I possibly sneak away to see Oliver when family is visiting?

"Haaah. That is what makes it meaningful," Aaji says.

I'm forced out of my reverie. "What do you mean?" I turn to face her. She's bundled up on the couch, an old shawl wrapped around her shoulders.

"You chose wisely. You may have developing notions now, but past choices must be respected. Look—her light is lovely still, after so many years."

My phone vibrates again; I need to deal with this Oliver thing in private, in my room, away from Aaji and the suddenly grating Christmas tunes. I turn to go, mumbling something about going to the bathroom, and glance at her on my way

188

out. Her milky eyes shine as she gazes at the half-decorated tree, at the cheap plastic angel topper. Her hands twitch, a few sprinkles of the angel's glitter stuck to her fingertips.

———

I ring Oliver's doorbell, shivering and sweating at the same time. He buzzes me in; I wave to Kate in her idling car and run up the stairs and into his arms. I breathe in his warm, spicy-soap scent as he murmurs something into my neck.

"What?"

"Nothing, nothing. Get in here."

He leads me into the apartment, my heart hammering.

"Wanna sit?" He gestures toward the couch.

I sit down stiffly, and he laughs, dropping onto the sofa next to me. His cat leaps down, glares at us, then stalks away in haughty-cat fashion, tail in the air.

I raise an eyebrow. "*Somebody's* pissed that I'm here."

"Who, Pepper? Nah. That's how he expresses love."

I grin and feel him absorbing me. "What?" I look at him.

"Huh? Nothing."

I cross my eyes at him.

"Do you . . . wanna watch TV or something?" He switches it on. We sit shoulder to shoulder, pretending to ignore the heat between us as an *E! True Hollywood Story* special on Paris Hilton blares. Oliver's eyes are transfixed by the screen.

"She's hot," I say.

"What?" He blinks as I wave my hand in front of his eyes.

A slow smile spreads across his face, igniting his features. "How dare you accuse me of scoping. Like I'd ever do that. In front of you."

I play-pummel him, and he digs into my armpits, tickling me without mercy. I shriek, giggling helplessly as the tickles grow more insistent. My eyes squeeze shut as the torture builds. I open them for a moment to see his face inches away . . . our eyes lock and then we're kissing. His body is taut, stretched along mine, brimming with an urgent, quiet energy. With my head swimming and my insides a molten river, he gets to his feet and pulls me up, leading me down the hallway.

———

"Okay, so at the risk of revealing my stupidity: What's the Juliet bit all about?" We're on Oliver's bed, our backs against the wall, having just exchanged Christmas gifts. I gave him a photo of us making hideous faces together at a café across the street from the Noyes Cultural Arts Center. The photo is framed in wood, upon which I painted a rangoli design. He laughed when he saw it. "A singular moment I wouldn't mind living in forever," he said. His gift to me was a literal work of art: a personals ad centered on a watercolor background—the abstract form of a tree, a blurry sand dune with a lighthouse, a grassy yard behind the Harley Clarke Mansion . . . our night spots.

When I read the ad, tears sprang to my eyes:

To Queen Rani, aka my Exotic Juliet:
Thanks for the tickling, kicking,

hugging, laughing,
shit giving, kissing, and, most of all,
loving.
You are the best.

I face him now, bending my knee so that my leg forms a triangle between us. It's my attempt at being civilized and having a conversation, instead of constantly caving to hormones. I try to suspend a thorny sensation scraping beneath the surface.

"Well, you're my Juliet," he says.

"Your *exotic* Juliet, no less." There. I said it.

"Right." He shrugs, smiling.

Is he really this clueless? Doesn't he know what a loaded word *exotic* can be for a brown-skinned girl in America? Then again, who wants to be a jerk about a handmade gift? "And you're my Romeo."

"Yeah. So we can now consume one another."

"Wow. You are a cheeseball." Despite myself, I turn away, hiding the stupid grin on my face. I am sucker-punched, powerless. Goddammit.

"You clearly haven't read the play," he says.

"I watched the movie. Wait. Maybe that was *The Princess Bride?*"

"Okay, an entirely different story. Have you at least heard the *song?* By Dire Straits?"

I shake my head.

"God, woman. What are we gonna do with you? No wonder you didn't get the subliminal meanings of my gift." He grabs a disc from the wooden crate that serves as a nightstand

and pokes it into an ancient-looking CD player on the floor. We listen to the plucking of a guitar, the jangly, wistful notes of the band singing about a love-struck Romeo.

"It's about heartbreak," I say finally.

"Well, part of it is."

"What's that got to do with us?"

"'Come up on different streets. They both were streets of shame.'"

I look at him blankly.

"The lyrics. You're just gonna have to read them online. Best song ever." He leans over and brings his lips to mine, and I feel myself fuse into him again. I place my hand on his chest and push myself up and away.

"So, what's Christmas like around here?" I say, straightening my shirt. "Your sister coming?"

"What do you *think* it's like around here? It'll be a bloodbath, no doubt," he says, his eyelids at half-mast.

"Now that's the spirit of the season."

"Does any of it even matter?" He trails a finger along my forearm. His hair's in tufts and he's wearing just jeans. I stare at the tattooed red hearts trapped among the branches on his arms.

"It *does* matter. We are *conversing*." I throw him his shirt; his bareness is distracting. Anyway, Christmas. What will you guys do?"

"Um, well, let's see. . . . There's sure to be some tears. . . ." He looks up at the ceiling, like he's thinking, then snaps his fingers and points at me, eyebrows raised, like a brilliant answer just occurred to him. "Oh, and accusations! Yes. Regarding who didn't call who, and who's been rude to who, and who didn't tell who that so-and-so is now on antidepressants, and didn't so-and-so think that her mother would like to know something like that? Oh, and by the way, I'm pregnant!"

He's pulling his shirt on. I fight the urge to take a photograph of the way the fabric's twisted, taut across his bare skin. I clear my throat, smoothing my hair. "Are you the one pregnant in this scenario?"

"Nah. My sister. She's three weeks along."

I stare at him. "She is?"

"That's why I wanted to see you tonight, before things got—crazy. Kathy's hoping to move back home so that she— and the baby, when it comes—will have some support. Because Mom is so supportive and all."

My eyes lock with his. "I can't believe you're gonna be an uncle," I say finally.

"An uncle. Heh. Yeah. Uncle Oliver. How fucked is that?"

"She . . . she is still with Richard?"

"Yup. Richard will, hopefully, be a decent dad, seeing that he already is one." Oliver scratches his ear. "But, I mean, he *is* still married. So you know how that goes."

I don't, really. My parents and aunts and uncles were arranged and married with the blessings of their families, and lived happily—more or less—ever after. I sit beside him on the edge of his bed, watching him chew a fingernail while staring off. "You and Kathy . . . you get along well. So that'll be good, having her around." I sound stupidly cheerful.

"Sure, yeah. I do love Kathy." He flops onto his back, staring intently at the ceiling. "But she and Mom together? Holy shit. You saw them that day. This house will need an exorcism when things are through."

I study the piece he made me, its details shimmering and full of heart. His profile is thoughtful, brave, and boyish in the dim light, and my heart throbs like a stab. I lace my fingers with his. "Hey. It'll be all right."

He looks at me, eyebrows raised slightly. "Yeah? Can we start seeing each other more, because it's literally the only thing keeping me from going off the deep end."

I fiddle with my rings. "Um. Maybe? At least my lighthouse paper is done with. And college apps will be over soon. . . ."

"Which means you'll try, right? To make time for us to be together more?"

"Making time" is a nonsensical concept. Time is marked by the fulfillment of one responsibility after another; where Oliver fits in is not exactly clear to me. And sneaking out regularly already poses monumental risks, risks he doesn't believe actually exist. . . .

But here I am, gazing helplessly into the soulful sea-gray depths of his eyes, getting sucked into their vortex. His need is all reckless desire and desperation—and the result is a dopamine surge. I am screwed af.

"Yeah. More singular moments. On the house. They'll crowd everything else out." I lie beside him, my face an inch from his. He smells peppery and clean. I can feel the ions in my body trying to meld with his as if they're confused that we're actually two separate people.

He slides his body up tight against mine. Murmuring into my neck, he says, "Where did you even come from?"

CHAPTER TWENTY-SEVEN

Christmas arrives, and we celebrate in our family's usual style—braiding Indian traditions with American ones. The day begins with Christmas music on the radio and me tearing open two gifts from beneath our tiny twig of a tree—hand-knit slippers from Aaji and an embroidered kurta. I gave my mother and father a calendar of photographs of our family over the past year, while Aaji got a mug with a black-and-white photo emblazoned with a close-up of our two hands in sand—she loves anything to do with her daily chai ritual. Later, we make vegetable biryani and eat with our visiting relatives, the *Nutcracker* ballet muted on the TV while my father's favorite, Ravi Shankar, suffuses the house with mellifluous notes.

I've been dreading all this family time devoid of Oliver, but now in the thick of it, I surrender. I vaguely recall Tanuja from the Spirit of Life intoning: *Whatever you resist will persist.* . . .

Aaji's eyes shine as she watches the dancers on the television: "Such grace. So lovely." Baba tells jokes in his dorky dad way, so dorky they actually become funny. "It was a wonderful fall, though," he tells our relatives. Eyes sparkling, index finger raised, he enunciates: "Arre! It was a *wonder-fall!*" My mother covers her mouth as she laughs, while my relatives shout, "PJ! PJ!" indicating that my father has again cracked a Poor Joke. There's something sweet and simple and comforting about it all, like hot masala chai during a blustery winter storm. I play with different lenses, snapping photos, and for once, I'm content to be home.

As snowflakes fall steadily for days after Christmas, I carefully craft last-minute college essays. Losing myself in the writing, deep in the zone, I barely notice the creak on the stairs and Ma's tentative knock on the door: "Rani? Would you like to take a break and join us for lunch, or should I bring your food to you here while you work?" I take full advantage, eating half my meals in front of the computer, relieved that my academic endeavors still have the power to inspire me.

I text Oliver daily. Kathy has had severe morning sickness and is now bleeding intermittently; her doctor has prescribed strict bed rest. He shares only the bare minimum with me—despite my million questions. I send supportive texts, but on some level, I'm relieved to be on the outskirts of his confounding family situation. For once, no worrying about sounding like a naive, privileged baby when responding about his family troubles, no stressing about how I'm going to see him without getting caught. Occasionally, we talk on the phone, male hooting or laughter in the background—he's spending most of his free time at Saul's. His voice sounds different—distant, distracted—and inevitably, amid the noise, he says he needs to go. "I love you," he always murmurs in that hoarse way that hitches my heart.

I miss him, but I admit that slipping into my familiar roles at home feels cozy and effortless: committed student, devoted daughter and granddaughter—roles untainted by lies and recklessness. Puttering around the house, days without his physical presence, it's like a fever has broken, and I'm finally tending to the other gardens of my neglected life—one being Kate.

I see Kate almost every day, just like in the pre-Oliver days. We meet up with Mimi and Irene for ice-skating at Ackerman Park, howling with laughter when we end up skidding across the ice. We head to the downtown library, where we trade and ponder one another's essays before strolling to the theaters to see whatever's playing at the moment. We babysit Salil together, sometimes playing Jenga or Pictionary with Henry. We buy ingredients for a natural face mask, spending the evening giggling as the masks flake off our faces like the powdery plaster walls in my grandparents' home. Time with Kate is like being on vacation, or like coming home after an exhausting, adventurous one.

Of course I miss Oliver. But I also missed this, and it's impossible, apparently, to have both.

———

"So which applications will you work on today?"

Baba's driving me to Kate's on his way to work. He just smiled when I asked if I could drive—maddening. I can't believe that despite the fact that I'm eighteen, have had my license for two years, and am actually a good driver, I'm still being driven around like a little kid.

"Not sure," I tell Baba. "Probably I'll apply to those East Coast schools we talked about."

Baba glances at me. "Good idea. Cast a wide net, as the saying goes. Interesting these sayings, na? How many people actually know anything about fishing?"

I stare at the passing scenery. The trees are leafless, their stark black branches interlacing against the gray December sky. New Year's is just days away. When I was young, it was my favorite holiday—anything to stay up late—but this year I can't seem to muster enthusiasm; I'm worried about the changes I'm sensing in Oliver, counting the days before I can see him again, revel in the fire of his presence. . . .

"Are you excited?"

I jump. "Huh?"

Baba glances at me, smiles. "What are you daydreaming about? I just asked if you're excited."

"For what?" My pulse quickens, panic igniting.

"For college." Baba glances over, his heavy brows drawn together, a furry cliff above gentle, worried eyes.

"Oh, sure, Baba. College. Yeah, definitely. Really excited."

"Are you still considering a career in medicine?" He speaks in his careful, formal way, and I feel a sudden pulse of sadness. If he even knew all the things I was considering.

"Yeah. I like kids, and I like biology, so yeah."

He drives in silence. I know he's formulating some kind of deliberate, prodding speech about the importance of ambition and hard work.

"Rani, coming to this country, we had only our practical natures and our intellect. I came here with just one hundred fifty dollars."

198

"I know, Baba. Pretty amazing, seeing all that you've accomplished."

"Yes. But the point, betiya, is that we made most decisions based on fear."

"Fear?"

"Yes. Fear of not being able to make it here. Fear of the shame we would bring on our families if we had to return to India not having succeeded in America. Fear that we would encounter great opportunities, yet not have the sense or strength to take advantage of them."

"So that's why you went into engineering."

"The choices in my family were either doctor or engineer."

"Right."

"We didn't pay mind to what would be 'cool.' We were taught to find a practical profession, one that would require higher education, afford us a good life, and ensure self-reliance. That philosophy shaped our ambition, our drive, our desires."

I adore Baba, but I honestly can't imagine allowing fear to be a driving force in my decision making. I know immigrant life is no joke, but how can people live this way? I want to make choices based on what I love: science, medicine, photography. Oliver . . . ?

"I realize things are different for the next generation," he says then. "But be open to learning from your elders. I feel I must pass on my perspective. Something to keep in mind."

I'm quiet, staring through the windshield, head low and eyes ahead. I respect my parents deeply, but their beliefs can be so zombifying.

"Keep your eye on your future and your mind on the

practical. It's not so easy here to create a comfortable life. Stay focused, and don't get swept up in distractions, betiya. People your age tend not to see the whole picture, so trust in knowing that our advice will help you attain a solid future."

"Sure, Baba. I know. Thanks." Where's this coming from? Does he know about Oliver?

"Enough lecturing from your boring baba." He winks. "How is Kate?"

"Good." I swallow. "She's . . . uh, she hopes to go to the University of Michigan. Her cousin goes there, so she's visited a lot."

"Michigan has top science and math departments. World-class."

"Uh-huh. And she's getting ready for the varsity soccer season in the spring."

We pull up to Kate's house. I climb out, strapping on my backpack.

"And, dahrrrling?" My father ducks to meet my eyes as he gives me a teasing smile.

"Baba, stop," I say, knowing what's coming, avoiding his face.

He points dramatically with a finger in the air. "I *lowe* you!"

I turn away, shaking my head and hiding my smile. It's our inside joke—a reenactment of a comically bad, Indian-accented line from some vintage Bollywood film. My mother loves old Bollywood with so much passion that it leaves Baba and me no choice but to make light of it—the dancing, the sari-clad heroine singing shrilly as she runs from her lovesick suitor, the peeking coyly from behind trees, the fluttering of lashes, the male lead breaking out in English when showering his beloved with endearments . . .

I lumber up Kate's steps, my grin fading as I turn to wave to Baba. He toots the horn happily as he drives off. "Love you, too, Baba," I murmur.

I try to fight the sixth sense that Baba's love is based on a fallacy. That if he knew me as I truly am, his love would cease to exist—like water left out on a silver dish, evaporated with nothing left but a calcified trace.

CHAPTER TWENTY-EIGHT

January is torture: with ACT scores in, references submitted, and college applications sent, we're left hanging. It seems unusually cruel to make us seniors wait so long, our fates in the hands of nameless, faceless admissions teams. Secretly, I regret not having applied anywhere early decision like Ma implored me to do—I'm not good with uncertainty.

Satisfied enough with my scores and essays, I attempt optimism. "I have a bright future!" I say aloud to the mirror, like a weirdo. It's the type of thing Aajoba would say those summers in India as together we'd water the wild, muddy garden. "Rani, your future is very bright, the power in *you* only. Never waste that power," he'd say, pronouncing *waste* as *west*. He was always making formal, old-timey statements, raising a long, knobby finger: "Your potential for greatness lies within your passion." It was gibberish to me then, but now I pan for these little nuggets of gold, sensing their secret power.

On the flip side of all this visualization is Oliver.

Getting together has been tricky all month. His sister, Kathy, has officially moved in and continues to be on bed rest. According to him, between the wild mood swings and aggressive screaming matches, a radioactive cloud hangs over the apartment. "It's like they're premenstrual at regular, extremely frequent intervals," he says. I inform him that it's misogynistic to attribute family arguments to women's menstrual cycles, but he just scoffs. Sometimes, he says, everything seems kosher. The two women will be planning a shower or shopping online for baby items, bantering. Then, without warning, the bickering will begin, and before long, it devolves into an apocalyptic scream fest.

He tells me these stories like he's telling a joke, but his eyes are shadowed. He's also constantly hunched over his phone. Once, I peeked to see what he was doing, and I saw him saving photos of what looked like India in a digital file. When I asked him about it, he said it was for a project and promptly changed the subject. Even his walk is different, more a trudge, really, the tattered hems of his jeans dragging like he's a character from *Les Misérables*. Has he always been this ragged?

As if these changes weren't worrisome enough, his moods are everywhere. One minute he's making a funny observation, and the next he's silent and brooding . . . now he's muttering something snarky about my family's rules in front of his friends, and then he's apologizing for being a jerk, begging me to meet him after school.

"You know I can't," I usually say, groaning. In the past, he'd have said, "You know I gotta ask." But one Wednesday in late January, he just stares down, his eyes like granite. "Please. Will you at least consider it? Please."

Startled by his desperation, I tell my mother I'm studying

at Kate's and instead ride the bus with him to his place. The house is empty—Kathy's on a rare hiatus from bed rest—so we spend the afternoon together in his room.

Alone with him, I'm blindsided by my complicated feelings: something feels off, but his kisses light a fire in me. His breathless restraint makes him seem bizarrely skilled, his touch urgent but gentle, intuitive, effortless. The humming heat between us weakens and consumes me.

Afterward, I lie in his arms, watching the dust motes in the afternoon light that slants through the blinds. Oliver trails a finger along the bridge of my nose, and I look up to see his eyes, liquid and smoky.

"What?"

"I dunno . . . ," he whispers. Pepper meows at his closed door. Oliver gets up and lets him in.

"Hey." I prop myself on an elbow. "What's up?"

"I just . . ." He clears his throat. "I want to be a part of you. I feel like I can't get close enough. I want to be with you every minute, I want to eat every meal with you, I want to hang out at your house. I want to go out together, in broad daylight, and do something boring, like . . . a bike ride. I want to be part of your life in a bigger way. You are . . . my life."

He stares off, silent for so long that I think, irrationally, the conversation is over. But then he looks back, staring into my eyes. "I really want to be with you. In every way. Bring me to your place for dinner."

"As in—with my parents?" My heart pings around my ribs. Pepper glares at me from a pile of clothes across the room.

"Yeah. And your grandma. I'll torment her with endless questions about India."

A part of me loves it, the idea of it all. Of being together, really together. But . . .

"Oliver." I keep my voice soft and low. "You know I can't do that. I thought we had an agreement. That you understood."

"I know, but you love me, right? I mean, what is this—the 1800s? Have you ever considered how it feels to be excluded from your life, like I'm some shameful secret?" He scans my face wildly. "I don't want to sneak around anymore, Rani. Introduce me to your parents. Prove to me that I'm worth it."

"Of course I love you and you're worth it, but please trust me. Now is not the time."

"When, Rani?" he demands. "When will be the right time? Because I'm starting to think it's never."

The truth is, I don't know the answer to that. Unbidden, some of Oliver's choice words for me run through my mind: *exotic, Princess Jasmine, sexy Indian princess.* . . . I think of his mom and that first fight, his views on my conventional life. I love Oliver, but with a quiet burst of clarity, I realize that so much would have to change before I can introduce him to Ma and Baba. Before I'm ready to bridge the gap between my world and his.

I take his hand, practically pleading. "We just need more time. I promise that one day we'll all be hanging at my dinner table. But for now . . . trust me on this."

He says nothing. Removing his hand from mine, he opens his sketchbook and rubs charcoal across the page. "Any Hindu happenings coming up?" he asks.

"Huh? Oh. I guess so." February is around the corner, which means the Indian holiday ushering in spring is soon. Not that I remember the name of this holiday. . . .

"What's on the docket? A—what was that called?—puja of some sort?"

"Yes, a puja. A ritual done in honor of a god or a goddess."

"Right. Who's the next one in honor of?"

I fidget with my rings. "Sarasvati, maybe? I'm not totally sure."

He taps something into his phone. "Vasant Panchami—the festival honoring the coming of spring and Sarasvati, goddess of knowledge and the arts." He studies his phone, then glances at me. "What you gonna wear? Those combats?"

"No. No shoes for pujas."

"Huh." He turns back to his sketch, the charcoal in his hand moving like a hummingbird, the smudges turning into my face. "What time's it at?"

"Usually late morning, after everyone's showered."

"You think anyone would mind if I popped by? Just to soak in a little cultural experience? In the name of being closer to my girl?"

I laugh nervously, moving toward the bathroom.

"No, stay. . . ." He pulls me down on top of him.

"So . . . all this togetherness means no going to the bathroom?" I say, my face inches from his.

"You can go—as long as you're willing to take your dumps with me in there, watching."

"Ha," I say, extricating myself from him and hoisting myself off the bed. Pepper scampers out the open door.

CHAPTER TWENTY-NINE

One week later, I'm standing beside Aaji in my parents' bedroom, where the wooden devghar—a small temple for the home—sits atop the dresser. It's Vasant Panchami, the holiday Oliver read about that marks the end of winter and beginning of spring. Aaji and I are both wearing bright yellow—she a golden sari, and I a neon, chunky sweater—the color signifying the vibrancy of nature, I just learned. She dips the tiny silver Ganesh, Sarasvati, and Hanuman into a silver bowl filled with water before passing each one to me for drying. With a white washcloth, I polish the gods' nooks meditatively, daydreaming about all the things I want to do with Kate this summer before we go off to college, all the ways I can make it up to Oliver once school is out, the days and nights finally warm, the outdoors an easy meeting place . . .

"Betiya?" Aaji gestures at me to wipe down the devghar.

"Hi, Rani, Aaji," Baba says genially, walking in with a small bouquet of daisy-like yellow blooms. "Want to behead the flowers?" He hands me the bunch.

I begin snipping the heads off, one by one. "I've always

wondered why killing flowers for puja is okay, but not other living things."

"Rani," my mother says sharply, whisking in with some matches.

But Aaji laughs. "What lines are drawn regarding God's honor? A true spiritual question," she says, lighting the incense sticks. I watch the mini cattails catch the flame and burn out with a hiss, sending up a slinky, curling ribbon of scented smoke.

We place the flower heads at the feet of each god, then tuck more around them—in the crook of an arm here, upon a shoulder there—until the entire inside and top of the tiny house is aglow with yellow flowers. The silver glints of the gods peek beneath the pristine petals like gnomes in a floriferous garden.

"Baas, that's enough," my mother says, waving her hand impatiently. "Rani, fetch the prasad to offer the gods. It's on the stovetop."

I bound down the stairs, and before heading toward the kitchen, I glance out the front windows.

I freeze.

Even from a distance, I know it's Oliver. Outside. Staring up at my house into my parents' bedroom, derelict and forlorn in the weak February light, there in plain sight.

And before empathy or sadness over everything he's going through, there rises an ugly, blinding rage.

I snatch the sweet roasted wheat offering from the kitchen and bolt up the stairs, accompanied by the wafting fragrance of ghee and saffron. I dump the pot unceremoniously in front of the devghar and announce, "I think I'm having a migraine. Maybe." I glance out the window.

"What?" My mother's brow wrinkles. "You don't get migraines."

"Yeah, but Lalita Mami does, and I just . . . don't feel well," I mutter. "I think I'm getting one." I inch toward the windows, right where Aaji is standing. "The sunlight in here is so . . ." I lunge at the curtains, and just before shutting out the view, my eyes lock with Oliver's.

My heart leaps.

Aaji's gaze is transfixed exactly where mine is.

"But, Rani," my mother says, "we need the eastern light to shine on the gods."

I arrange the curtains so they are blotting out the outdoors, then squint and rub my temples. "My head's killing me," I murmur. "I think the gods will be okay with it." I wrinkle my face in pretend pain.

"Arre Rama—not you also." My mother stares at me, unblinking. "I pray you did not inherit those horrible headaches from my sister." She touches my forehead. "Can you do the puja or do you need to lie down?"

I exhale. "I think I can make it through the puja," I mumble. "But no sunlight." I carefully avoid Aaji's eyes.

Tinkling the tiny bell, we chant our prayers in unison, staring at the flickering oil lamp's flame shining upon the silver gods. They're ancient Sanskrit words, gibberish to me, my mind far away, outside with Oliver: Is he still there? What if he rings the doorbell?

But instinctively, I know he's gone.

I've worked so hard to keep the balance, and to think that he could obliterate it in an instant . . . I glance at Aaji. Maybe he's already done all the damage. . . . How can she not know everything now? And what reasons would she have for keeping my secrets?

With our ring fingers, we apply powdery orange haldi, or turmeric, upon the forehead of each god like a blazing third eye as my anger gives way to a twisting in my heart.

Did he park far? Did he take the bus? Worry and shame and fear mushroom in my gut like a cancer.

We prostrate ourselves, doing a reverent namaskar on the floor before the gods, the short period of bowed, silent prayer that concludes every puja. I pray to Sarasvati that Aaji didn't actually spot Oliver. I pray for her to fix whatever's breaking down between me and Oliver.

I pray for the wisdom to know how to give Oliver whatever it is he needs—without losing myself.

CHAPTER THIRTY

"Rani, did you even eat today?" my mother asks. "A major cause of migraine is not eating properly! And ay, when you're feeling better, set up the Zoom so we can speak to Aajoba."

"'Kay."

I shut my door, grab my phone, and tap out a text to Oliver with trembling fingers.

> I'm sorry I couldn't let you in. Can we talk?

I stare at my phone for a full minute. Nothing.

> You there?
>
> ?

Now that my initial anger has faded, his silence pierces me. I begin to imagine how he must have felt, standing there outside, shut out, desperate to be included. . . . I leave a few voice mails: first an apology, then a polite request, then a plea. All the restraint I've practiced over the months of our relationship unravels within me, quietly, rapidly.

My phone sits, silent and stupid.

I settle at my desk. I have a ton of reading, along with a reader's response page, a huge problem set, a pointless French project. I set up my desk, sharpening pencils, laying out my calculator, organizing papers and folders. I stare at the spindly branches of a tree scratching my window, crafting possible texts to Oliver in my head, obsessing over every word.

I tap in what I decide will be my final text of the day:

> I'm sorry. Want to see you.
> Please write back.
> Love you.

I read and reread it, trying to feel what he'll feel.

I'm begging. Something I vowed I'd never do for a guy, or anyone. Kate would be horrified.

My finger hovers over the send button on the phone, friendly and innocuous. I hit it, then stare at my phone, willing it to give me a sign.

Nothing.

I swallow my rising sobs, throw myself on my bed, and curl up with my phone like it's Oliver himself.

I must have fallen asleep, because when a text dings in, I'm middream. It signals again, and I pry my eyes open:

> Hey

I blink hard. Relief and desperation sweep over me: I decide on efficiency.

I know you're upset
can I call you

I stare at my phone. Three dots appear, and then they vanish.

Not upset. Cool I'm not worth introducing to your family.
Feels great

That's not it. Let's talk. Please

Can't. Helping Kathy puke.

You're a good bro. When can I call?

I don't know

Please? I'll make it up to you...

will call later

I check my phone every few minutes like a maniac. I putter down to the kitchen, where Ma asks, "Rani? Is your head better?" I look at her blankly before flooding with relief: I have an excuse for acting weird.

As the night drags on, I'm beside myself with despair, imagining that it's over. My mouth is parched. My limbs are filled with sand. I'm barely breathing.

Is my heart even beating?

When he still hasn't called by ten, I call him.

"Hello."

"Oliver?"

"Yeah." His tone is flat and cold and deep.

I pause, suddenly unsure of what to say. For a fleeting moment, I consider demanding why he hasn't called me as he said he would. "Is Kathy okay?" I ask instead, tentatively.

"Yep. She's asleep now."

"Wh-what are you doing?"

"Just catching the end of this basketball game."

The cell connection crackles. "Wanna come get me?"

A long pause. And then: "Yeah."

———

The air smells of earth and dirty, slushy snow as I sneak out to the alley, where Oliver's car idles. I've prepared a little speech, a passionate statement that will get him to understand. Maybe even forgive me.

"Hey." I grab his hand through my fingerless gloves. "I'm sorry about what happened."

"It's okay. I get it."

"I know it was beyond shitty to shut you out like that. You know I love you. But you coming to the house—" I stop. I don't want to sound blamey.

"Rani, look: I know. I just really needed to see you today, and thought that if you saw me outside . . . I don't even know." He flicks on his turn signal with irritation. "Can we just not talk about this right now?" He roots around in his coat pocket and pops something into his mouth.

I spin my rings as he drives in silence. "Yeah. Totally. Um. Tell me about your latest piece."

"Needs a lot of work. But I got permission to install it as one of the artists featured by the Art Café." He turns slowly onto Lincoln heading east. "Show's in May."

"May's still three months away," I say encouragingly. Maybe we can move past this, enjoy our night together. "Hey, I'm perfecting my bokeh technique. After all these months, I finally get how to use a narrow depth of field when shooting something like city lights on the water . . . the effect is kind of amazing."

"Sounds great." Everything about him is monochromatic. "Um. How's your job?"

"Huh?"

"Your sexy janitor-teacher gig." Have we ever small-talked before? Why is this so awkward?

"Ha. Well, I kinda don't have that anymore." He scratches at his chin, squinting out the windshield.

"What? Why?"

"I quit."

I stare at him. "Wh—?"

"I couldn't show up to the workshops, uh, in a reliable fashion."

"Why not? You love it there."

"Because sometimes I'm high and can't get my shit together to make it in."

I stare at him, slack-jawed.

"Kidding!" He looks over at me, his eyes lit up. "I'm kidding. I just can't always make it in, that's all."

"But I don't understand . . . ," I say slowly. "You . . . you said it was a place that inspires you, all that art, the kids . . ."

"Because I've got a lot of shit going on, Rani, if you haven't noticed. Plus, I'm spending all this time on the one piece for the show, but I need to make some *money*. That place barely pays. I've got my unstable, bedridden, puking ten-weeks-pregnant sister living in the apartment with my alcoholic mother. Can you imagine a better environment for a baby to come into the world?" He pops another something into his mouth and flicks on his turn signal with annoyance. "Anyway, I've been looking for actual work."

"Of course." I stare out the windshield. "That all makes sense. I'm sorry." We've reached Lighthouse Beach, and he pulls into a spot with a perfect view of the lake. The water's frozen a frosty white along the lip of the beach, and glacial plates of ice bob in the middle distance. I think fleetingly of the *Titanic*.

He leans his head back and inhales deeply, eyes closed. "Okay. Better." He turns to me, pushing a wavy lock from my face. "Don't worry." He lightly touches my jaw with his fist. "I will survive, as I do." He clasps his hands together and shakes them high, like a champion accepting applause. "Let's forget all this and go have some fun." We get out, and he wraps an arm around me as we amble toward the beach.

"So—where have you looked for jobs so far?"

"I remember the first time I ever saw you," he says, ignoring my question. "I couldn't tear my eyes away." He leans down and kisses me, tasting sweet like candy.

"I remember."

"And then," he says dramatically, palms open, "you actually

talked to me. And I thought I might combust." He shrugs. "Possibly die."

I laugh. "Talking to me almost killed you?"

His brow rises lazily. "Pretty much. I mean, the realization that your soul outweighed all this"—he gestures at my face and body—"and that you might actually agree to meet up with me? Yep, I died that night."

I can't help but giggle, still in awe that someone like Oliver could think of me *in that way,* despite my armor and road-blocking, my limitations. . . .

A cold gust of wind blusters off the water, and I shiver. But Oliver's unfazed by the freeze, holding me against him, strolling along the shoreline. He seems different somehow from our time in the car . . . weird. Suddenly, we're at the breakwater. He hops up onto it.

"Um. The breakwater?" I say. The wind's whipping hard, the moon close to full, like it was on our first beach date. But he begins casually stepping along the rusted structure, moving out toward the black horizon, the waves below angry and frothing.

"Oliver. This . . . is maybe not a great idea?" Confused, I follow behind him.

"Aw, come on, baby. A little adventure isn't going to kill us." He's moving farther out. He glances back, flashing me an easy smile.

I halt. "Oliver, stop. This is dangerous."

But he's already approaching the end of the plank, surrounded by white waves, white icecaps, and black, crashing water. I step up cautiously beside him, and he reaches for my hand, staring out at the giant waves, the endless horizon. Our first night here, Oliver froze in fear after just a few steps on the breakwater; walking down to its end point had been out of the question. What is happening?

Finally, he turns to me. "It's fucking beautiful here." The blue moon shines behind him, shadowing his features. "It makes me want to be, like, *one* with the water." He laughs, sweeping an arm across the vista.

The hairs on the back of my neck rise. Everything in this moment feels wrong. "Oliver?"

"I mean, what if I just decided to become a merman right now and dive into this water?" He peers out at the furious waves and grins widely. He takes my hand and gives it a squeeze before letting it go.

"Well, for one thing, you can't swim." Fear grips my heart. Something feels beyond off.

"But being a merman and all, I can totally swim," he says, still grinning.

"You're *not* a freaking merman. Oliver. I want to leave. Now."

Arms out, eyelids heavy, he steps closer to the edge, the toes of his battered Vans inching forward above the hungry waves. He closes his eyes like he's reveling in a summer breeze. "So let's say I, a nonswimming merman, decided to jump." He turns to face me. "You'd jump in after me, right?"

A sickness seizes me, the realization that it could all end, in an instant, right here. Lake Michigan is wild and deadly, especially on nights like this. A sob gathers in my chest. "Oliver?"

"Think of it," he says dreamily. "You'd be my mermaid savior forever girl." His body wavers like he's practicing tai chi, his torso suddenly dipping low. My heart drops.

"Oliver, I'm leaving. This is ridiculously dangerous."

He laughs, his body swaying. "I could just—" And then—his foot slips.

I gasp.

He grabs my arm as I bend, seeking gravity for both of us, my heart in my throat. . . .

"Whoa," he says as we regain our balance. He shakes his head like he's clearing it. "What the fuck?" he says, straightening up. His eyes meet mine. Barely breathing, I stare into the gaping dark of his pupils, his eyes almost black. . . . "Yeah, let's go."

Silently enraged, I take tentative steps backward along the plank, praying we don't hit a patch of ice. I keep my eyes trained on his feet, trying to steady my heartbeat by watching the shuffle of his shoes—right, left, right, left—heading back toward land.

He stumbles a few times, giggling while my heart plummets . . . but the placement of his feet is precise—sheer miraculous luck. Finally, I turn so that I'm heading forward, gripping his fingertips behind my back.

"Okay, we're above land," I murmur. I step down before turning to help him. The last time we were here, he was the responsible one, suggesting we get back to land, to safety. . . . My mind whirs. . . .

Back in the car, he sits, slow-blinking like a lizard and staring through the windshield at the moon. I try to process what just happened: What if he *had* jumped, fallen? "Are you okay?" I say finally.

"What? Of course I'm okay." He produces a cigarette, squinting as he lights it, like life has not just been irrevocably altered. I watch him, saying nothing. I've never seen him smoke before, and yet, it's the least of our problems. "I'm sorry for that back there," he murmurs.

"Do you mind telling me what is going on?" I hear in my voice the same quiet tone Baba uses in the rare times he's upset.

He glances at me, then does a double take. "Hey, whoa. You're pissed. And you know, I get it. That was seriously fucking weird. I was just messing around, but I mean, it won't happen again."

"Are you . . . ?"

His features rearrange in comprehension. "What? No! Rani." He faces me, taking my hand in his. "Look, I'm not a drunk. I'd never drink. After watching my parents . . ."

"No, sure. Of course not, I know. But so you're not . . ." I can't bring myself to ask about drugs. What if I'm just being paranoid and my suspicions are off base? He'd be so offended. . . . Plus, I've already upset him enough today with the puja fiasco—is now really the time to interrogate him? "I don't know what exactly I'm trying to say." I shrug helplessly.

"Rani, look." He twists a tendril of my hair around his finger. "I'm just . . . seriously tired. I haven't been sleeping well. Things at home are weird, so I'm . . . a little delirious, that's all."

"Oh." I look into his eyes, soft and earnest. He *is* going through a lot, and I have to trust him. Aren't all good relationships based on trust? "Not sleeping usually signifies underlying issues," I say. "Have you thought about talking to someone again, you know, who knows how to help?"

He laughs. "Always the pediatrician." He ducks his head, squinting at the full moon through the top of the windshield.

"I appreciate the concern. I had a shrink. Back when my dad left, and anyway, this was a blip. I'm cool, okay?"

He leans in and kisses me gently. He tastes like smoke, with that trace of sickly sweet.

I pull away. "I'm sorry again about what happened at my house today. You deserve to be . . . included." I swallow hard, trying to work out my guilt amid what was basically a reckless, near-death experience led by Oliver.

"Yeah, I'm perfect and I deserve perfection," he says, smiling lazily and turning the key in the ignition. He's surprisingly chill despite everything. He makes a little wavy hand gesture ending with a touch at the tip of my nose; a spark of annoyance flares inside my chest.

We drive in silence.

He pulls up to the back of my house in the alley and turns to me. In a flash, I see it: the hollowness in his eyes, pupils huge and blank . . . a vapid emptiness that suddenly reminds me of Nilesh, years ago, that night at Pratap Uncle and Indu Auntie's—the night of a public showdown between him and his parents.

He kisses me again, the earlier sweet of his mouth now turned sour. "Later, Jaz."

Too exhausted to call him out, as Tonio did on my behalf, for this mildly racist nickname, I steal through the backyard into the slumbering house and slip into my room. Beneath my covers, I let my mind replay the night's events: Oliver's foul mood, him popping something from his pocket, and then . . . his irresistible charm. I think about drugs, about everything I know and fear—their impact on neural pathways, the difference between infrequent use and desperate escape. . . . I think about the ways I've watched drugs affect personalities, families, communities, futures—the tumult of a hurricane that has the potential to destroy lives.

But Oliver drove tonight. He'd never drive high, putting me at risk.

Would he?

CHAPTER THIRTY-ONE

Just when it seems as though winter will never end, the snow vanishes. Tiny pink buds dot the black trees, followed by an explosion of fuzzy, flowering branches—a shocking spring spectacle.

One warm Friday afternoon, I come home to find my mother working the soil in our narrow back garden. She digs out half-frozen cylindrical chunks of earth with a foot-operated bulb planter. Baba bought the planter from a man selling door to door, and when Ma first saw it, she was furious. "Why not just invite every stranger into the house?" she cried. "Have them tour the place. Show them where we keep my wedding jewelry! And give away more of our money in exchange for useless things." Baba shrugged and smiled in agreement. "Correct," he said, admitting his naivete.

"Looks like you're making good use of that thing after all," I say.

She glances up at me. "Betiya, we are going to India this summer."

I drop my backpack. "What?" I croak.

She nods, avoiding my eyes. She rips open a netted packet

of bulbs and places each one into the freshly dug holes. "Your aajoba . . . he's not coping well with Aaji gone. We must go to him."

"That's . . . that's terrible. But—it's also the summer before everyone leaves for college!"

"Your friends won't be far. You'll see them again."

"Were you even planning on *asking* me? Have you already booked the tickets?"

"Not yet. We'll talk to Aajoba this weekend and make a final decision. Will you set up the Zoom so he can see us? It's organized on their end, but we need your help with it. You know Baba and I are not tech-savvy."

"I can't believe I don't have a say in where we spend our summer." I feel a twinge of guilt even as I say this. I do love Aajoba, and want to be with him, but I was counting on spending more time with Oliver this summer, making things up to him. . . .

"Rani." She flashes me her stern look while I stare at her plantings. The tip of each pale bulb points up, like soldiers in a line. Or headstones. "This is your aajoba. He needs us. I think you understand what would be best."

She's piercing my heart and she knows it. I turn and march into the house.

"Rani! How many times more must I ask you to set up Zoom so we may speak with Aajoba—" The screen door bangs shut behind me just as a call dings in from Oliver; lately he's been contacting me outside the safe-zone hours. What even?

"Hi, betiya," my grandmother says from the couch. "Is it truly warm out, or only a trick?"

I grunt and stalk to my room.

"Can you please not freaking call me when you know my family's around?" I whisper into the phone. "I *told* you—"

"Sorry, baby. I've been dreaming about the rock mermaid. The three of us need more sexy times together. When can I see you?"

I bristle at his mention of the rock mermaid, whose significance will forever be altered since that night on the breakwater. To make matters worse, I have to break the news about spending the summer in India. "Later tonight?"

"Excellent. But I don't have a car tonight."

"I do. I mean I could . . . steal one."

He laughs. "Damn, woman—you know how to hot-wire?"

"I'll be there by eleven-thirty," I say, my heart pounding.

"Everyone'll be home here, so maybe—"

"The police'll be trolling campus by then, so no mermaid, but we'll find someplace." Knowing I'll be in India this summer is making me jittery, desperate.

"Fine," he says. "We'll do her another time."

Ugh. "Okay, so I'll see you tonight?"

"Yeah. But I have a request."

"What's that?" I wait to hear the request.

But all he says is "Okay. Eleven-thirty."

———

The engine idles in Oliver's back alley. This is the first time I've driven my parents' car without asking, and I try to blow it off like it's no big deal.

225

I'm muttering to myself to stop obsessing over the thought that this could be the one night I get caught, the one night that could end my life or result in a permanent move overseas, when I hear the rap on my window. I jump.

But of course it's only Oliver, pale and quizzical, his dark hair whipped by the night wind. I lower the window. "You scared me."

"Yeah? Well, you were talking. To no one. I'm the one who should be scared. Unless you were on speakerphone, finally telling your parents you're out meeting me. In which case, I'd rejoice."

I smirk. "My parents would freak over me driving, not to mention driving while distracted, so no, that would never be the case."

Oliver snorts. "Your parents and their freaking. Don't get me started." He walks around to the passenger side, and my heart sinks like a stone. Great—he's already pissed at my parents, and he doesn't even know yet that they've decided the fate of our summer in one fell swoop. He tosses a backpack onto the floor, slides into the seat, and slams the door in one fluid movement.

"What's with the backpack?" I ask.

He leans in and kisses me quick on the lips. "You'll find out, nosy. Let's go."

I head north, glancing at him.

"How—how are you doing?" I should tell him about India, but he's in a decent mood. . . .

"I'm great. The question is, how are *you* holding up," he says, drumming his fingers on his thighs, "seeing that you are now officially a criminal who has stolen her parents' car?"

"I mean, not great? It's the middle of the night, and if they realize what's happened . . ." I gulp, hoping desperately I get away with this. "But no doubt, it's worth it. To see you. Of course."

"That's my girl." We drive through the corridor of trees, their black branches looking smudged amid a suddenly dense fog. "But, um, remind me again why we're *still* sneaking around?"

"Do I really have to?"

He laughs. "Nah. Fuck your parents. Let's forget that shit tonight. I've got something I think you'll love." After recent events, I admit that sounds better than another heavy talk. Maybe a spectacular night together is all that we need. I'll tell him about India later.

Driving in silence, we pass the schools and churches and the tiny golf course on Lincoln cloaked in heavy fog. Instead of turning toward Lighthouse Beach, I head south on Sheridan, searching for a low-profile spot where we can stay awhile.

We pass the university campus, veer east as the road hugs the shoreline, before turning onto a side street. The fog's so thick it's like entering a silent white car wash. Slowing to a crawl, I finally spot it—the foreboding iron fence surrounding the giant corner lot of a long-since-foreclosed home. Giant fir trees shroud the property from public view.

I park, kill the engine, and stare into the dense white cloud that envelops us. I turn to Oliver, regarding him for the first time tonight. "This okay?"

"Wow," says Oliver. "Um, yeah. It's perfect, actually."

I take his hand. "How are you feeling? How's your sleep? I still feel terrible about that day at my house. . . ."

"Shh. Okay. You're sorry, I know. You drove a stake through my heart, but I'm alive. My sleeping is fine, everything's fine. I want to show you something. Something I think you'll dig."

As he pulls things out of his backpack, relief floods me. He does seem fine. Maybe we'll be okay, despite everything. . . .

And then I see it: neatly folded red fabric, its edges embroidered in gold, several tiny cattails like the ones Aaji lit during puja, a miniature wooden canoe-like thing, colorful plastic bangles, a sheet of what looks like stickers covered in cellophane. . . .

"Wh-where did you get all this?" My heart's pounding.

"Some from Goodwill—can you believe I found the sari there? Of course, I washed it to remove its Eau de Thrift top note. The rest was from Devon Avenue. Little India. That place is authentically gritty. As close to the real thing as you can get around here."

I stare.

"The coolest part is"—he rummages around in the front pocket of the backpack and presents me with a tiny cardboard box—"this. For you."

I laugh nervously. "A gift?"

The box is red and decorated with a mehndi dot pattern that's quintessential India. It's surreal to see it here—in America, with my boyfriend, in my parents' car, in the middle of the night. I lift the cardboard lid, and out wafts a smell that's pure nostalgia: incense, gasoline, cardamom. I unroll magenta tissue paper and find a gold chain nestled within.

"Okay, so it's not real gold." His words are coming fast. "It's gold-plated, just to get that out there. But what's so cool is that it hooks up to your ear, like this. . . ." He leans over and somehow fastens one end to the gold stud in my earlobe. I inhale the scent of him—soap, rain, earth, leather—and close my eyes. "And the other end's a regular nose ring." Our eyes lock. "Could you . . . ?" I nod, speechless. "I just don't want it to hurt," he mutters. I remove the nose ring I'm wearing and insert the new one.

He sits back, studies me. "Holy mother of God."

Seed beads brush my cheek, trailing an arc across my face from ear to nose. I shake my head, and the beads tickle, tinkling, tiny little bells. I pull down the vanity mirror and stare. "Wow," I mumble. "Suddenly, I'm about to . . . get married. Old-world style."

"Huh?"

"This is bridal jewelry. My mom's wearing one of these in her wedding photos."

He stares at me for a full five seconds. He clears his throat. "Um, okay. I did not know that." He looks out the window at the white night, then back at my face. "But um . . . remember my request? Would you . . . maybe put some of this stuff on? You'd look so amazing," he adds.

His face is full of earnest longing—eyes liquid and hazy, a sheen of sweat on his skin. My eyes wander to his lap; it's like he raided my family's basement closet. "Now?"

"It's late." He shrugs. "And foggy."

"You want me to play Indian bride dress-up? Here in the car?"

A shadow crosses his face. "Only if you're cool with it."

"I . . ." I stop. This is my chance. A chance at making everything up to him, maybe my only chance. There's so much I can't give him. Maybe this is something I can . . . ? "Hey." I take his hand. "If this— Sure." I rub the skin along his thumb and swallow.

"Do you love me?" he says.

"You know I do."

He stares into my eyes, trails a finger along the gold chain across my cheek, and cocks an eyebrow half comically. "Let's do this, Jaz."

Wordlessly, we climb into the back seat and begin stripping off layers. He slips a fitted sari blouse over my bare shoulders, fastening the hook-and-eye closures over my chest before wrapping me in the crimson sari, slipshod and mummy-ish. ("You mean you don't know how to put one of these on yourself?" he asks in disbelief.) I shove glassy plastic bangles up both wrists, while he peels off a bindi and places it between my eyebrows.

"You're so sexy, you have no idea," he murmurs.

I get a glimpse of myself in the rearview mirror: I am an Indian bride.

At a family friend's wedding once, I admired the bride in her gorgeous silk sari—a symbol of elegance, pride. . . .

But nothing about this moment feels like pride. It feels terribly, utterly wrong. . . .

Once I would have called him out for this. I'd have scoffed and ridiculed and maybe even started a fight over it. But now, after everything, all I can think, over and over, is: *This is something I can give him.*

He places an incense stick into the canoe-shaped thing on the dashboard, which I now see is an incense holder created to catch the ashes in a perfect line. He lights it, and just like during the Sarasvati puja in my parents' bedroom, I inhale its spicy scent.

He lifts a garland of fake marigolds over my head and climbs on top of me. After peeling away layers of fabric from my body, he unbuttons the cropped blouse he's just done up, baring my breasts, and nuzzles my neck, running his tongue and lips over me. . . . Trembling, I pull off his shirt, move my hands across his body, and fumble with the zipper on his jeans. I tug the condom out from its customary spot in his back pocket and tear it open.

"Hey. You sure you're okay with this?" Oliver's shaking, the air between us weighted, heavy, as though before a tropical storm. Our eyes lock: *This is something I can give him.*

I nod.

In the reflection of the window, I can see the bridal crown glinting along my cheek as the cherry bangles clink and slide along my wrists. . . . Our bodies bound together, the garland crushed between us, I feel the beating of his heart against my chest. I wonder if a person could die of pleasure, or lovesickness, or sensory overload, enveloped in his heat and the gorgeous vibrant colors and the scent of incense. . . . *This is something I can give him.* His body trembles, eyes saturated with lust and longing . . . but there in the heat of everything between us flashes a bolt of fear, and something darker . . . something different. . . .

We lie there, breathless, in a pile of sari fabric. The incense smoke trapped in the car is suddenly cloying, and there's a dull burn at the site of the new nose ring. I try extricating myself from the billows of sari, noticing only then that a plastic bangle's broken off, leaving a delicate red track along my inner arm.

"Holy shit," he murmurs. "You don't know how many times I've fantasized about that."

I close my eyes, a dark, liquid lead spreading heavy through my veins.

CHAPTER THIRTY-TWO

"Holy crap. Indian bridalwear?" Kate says, her jaw half open.

"I know."

It's three weeks later, a Monday afternoon, and Kate and I just split off from Henry as we head to PE.

"Was Oliver embarrassed when you told him they were for a wedding?"

"Not exactly. But he was being weird."

"As in stalker-boy-out-front weird, or a different brand of weird?"

I hesitate. Just as I couldn't tell her right away about the L-word, I've been putting off revealing the latest events with Oliver. I did tell her about Oliver appearing during the family puja (over which, I note uncomfortably, she's now calling him a stalker). But I can't bring myself to tell her about the devastation I felt while being ghosted by him before meeting up that night we went to the breakwater. And I don't even know where to begin talking about the weird role-playing that happened a few weeks ago. I open my gym locker and start undressing for PE.

She's about to pull on her Frances Willard Bobcats shirt

when she stops. "Hey." She lowers her voice. "Something has been up with you. Are you gonna tell me what it is, or do I need to wrestle it out of you? Because you know I'm good at that shit."

Dang it, Kate's sensory powers. I glance around nervously—we do have the row to ourselves, and there's plenty of talking and laughing in the other aisles. . . .

"Tell. Me. Everything," she says.

And in that moment, I can't help it: I do. I talk about how Oliver ignored my texts and calls after the puja. How frantic I became, how unreasonably thrilled I was when he grudgingly agreed to meet up that night, the terror on the breakwater, my suspicions about him using drugs, India this summer and how I can't bring myself to tell Oliver . . . leading me to cave to his desperate "request" that foggy night, the sickness and heat and stress of it all . . .

I look up. She stares at the blue stripe painted along the top of the locker-room walls, avoiding my gaze.

"Okay," she says, in a way that reveals that none of it is, in fact, okay. We move toward the indoor track, now late for PE, heads down.

"I know."

"I'm just thinking . . . damn, how does anyone get together at all? I'm sorry, but Oliver was my last and final hope for mankind. I'd pinned all my aspirations on you two. I mean, the breakwater: That's really scary, Rani! He could have taken both of you out that night!"

"I know."

"And this followed by an *Indian bride sex fantasy*? And here I thought Oliver was kind of . . . your rock."

We begin stretching with the class. Coach Morris—who's also Kate's soccer coach—is leading, her tube socks pulled high. My mind whirs: Does the car scene with Oliver really qualify as not okay? Kate can be a little over-the-top with her judgment . . . though, of course, the whole experience felt beyond off. I decide to push deeper. "And now . . . ?"

"I mean, I know he loves you and everything. . . ."

"He does," I hear myself say. "He really does."

"But . . . that breakwater incident," she murmurs, stretching her hamstrings.

"I know. He insisted he's just stressed and sleep-deprived." We begin jogging around the track. "But it felt like more than that." I struggle to keep up with Kate's pace.

"Also . . . I'm not clear on something." She swipes her hair into a low ponytail as we jog. "Why'd you go along with that last bit in your car?"

I take a deep breath. "I felt guilty about the puja episode—shutting him out was cold. Plus, I feel bad about all that he's going through at home . . . and I can only support him to an extent. . . ."

"Rani, you're the most supportive person I know. But let's get real: sexual favors or whatever you want to call them won't solve his problems." I start lagging, and she adjusts her pace to mine.

"I mean . . ." I try to patch up the picture. "He was really tender. And he asked if it was okay."

"And was it?"

"I told him yes." I'm losing steam, all this jogging while talking. "There's no way I can do what he really wants, which is bring him home to my family. So granting this was the next best thing. Whatever. It's hard to explain."

We run a lap in silence, my mind replaying the end of that foggy night with Oliver, as grainy and surreal as an old black-and-white film.

"Rani?" Kate's glancing at me, her brow furrowed.

"Enough about my ridiculous life," I puff. "Tell me what's going on with you. How's soccer?"

"Okay. Um. Yeah. Soccer's good. I do have some news."

"What? What news?"

"Henry just asked me to prom."

I stop in my tracks, and Kate jogs in place, grinning at me. Coach Morris shrills her whistle and gives Kate a pointed look. "Ladies, let's hustle."

I start moving. "Whaaat!" I breathe. "Kate! That's so great!"

"I mean, whatever. It's Henry. It'll be fun, but we're just friends."

"Which will be nothing but awesome! Oliver will actually agree to go if he knows it'd be with you and Henry."

"And if Henry and I *weren't* going?"

"Then it'd be all snide remarks about prom being conformist or a lame excuse to show off and be fake or whatever. I will be spared that nonsense now, so thank Henry and thank you for saying yes." *And you'd better treat Henry well,* I can't help but think.

"Hopefully I'll be less pissed at Oliver by then." She sniffs.

Jogging around the track, we talk details—where should we go for dinner, do we want to stay overnight at a hotel with friends . . . ?

But our casual conversation can't conceal the fact that something's changed: she's lost some respect for me. The me who's pining, the me who's jumping through hoops . . . the me who's compromising myself in ways we vowed we'd never do for a guy.

After PE is over, I text Oliver.

Meet me after school. Need to see you.

The thought of being with him soon hits me like a rush of dopamine. The discomfort I felt around Kate falls away like the peel of a blood orange, revealing something sweet and taut.

My phone buzzes a few seconds later:

K. Where?

CHAPTER THIRTY-THREE

Sitting on a bench in Ellingwood Park, I wait for Oliver. He said he had yet another meeting at Noyes right after school with his mentor, Valentia, about his May show. To kill time, I went to the library to do homework, but instead stared out the window, thinking about how things fall into oblivion when it comes to Oliver. . . . About the fact that, unbeknownst to Kate, he and I have been together multiple times since the night in my car, each time more charged and confusing than before. . . . About the fact that I still somehow haven't told him I'll be in India this summer. I wait, breathless.

He comes speeding up Hartrey on his bike, dark hair flying. I rummage in my backpack for some gum—my mouth is suddenly parched—then I sit on my hands to hide their trembling.

He hops off his bike, shoves it against a tree, and grabs me in a bear hug. "Hey. God, it's good to see you. You read my mind—I really wanted to see you today. Then again, I'm obsessed and can't ever get enough, if you couldn't tell."

The fact is, our strange addiction fuels us both in ways that don't make sense.

"I know . . . ," I manage. I clear my throat. "What's going on with you?"

"Well, I've got news," he says, settling on the bench beside me.

"Is your sister . . . ?" I search his face.

"Kathy's okay. Still on bed rest, though at least she's past four months and throwing up less. But this." He pulls an envelope from his back pocket and hands it to me. "Acceptance letter."

Rhode Island School of Design.

"Scholarship." He's grinning wide.

"Wait. RISD? You got the letter today?"

"It was postmarked almost two weeks ago. The fool people I live with are so wrapped up in their drama that they stash old mail beneath the body lotion on the toilet tank. I just found it."

I open the letter and skim the words, my chest filling up. "God, I'm so happy for you, Oliver."

"It's just— Man. *Scholarship*."

"You deserve it."

I hug him hard. His eyes are shining, filled with the impish light I haven't seen in so long. I try to smile at him with my eyes, with genuine feeling, but my throat is thick.

"So," he says, "needed a fix after school on a Monday?"

"Yes—an Oliver fix." I smile wanly.

"Rani." He leans down, poking his face into my line of vision. "Hey. Come here."

He strokes my hair, kisses the top of my head, and holds me tight. "We're gonna make it work. We can talk every day. We'll visit each other. I mean, I *want* to make this work with you. And this summer, we'll have so much time to—"

"Oliver. I'm going to India this summer. My mom informed me the other day."

He freezes. He lets me go, sits up straighter, and blinks. "The other day? When? When did she 'inform' you? Do you have a say in *anything* regarding your life?"

Instantly, I regret my phrasing. "No. Yes. Well, I mean, my grandfather's not doing well. We need to be with him. It's going to suck being away from you this summer. But I guess I was thinking—"

"What? What were you thinking, Rani? What were you possibly thinking?"

Invisible shards prick at my eyeballs.

"I guess I was hoping that maybe you'd go to school nearby. Like the Art Institute of Chicago . . ."

Last week, I was offered a spot at the University of Chicago, and I accepted immediately, though I hadn't yet heard from other schools. When Oliver asked why, I shrugged, saying: "It was the best school I applied to."

He countered, "Best how? And according to *who*? What's their photography department even like?" I didn't answer, and he sneered, "Do they even *have* a photography department?"

A part of me was outraged: How dare he treat me with such blatant disrespect? What does he even know about my life and how photography fits into it? But deep down, I understand: He *doesn't* actually know much about my life, and maybe that's my fault for keeping him and my family separate. Plus, I've lied to my parents about practically everything, and it's hard to respect a liar. Not creating space for photography is just one facet of the complicated prism of my life.

"But this is a *scholarship*," he says now. "They don't even offer scholarships for students at the Art Institute."

"Yeah. I guess I hadn't thought of the scholarship stuff." Somehow, talking about colleges in this moment reminds me of that fateful conversation I had with Nilesh the summer before my freshman year. . . .

"Of course you hadn't. It's all 'Wherever you'd like to go to school, Rani, we will send you, no problem,'" he says, mimicking an Indian accent. And did I just detect a slight head bobble?

I swallow hard. Fear and anger coagulate in my gut.

"Anyway, it'd be nice for me to get the hell out of here," he says.

Get the hell out of here? We stare out at the street in the fading light, the occasional car swishing by. I feel exposed, like we're on a movie set, or inside a terrarium.

"I'm sorry about your grandfather," he says quietly.

"It sounds like he's been struggling. He'll be okay once we're all there." I shiver. Why am I revealing details about Aajoba? Then again, why do I feel this need to protect my family when I'm with Oliver?

"So after graduation we have . . . what? A month of summer before you leave?"

"Sort of. Well, not quite. We leave in late June." Is it possible that I only imagined him mocking Baba using a stereotypically Indian accent?

"Shit," he mutters. "Late June." He twists a spindly branch

241

off a nearby tree and flings it into the street. "Let's double-bike to the rocks."

———

"So how was your group project?"

"Ma!" I swallow. "You scared me! I didn't hear you come down."

"Sorry. You really should eat properly, with everything warmed up on a plate."

She's standing in the kitchen doorway in her old pink robe, her face greased up with Pond's cold cream. I turn to fill up a glass of water, not meeting her eyes. I wonder what I look like after my Oliver time: Is my mascara smeared? Is it possible that I have visible hickies?

"So you got my message about the group project meeting," I say, settling at the kitchen counter as I take a bite of my late dinner. Oliver and I were together six hours by the lakefront on Northwestern's campus, and we forgot, in all that time, to eat.

Silence. And then: "Rani. Do you not remember what you'd agreed to help with when you had a free moment?"

"Huh?" I stop in my tracks, looking at her fully for the first time. I search her face, and then it hits me. "Oh, jeez. Zoom."

"I'm glad it finally came to you. You had many chances."

"Oh no. I'm sorry. I can set it up now. . . ."

"We already called him this evening—which, you know, is morning in India—and spoke on the phone. But he was disappointed. He really wanted to see you and Aaji. He sounds lonely, and it would have been good to . . . well, *see* him. For him to see us."

"I'm sorry, Ma. I'll do it tomorrow, I promise. . . ."

"No need. Your cousin Vineet is the only one who can set it up at Aajoba's, as Shalini has still not yet received her job transfer to Pune. He was in town several times for business and visited Aajoba but is now back in Bangalore."

"Ma, I'm really sorry."

She stands and looks at me for several seconds. "Get some sleep, betiya," she says, her voice tight. "It's a school night." She disappears up the stairs.

I tear off a piece of roti, but suddenly have no appetite. My eyes well, a storm gathering in my chest. Things are spiraling with Oliver, Kate is losing respect for me, and I am also somehow failing the one person who always found a way to support me, despite living on the other side of the world.

CHAPTER THIRTY-FOUR

Mid-May, as we get ready for prom, Kate dances to the Top 40 station in her strapless dress, testing out her heels.

"Nice moves," I comment from her bed, observing an extended shimmy. My nails are bitten down to nubbins. I told my family I was going to prom with Kate and some girlfriends. They were distracted at the time, so I seem to have gotten away without the usual inquisition, but I can't help but feel that I got off too easily. As I self-consciously tuck my thumbnails inside each fist, Kate wiggles her shoulders, doing the limbo beneath an imaginary bar. "How are you even doing that?" I laugh.

"I'm *so* ditching my shoes during the dance," she says, flinging her pumps across the room. "Whoever invented heels clearly never danced. Undoubtedly some chauvinist." Her eyes are bright, and tendrils of hair have escaped her updo—she looks gorgeous and bohemian. Jealousy squeezes at my heart.

She seems so free.

"So I went with my mom to that Mexican place in the city Henry mentioned to us the other day," Kate says as she curls her lashes. Obsessed with exploring his new city, Henry loves googling its top spots. "The enchiladas there are incredible, nothing like the Tex-Mex around here. Anyway, right in the open, she starts talking about sex. As in *me and Henry*! Things like 'Have you guys talked about this? What kinds of stuff, *physical stuff,* have you done with him?' et cetera! I almost died I was so embarrassed. I mean, really. As if Henry and I are a couple." She futzes with the mascara wand, and a huge glob clumps beneath her eye. "Oh, jeez. Why do I even try?" She heads to the bathroom to rinse, and I follow.

"But I'm sure you've thought about it," I say.

"No, in fact, I haven't. He's just a friend."

She towels off her face, and our eyes meet in the mirror. We burst into giggles.

"Okay, yeah, I've thought about it. Like I do with everyone, everywhere, heh-heh. But really! *My mother!*"

"Why do you think she brought it up?"

"To get a sense of where things stand with Henry, I guess? And to tell me that sex kind of 'raises the stakes'—her words. That it's not a great step to take if you aren't sure where things are going with a guy. Especially if it's prom night—so much pressure." She applies coral lipstick and then blots most of it off. "I think she was worried I'd have sex with Henry because it's prom. I mean, I haven't even kissed Henry. We're for real just friends. So sex is out of the question." We head back to her room.

"But . . . it's actually really sweet that she cares?" A tiny part of me wishes Kate and Henry *would* have sex so I could talk to her about some of the confusing stuff with Oliver. Once, sex felt like a revelation, but lately I've been feeling kind of terrible afterward. Like, it's supposedly the truest form of intimacy, but half the time it leaves me feeling more alone than ever.

"Yeah, it's sweet. Bonnie's surprising me nowadays. By the way, you decided no about getting a hotel room with Oliver and that huge gang of people tonight, right?"

"Right. No hotel room," I say.

"Good. That business sounded seedy. So back here afterward?" She squints, gazing at my face. "Hey. Maybe use some blush? You look a little . . ."

The doorbell rings.

It's time.

———

In the Aon Grand Ballroom at Navy Pier, girls sail by, dressed to destroy in their vintage frocks and glamorous evening gowns. Everyone's snapping selfies and laughing and dancing, the party loose and already in full swing. "Hey," Oliver says, glancing at the black shift dress I found last minute with Kate, "you could have worn the sari tonight." When I shoot him a look, he says, "What? With you in that thing, we could have gone to *your* place for pictures. Your parents would've fallen in love with me for buying you a traditional sari, proving that all that sneaking around was for nothing. Plus, you'd look hotter than everyone here."

I clench my jaw. This guy. I wish he would leave me in charge of my own external identity. Of course I could've worn desi clothes tonight—our school celebrates its diversity, and it clearly would've made my date happy. But I have complicated feelings about my Indian clothes: I love to wear

246

them, but wearing a sari to school to me feels unsafe, like exposure—exposure to gawking, othering. . . . Traditional Indian clothes hold deeper meaning for me—and Oliver seems to not get that.

The shameful scene that Halloween night at Brittany's all those years ago flits into my mind, those hushed, mocking voices as I returned from the bathroom. . . .

Kate, Henry, Oliver, and I run into Irene and Mimi and their dates, and before long, we're hitting the dance floor, we girls inventing moves that the guys then riff on. The guys watch in rapt attention before mirroring us, lit up and laughing. Oliver, however, is in a different zone, arms sweeping out like that night on the breakwater, crouching like he's surfing, eyes glassy. . . . He soon floats away.

I get swept into various tottering circles on the ballroom floor, surveying groups of kids I've known over the years— girls from cross-country, kids from National Honor Society, friends from photography. A wave of gratitude, nostalgia, and melancholy swells within me—*this is the end of a chapter!* I was so distracted this year—I'd already drifted from everyone before senior events ever began. Burly Charles Black takes the floor with several girls on his arms, prancing and lip-synching as "We Are Family" booms from the speakers. I giggle, a kind of hysteria taking hold as we surround them, dancing. . . . On this night, our class is a unit, bound together by shared history. Euphoria rises in me, a feeling of freedom. . . .

Later, I spot Oliver talking to Irene and Joren, who are listening politely with vaguely pained expressions. I inch closer, hiding in the crowd, and strain to listen.

"It's obnoxious," Oliver's saying with an angry laugh.

"What kind of people wouldn't accept me? Okay, so I'm a little rough around the edges, sure, but I'm someone who loves their daughter *with my life*. Like, what brand of discrimination are we dealing with here?"

My blood freezes.

"Rani's parents can't be that bad, Oliver," I hear Irene say defensively. "I don't think you . . ."

I slink away, and I avoid Oliver for the next hour.

As the dance winds down, he signals to me and we move with the crowd toward the lobby, where a school-sanctioned after-prom party has begun. People toss sandbags or mini basketballs in hopes of winning a stuffed animal for their dates, and chaperones snap pictures and chat while eating popcorn from an old-fashioned popcorn maker. The prizes are good: an iPad, Cirque du Soleil tickets, and tees donated by Kumail Bukhari, a classmate who makes screen prints of his pen-and-ink designs.

Oliver and I look down on the festivities from a mezzanine, where a bar is stocked with soft drinks. We spot Henry and Kate playing mini golf, both sets of hands on a club as they take a swing together, laughing. Even from afar, I can sense their chemistry.

"You want a Coke?" Oliver asks, gesturing toward the bar. He searches my eyes wearily, like looking at my face exhausts him. I nod, watching him go.

Maybe I'm to blame for his attitude about my parents. Haven't I been the one lamenting Ma and Baba, and how they'd never accept us being together? Someone below hoots, winning something big.

He saunters back, hands the drink to me, and stares dully

over the railing at the spectacle below. Inhaling the smell of popcorn and ballroom carpet, I try to think of what to say. I trail my fingers along the cold metal railing, suddenly in a different universe from my carefree classmates. Oliver breaks the silence.

"So, are you gonna tell me what's up with you?" He looks at me, eyes flashing. "I spent a ton of money to rent this damn tux, and then you ignore me all night."

Where do I begin? Do I tell him I overheard him trashing my parents and that nothing feels the same now? "I got caught up seeing everyone," I say finally. "Sorry."

His features soften. "Hey," he says, "Saul's having an afterparty. Sans babysitters. Want to . . . ?"

And because I can't imagine any worse torture than this moment, I nod. "Let's go."

CHAPTER THIRTY-FIVE

The last time we were at Saul's, we declared our love to each other for the first time, after the screening of *Sex 4 Ur Soul*. The whole ride over, I debated whether to tell Oliver I want to go back to Kate's as planned, but once we're on Saul's doorstep, he squeezes my hand and smiles with what feels like genuine love.

"What the . . . ? Where is everyone?" Oliver squints into the dining room, strewn with beer cans, jackets, overturned shoes. Unfamiliar music pulsates through the speakers, and the house smells like beer and feet and something sweet—brownies?

"Saul?" Oliver calls.

"Ollie, that you? Back here!" We move through the kitchen, stepping over liquor bottles, a puddle of something suspicious, and half-open trash bags as we make our way onto the back porch. Saul, Fiona, Jared, and a couple others are squished together in a hammock. Two guys in a wicker love seat take turns inhaling from a little glass pipe. On a battered recliner lies a girl I recognize vaguely from Open Mic, faceup, immobile. I study her before deciding she's taking a nap.

"Ollie! Princess Jasmiiiiine!" Fist bumps and special hand-shakes all around. A prescription bottle is on the floor.

"People! How was prom?" asks Saul. The apples of his cheeks are flushed, his hair curled along the nape of his neck like that of a cherub who's arisen from a deep and sweaty nap. "As you can see, none of us made it out."

I stare at the smokers on the wicker sofa. A blue-gray haze swirls around their heads.

"How was it?" Fiona asks. "Was everyone losing their virginities left and right, like in the movies?" She's slurring, peaceful in her undead makeup and a black lace dress. She wiggles her fingers at me.

"Nah. Nothin' like that," Oliver says. "Lots of parents and teachers. More like conferences."

A bag of chips is passed around. A tall guy in a hoodie balances a pan of brownies in one hand, offering them like a host. Shrugging, I pluck one away from the gooey bulk.

"Whoa there, partner," Oliver says, lifting the brownie from my hand. "Those, judging by this scene, are potent."

The reality dawns on me as I stand inhaling the herbal, skunky scent of marijuana wafting about, and my face burns with shame. Still clueless after everything that's happened.

———

When I was a freshman, the Bears had just made the playoffs and the kids were bursting with pent-up energy from hours of watching TV in the Sobtis' white-carpeted basement. To everyone's shock and delight, Nilesh was there—and not the funked-out version, but a toned-down yet still-benevolent version, not unlike the Nilesh we remembered. The adults were in the living room, but he was down in the basement with us like old times, teasing the squabbling kids in his trademark way ("Ey! You two! You know that arguing is a sign that you secretly love each other, right?") and smiling as they tripped over each other trying to tell him stuff.

With the game over and the promise of more football frenzy on the near horizon, the kids began pinging around the basement like pinballs, passionately debating which teams the Bears were likely to beat. They gorged on chips and pop and were generally ornery, while Nilesh and I minded them like kindly grandparents as we sipped at our Cokes and made small talk. Seven-year-old Rahul bounded over to us, and Nilesh busied him by offering his fist—fingers crossed, clustered and bound with his other hand—telling him to locate his middle finger by fingertip sight only. When Rahul touched and pulled out Nilesh's index finger, Nilesh said, "Try again try again try again, child. Remember: two times a charm." This time, Rahul pulled Nilesh's middle finger from its cluster, and Nilesh stood up, raising his middle finger to the group of kids with a look of sheer joy. "Look what my buddy Rahul just found for you guys!" he said, which resulted in a cascade of giggles.

I sat there trying to have some chill, my secret excitement at hanging with Nilesh like old times barely contained. I started babbling, telling him about high school as I knew it so far: new friends, new teachers, running cross-country while balancing homework and studying, figuring out the bus system and all the places in the city it could take you.

"Any dudes you got your eye on?" he asked casually. The

kids had found a basket of Nerf blasters in the furnace room and were tearing into it with grating gusto.

"Ew, no," I said, as though I were above all of that. The truth was, I'd just started at Frances Willard, and picking my way through throngs of giant humans to get to my classes on the college-size campus kept me pretty occupied. Guys were not yet on my radar, and it was clear that I was invisible to them anyway. Girls like me didn't capture the imagination of freshman guys, and I said as much.

"And what the hell does that mean? Listen, Doc. You are a catch," he said, regarding me seriously. "To *some* fool out there." I shoved him and got a whiff of what now seemed to be his signature scent, a grown-up scent I couldn't place then—something simultaneously smoky, skunky, sweet. "But really," he said, squaring his shoulders, "choose carefully. Guys are generally dicks. Have the guts to be yourself, not something else for someone else."

"I don't even know what any of that means," I said. But he was gazing mildly, heavy-lidded, at the kids, who were now engaged in a full-on Nerf blaster battle. "Um. What about you?" I said. "Any girls?"

"Nah, man. They require too much presence."

"Meaning . . . ?"

"You're in a relationship, and you have this . . . I don't know . . . privilege. *Power.* To have an impact on someone, you know? Which means you've got to be a whole, present person first, so that you don't inadvertently screw them up. Nah." He gulped at his Coke, his hair—still streaked with bronze—hanging over half his face. "I'm too incomplete a person for a girlfriend."

Five-year-old Sonu shrieked as a group of boys snuck around the corner and showered him with darts.

"You *seem* like a whole person now, though," I said, glancing at him sideways.

He smiled sadly, swirling the ice cubes in his drink in a way that reminded me of the dads upstairs with their scotch and sodas. "Yeah. But not so, Doc."

"I mean, you're graduating soon, right? What's happening with college?"

"College?" He barked out a laugh. "I mean, it's a miracle that Niles West High School hasn't kicked me out yet. My theory? They're in disbelief that the kid of South Asian immigrants could veer into effed-up territory." I watched him, grinning. The old Nilesh would never drop the actual f-bomb in front of the kids, just like this version. "I may be the only one in history, in fact! Maybe I should include *that* in my college essay."

I continued to sit there smiling, because I was fifteen and because I knew nothing about college or essays or what to say to someone who had fallen into whatever it was he'd fallen into, and because I was still secretly in awe of him as my hero who seemed to have miraculously returned from the dead.

"It's like," he said, gaining momentum, "the school officials anticipate that any day now, I'm going to pop in, shouting, 'Just kidding, y'all! I secretly applied and got accepted early decision to Yale!'" He leaned back and snickered good-naturedly, kids scrambling around him after their darts.

"Okay, so forget Yale," I said. "You've applied *somewhere*, right?"

He regarded me a moment. "Doc." He closed his eyes for a few beats, like he did that day we visited him after the hospital.

"Ey! *Guys!*" Salil was on the floor, curled into a ball and giggling, while three older boys sat on him, using him like a perch as their Nerf blasters spewed darts. "No. Sitting. On. Little. Men!" We exchanged a look and he muttered, "I mean, Jesus."

"They're turning into gremlins before our very eyes. And we didn't even get them wet."

Nilesh rose. "All right, gremlins!" he bellowed. "Outside, touch football, ASAP! Shoes! Coats! Meet on the field in approximately two point five minutes. Hut!"

The next two hours, I watched Nilesh lead the group in touch football in the frozen tundra yard, Salil at his side. He was funny. He was patient. He was as worship-worthy as ever. At the end of the night, after a dinner of spicy sambar and masala dosa with the parents, he leaned in—enveloping me in that scent of his that I now fully understand—and said: "Doc. When I'm gone, make Salil your right-hand little man, okay?"

Without a moment's pause, I said, "Of course." Salil would need someone in his corner once Nilesh was gone to college.

Five months after the Sobtis' playoffs party and just before his graduation, Nilesh was found by his mother, hanging by his neck in the shower.

Two times a charm . . .

It dawned on me with languid precision: I was the one who'd missed all the signs. I was the one beating a dead horse about college in that white basement. Nilesh had had no intention of college in the near future. He had had no intention of having a future at all.

And I—because I'd do anything for him—was too stupid to notice anything out of the ordinary. Not even the most obvious cry for help.

CHAPTER THIRTY-SIX

"So this is what happens when I'm not around."

We're in Saul's music room. Faint hoots and laughter drift through the open window. I shut it.

"Rani. Come here. It's not like that."

"No, I'm cool with it. I mean, why *not* be part of it? They sure *looked* like they were having fun. Zoned out, sweaty, immobile . . . awesome, all of it." I stand by the window, arms crossed tightly across my chest, shivering.

"Rani. I'm not 'part of it.'" He tugs at his ear. "They're just . . . friends of mine, some of them. I didn't realize they'd be fucked up like that or I wouldn't have brought you here."

"I guess I'm in your way, huh?"

"Rani, STOP. You know that I respect you for—"

"Respect! Yeah. That was super respectful at prom, putting down my parents to Irene, and insisting I should have worn a sari."

"Okay, now we're onto different topics. Sweetie . . ."

"So answer my first question. Is this what you do when you need to let off a little steam and I'm otherwise occupied?"

"No, I . . ."

"Or is it after we're together, once I leave for home? You head here to Saul's to get blazed?"

"Rani. You're overreacting. I'm not even high."

"You're not high now, or you don't get high—which is it?" He's silent. "Look, I don't even care. I mean, do what you wanna do. I don't own you. I don't *want* to own you."

"Well, what is it, then? Why is this such a big deal? It's not like I was even fucked up tonight."

How can I explain to him that drugs caused me to lose the closest thing I ever had to a brother? How can I tell him that just being around them makes me feel stupid *and* enraged? But all I hear myself say is: "Were you high that night on the breakwater?"

"Rani." He tries to take my hands, but I shove them into my coat pockets and stare steadily into his eyes. "Okay." He sighs deeply. "Yes. It was stupid and I'm sorry."

"What drug?"

"It was . . . an edible. It was more potent than I—"

"So . . . you, someone who can't swim, took me out along the breakwater . . . while high?"

"Rani, I said I'm sorry. It won't happen again."

"You drove me home that night . . . while high?"

"Rani, I suck, what can I say? The drugs occasionally help—"

I begin pacing the room. "I mean, recreation is one thing, but you're . . . using it as a regular escape, it feels like. And making garbage decisions. And I don't know if you care, but that shit can stunt your brain development at our age, and . . . I . . ." I hear what I sound like, but I go on. "What other drugs do you use?"

He hesitates.

"You know what?" I say, waving my hand. "I don't even wanna know."

Oliver stands and wraps his arms around me. I inhale his peppery scent, and my body relaxes, weakens. Despite everything, he's like a dopamine hit. *My* drug of choice . . .

"Rani. Listen." He pulls away, levels his gaze at me. "I am not what you think. I'm not some druggie. Come here."

I ignore him, the floorboards creaking beneath my flats.

He grabs my hand, pulls me to the couch. He sits, smiling up at me, that warm, disarming smile. I recross my arms over my chest, but he grabs my hips and brings me closer.

"I love you," he says, his voice hoarse. His hands slip beneath the hem of my dress, trailing the bare skin of my calves, thighs. "I would never want to hurt you," he murmurs. "Or do anything that would make you upset. I'm sorry for bringing you here."

"That's not really the point. . . ."

"I just want more of you."

"Oliver . . ."

"I want you. Every little bit of you. I want to be part of every dimension of your life, and I know that's kind of batshit. But I can't help it." His hands travel up my hips, caress the small of my back beneath my dress, his touch awakening every nerve of my stupid, traitorous body, fiercely, irrevocably. "You're a part of my art, you're . . . everywhere. Do you know what I mean?"

I gaze down at him: his loosened tie, his untucked shirt, the shiny shock of hair hanging in his wounded eyes. The essence of us together gathers energy like a twister, and I feel myself softening. Maybe I've driven him to this point by not meeting his needs. Maybe the best way to support someone is to trust him, accept him, forgive him, like the books say. . . .

"Do you?" he asks again.

Yes. I nod. *Yes.* . . .

He pulls me down.

CHAPTER THIRTY-SEVEN

"So where did you two disappear to Saturday night?" Henry asks. It's lunchtime, the Monday after prom—yearbook day, and the cliques have temporarily disbanded as people mingle in the East Courtyard, exchanging signatures.

It's also the day of Oliver's big opening at the Art Café, a show I somehow know nothing about, other than the fact that he's been working tirelessly toward it.

"Well." I clear my throat. "We went to Saul's. Which . . . was interesting."

"*Real* interesting," says Oliver through a mouthful of chips. He's sketching me in his notebook, my expression on the page so dour it's no doubt accurate.

I sit up straight. "It seemed like *you* guys were having fun, though."

"It was great," Henry says. "*This* girl whupped me at my own game."

Kate laughs. "I did not whup you, please. I suck at golf."

"What'd you guys do?" asks Oliver, stuffing four more chips into his mouth while shading my lips.

"Well . . ." Kate flashes an unreadable grin at Henry. "After the after-prom thing . . ."

"Where Kate not only became a golf whiz but also won me a bear . . ."

"We drove back to Evanston, and Henry showed me the Merrick Rose Garden. Have you guys been?"

We shake our heads dumbly, and Kate describes a hidden patch of heaven just south of downtown Evanston where hundreds of roses bloom. "I mean, I've lived here my whole life, and I'd never even heard of the place," she says.

"Google, the best-kept secret," says Henry with a grin.

"Right. Why would *I* ever google my hometown? You need New Guy to do that." Kate shrugs happily.

"So then we walked to the beach," Henry continues.

"And there was this crazy beautiful moon, right over the water. . . ."

"Yeah, huge and yellow. . . ."

"And the air was warm, you guys," Kate says. "Despite being that close to the water. So we just played Frisbee there and hung out until the cops made us leave."

They seem so comfortable. Then again, it's Henry—he brings out the chill in everyone. I'm examining subtleties to determine if they might have held hands or even kissed: body language, eye signals . . .

"Hey. You two would be good together," says Oliver. "Rani, get a shot of them."

So much for subtle. Damn Oliver. I fumble for my camera and snap a photo of them as they pose, arms crossed, backs to each other. They might have kissed, for chrissakes. Why didn't

Kate call me yesterday to give me the play-by-play? And why am I feeling . . . *weird* about this prospect?

Henry gets up to leave, saying he needs to check in with his counselor before class. He and Kate fist-bump—is it just me or was that a mildly intimate fist bump—before she offers to give him a ride home after school.

"So, wait," says Kate, seemingly unfettered by these new developments as she swipes a wavy lock from her eye. "What was happening at Saul's? I didn't even see him at prom."

"No." I wrap my half-nibbled sandwich into a cocoon of cellophane so tight it's now unidentifiable. "You wouldn't have seen him, because he spent the night having a stoner party."

"Rani. So dramatic," Oliver says. "He just had a few people over." His pencil is filling in the waves of my hair. "Though some *were* kinda fucked up."

"By 'some,' Oliver means everyone but me and him. Or maybe just me, who knows?" I flash a fake smile at Kate. "It was loads of fun!"

"Hey," says Oliver, looking up at me. "*We* had fun together."

"Sure. In a locked room, alone. But that's not exactly 'attending a party.' "

"Those dudes had nothing compared to *our* party."

I shove Oliver, suddenly embarrassed. "The point is, I almost slipped in vomit and the whole thing was infuriating."

"Okay, who walks into a kitchen for a glass of water and steps directly into the *one* spot where there's vomit?" he says. "I mean really, Rani. That's on you."

"Maybe you should find some nondruggie friends so we don't . . ."

"Oh, right, because you and your friends are so perfect. Because you're so close and you tell each other everything."

"Dude . . . Rani and I actually *do* tell each other everything," Kate says, coming to my defense.

"It's true," I say.

"Oh yeah?" Oliver glances up at me and laughs. "So you're telling me Kate knows what you really think about her torrid past with random guys?"

I freeze.

Kate turns to me, a sudden hurt in her eyes. "What?"

"Kate. No. The truth is . . ." I gaze out across the green at my classmates signing yearbooks, collecting my thoughts on how to have this conversation. Damn Oliver! I square my shoulders. "I once told Oliver that I thought you deserved someone special after all the guys who—didn't work out," I say carefully. "I mean, you barely knew most of them."

The bell rings, signaling the end of lunch, and people start streaming back inside. We don't move.

"So . . . you think I'm some kind of . . . slut?" Kate's eyes have gone wide.

"Oh my God, no! Never. I mean, I kind of understand why you were with those guys. And I've respected you for not—you know. But you deserve someone great, and I'm . . ."

"Rani, I chose to be with different guys because that's what felt right at the time. It's my choice and my freedom, which is everything to me."

"And I respect that. I just don't always . . ." I search for the right words.

She stares at me. "Look, it's simple. I don't want to pine after some guy—pining is so freaking disempowering! Look at Bonnie, how far it got her! Why would I want to repeat that pattern?"

"But . . . you're allowing your dad's issues to set up a construct for *your* life. Isn't that giving *him* . . . too much power?"

"Avoiding my mother's choices is not giving him power, Rani. I mean, I *could* have just avoided boys altogether. . . ."

"That's also kind of extreme. . . ."

"But having no dating experience and being clueless in college doesn't sound great, either. Plus, it's fun being someone's dream girl without trapping myself. I don't want to build my life around someone only to discover that he's a bag of shit."

"But—isn't it fatalistic to assume he's . . . a bag of shit?"

"Is it, though? Damn. I didn't realize you of all people would judge me on this."

"I'm not judging you, Kate. I just don't *totally* understand the point of skipping through guys. It's like you don't even give them the chance to be great, or be shit, or reveal who they really are. . . ."

"Maybe I don't want to be let down. Maybe Bonnie and Ron's story is everyone's story. Any guy seems decent at first but winds up not caring. Not showing up. Being a stupid piece of shit. I don't want to play into this phenomenon, Rani. *I* control things. Who I date. How long I date them. What I do with them. I thought you'd understand that—you're my best friend!"

"I do understand . . . but, so these guys to you were just—"

"Distractions? Maybe." She's making strange little shakes with her head. "Think what you will about me, Rani, but I'd

264

rather be a slut who makes her own choices than be under someone's . . . spell."

I wonder if she means me and Oliver—Oliver, who is still sketching me like everything's cool. My hands are trembling. Kate and I have never before had a single argument. "Okay, for the record, I never thought you were a slut," I say. "I've just really wanted you to find someone amazing, like Henry—"

"Not that it's any of your business, but . . ." Her eyes are hard as she gazes across the almost empty courtyard. "I'm not planning on *being with* Henry. I'm training for regionals."

My stomach drops. "Oh. Okay, sure. Regionals. But I mean, you guys seem—"

She looks at me evenly. "Sorry to disappoint you, Rani. But Henry's not what I need right now."

And out of nowhere, I'm seized by a blinding, destructive rage. "What precisely is it about him that you don't need?" I splutter. "Because he's a kind, funny, real guy who knows and accepts you and who's actually your friend?"

"Look, I know he means something to you—that he's Salil's neighbor and all. But I've got to do what feels right."

"But—you both seemed . . . like there's something there. He's been interested in you since forever! I knew I should never have . . ."

"Should never have what? Introduced perfect Henry to your fuckup of a friend? Tarnished his world with me?" An ambulance comes wailing up Dodge. "Yeah, you shouldn't have."

"Kate. Here's a chance to be open to a healthy relationship with someone who gets you. Someone for whom you're not just some empty fantasy."

"A 'healthy relationship'? You mean like you and Oliver?" She lets out a sharp bark of disbelief. "Whatever. I don't even recognize you anymore."

I stare at her, stunned into silence.

"And thanks for ditching me at prom. Not to mention all the other times you basically used me to be with Oliver. And, Oliver, thank you. For helping me see clearly." I watch her stride toward the doors, my heart collapsing in on itself, shattering into ten thousand shards.

"Dude," says Oliver, glancing at Kate's retreating form, "I think that was my bad."

I barely even hear him. I've never been on the receiving end of Kate's fury. All I can think is a single, gut-wrenching thought:

What if those are the last words I'll ever hear her say?

CHAPTER THIRTY-EIGHT

That evening, still blinking back tears over the nightmare with Kate, I drive my parents' car down Chicago Avenue toward Oliver's show. I told my family that a girlfriend of mine was having a gallery show nearby and I was running late for it. I left in a rush, leaving no time for the usual insistence on them driving me. I try not to focus on the fact that this time, Kate won't be covering for me.

What piece is Oliver even exhibiting tonight? He's mentioned that he was installing something, but I know nothing else. Usually he tells me about his paintings, their mood or color palette, or some new technique he's trying out. But this one's a mystery.

The fact is, it's hard to be excited for him. I'm destroyed by what he instigated between me and Kate. What on earth was he thinking, blurting out something I told him in confidence months ago that I barely remember saying? I fume, jabbing at the radio.

And then—my eyes settle on the clock: 7:04.

I find parking, scramble out of the car, and half jog toward the Art Café, slowing as I spot a large crowd gathered out-doors, across the street from the café, beneath the L viaduct. When I reach the café, I see a sign in the window:

OLIVER JENSEN'S NEWEST PIECE
WILL BE UNVEILED AT 7 P.M. BENEATH THE VIADUCT.
RECEPTION INSIDE TO FOLLOW.

Groups of artsy people I recognize from school are mov-ing toward the viaduct. I tug self-consciously on the basic skirt I bought at Plasma—is it just me, or are people's eyes on me? As I approach the crowd, it hits me: his work must be a mural. Of course—his mentor is Valentia, the artist who created the amazing *We Are All America* mural at Noyes. I feel a pulse of pride: Oliver was given the honor of making an Evanston art mural? I've always loved the murals around town, intrigued by how social commentary can be tucked into soaring, shocking public art. . . .

As I inch into the crowd, a path clears—as though people are making way for me. I try to shake off the feeling that people I don't know seem to be watching me, studying me. I look up at the giant brick wall just beneath the tracks, black on white with pops of color. . . . I stop.

Streets of Shame
Oliver Jensen

And suddenly, everything clicks.
The sidelong glances, the quiet murmurs. Oliver's evasive-ness about this night . . .

I stare up at the giant mural of a girl whose face is split down the middle by a prismatic leading line. Her left side features a smoky eye glaring like a challenge, body in black, fishnets, and a combat boot. Her opposite side is traditional Indian: a lashy eye lowered, half a blazing red bindi between heavy eyebrows, a nose ring attached to a wedding crown hooked to the earlobe, body wrapped slipshod in a scarlet sari—a giant replica of the one I wore that foggy night in the car—light and shadow carving out her naked shoulder, clavicle, and cleavage visible beneath the gossamer fabric. . . .

I take in a sharp breath.

Along the length of both her overly hairy arms are words. Words in red—painstaking, delicate-cut words. Words running into each other, transposed, words I'd said to Oliver in private, now in blood-red print, my truths and mistruths cast out for the world to consume:

MY PARENTS HONESTLY WOULDN'T UNDERSTAND
I JUST REALLY NEEDED TO SEE YOU
MY FAMILY'S SUPER TRADITIONAL
YOU KNOW I LOVE YOU
I COULDN'T LET YOU IN
MY MOM INFORMED ME THAT WE'RE GOING TO INDIA
I TAKE PRIDE IN MY INSECURITIES

The punk side of her head is shaved just above the ear, the rest an edgy shag. The Indian side is all loose waves of hair fanning out and winding luxuriantly around the too-high cheekbone and too-long nose in a dark face. Her wrists are shackled, and animal demons (or are they meant to be gods?)—monkeys, goats, and elephants with multiple arms—gaze up at her, beseeching. At her feet lies a bloody heart, the valves, chambers, and muscle walls so lifelike that I wonder idly if Oliver borrowed my anatomy book to get them right.

A pale arm, covered delicately in tree-branch tattoos, reaches from the edge of the giant frame, fingertips dripping—the hand has dropped the bloody heart at her feet, and beside it lies a camera, smashed into shards. The backdrop is split into shattered sections like a cracked windshield. Over her right shoulder is a dusty, quaint scene of India, like the kind on the cover of a *Visit India!* DVD series: a quiet, tree-lined dirt road, with a single figure riding his bicycle rickshaw—a burnt umber silhouette against the backdrop of a peach sunset. Over her other shoulder is a scene from a bedroom—the silhouette of a couple wrapped in a passionate embrace, the slatted window in the corner by the bed framing a glowing moon, a dark figure lurking outside the door. . . . I look back to the girl's hooded eyes, the furrowed brow, the lips, my lips . . .

Light-headed, I stumble, pitching into a hulking body. "Whoa, hey." Dante, from Open Mic. "Oh," he says, his face registering recognition, though I've never formally met him. "You—you okay?" I can't seem to look away from the mural, like it's a distorted mirror. . . .

Is this how I'm seen? The face is mine, but not mine—it's stylized, a mermaid's. I stare at the body wrapped in the sari. The shapes of her breasts are mine at their largest, full beneath the fabric. And then I see it: the one word etched artfully in red atop the left breast . . .

Blood roars in my ears. I glance around for an easy escape. I'll have to push through crowds of people back the way I came.

But then Oliver appears. He stands behind the owner of the café as she taps on a mic and makes a few insipid jokes to warm up the crowd. I absorb him: white button-down shirt and dark jeans, wet hair combed away from his clean-shaven face, glancing at the owner, humble, nervous. . . . *It is my pleasure to introduce you to an amazing new talent . . . Oliver Jensen!*

Oliver steps up to the mic. He speaks quietly. Bodies push in as a wave of nausea hits me. . . . I wonder if I'm about to pass out. I try to take deep breaths to slow my pulse. His voice comes through an echoey cave. . . . I understand nothing. The crowd erupts into laughter, then rapturous applause. I start backing away. Oliver's on a roll, and amid the ripples of appreciative titters, I slip into the crowd, moving toward the street. . . . Some may notice my exit, but probably no one does.

Shaking, I stumble to a tree just out of sight of the crowd and rest my forehead against its smooth, bluish bark. Unzipping my jacket, I choke back nausea, sweating bullets and gulping deep breaths of Evanston spring air: wet earth, dirty rain, gasoline. All around me, people are driving and walking and laughing as if it's a regular Monday night. I hear the crowd swell again with applause. I slump against the tree and stare into the street like a zombie, minutes slipping by.

"Rani?"

———

He stands before me, and it's like I'm seeing him for the very first time: the only boy I ever loved. A wretched fist grips my heart, squeezes. I practically dry heave.

"Rani. Are you okay?"

I blink. He looks so fresh-faced and clean. Riding high on all that attention from adoring fans.

I step back.

"Rani? Look, I know you're upset."

"I'm not upset." I cross my arms over my chest. "I'm great."

"I know the mural is a lot of . . . exposure," he says quietly.

I stare at him. He looks different. Even his hands are unfamiliar; I thought I'd recognize those hands anywhere, for the rest of my life.

"And I know that's hard," he goes on. "But I had this great opportunity to push myself out of my zone, and . . . it's just what came out. It's what's been on my mind."

"So"—I clear my throat, jolted alive—"what's been on your mind is how to best humiliate and ruin me?"

"Come on, Rani."

"There's a risqué, semiracist image of me and my life on an outdoor mural right now. On display for the world. And etched there are my words to you—words I spoke in private."

"Semi-racist," he mutters, shaking his head. "Okay. May I point out the irony here?" He shoves his hands into his pockets, eyes lasering beneath raised eyebrows.

The temperature seems to have dropped twenty degrees. I shiver in my pleather jacket. "No."

Oliver leans in. "I create a piece—which, by the way, people seem to really be digging—highlighting . . . you. You and your amazingness. I'm in it, too, in case you didn't notice, only my ugly ass has ripped out my pathetic heart and dropped it at your feet. And now you're pissed? I mean, what the hell, Rani? Don't you see what this mural says about us? About everything?"

"It says you don't care enough to tell me the truth. And that you'll use my words, my thoughts, *my life* to forward some artistic agenda."

"It means *I love you*. That I gave you my heart."

"It means you see me and my culture as some kind of exotic fantasy to exploit."

"The piece," he says slowly, taking another step toward me, "shows how you're bound to your *culture* more than you are to *me*. The piece shows how much that sucks for me, because I need you so much it hurts."

The L rumbles by, bursting through the leafy brush on the elevated track above our heads. It stops, letting off a few passengers, and trundles on, out of sight, like a dream.

"Rani, did you hear anything I just said?"

I close my eyes, struggling against the feelings he brings out in me, resisting the current that pulls me back to him every time. His words are like sugar: addictive, toxic, empty.

"Rani?"

"If you loved me, you wouldn't have publicized *this* piece, of all things. You'd confide in me openly about your family, your problems, instead of using me as some kind of escape. And you wouldn't have risked both our lives while using drugs on the sly."

"The drug thing is under control, Rani."

I stare into the street. "We're just . . . so different. It's like we're from different worlds, and it's impossible to weave them together—"

He interrupts: "Oh, so you want someone from within *your* world, huh? How fucking conventional."

"That's not what I mean. And some conventions and traditions *are* a part of my culture, and I'm tired of you making me feel ashamed about that."

"So you'll just continue to fulfill your parents' expectations and conventions, forevermore, is that it? Despite our love?"

"If you loved me, you'd trust me when I say my parents are not ready to know about you and me. You'd accept and appreciate what I *can* give you. If you loved me, you'd share your real world with me, so that when it *was* time to bring you to my family, I'd know who you were. I'd know who I was fighting for."

I can feel him studying my face, but I avoid his eyes, knowing their power.

"That," he says, "is bullshit. You never intended to bring me into your family." He kicks at the tree's knobby roots.

"I mean, no. Not now. My parents forbid me to date in high school. What am I—"

"For fuck's sake—you're almost nineteen! You're a *grown-ass woman*, and you're still living by their rules. Don't you see? Keeping up this secretive shit has gotten ridiculous, Rani. You've taken it way too far."

"I know you can't understand it, and I'm sorry."

He leans in close. "I understand everything. I understand that our love is worth more. You and me and your culture and my crazy life fused together is this . . . *force*. Something that

274

transcends us and our stupid families. I thought this piece, when I first started it, would reveal this kind of . . . truth."

"So . . ." I swallow. "What *did* it reveal?"

He gazes into the distance, unseeing. "It's like we're just . . . cursed. Like . . . I can't get close enough to you, no matter how hard I try. And you're always going to cave to your parents."

"My dad arrived from India with nothing," I say quietly, "and had to make it with no reserves, and in the face of a lot of racist garbage, Oliver. In their minds, people don't survive by dating in high school and making art and doing drugs. They survive by sticking together and accruing a ton of education and working hard against the odds, and they want that for me. There's a lot about our American culture that terrifies them. I just . . . I wanted to protect you from that viewpoint, and to protect them from the fact that I don't totally subscribe to their ways."

"Why is everything always about protection? It's so cowering, so pathetic, Rani."

I blink. "Have you ever stopped to think that maybe . . . maybe I also need to protect my parents from you?"

The air between us stills. "What the hell are you talking about?"

"How your microaggressions might make me not trust you?"

"Microaggressions? What microaggressions?" He barks a laugh in disbelief, and my gut curdles at the cruelty of it.

I break into a sweat. "Calling me Princess Jasmine . . . dressing me in an Indian bridal sari . . . mocking my father's accent . . ." I keep my voice low, quiet, ashamed to say the words out loud.

"Oh, come on, Rani. First of all, I thought you liked being called Princess Jasmine—it's cute! And you in that sari that night, I mean, we *both* thought it was hot. And you know what? I never mocked your dad. I don't even know your freaking dad!"

Kate once forwarded me an article from the *New York Times* that claimed that calling out microaggressions is risky: You risk appearing petty, hypersensitive, unstable. You risk your credibility. You risk having to watch the offender— in this case, the one I love—justify. Backpedal. Flat-out lie. And yet . . .

I take a deep breath. "I can't introduce you to my family until you make an honest effort to listen. Hear me. *Read me.* Try to understand my views and perspective." I work to keep my tone steady as my throat thickens. "If you can't put my needs first, and instead demand that I serve as some silent, exotic, erotic muse, how can you ever handle the reality of my family?"

I sense once again I'm betraying my parents, portraying them as difficult. My phone dings in my pocket. I silence it.

"Unbelievable, everything you just said." He laughs again. "The most screwy thing of all?" he says, taking a step closer, his palm flat and stiff, like he might karate-chop me. "You're actually supporting your parents' narrow way of thinking by pretending I don't exist."

"You still don't understand: it's our freedom, Oliver. Their punishment, their disappointment in me would—"

"Oh my God, Rani. Their 'disappointment.' Did you ever stop to think that maybe lying and sneaking around and pretending to be someone you're not would actually be more disappointing than just telling them you're in a relationship?"

"Of course—it's horrible and I hate doing it. But that doesn't give you the right to force the issue into public like this."

"Do they expect you to be celibate all through college, up until you're married?"

"Probably, yes. Look, I don't really know. It's not something we've ever . . . discussed."

He peers at me incredulously.

"I'm sick of you acting like they're crazy. Look—they've made it clear that dating's off-limits. Indefinitely. I mean, they've said stuff about me eventually finding someone I'd have a lot in common with, someone from a good family . . ."

"Good family? What the hell does that mean?"

"How am I supposed to know?" He raises an eyebrow at me as if to say, *Nice try. Of course you know.* "Look, it doesn't help that you and your family don't share my culture, and that you've had your unfair share of struggles. But more than that . . . they wouldn't accept me being with *anyone* right now. Like it's a risk to my education and . . . future. They're not ready to come around on this. Why can't you trust me?"

People begin streaming toward the café for the reception.

"Because it's bullshit, Rani! Tell me this. How is my creating a painting of our love tied up in a cultural conflict worse than your parents' intolerance?"

"My *parents*' 'intolerance'?" I'm shaking, emotions searing through me. "Oliver, they regularly deal with racism, like when they're suspiciously asked their thoughts on some terrible news involving Indians, like crimes of violent Hindu nationalists—as though they are somehow personally involved with those atrocities and need to prove that they're not 'those kinds of people.' They are ignored and excluded from

277

social events, told to 'go back to where they came from,' and mocked for their accents or worse, like immigrants everywhere." Images flit into my mind: the man screaming at us outside the Spirit of Life retreat, the mean girls of my tween years, the racist middle school boys, the countless silent and not-so-silent attacks by strangers, friends. . . . "We deal with bigotry and suspicion on the regular, being made to feel 'other' and 'less than' at best, like terrorists and threats at worst. So just stop about my parents' 'intolerance.'"

His eyes burn with contempt, scanning my face.

"Okay. Sure, I get it," he says finally. "People are shitty and racist and your parents have created a protected life so you all don't have to face the ugly outside world. I totally get it."

I watch him warily.

"But I still think you need to stand up for what you want," he says.

A couple exits the café, arm in arm, the girl's hundred tiny braids hanging like sparkling onyx down her back. Our eyes meet, and I realize the guy on the left is Tonio. He holds my gaze and, with a fist to his heart, mouths, *I'm sorry.* I nod and he lopes away with his girl, that uncanny "Romeo and Juliet" song tinkling from the café's doorway.

"Jaz." I flinch at the nickname as Oliver leans down, gazing into my face. "*Do* you know what you want?"

I regard him, unblinking. "How could you not have told me about the mural?"

"I don't usually talk about my work."

"That's not true. And this piece involves me. And you. This piece is personal, and I told you from the beginning that our personal stuff has to stay under wraps. You agreed to that."

He steps so close, I can smell his rain-and-pepper scent. I swallow a sob. "That was before I went batshit crazy for you," he says, enunciating every word. "Before you became the one real thing. Before you shut me out in so many ways."

We stare at each other, jostled by more bodies leaving the café.

"What if my family sees it?" I whisper.

"What if they do? It could open doors, avenues, conversations! Isn't that the point of art?"

I shut my eyes—I'm suddenly exhausted. "You respect none of my boundaries."

"If I lived by boundaries, I'd never discover my truth." He scans my face, and whatever he sees there softens his features. "Hey," he says, touching my hair, "I love you."

"Is love supposed to hurt like this?"

He looks at me evenly. "Love and pain are the same thing."

And as he's moving toward the café, muttering that he's got to get back to his event, I hear myself utter the words I wasn't sure I'd ever have the courage to say.

"It's over."

His hand is on the door now. He stares at me, scoffs in disbelief. "Rani. We'll talk about this later, okay? I need to get inside for my reception. . . ." And with that, he steps inside the café, the door banging shut behind him.

I stare into space, and the tears finally burst forth, rivulets of rage and grief making cold tracks down the length of my face. With the sudden, violent recognition of all the ways I was willingly deceived it dawns on me:

I do know what I want. And it isn't this.

CHAPTER THIRTY-NINE

I'm careening toward my car when my phone buzzes. I pull it out, glance at the screen, and stop.

Today 7:10
BABA: Rani, where are you? We must speak to you. Come home.

Today 7:15
KATE: Emergency!!
Ur fam insisting on seeing you NOW.

Today 7:18
KATE: They want me to drop them by the café??

Today 7:23
KATE: Where the hell are you???

Today 7:25
KATE: ??

And then another texts pops up:

BABA: We are at Art Café. Are you here?

I whirl around to see my father, mother, and grandmother standing halfway up the block, Oliver's mural as backdrop.

For a split second, I consider fleeing.

They're strangely still, like three wax statues.

A new dread grips me: they must have seen the mural. Oh God . . .

I move toward them.

"Hi?" I say, approaching. Their faces look strange—my mother is . . .

"It's Aajoba," says Baba. He steps closer to me. "He's . . . Rani, he passed away."

I stare into his eyes and he nods. My mother touches my arm.

"What?" I say, half laughing, jerking away from her hand. "What? No."

"It is okay, betiya," my father says in his gentle way. "It is a shock. To all of us. . . ."

"He should have waited." My mother wipes tears from her face with both hands. "We were going to visit so soon!" Her face is stricken, as though she's aged twenty years since I left the house.

My grandmother hangs behind. Her face is ashen, her lips colorless, moving silently.

I wrap my arms around her, inhaling her coconut scent. She is impossibly tiny.

"He was sick, betiya." Hoarse words rumble deep within her chest against mine. "And yet you were all he kept asking about." She looks at me, beseeching.

I swallow a deep sob. My grandparents, a bottomless source of warmth with their friendly ribbing and mock arguments, the way my grandfather's eyes lit up when I walked into a room. His love for me was so pure that I've been unprepared; I've had no reason to ever question love.

"He wanted those small lemon cakes only," she murmurs. "He said, 'Just bring me Chotu and the lemon cakes, that's it, baas. Nothing more do I need.'"

Chotu. My heart implodes at hearing Aajoba's pet name for me—the name I've more or less forgotten. It means "little one."

"Lemon cakes?" I say stupidly.

"Madeleines, madeleines," Ma cries. "Why he likes those, God knows. He's not to eat such things as a diabetic!"

We move toward the car. "Rani." Baba turns to me, gesturing behind us, and in his heavy accent says, "Why is there a strange outdoor painting of you beneath the bridge?"

I glance at Ma, whose eyes skitter to the mural. She wipes at her eternal tears.

My mother's worst nightmare has just come true.

CHAPTER FORTY

Forty-eight hours later, I wake up in a strange room. I squint through a sheer white tent of mosquito netting, the air smelling of soil and soft, rotting fruit. And like a dirty river, it all comes rushing over me: the mural and the fight and breakup with Oliver, Aajoba's death and the slow, sick realization that my callousness and loss of awareness were to blame . . . I am in Pune, India, in the room I share with my cousin Shalini . . . here now for the mourning period. Though I know that Hindu funerals and cremations happen at the first dawn or dusk immediately after death, I'm upset that we missed Aajoba's funeral. My heart's swollen with sorrow at the idea that I will never see his face again.

On top of everything, I told Baba I had no idea about the painting, that it was a shock to me. Not a lie, but . . .

Aajoba, I learned, had a fatal stroke. By the time the paramedics came, he was dead. I'm still half in denial that my aajoba is gone.

We took the first flight out to Mumbai so that we could at least be here for the days of mourning at home with the family. I got a text from Oliver just before we left, asking to meet, but when I told him what had happened and that we were flying to India immediately, all he said was *Oh no. Sorry to hear that. No time to meet then?* I texted back: *No.* And then radio silence. I considered texting Kate but couldn't lean on her after our unresolved fight. I even thought of texting Oliver out of desperate need, but stopped: If I hadn't been so obsessed with Oliver, I would have set up Zoom when my mother asked. We would have seen Aajoba, and he would have seen us. He would have cheered up, been reminded that we're here, still with him . . . that we're worth hanging around for.

If it weren't for my selfishness, he'd still be alive.

———

"Chotu?"

I blink stupidly in the piercing morning light—did I drift back to sleep? My cousin Shalini peers at me through the white netting, her perfectly threaded eyebrows raised in concern. "Good. You're alive. Let's go to the market to get stuff for the ceremonies. We must get you out of that bed or you'll never adjust to India time. Challo, let's go."

Shalini is my only girl cousin, and I adored her growing up. The summers we'd visit India, she and her two brothers, Tejas and Vineet, and their parents, Lalita Mami and Ramesh Mama, would abandon their bungalow to come stay at my grandparents' house. We'd play gin rummy on the rooftop terrace, or she'd dress me up in various salwar kameez and saris, snapping glamour shots with an antique Canon. As Tejas and Vineet organized carrom tournaments with kids in the neighborhood, she taught me how to play the game in the privacy of the kitchen so I'd be confident when it was my turn. It was she who showed me how to apply mascara, how to shave my legs, and how to create intricate designs of the grassy-scented mehndi along my palms. She was my protective big sister and, along with Aajoba, the basis of my best memories of India.

Now, at twenty-two, Shalini was finally transferred from Mumbai to her IT company's headquarters in Pune, only after Aajoba's death. She just moved in with her parents and Aaji in my grandparents' house. Her older brothers—Tejas in Indore, and Vineet in Bangalore—are both married now with families of their own.

When Shalini met us at the airport last night, I almost didn't recognize her. Tall and elegant, she wore jeggings under an embroidered tunic and layers of jangly jewelry. She did a quick and reverent namaskar to Aaji before hugging the rest of us, briefly holding each of our faces in her palm; her eyes, like ours, were rimmed red.

I'd been bracing myself for the chaos of Mumbai, but Shalini took charge. With finesse, she argued with the customs officer who hassled us about a suitcase, sweet-talked two officials so we could bypass a long line, and got us a cab that got us to the station in time for the Pune-bound train. Shalini followed the cab, expertly weaving her tangerine scooter through traffic with her dupatta and long hair blowing behind her. . . . All these years later, she's still my idol.

Shalini dresses me in a white salwar kameez—the color of purity worn during mourning. After a muttered debate with herself over whether she should or should not have someone named Ronak pick us up, we take a motorized rickshaw into the central business district. Bleary-eyed from jet lag and bouts of sobbing, I gaze out at the roadside shops selling everything imaginable: bindis and bangles, mangoes and sapodillas, plastic toys, crispy veggie pakoras and grilled corn, silver-plated religious paraphernalia and pirated DVDs. . . . Huge billboards showcasing the latest Bollywood films loom in the background. There is so much color, movement. . . . Could a camera lens capture even a fraction of it?

We stop at a jewelry shop, where Shalini pulls out a sketch pad. She flips through dozens of detailed drawings of necklaces and rings and bracelets before smoothing down a sketch of a ring. Speaking in Marathi, she tells the jeweler that she's designing it for Aaji for after the mourning period. The jeweler studies the drawing, tracing a finger over certain sections (the design's so exquisite, I'm still catching up to the fact that Shalini drew it). Once they agree on the specifics, we weave through the endless bazaar. Trailing Shalini while she collects items for Aajoba's upcoming ceremonies, I'm filled with an overwhelming, gaping grief. I watch listlessly as she buys dried coconuts, flowers, sesame seeds, garlands of marigolds, incense, and betel nuts. I wonder idly whether my parents have gotten me officially waived from the last weeks of school and graduation (knowing gut deep they somehow remembered to). I think about the AP exams I took early this month and how it feels like a lifetime ago. . . . Finally, we take a break at a rooftop café.

"So when were you going to tell me that you're a legit designer now?" I sip my icy Limca from a shapely glass bottle and rub my eyes. A group of neighborhood boys are playing cricket in the dusty park across the street.

"I'm a boring IT person," Shalini says, smiling sadly. I feel a sudden pulse of guilt: Aajoba's death is hitting her hard—probably harder. Her too-late job transfer meant she didn't see Aajoba in his final days, wasn't here to help as planned. "I'm no designer," she finishes.

"But your sketches are amazing," I murmur. I flip through the notebook between us. "How do you come up with the designs? Or, as the artists say: 'What's your process?' "

She smiles and hands me a silver ring from her finger. "Lots of ideas are inspired by pieces our ancestors wore—Aaji still owns some of them. Other designs come from the garden, or art, something I see at a wedding, even Aaji's knitting—I'll see a lovely stitch pattern on something she's made, and off I go to sketch." She shrugs. "It's just a hobby."

"Beautiful, Shal," I say, slipping the delicate garnet ring onto my middle finger. "I love your style."

"Aw." She covers my hand with hers. "Just for that, after the mourning period, I'll design you something. Something that captures your spirit."

"That— I would love that." Tears well in my eyes.

"It will be my pleasure."

I swipe at my tears and take another swig of my lemony-lime soda. "So . . . speaking of weddings . . ."

"Oh no, not you, too, Chotu."

"Who's Ronak?"

She groans, shaking her head, straw between her lips.

"Come on," I say. "It's *me*. I'm not going to hound you, or blab to anybody."

She looks at me as though determining whether I'm trustworthy enough to keep her secrets.

"I'll tell you stuff if you tell me stuff?" I say.

"You've got 'stuff'?" she says. "Well, of course you do. Chotu has turned into a swan." She chucks my chin lightly. "But no sharing secrets here—too public. Plus, I told Ma we'd be home by two. I'll think of someplace we can privately divulge saucy news."

CHAPTER FORTY-ONE

I've stuck close by Aaji throughout the mourning rituals honoring Aajoba. When I asked if she was sad we missed the funeral and cremation, she said, "I was told that Lalita Mami and Ramesh Mama managed them beautifully and drove the ashes to Alandi—you remember the sacred site where the rivers converge that we took you last time?" I nodded, tearing up. "Betiya, in India, the funeral happens immediately, just after death, on account of the heat and such. Not seeing your aajoba beforehand . . ." Her eyes become misty as she wipes the tears off my face. "It's just as he would have wanted."

A brass pot and a lit diya sit upon a tray in Aajoba's bedroom. I've become the one to change the water in the pot and light his diya every morning. Aaji says that we can mourn but need to keep a positive atmosphere in the house because Aajoba can sense the emotions we feel on his behalf, which could hinder his progress into the next realm. Each day, Aaji and I sit in his room and meditate together, seeking his presence, channeling our deepest love into his spirit.

The thirteenth day after Aajoba's death, our family members gather to reminisce about Aajoba and pray for his soul to travel safely to the next world. We each place a flower before the photo shrine of him in the living room, where Shal and I have draped marigold garlands. Several relatives sing his favorite shlokas, or religious mantras, and as I listen to my cousins and aunts and uncles tell stories about Aajoba, I can't help it: I feel envy for all the time they got to spend with him as opposed to my measly occasional summers. I hold Aaji's hand, reminding myself that whatever I feel is nothing compared to what she's going through. Just before we sit to eat his favorite meal—spinach masala, chapati, and simple yellow split pea dal over a mound of rice—I help Aaji spoon a small amount of each onto a silver thali, and she places it before his photo, which is uplit by a flickering diya. *Shahbaas, betiya, brava,* he would have said. *But add more ghee to that chapati, na?*

Hearing his voice in my head, I can't help but grin.

———

"I have something for you," Aaji says, sitting on my bed.

With the monsoon rain falling in steady silver lines from the sky, a stream of neighbors and friends have been stopping by to pay their condolences now that the mourning period has passed. I set down my guilty pleasure, my *Archie* comic. "Something for me? As a reward for leaving you to deal with the respects payers on your own?"

She smiles. "I told them I needed to have my nap, so they left finally."

"Good one." Aaji never takes naps during afternoon siesta, but lies awake reading, like me.

She holds out an ornately carved box the size of a shoebox. "For you," she says again.

"What . . . what is it?"

"It was your aajoba's," she says, placing the box gently in my hands. "He would have wanted *you* to have it only."

My throat thickens. I trace my fingers along the deep carvings, sliding a finger over the smooth mother-of-pearl vine inset. "Why do I remember this . . . ?"

I unhook the little brass latch and lift the lid. Nestled inside the molded cobalt velvet is the ancient Canon from my memories with Shalini, lying in its hard leather case. I lean in, inhaling the scent of sandalwood.

"I was just thinking about this camera," I murmur. "But . . ."

"This is for you, Rani, I am very certain about this," she says quietly. "I have many things of his. Too many things . . . he liked collecting. See, this level lifts up. . . ." She pulls on a satiny ribbon at the edge of the box, revealing a little secret space beneath—a silky vault. A small yellow envelope lies inside. With trembling hands, I unravel the string on the envelope and peek in: the unmistakable gloss of photographs.

I look up at my grandmother. "What are these . . . ?" My heart races.

"They are photos you and Aajoba took together, when you were young," she says. She takes the envelope from me and slides out the square chunk of photos. "You were always so interested in the camera. The early ones were of those silly plants the two of you watered together. You named each plant. 'Now I shall take a picture of Marta. Aaji, pose next to Louisa!'" She chuckles. "All named after *The Sound of Music* characters. Of course all the plants were female only."

"Of course," I say, smiling. She studies a picture before passing it to me.

"See how the photos became better as you grew? Better quality and focus, and more interesting subjects also." I stare at the image: Aajoba standing in an elegant linen outfit, like he's about to leave on safari. He's leaning on a spindly tree, finger raised, laughingly telling the photographer something. And along the yellowed border, in what must be my grandfather's print, is written: *Aajoba and "Maria," photo by Chotu.*

"Yes . . . ," I murmur. I wish I could time-travel back to that moment and find out what he's laughing about.

"Look at this one," she says. "A mongoose in the garden! You were frightened but couldn't pass up the opportunity to snap the photo."

"Hmm," I say. "Yeah . . . this one's not bad."

"'Chotu has a gift for the photography,' he would say to me always."

"Aw, he's just my biggest fan," I say. "Anyone can take pictures."

The rain outside has paused, the giant leaves of the banana tree heavy with droplets.

"Betiya, I know he felt strongly that you should continue with your photographing," she says carefully.

"Ma and Baba think it's a waste of time," I say, not looking up. I hold a close-up of Aajoba looking more serious, but with a conspiratorial light in his eyes.

292

"And do *you* think it a 'waste'? Do you think they know everything about you, everything that is right for you?" She looks directly into my eyes as she says this; shivers run up my back.

"Well, no. They don't know everything."

The air is heavy with humidity, smelling of jasmine and rotting jackfruit. I shift; does *she* know everything? Next to me, she thoughtfully traces a finger along the edge of a photo of a puffy cat, titled *Lucy on the Garden Wall.* "Moving to another country," she says, "can be very difficult. Your parents work hard to ensure that you can succeed, that you are not limited. No doubt your studies are very important." She reaches to tuck a curl behind my ear. "But true contentment is more than academics. This is something your parents may have . . . forgotten."

True contentment. When was the last time I felt that? The early days with Oliver? Or was it *before* Oliver . . . ?

Aaji's gazing at me like she can see my thoughts.

"Rani, we saw the big painting. You were close with this boy."

It's not a question. I'm silent, my fingertips following the intricate carvings of the wooden camera box. "Yes." I'm too exhausted to keep up the charade.

"Haaaah. You never mentioned."

"Sorry. It was—rough. It's over now, anyway. I've moved on." So I tell myself.

We watch the rain drip off the eaves.

"The best masalas use spices slow-roasted over the flame," she says, "browned, even a little burned."

I smile. "Are you saying that human beings are like masala?"

"Ho. And that burning, the pain . . . one must not avoid such pain. It is part of a . . . rich life." She shrugs as if to say, *I didn't make the rules.*

I feel nothing but searing pain right now, so I must be destined for richness or whatever.

"He is a good painter, your friend. Is he a good boy?"

"Is he a good boy . . . ? Yeah. Sometimes. We just—we had issues."

"Haah. Maybe this American boy was not right. But by no means does this mean that no American boy is right."

I look up in surprise. "Huh. So I get to marry anyone I please? Even a dude with a bald tattooed scalp and a pierced septum? A traveling musician maybe?"

"Arre Rama. What have I done?" We're both grinning as she covers my hand with hers. "You know you can talk to me, na? I am good with the secrets." She winks.

I can't believe I'm having this conversation with my grandmother. I hug her tight, trying to suffocate the sob that's suddenly expanding in my chest.

"What were you into when you were my age?" I mumble into her shoulder. Maybe pain is an essential element for living life deeply, but we have to get off this topic before I combust.

"Me?" She chuckles. "I used to sing, as a child mostly. My friend's grandmother taught the neighborhood children classical singing. My brother played the harmonium, my cousin-brother played the tabla—he was quite good. We would all make music together." A fat mosquito floats by, settles upon Aaji's arm; she slaps it deftly, sweeping its flattened body to the floor. "I had quite forgotten about all that."

"So you loved singing."

"Yes, I believe I did quite like it. Instructed by my friend's grandmother, we sang the classical ragas. But out of her earshot, we would sing the popular songs, from the films, you know. Those songs were then considered quite naughty, though they are nothing compared to today's films. Especially your American films."

"Do you still sing sometimes?"

"Nahi ga. I don't even remember the songs. It's been too long."

I imagine Aaji as a girl with thick braids, singing pop songs with her friends.

"But we are discussing you, betiya. Your photos are good, and they bring you joy. Your aajoba believed in joys," she says softly. She's wrapped the end of her soft pink sari around her hair, forming a little hoodie head scarf. She looks like a queen.

I blink. "Huh. And that's how he chose you."

Aaji looks at me blankly.

"You know, your singing voice. You told me back in Evanston that you thought it was a weird thing to . . . to care about. But Aajoba saw the joy in it, and I think he actually had it right."

Her eyes become moist. But she smiles.

"Yes," she says, laughing lightly. She squeezes my hand. "He did."

CHAPTER FORTY-TWO

While Ma and Baba visit Aajoba's lawyer regarding his will, I follow Lalita Mami on her pediatric rounds at the hospital. I study the way she deftly tends to the babies, chatting with anxious parents while efficiently completing her examinations. We then pick up Shalini from work and head to Bollywood Tandoor for lunch.

The place is lively, bustling, with Bollywood movie posters plastering the walls. The dining area is open to the kitchen, where a huge, circular clay oven stands, chefs plucking naan from its inner edges.

"What's that thing called?" I ask.

Shalini glances over. "A tandoor. They build a fire, then let it die down—the coals are hotter than anything, and they stay hot. You know, tandoori chicken? That's what's used to make those."

"That's . . . cool. Like a little hell."

Shalini snorts. "Certainly," she says, settling into a tiny table near the tandoor.

"Rani, did you like anything at the jewelry shop that day

you went with Shal?" my aunt asks, inspecting the table glasses.

"Um, no. I mean, I liked stuff, but . . . I'm not a huge fan of shopping."

"Arre! Just like your mummy." My aunt grins. "You remind me of her."

"Really? What—what was she like? When she was young?"

"Arre baap re," she says, the heel of her palm on her forehead. "Your mom was a lot to handle. We didn't know what we were going to do with her. So difficult, like a Kali warrior. But bright as anything."

"What do you mean 'difficult'?"

The server arrives, sloshing water into the glasses. My aunt glares, insisting on Bisleri bottled water. He stares at her and grabs the glasses back, water dribbling down their sides.

"Badmash man," Lalita Mami grumbles. "As though I've asked for fine aged wine!"

"Your mom," Shalini says, ignoring her mom's mini tirade, "was brilliant, but that made her difficult to raise. I've heard grand stories."

"Yes," Lalita Mami says. "She was—what did Aajoba used to call her?—belligerent. He was into fancy English words, as you know."

"She was always in trouble at school," Shalini says gleefully.

"Ma got in trouble at school?" I ask in disbelief.

"Yah yah," says Lalita Mami, dipping a pepper papadum into the tamarind sauce. "For questioning the teachers."

"But she was an excellent student, na?" Shalini says.

"Yes," my aunt says. "She had revolutionary ideas—"

"Revolutionary ideas?" I can't imagine my mother being anything other than practical.

"Your mum was a champion of the poor long before it was considered fashionable."

I stare at my aunt. *"What?"*

Our waiter delivers a plate of samosas and vividly hued chutneys.

"Betiya, do not touch those chutneys. They use tap water to make them, not boiled. No sense in you contracting some disgusting parasite the short time you're here."

"Wait, so Ma was some kind of . . . activist?"

"Yah yah." My aunt nods, popping a samosa morsel into her mouth. "While studying toward her degree in chemistry, she worked at a local shelter that found jobs for village women."

Who is she talking about?

"It was dangerous work, especially back then. People had never seen such a thing, a young university woman working in the villages. She would work late into the evening, then come home and study half the night."

"People must have thought she had gone mad," murmurs Shalini, swiping a samosa through the green chutney.

"Yes, everyone worried." My aunt nods. "'Who will marry such a headstrong girl?' Your poor aaji spent nights crying over it. Silly to think of it now."

I finally find my voice. "Did my mother—want to get married?"

"In those days, marriage was discussed and even arranged when a girl was still a teenager. But your mom said, 'Nothing doing!' She believed it would interfere with her life's mission."

In a daze, I watch cooks slap triangles of dough along the mouth of the giant tandoor, swiping beads of sweat from their faces with their sleeves.

"So how'd she end up with Baba?"

"She met him at the shelter. He had arrived on holiday from the States, where he was studying industrial engineering. He had been called upon for his American-educated advice on cutting costs."

Ma had initially scoffed at Baba's supposed expertise. But then Baba began assisting at the shelter regularly, negotiating with employers about wages, finding companies to help fund the program, working alongside Ma. It was clear that he admired her, and people began to see a change in my mother. She was relaxed when he was around, playful even. By the end of the month, just before returning to the States to continue his education, he asked her what she thought of marrying him.

"Rani Betiya, we were shocked, uh?" Lalita Mami goes on. "Your mom was never interested in matters of the heart. She was focused on her own ambitions, her studies, her philanthropies, and was stubborn as anything. Never had any of us imagined that a man might steal her heart.

"But one night, she returned home and informed her family that she wished to marry a boy named Alok. The news stunned everybody—her parents, her siblings, her friends. 'Uma has met her match,' they said. Theirs would be a 'love marriage.'"

"Wait, but I thought Aaji and Aajoba arranged their marriage. That they knew Baba's family beforehand."

"They did. That's the great brilliance of it all. They'd heard of this boy Alok, of this respectable family, through friends of theirs. Your aaji and aajoba had hoped their daughter would meet this son, but they knew that convincing their headstrong Uma to begin the process of finding a match would be impossible—she would fight them. It so happened that their mutual friend—you remember Suresh Uncle—was associated with the shelter. Your father's parents—your dada and dadi—suggested that Suresh ask Alok, who was also in the dark about the matchmaking, for his advice about the shelter when he arrived on holiday. So although there was some undercover arranging, the two met seemingly on their own terms."

I'm dumbfounded. "But—why don't I know any of this?"

"My guess is that your parents are focused on the present task at hand—succeeding in America. These stories are useless tales from their past."

"But—it's important. How my parents met. The fact that they chose each other instead of being told they were taking part in this . . . process."

Lalita Mami says, "Rani. It's disrespectful to believe that a couple's union is the sole result of their personal choice. Our elders know what is best for us. Your parents may have taken to each other at the ages of twenty and twenty-three, but it was the masterminding of the elders that brought it into being."

Shalini looks at her plate in silence.

A group of college-age boys one table over gaze openly at Shalini, smiling and elbowing and whispering. She is oblivious to them.

"The funny thing is," Lalita Mami says, "your grandparents weren't ready to send their daughter off to another country. They were frightened at the prospect."

"So what happened?"

"Well, you know your baba—charming, earnest. They learned more about his impressive family, full of doctors, engineers—a highly educated bunch and kindhearted, too. But still they worried."

"What changed their minds?"

Our salty server drops a basket of piping naan slathered in ghee onto the table, along with aloo spinach and dal. Shalini dishes out the food.

"Uma herself changed their minds." My aunt rips off a piece of naan, scooping it through her dal.

"What exactly did she say to convince them?" asks Shalini, riveted.

Lalita Mami smiles. "Not much."

"How'd she get them to let her marry him, then?" My throat burns from the chiles, though no one else seems to find the food spicy. I gulp the Bisleri.

Lalita Mami shrugs. "They just saw it in her eyes, her whole . . . persona. We all could."

"So her *eyes* convinced everybody?" I look at Shalini, incredulous, but she gazes at her mom, waiting.

Lalita Mami waggles her head sagely. "Your mum was a better version of herself with your dad, and no one, not even your aajoba—who loved and admired her deeply—could deny this truth."

The server slinks by, slipping us a plate piled with sticky-sweet jalebi. My aunt protests, saying this was not part of our order, but he insists with a few short words and a little head-shake that says, *No worries. Enjoy.*

"Hmph," my aunt says, her brows arched high.

"He's all right, huh, Mummy?" Shalini says, side-eyeing her mother. She winks at me.

————

Once we arrive back at Aaji's, I hurry to my room and pull out the stationery I bought at a roadside stand. It's as thick as bark, translucent dried flowers pressed right into the paper. The only way to text amid spotty Wi-Fi, Shalini told me, is through WhatsApp. I'm pretty sure Kate doesn't have the app, and even if she did, would she respond to a message from me? I smooth down a rough-hewn page and begin to write.

> *Dear Kate,*
>
> *I'd understand if you're still mad at me. I'm hoping if nothing else, you'll read this through because of the amazing paper. It reminds me of you.*
>
> *My grandfather passed away, as you might have heard. We're in India for the mourning period and to help my grandma adjust. I guess I'm still in shock. I've needed to talk to you so badly. Being here without him is so painful, it hurts to breathe. I don't mean to be dramatic, but it's hard to write about.*
>
> *I think of you constantly here. Kate, there are seriously elephants in the streets. Okay—I've seen one elephant. But also cows. And goats led by, like, a real goat herder along the side of the road. It's not my first time here, as you know, but it always feels new. You'd*

302

die over the traffic—moving one block can take half
an hour. But it's beautiful, too, the chaos. It's hard to
explain. And you won't believe the things I'm learning
about Ma . . . super weird but cool stuff, Kate.

I gaze out the window, massaging my cramping hand. A
cow moos in the distance. I crack my knuckles, staring at the
rain drumming down steadily, washing everything clean. I
bend over the textured paper.

> *I'm babbling. The real reason I'm writing is to*
> *tell you I'M SORRY. I feel awful about everything*
> *that happened between us. I shouldn't have talked*
> *to Oliver about your past relationships. It was hard*
> *for me to understand why you'd want to spend*
> *time with someone not special to you, and why you*
> *wouldn't want to move forward with Henry. Though*
> *I don't want him to get hurt, of course you need to do*
> *what feels right for you.*
> *And now I see it: in real relationships, people DO*
> *get hurt, like with your parents, or me and Oliver.*
> *Maybe you avoiding that pain is actually kind of*
> *brilliant? (On the other hand, Aaji says that pain*
> *is part of living a "rich life," or some such thing, so*
> *what the hell do I know?) Anyway, what I do know*
> *is that those guys were great in their own way: they*
> *made you feel good about yourself, and you were*
> *always honest and straightforward with them, which*
> *is more than I can say for myself.*

The fact is, I was stupid to be judgy, and I'm so
sorry. I understand if you don't feel like you can forgive
me, but I hope eventually I can make it up to you.
                          Love always,
                          Rani

A faraway train whistles. I pull on the sweatshirt Kate got me for my sixteenth birthday—the one that says YOU'RE WEL- COME across the chest. I stamp and seal the letter, then sit on the leafy front veranda, waiting for the mail carrier to come cycling up the dusty road.

CHAPTER FORTY-THREE

Shalini decides we'll take her scooter—rather than a rickshaw—to a small business district on the outskirts of town; the roads there are peaceful, rural. Kicking on the brake, she parks the scooter and helps me off. We stand before a restaurant, its name strung in white lights.

"How'd you find this place?" I ask.

"Ronak and I come here in secret. It's called Samudra."

"'Ocean.'"

"Yes. Technically, in Sanskrit it means 'the gathering together of the waters.' Your language has gotten good. Anyway, no one local knows us here. Come." She strides inside, her silk dupatta and black hair flowing down her back. I follow.

The place is cavernous, but also packed. A server gestures toward a nearby table, but Shalini points to one in the far corner.

We settle onto cushions on the floor. Trees grow inside amid the tables, their gnarled roots half concealed by dozens of potted plants. Strings of lights crisscross in midair. Heavy logs stretch above, a rustic trellis framing the twilit sky.

"Wow."

"Yes. The owner of this café is from Rajasthan. He designed it to look like one of those old, opulent Rajasthani palace hotels."

I fold my hands beneath my chin, elbows on the table, and look straight into her eyes. "Okay. Spill it."

She smiles shyly. "So . . . Ronak is my boyfriend. Although of course I don't use that term with Ma and Baba. They'd kill me. So he's a 'friend.' Part of my group of friends."

"Sure."

"On some level, they must know we're a couple, but no one properly discusses such things."

"Ronak. Sexy name."

Shalini giggles. "Okay, yes, he is sexy." She pulls up some photos on her phone of a young man with a genuine smile, his face covered in the colorful powders of Holi, the festival of spring.

"Ooo, he's cute. And somehow looks really kind."

They met working together on a project in Mumbai. He asked her to lunch, and afterward they walked along the Arabian Sea, their fingers barely grazing.

"We were comfortable together even then, but not too comfortable, you know? We have interesting conversations. Some would call them arguments," she says, grinning.

"Keeps things spicy, passionate."

"Yes. Passion is underrated. Parents say they value compatibility, but the focus seems more on background and socioeconomics." Mimicking a traditional-minded elder, she wags her index finger: "'Is he from a good family? Will he be a good provider? And above all, does he have a wheatish com-

306

plexion?' Purely practical things, except that last one, which is pure stupidity."

"Um, what exactly is a 'wheatish complexion'?"

"Fair-skinned, like the color of wheat. Everyone's matrimony bios state they either have it or are looking for a mate who possesses it, especially the female. Such nonsense."

Our server tries to pour water into our glasses, but Shalini raises her hand. "Bisleri for her. I will have chai."

The man bows, then swans away.

"And it's such a shame, na?" she mumbles, her long lashes low as she gazes over my left shoulder. "I'm not sure that passion was discussed as an essential between a man and a woman."

Of course I know passion. It's what Oliver and I had—too much of, maybe. Something about him lit a fire in me. Was it the way he looked at me, his eyes liquid with love and lust? Or maybe it was the way we bantered and bitched about everything and nothing, until one of us got fed up and grabbed the other hard and close. There was a point when we struck a sensual, delirious balance—it was ravishing. And also ravaging.

The server comes and sets down our drinks with a flourish. "There's a fine line between fun, sexy passion and I'm-so-obsessed-with-you-that-I-want-to-destroy-you passion," I say.

She looks at me quizzically. "Okay. Now *you*. Tell all."

I gulp my Bisleri. The hook of a song trills through the speakers. A group of young women sing in unison, chair-dancing to the Bollywood beat.

"Chotu?"

I study my hands, shame welling up inside my chest. How can I possibly put into words everything that's happened? Will she judge me?

I swallow. "There is this . . . boy. Back home." I look up at her. "His name is Oliver."

And then, before I know it, the story tumbles out. The day we met at the gallery last fall, the intro to his art world, the beef tacos with his family, the night at Saul's, the torrid, clandestine nights at the beach, in cars, in his room. The lightness and darkness of being in love. The secrecy and shame. The fights about drugs and racism, the way he pushed my boundaries, and, finally, the end of it after seeing the eroticized mural that advertised our struggle for all to see.

Pakoras arrive, and she eats carefully, watching me as I pop one into my mouth. The fried morsel bursts with flavor.

"Oh, Chotu." Shalini's eyes are moist. "Love . . . Love is . . ."

I swallow. "Love's a burning tandoor."

"Eh?"

"Hot as hell, and when you're in too deep, you get singed." I take a swig of water. "It's a slightly less inspirational version of something Aaji said."

She smiles sadly. "Yes. Love is a bloody-hot tandoor." Our server hovers, and she waves him away. "Chotu. When was the last time you spoke with him?"

"That night. Outside the café."

"You haven't been in contact since?"

"Not really." I mop at the saucy vegetables with a piece of roti and scoop the whole thing into my mouth.

She laughs, watching me. "Well, despite this deeply American love story, you're becoming an Indian as we speak. Look at you, dal dripping off your chin. Well done."

I wipe at my face. "Well, do *you* see any napkins anywhere?"

"No. You're supposed to lick your fingers clean, my dear girl."

"*God*, I love India. I could live here, if it weren't for Kate. Of course, she hates me now, so . . ."

Our server arrives, half bowing as he presents a tray lined with steaming hot face towels.

"Thank you," I murmur, taking one.

Shalini says something to him in Hindi, and he disappears. "Tell me more about Kate."

"Kate." I puff air out of my cheeks. "I was a crap friend. I told Oliver I wondered why she wasted her time on—unsuitable boys, you could say. He repeated this to her, and she's not speaking to me now."

"Because you never mentioned your feelings earlier?"

"No. Her parents went through a divorce, and I figured it was her way of coping. . . ."

"Sounds like Oliver should have kept his trap shut."

"Right? He made me sound like a monster."

"You just wanted the best for her. You didn't mean for her to know your concerns."

"Maybe I should have told her. . . ."

"No, you were right not to. There is *too much* openness in America," she says, karate-chopping the air for emphasis. "*Honesty.* I see the movies, Chotu, so don't think I don't know. Americans could learn a thing or two from Indians. You're

309

dying of cancer, sprawled in a hospital bed? Here, everyone will tell you you're healing beautifully, absolutely *pukka*, even your doctor."

"Oh, stop. That's not true," I laugh.

"It is, Chotu. So you had opinions about her bygone fellows. What does it matter now?"

"I don't know—it's complicated. Partly, I was so *involved* with Oliver, I barely gave much thought to her or anyone else."

"Well, that *is* different. You will rot in American hell for that one." She grins, motions to the server for our check. "Seriously, Chotu. Kate will forgive you."

"Well, that's not all. I kind of tried to pressure her into a relationship with my friend Henry, who really likes her."

"Arre baap re! More drama than expected." She studies me. "Why so invested in her and Henry?"

"He—well, he's Salil's next-door neighbor. And is really kind to Salil, like Nilesh was."

"Ah" is all she says.

"I just couldn't believe she wouldn't give Henry a chance. I mean, if not him, then who?"

"Maybe no one, Chotu. Perhaps she's not in the state to be with anyone right now. Heartache won't kill Henry."

"I *was* pretty judgmental."

She smiles. "You two will move past this, I promise."

"I just— Living here seems easier. People don't really date, meaning they don't stupidly self-destruct. . . . I wish I'd never—"

"Chotu. Love affairs happen everywhere, including here. Obsessive and dramatic ones, like yours and Oliver's. We here experience all the highs and lows that you're going through."

"So people here give their heart and soul to someone who'll then throw you under the bus the first chance he gets? No, people don't do that."

"And how do you know that?"

I regard her, my eyeballs pricking.

"Look, Chotu. You're hurting. But do you regret anything? Tell me honestly you wish that you'd never met Oliver."

I blink away a tear. "I don't know."

She sighs. "What's so difficult about our family is that what's unaccepted goes undiscussed, leaving us to handle it alone. Much harder that way."

"Do you know what happened to Nilesh after everyone found out he was using?"

She takes my hand in silence.

"I overheard some uncles talk about how he was making the Indian community look bad and squandering precious opportunities. And the aunties were silent—no one really defended him, not publicly anyway. He was suddenly taboo. Nilesh—our Nilesh!" Ice shoots up my spine.

She squeezes my hand. "And that affected you. Of course it did. Maybe it's partly why you couldn't tell your parents about Oliver. You are a young heroine in that community, na? Adored by aunties everywhere."

I gaze up at the stars through the trellis above. Being open about Oliver meant risking isolation, alienation from my family . . .

"Chotu? You don't need this Oliver. You were correct in finishing it with him."

"Then why do I feel so terrible?" I whisper.

"Because you were in love, for better or worse. And since

311

he has struggles, you feel guilty. But nothing here is your fault."

I affix my stare on the brightest star I see.

"Rani," she says, leaning in, "you must believe in your choices and stay true to your heart, your goodness. You cannot go through life this way."

"What way?"

"You were honest with him, made a deal from the start, and were strong to end it when he betrayed you. And now you're free to have new experiences, with this newfound awareness making you stronger. Trust me."

Riding home, my arms around Shalini's waist, I gaze up at the full moon hanging low in the sky and think of Oliver. I wonder if he's looking up at the same moon, but then I remember that it's daylight in America and no moon would be shining there now.

CHAPTER FORTY-FOUR

The next day, after Shalini leaves for work, I roam around the neighborhood in my white salwar kameez, snapping photos with Aajoba's camera. People stop and stare, their confusion clear as they work to categorize me. I'm not a white Westerner in an ashram robe, nor am I a native. I'm an Indian American in Pune, looking to capture "daily Indian life," which places me in my own odd category.

I follow Aajoba's walking route, past the old Anglo-Indian mansions—grand and stately, in various stages of disrepair. I take shots of the wild, rambling gardens and the spooky banyan trees outside the iron gates. Shalini once told me horror stories about how the banyans' twisted, hanging roots were actually the limbs and entrails of English ghosts. . . . I shift the lens, highlighting the hanging roots with refracted light to suggest the spirits that haunt them.

As I start home, my thoughts are a wide-angled color wash of Oliver. How badly he wanted into my world. How he had only a romanticized idea of what that world was. How burned he was by my parents' views—and my lack of courage at challenging those views—and how he retaliated with racism. It still eludes me how to share my culture with another person. With Kate, everything just fell into place, but with Oliver . . . that trust and understanding kept collapsing, time and again, despite us both wanting it so badly. Here, in India, I can see a side of our love I couldn't back then. And yet, most of it still feels unforgivable.

I tread the rest of the way home blindly. It's a walk I know by heart.

———

That night, Shalini and I lie in the double bed in our room, listening to the lonely sound of a distant train. I turn to face her, the moonlight glinting off her hair. "So what's the story?" I say quietly. "Are you going to marry Ronak?"

She blinks. "I think so. He's now officially been transferred to Pune, is about to get promoted to supervisor, and then . . ."

"You haven't yet told your parents about him."

She chews on a hangnail. "He wasn't 'top of his class.' He would never want to go to America—though, ironically, he works in a call center offering tech support mainly to Americans. And he's good at his job. But he's not from some wealthy, well-known family. They're perfectly respectable, but not what our family has in mind for me."

"But you both do basically the same work, it sounds like."

"Yes, though my position is one level above his, currently. But our family wants me with someone who's well above that, of course. And they don't trust or understand modern India: men and women working together, often through the night on Eastern Standard Time, dating one another . . ."

"They may not understand now. But over time . . . ?"

She turns onto her side, facing me. Her eyes are wide—suddenly she looks like she did when we were kids.

"You'll stand up for him when it feels right," I say. The paradox of this conversation.

She sighs quietly. "Ronak's bright, in a scrappy, street-smart kind of way. He makes me laugh even when I'm in a vicious mood. And mostly . . ." She props herself up on an elbow, looking at me intently. "Mostly, I feel *good* when I'm around him. And I don't mean just the sexy stuff. He sees things in me—things he admires, qualities I didn't think I possessed. He's not exactly what I'd dreamed. But in many ways . . . he's better."

As the mating call of garden frogs shrills through the window's iron jalis, I can't help but imagine Shalini in a wedding sari that reflects her unique style, standing beside Ronak, the handsome guy from the photos. *I feel good when I'm around him.* I once, long ago, felt that way with Oliver. I smile in the dark, pride for Shalini filling my chest.

If that feeling can be a lasting thing, what more even is there?

CHAPTER FORTY-FIVE

The next day, I find my mother alone on the living room couch, dabbing at her eyes with a balled-up tissue. She sees me and stuffs the tissue beneath her thigh.

"Hi, Ma," I say, sitting next to her. "What're you watching?"

"Just an old Bollywood film. It's not too good, actually."

"What's it about?"

She scans my face in surprise. "Oh. Well, this mother-in-law, that one there, is quite awful to her daughter-in-law. For years, awful. But then the old woman discovers that she has a mysterious disease, and . . ." She glances at me again. "It sounds silly. I know how you and Baba detest these films."

"No, no. They're kind of fun. Drama is the spice of life."

She smiles. "I suppose." She winds a chunk of my hair away from my face. "How are you, betiya? Is doing rounds with Lalita Mami keeping you occupied now that Shalini is back at work?"

"Yes. I love rounds. And I've been taking good walks."

"I see you took Aajoba's camera with you. A treasure."

I take the strap off my neck and set the camera in her hands. She strokes its leather case as we watch the screen.

The daughter-in-law caresses the mother-in-law's face with a melodramatic flourish, then begins dancing and singing to her, together with a troupe of women who appear out of nowhere. Whoever they are, all their midriffs are bared as they gyrate in unison to an upbeat tune. It's basically a musical, or a Disney cartoon. Undeniable mass appeal.

We watch in silence as drama unfolds: mother-in-law drama, hospital drama, lovesick suitor drama.

"Ma?"

"Hmm?"

"How are you doing?"

She glances at me, then down at her hands. "Mostly, I'm angry at my father for not waiting until after we arrived, but I suppose that's silly."

"I do wish we could've seen him one last time."

"It's selfish of him, isn't it? To leave us like this." Her eyes settle on my face, and we both burst out laughing.

"Okay, that's probably the craziest thing I've ever heard you say. But you're entitled this time."

"Just this time, yes." She giggles, wiping at her eye.

I rest my head on her shoulder. "I went out to lunch with Shalini and Lalita Mami while you and Baba were with the lawyer," I murmur. Being close to her like this feels comforting but strange—a nostalgic song echoing through the wasteland of my life.

"Were you careful about the food? I don't like you going around to these restaurants. Who knows what they—"

"I heard some amazing stories about you."

She sniffs. "Huh. What nonsense was my sister filling your head with?"

"Nonsense? No, it was—well, the opposite. How you used to work in a women's shelter in the village, and that's where you met Baba."

"Oh, your mami. Always bringing up the past."

"How come you never told me any of that stuff, Ma? She said the women's shelter was your 'life's mission.'"

She sighs deeply, gazing out at the garden. "I don't know why I never told you, betiya," she says. "It was—another life. I haven't thought about it in years."

"But it was your passion, she said. To help those in need. And at a time when it wasn't even trendy to care about that. When it was considered dangerous work. Especially for a woman."

"I guess when you put it that way, betiya, yes. It makes me sound like a young heroine." She strokes my hair. Dramatic music swells on the television, but my eyes stay on my mother's weary face. She looks like she's working through something in her mind, blinking rapidly. "I'm sorry, Rani," she says finally. "That I've not shared any of that with you. You're right—I should have told you all of this. Our family stories."

I say nothing.

"Why?" she says. "Why do we do the stupid things we do? I don't know, betiya."

The silence stretches between us while an up-tempo beat throbs from the television. Is that it? I close my eyes. I will never connect on anything of importance with my mother. Our relationship consists of discussions of dinner and schoolwork and chores, and that's all it will ever be.

She clears her throat.

"When we moved to Chicago, I tried to find work in women's shelters, similar to the work I'd done in India," she says, her voice tight. "But the logistics were more complicated in America. The shelters were located in rough sections of the city, and your baba wasn't comfortable having me take the several buses necessary to get there. Of course, I couldn't drive at the time, since I didn't yet have a license. I almost had an accident while learning the highway system, and I never—well, you know me and driving."

I hold my breath, listening.

"Most important was the issue of income—the pay was frightful. In most cases, nonexistent, especially for someone like me, a foreigner. . . . Add to that the fact that my Indian degree and accreditations were of little value in the States. Plus, my heavy accent—" She laughs, a little bark. "We couldn't survive without a steady double income. Baba was a graduate student, getting a small stipend each month. I eventually found a job at Aubergine in the quality control department, as you know."

"Did you like it?"

"Oh, betiya. You're . . ." She searches my face, then looks down. "I didn't think of whether I liked it or not. The fact was, I was already pregnant with you, and you—became the reason for everything I did from then on."

A sparrow lands on the window's iron jalis behind the TV. It stares at us with black bead eyes.

"When you arrived, there was so much to worry ourselves over. There still is, of course. Worry over not raising you well, over not properly providing what you'd need to thrive in America. No relatives there, and very little money. It was—"

She shakes her head, a quick jerk. On-screen, a child pushes an ailing grandmother in a wheelchair toward an ornate temple, singing shrilly, while neighborhood children trail them. "I wonder how we did it. Sometimes, I wonder how we still do it."

I give her a hug, hiding my face in her neck, inhaling her spicy gardenia scent.

"We're doing okay, Ma," I murmur.

She says nothing. She turns the camera over in her hands, her fingers running along its ragged leather straps. Her brow is furrowed, her mouth curved down in the slight frown I know well.

"I know," she whispers. "But I worry." She turns to me. "We saw the painting. Outside by the café."

My mind whirls; this is the moment I have been dreading with all the fibers of my being.

But then—a sudden surge of resolve. *No more lies.*

"The mural," I say carefully, "was created by a friend of mine. Someone very interested in . . . India. Someone I met at my gallery show last year."

She watches me, her eyes wide.

"I— We're not friends anymore," I say breathlessly. "He didn't understand—things—even though he wanted to. I didn't know about the mural until the night you saw it." Am I actually talking to my mother about Oliver? Fear rattles through me.

"I see." She turns the television off and faces me on the sofa, her hands settled in the folds of her brilliant purple sari. "What is this young man's name?"

"Oliver." As I say his name aloud, terror seizes my heart.

"Hmm. You and this Oliver. You spent time together?"

My breath is ragged, catching in my throat. "Yes," I say finally.

"I see." Tears well up in her eyes.

"I'm sorry. He was—a friend. But—"

"Arre Rama . . ."

"He—" I don't know how to proceed with this conversation. But then: "When would you see him?" My mother's studying my face. "This Oliver?"

The door to my resolve slams shut. I can't tell her everything. I just can't.

"Tell me," she says, "that you didn't have sex."

My face gets hot. "Of course not." *One lie per day . . .*

"Because that would have been so stupid. And risky. To you and your future. The sex complicates things."

No kidding. But . . . I chose to. And wouldn't I do it all again, as Shalini said?

We sit in silence and watch the blank television screen.

"Was he a smart boy? Did he work hard?"

"Yes." I exhale silently. "He was the boy you noticed at the gallery. With the tattoos." Recognition—then fear—crosses her face. "He—is a talented artist. With a tough life," I say. "And he needed more than I could give, and it led to . . . a lot of pain."

Fresh tears form in her eyes. "I'm sorry—for him," she whispers. "Kids should not have such troubles. And you—you were managing all this."

I say nothing, stunned that we're having this conversation.

Stunned that she's taking it so calmly, that she's not disowning me, the way Nilesh was disowned for all his flaws. Stunned at how close I am to admitting how my obsession with Oliver led me to neglect our family. . . .

"Ma?" I clear my throat and in a tiny voice say, "I'm . . . I'm sorry for not setting up Zoom."

She holds my face in both her hands. "Oh, betiya." She kisses my brow. "You're not blaming yourself for what's happened with Aajoba, are you?"

She hugs me long and hard, the sort of mama-bear hug she used to give me as a kid. "Rani," she says, still holding me tight. "He was . . . sick. He was very sick. He had diabetes and was rather careless about it. He had heart disease. His knee troubled him daily, so he barely walked by the end. He . . . well, none of us knew that he would go so soon. But he was struggling, was going to die, and Zoom would not have changed that, betiya."

Tears spill from my eyes, seeping into her gauzy sari as she holds me close. "But it might have," I whisper.

"No. He was always connected to you, Zoom or no Zoom. He loved you so much. I believe he cared for you more than anybody," she says.

I sob into her shoulder, her arms tight around me. My mind empties. She strokes my hair lightly, as if any sudden movement might break the spell, she a touch point of connection to the generations before me: their love, their trauma, their wisdom.

And then a thought alights like a butterfly: this kind of understanding from Ma feels . . . new. Her reaction to Oliver ordinarily would've exploded, gruesomely, all over the world.

I may have fallen from the ideal betiya, but somehow, my place is still here with her.

Maybe her quiet acceptance comes from being reminded of her Wonder Woman past. Or her and Baba's sweet beginnings. Or maybe it's the fact that together we're grieving Aajoba, who's found a way to save me once again.

CHAPTER FORTY-SIX

After over three months in India, we board the 5:23 a.m. Mumbai flight for Chicago. As I settle into my cramped seat, the morning's goodbyes are on my mind. "Are you sure you can't come with us, Aaji?" I begged.

"No, betiya," she responded with a sad smile. "My arthritis is much improved, thanks to the treatment I received in the U.S., so now I rest. Maybe after your first college year is over, then I'll visit, uh?"

Then Shalini presented me with a gift—a stunning ring she designed for me, as promised. A silver bezel surrounding a flat, irregularly shaped moonstone. "Moonstone gives you strength," she said. "It's used to facilitate emotional journeys, clarifying inner truths." I hugged her, promising to stay in touch. Now I gaze at the ring, tracing the stone's edges, hoping to activate it. I'm going to need clarity. The task of suturing the wounds in my life lies before me: a bloody, complicated mess.

Tropical trees whiz by along the runway. The plane then soars above the City of Dreams and a nation of extremes.

As we careen higher and higher over the slums and the sky-scrapers, the sea and the clouds, my heart contracts. I think of Aajoba: Is he watching us?

Sweet sleep must have saved me, because next thing I know, a boxed meal is plunked before me, the word HINDU stamped on top. Groggy, I peel off the lid to see spiced vegetables, pulao with dal, and a respectable-looking roti. I tear off a piece and scoop up some of the mystery veggies. "Mmm," I mutter.

"It's quite good, na?" Baba says, smiling at me. "Aren't you glad I preordered the Hindu meals? Might even be better than your mother's food."

"Arre!" Ma swats Baba's arm. "Maybe I should stop cooking, then, and we will order from the airline only."

I smile. My love life may be decimated. But thank God I still have these two.

———

"Rani Betiya? We are home," my mother says softly. "And it looks like there's someone waiting for you."

My eyes flutter open. Bleary-eyed, I peer through the taxi window. Kate's standing on the front steps, holding an enormous handmade sign whose lettering I can barely make out in the dusky light:

WELCOME HOME!

I blink, half believing it's a dream.

My father pulls me out of the car, grinning. "Go! Say hello while I get our bags."

I stumble up the walkway. Her auburn hair's short and sassy and streaked with blond. She's grinning huge.

"Your hair . . . ," I say stupidly.

"I know!" she says, twirling a finger around a golden lock. "See the mess that happens when you're not here to stop me?"

I gaze at the stenciled block letters of her sign. "Dang, professional-looking sign. What else have I missed?"

"Yeah, I'm a master sign maker now." She shrugs comically.

"Kate." I still can't believe she's here. "I'm so sorry."

"Girl. Is my hair that bad?" She flings the sign over the railing and brings me into a bear hug. "I know you are," she whispers. "I got your letter. You got mine, too, right?" She searches my face.

I shake my head. If I say anything, I'll burst into tears.

"What? You didn't get it? *Shit*. I mean, there are *things* in that letter—"

"Wait, so you haven't left yet for college?" I say. "I thought—"

"Actually, I *have* left. I'm all moved in at Ann Arbor. I'm just back for the weekend."

"How did you know when—"

"I asked your neighbors. Good ol' Greg and Angie. We're besties now."

My mother comes up the walk, smiling. "Kate. How lovely that you're here. Did you cook dinner for us, too?"

"Dinner? No, Mrs. Kelkar, I thought I'd come help consume the first dinner *you* make back in America."

We laugh, and Kate helps drag our luggage inside. We throw open some windows, order a pizza, and lug the three bins stuffed with mail in from the porch. Then Kate and I slip out for a walk together in the summer night.

Wobbly with exhaustion, I listen to her voice in disbelief and gratitude: I still have Kate. I have a great family and I have Kate. Everything's going to be okay.

CHAPTER FORTY-SEVEN

Kate and I wander the twilit streets, the buzz of cicadas rising as a fearsome crescendo. There's a subtle awkwardness between us—we've not spoken in so long. As she tells me about her week at college and her summer job and her work with Habitat for Humanity, a light breeze blows—it's an alternate reality from the heavy monsoons and humidity of Pune. I try to listen to Kate but only half hear the details, so shocked am I in my new-old surroundings. Surroundings that remind me so much of Oliver.

"So: Bonnie. It's weird, it's like she's becoming a new and improved version of herself. She's still learning the ropes at work. She's begun running, and she sees girlfriends sometimes. She's, like, 'getting her groove back.'"

"That's amazing. You must be so proud of her."

"You know what? I totally am. She's come a long way. I feel like I can actually talk to her." Kate is grinning in the dark. "Even about boys."

Boys, plural. As in, Henry is probably long gone.

"In fact, I talked to her the other day about sex," she goes on. "Voluntarily!"

"Whoa. What exactly did you tell her?"

"Well, if you'd gotten my letter . . ." She sniffs.

"All I did this summer was suffer and stalk the mail carrier. And you know the Wi-Fi there is ridiculously patchy, so I couldn't even email or text!"

She grins. "I know. So I asked her whether having sex changes things for the better or worse. I was seriously thinking about doing it. With Henry."

I stop. "Wait, you and Henry . . . ?"

Her jaw drops. "Oh my God. I need to back up."

"Yes. Back. The. Hell. Up." We laugh, and I twist Shalini's ring.

"Okay, so . . . I guess I should've opened with that."

"I—I'm just so happy."

"Me too. I just—I freaked out after prom. Like, I had all these feelings for Henry, and I worried that I'm basically Bonnie, falling for the first guy who sweeps her off her feet."

"I get that," I say. I want to weep with joy.

"I actually did put things on hold after that day in the East Courtyard. He was disappointed, but sweet about it."

"Okay," I say, tugging the moonstone ring off my finger and rubbing at the flat stone.

"You and I'd just had that awful fight, and your grandfather died, and you left, and I saw that fucking mural, and I felt just . . . totally unmoored. I was trying to train for regionals, but I kept brooding about everything: you, me, your family, Oliver, Henry . . ."

I nod guiltily. She was brooding over me, but I didn't even remember her big game.

"I couldn't focus at all, but then, the day before the game, there was this handwritten note in our mailbox. All it said was something like: 'I know you're going to kick ass tonight. You won't need it, but best of luck! Henry.'"

"Wow. He remembered," I say. Unlike some of us.

"Yeah. Like, my *own dad* didn't remember the game. Anyway, so we won, and . . ."

"What? Holy shit!"

"Yeah! Three to two. Last two minutes of the game, Janaya scored! Henry then texted, congratulating me on the win. Of course we then lost sectionals, but that's okay. A few days later, I ran into him and asked if he wanted to join me at Habitat. Then we went on a quasi date and had our first kiss. And my first thought was: *Where's Rani? Must dissect this kiss!*"

I laugh. "Sounds, wow. I'm sorry I wasn't here for any of it."

"It was probably for the best, to be honest. I had to actually make decisions on my own."

Kate goes on to describe how they spent the summer—running together most mornings with the ever-growing plogging club, volunteering at Habitat, filling in for me at Salil's, biking to the beach. . . . They had the kind of summer Oliver and I could have had, if only . . .

"Anyway, you weren't here, so I'd talk to Bonnie. She said that the choice to have sex depends on 'the nature of the relationship.' All professor-like. That in a healthy relationship, based on friendship and 'deep love,' sex can make things even better. But if it's dysfunctional and stressful and clingy, then sex *compounds* all that. So, basically, sex intensifies whatever's already there."

"Dang, Bonnie." I could have seriously used this wisdom, like, nine months ago.

"I know, right? We might have to consult her when we write our book together."

"Our book?"

"Sex with Boo: When Y'Know It's Right."

I laugh. "I'm assuming you still have that napkin some-where." We take turns kicking a rock, neon fireflies floating in the darkening night. "You're lucky to have your mom to talk to."

"I know. But this is seriously new. I used to think she was so fragile. But now that she's not expending all that energy appeasing or resenting my dad . . ." She kicks the rock toward me, but it scuttles off the sidewalk, lost in the grass. "She's not just surviving—she's actually thriving. It kind of gives me hope." She grins. "Listen to me, all yoga leader . . ."

"Yeah. You could lead the Spirit of Life sessions, no problem."

"Yes! The Spirit of Freaking Life. We *could* lead them with the life lessons we've had this year."

I smile. "Actually, I told my grandma *she* should become an instructor. She put the teachings to major use these past few months."

"Oof. How is she?"

"She's—doing okay, I guess. Aajoba—" I shake my head.

"He's a huge part of your heart, isn't he?" Kate says softly.

I nod, gazing into the canopy of trees overarching Colfax, my heart aching.

"Hey." Kate stops walking and holds me tight. "I wish I'd been there for you. Tell me everything." I inhale deeply; her hair smells of lavender and mint.

"Did I ever tell you that it was Aajoba who first got

me taking photos?" I pull away and look at her face. "I was nine."

"So it all began with him." An owl coos from a nearby treetop. "What would you two photograph back then?"

I smile. "The garden, our family, things like that. My grandma gave me some of those old photos, along with his camera."

"Holy mama."

We gaze in silence down the block at Kate's old elementary school, and out tumbles everything.

I tell her about the mourning period and its rituals, Shalini, and my mother's superhero past. I tell her about being entangled in guilt over not setting up Zoom but how Ma cut me loose with her kindness. I try to describe India to her, but out loud, it rings inaccurate, or carelessly dramatic.

"God. What a backdrop to everything you were dealing with—including Oliver." She squeezes my hand.

We wander westward, passing the school and turning south until we reach the entrance to Perkins Woods at the edge of the school grounds. Stepping along one of four converging pathways, we stop at the heart of the forest, where a picnic table stands beneath the towering trees. We lie across it and stare up at the patches of sapphire sky visible through leafy branches.

"So . . . I saw the mural," she says quietly.

I keep my eyes on the inky sky. "You and everybody."

"Did you know about it? Before it went public, I mean?"

"Hell no. Who would okay that?"

She sits up, staring down at me. "You mean he made it without your knowledge?"

I nod.

"Holy shit."

"Yeah." I close my eyes.

"What— Did you *talk* to him that night?"

"Oh yes. We talked. Outside the café, with droves of people streaming by to witness my humiliation."

"Oh, Rani."

"He said the mural was a romantic gesture."

"No."

"And that our problems were rooted in my own issues and hang-ups, like my refusal to be up front with my parents . . ."

"But—he obviously didn't understand. They're awesome people, but accepting that a horny teenage dude's dating their daughter? It's a lot to ask of people who come from a traditional culture, where dating's not the norm. And anyway, you're the best to read the temperature on that, not him."

"He felt it was hypocritical for me to be upset about the racial overtones of his work when my parents forbade me to date," I say, sitting up, "like it was reverse racism or something. And he said I'm just as bad because I won't stand up to them."

Kate's back is ramrod straight as she absorbs it all.

"How dare he?" she blurts. "Your parents aren't bigoted. And I can't believe he'd accuse *you* of reverse racism. That is unbelievable white privilege bullshit."

"I thought what we had . . ." I trail off. Suddenly, I am beyond exhausted.

"I'm so sorry, Rani. That's seriously so shitty."

We sit in silence. "Did your family end up seeing the mural?" she says finally.

"Yes."

I watch her eyes go wide.

"We didn't talk about it until after the mourning period in India. Eventually, I told Ma about Oliver—that he was a 'friend' but not anymore."

"Holy crap."

"I know. She was shocked. And upset. But she didn't disown me."

She smiles sadly. "You didn't think Ma would actually disown you, though, right?"

I shrug. "I've seen it happen."

"God, how did things devolve? Oliver seemed—kind of great once."

"I don't really know. There was always so much tension between us. My cousin Shalini calls it *passion:* the secret, exciting ingredient to a great relationship."

Kate snorts. "Irony."

"Right?" I sigh. "It *was* kind of thrilling. I mean, he was passionate, and tender. . . . But then things got kind of weird. *I* got weird. He got weird. It's like there was more at stake, and everything felt heavy."

"Hmm. Heavy how?" She slaps at a mosquito.

"Like clingy-heavy. He needed so much from me. And when I wouldn't or couldn't do the things he wanted, he basically went batshit. The drugs and putting both our lives at risk at the breakwater . . . At prom, he actually had the gall to ask why I wasn't wearing a traditional sari."

"Jesus." Suddenly, we're both being attacked by mosquitoes, and wordlessly, we leap off the picnic table and step quickly down the path out of the forest. "It's like he was obsessed with my culture," I say as we cross the schoolyard beneath the open sky. "But he didn't truly understand it, and the less he understood, the less he seemed to respect it, which felt like he didn't respect *me*. I wanted so badly to give him what he wanted, but after a while, it's like he didn't even see me as a person. . . . Like the role he wanted me to play meant more to him than I did."

"He fetishized your love—I mean, that night in the car with the sari is the ultimate example," Kate says slowly, hooking her arm in mine and falling into step beside me. "Like . . . he objectified your culture as much as your body."

I blink. "Yes. And it wasn't about *us* anymore. It was about him indulging his need for art or culture, or whatever. But when I pointed out his microaggressions and how they hurt me, he was outraged. It's like he has this inability to see past his own needs . . . the mural being the low point. That night, I ended things."

"I heard." She hesitates. "You know his sister had her baby."

"No."

"Yep. Prematurely, according to Saul, who I ran into the other day. Sounds like Oliver was busy at home this summer."

"Girl or boy?"

"Girl."

I'm silent a moment. Was I wrong to have ended it that night? Should I have given us another chance?

"Rani. You did the right thing, and you are *not* calling him over this," Kate says, reading my mind. "Would he have ever apologized for what he put you through? For belittling your family's values, for driving an intentional wedge between *us*? The secrets, the drugs, the disregard, the mural . . . I mean, those are a lot of strikes against him that I'm not sure he'd even see as strikes."

"They are. And somehow, *I* feel guilty, like . . ."

". . . like it's your fault. But it's not, Rani. It's okay that you couldn't give him everything he wanted—you didn't owe him that."

"I know. . . . I'm still so mad, but I also miss him, which makes me even more mad. Then the fact that things have been so hard for him . . ."

"And that's why you're going to make an amazing pediatrician one day. Being sympathetic and having heart is in the job description, and the world will be lucky to have you. But this—"

"I know. It's wrong. In the end, he saw me through a certain, like, *lens*, and it was disturbing. Why he even needed that lens . . ." My throat thickens.

"God, Rani, I'm so sorry. It just sucks, and will take time. But let's look at the bright side: you're qualified now to manage the pitfalls of college relationships. Also known as 'college hookups.'"

"Great. That sounds right up my alley."

A couple walks by with a huge white poodle wearing actual pink bows in its fur. I wonder idly if my parents will get a pet after I leave for college, something to fill their empty nest. . . .

I clear my throat. "Hey, so you never told me what . . . *transpired* with Henry. Did you guys . . . you know?"

"I can't believe you didn't get my letter."

"I literally stalked the mail guy!"

"Short version: we tried to have sex and it didn't work and now I can't seem to take the plunge."

"Long version, please."

"Well, we recently started having these . . . sessions. Things got pretty heated, actually. . . . We even tried one night, but it wasn't *working*. I was like, 'Do I even have a vagina, because it seems to have disappeared?'"

I laugh. "Virgin vaginas do not know what they have coming. But they suspect."

"And the whole condom deal? On that alone, I could have used a tutorial. Anyway, we went to Blind Faith Café beforehand, then to his house. But he got a text from his grandma saying she'd be home soon, so things were rushed and I simultaneously freaked out, feeling like everything might change between us, so we didn't end up doing it."

"Oh. But that's cool, Kate."

She glances at me. "'Cool'? Name one thing cool about this . . . fail."

"It's cool to wait until it feels right—not be swayed by some . . . *societal pressure* about how or when. . . . Plus, I believe you haven't passed the four-month mark yet," I say, winking.

She snorts. "As if *you* waited four months, bish."

"Exactly! See how well that turned out?"

"Humph." She grins. "Anyway. We may end up waiting four years at the rate things are going."

"Which means the sex'll likely be even hotter." She raises her eyebrows, waiting for me to elaborate. "In theory, the deeper you know each other, the better the physical stuff. That's why people get weird when they run into a one-night stand on the streets—too much intimacy too soon means too awkward." Shalini and I had a long talk about this.

We reach Independence Park and settle into the swings. "So where does Oliver stand amid all this great advice?" Kate says.

"Good question. I thought we were really close, but apparently . . ." We start swinging high.

"Do you regret having sex with him?" Kate asks carefully.

"I'm not sure I . . . *believe* in regret. As in, what's the point? The deed is done and over with. . . ."

"Right. Dumb question. Regret is stupid."

I stretch my legs out and lean back into the pendulum motion, feeling both heavy and free. I think of the earnestness in Oliver's eyes our very first time, the comfort and laughter between us, the intensity of feeling that being with him awoke in me. . . . "I wouldn't trade the experience of being so deep in love, our connection like this . . . comet. But if I knew then what I know now? If I'd known that things were going to detonate, crash, and burn—"

"But you couldn't have known."

"There were enough signs. . . ." My legs have stopped pumping.

"Most of those signs revealed themselves after you had already done it. . . . Hey." She stops her swing. "This isn't your fault, Rani. You took a risk. And sometimes shit happens."

"Aaji said going through shit actually makes life more complex and rich, and that we shouldn't spend our lives avoiding it. Something about being burned, spices in masala . . . ?"

"Ah. So shit inspires a fuller, more vibrant life."

"Who knew shit could be inspirational?" My swing now slack, I yank off a wispy branch from a nearby bush and begin decimating its leaves. "Still, it's a mindfuck when the person you love screws you over."

"Totally. We *expect* humanity. Bonnie struggled over my

dad—but look at her now. And Henry . . . did you know that his mom was in a huge car accident when he was in fifth grade?"

"That's awful." I stare at my chipped toenails peeking through my sandals. "I always wondered about his mom."

"Yeah. She had extensive injuries, and was on doctor-prescribed painkillers that eventually led to addiction. She's been in and out of rehab ever since, which is why Henry lives here with his grandma."

"Oh my God. Poor Henry."

"And it sounds like she was a really great mom before the accident, you know? So maybe sometimes a person's struggles overpower everything, no matter how great things once were. The pain can be so . . . *gaping*, so dark, that it, like, eclipses the love?"

I'm silent. An undercurrent of jet lag and sadness tugs at my lids, threatening to pull me under.

She sighs. "Oliver clearly went through some shit, but attacking you and your family was just . . ."

"Aggro."

"Selfish."

"Gaslight-y."

We high-five, smiling. "Wish you'd been there that night," I say.

"Me too. But neither one of us could have taught him—or saved him." She gets up from the swing and holds out her hand. "He's going to have to save himself."

When we reach my house, we promise to meet up again before she leaves for school on Sunday. With a knot in my stomach, I watch her drive away.

Like Oliver, I will have to save myself.

EPILOGUE

NINE MONTHS LATER

"Arre! Do they feed you at all at that college? You are bones only." These are Ma's first words to me when she meets me at the train station, despite the fact that I see her all the time. "Come. I'll take you to your event," she says. "And afterward, home for some real food. Your friends from school are joining later tonight, yes?"

"Yes," I say, maneuvering my bulky portfolio into the car and ducking in after it.

She chatters about Shalini's upcoming August wedding to Ronak, and I show her WhatsApp photos of top-contender wedding saris and the jewelry pieces Shalini's designing. As we drive, Ma tells me about a new family at Apna Ghar ("Our House"), the domestic violence shelter for South Asian women and children where she's been volunteering. She then updates me on Baba's search for a hobby. ("He read some silly article about the empty nest and decided that he will now fill his time with bonsai. Expensive, these tiny baby trees! Clipping, watering . . . talking to them, even. Such madness!")

We pull into the Lighthouse Beach lot, and the Harley Clarke Mansion comes into view, majestic and laced with ivy. It's the new venue of Kindness and Nonviolent Action, an Evanston initiative where people of all ages and backgrounds come together to celebrate the power of art, social justice, and inclusivity.

"Rani," my mother says, throwing the car into park, "I'm proud of you. Being part of this event is an honor, I understand, in the arts world—and such an important cause. It is lovely to see how your photography work has paid off." She smiles, and I get a glimpse of the dynamic young woman she actually still is: strong, independent, and unwilling to settle. I want to tell her that her grit and service-mindedness inspired me to apply as one of the youth artists. But all I squeak out is: "Thanks, Ma."

She gives me a fierce hug. "Do you need me to come into the gallery with you, or can I go get Baba while you set up?" Her hair is shiny and her face glows. Empty-nesting suits her, apparently.

"No, go. I'll see you inside. And oh, so I don't forget." I pull out the silvery blue poncho I knit for Aaji, the result of a meditative practice I've started doing between studying. "Can you include this the next time you send Aaji's meds, so she'll have it for the monsoon?"

She nods, her eyes suddenly moist. "Aaji will love it. Now go."

———

Six o'clock approaches. My photo series, *Dawning*, hangs in the mansion's octagonal gallery, overlooking the lake. As a student blues band warms up on the far side of the room, I scan my exhibit: iridescent bokeh dots of the city skyline; images of my roommate, Cara, overlaid with geometric shapes made from patterned paper; and detailed black-and-whites of Shalini. My eyes settle on the lone photo of Oliver: a sepia image of his profile, his single eye singed by a burning match. This burn technique I learned from a friend at U of C's photography club—the most cathartic technique that ever existed. Satisfied with the installation, I slip into the restroom to check myself in the mirror.

I'm in a sari blouse covered in kantha embroidery, a cropped blazer, and a sleek, high-waisted skirt. Tied at my throat is a brick-red dupatta, and I have loads of black bangles up my arms. Kate visited me at school last week and helped me choose tonight's color-season-theory-based outfit, knowing she'd be on a Habitat trip to Nevada with Henry at the time of the opening. "Dang, girl," she said, fingering the top's embroidery. "Way to rock your own aesthetic." The truth is, I've had lots of role models, from Veena Auntie to Shalini to late night talk show host Lilly Singh to my college roommate, Cara, a Korean American who somehow weaves together her love for K-pop with her gaucho-pants-over-Victorian-booties look. A tiny diamond from Lalita Mami—who said my nose piercing gave my face "dignity"—twinkles on the side of my face like a star. My hair is wild and wavy, and my eyes are lined with the sparkly gray kohl that's now my signature. Today there's a brightness to my skin and a shine in my eyes. Getting into this show was no fluke—and I know it.

I step out just in time to see my parents striding toward

me, arms outstretched. Baba gives me two thumbs up as he approaches, and I give them both tight hugs.

"So lovely in here," Ma breathes. "All these years and have we ever come to this prestigious gallery, Alok?"

"No. We are fools." Baba grins, planting a quick kiss on my cheek. "All this time we could have been giving our Rani a window into the world of art, but we are engineers and scientists by training, betiya. Forgive us."

I laugh. "You're forgiven. I'm a scientist in training, too. I get it."

"Betiya, before the show opens . . ." My mother presses a set of keys into my hand. "Yours."

Stunned, I study the them—house and car keys on a keychain with a tiny plexiglass-framed image of the famous photographer Annie Leibovitz. Its caption reads: "A thing that you see in my pictures is that I was not afraid to fall in love with these people."

I smile. "'Fall in love,' huh, Ma?"

"I thought you'd appreciate such a quote," she says briskly. "Baba and I will walk home; you come with the car when you're ready." Baba winks at me, and the two turn toward the photos in my installation, their faces open, curious.

People filter in—people of all ages, and from all walks of life—grabbing food and even dancing to the music. I stand relaxed, smiling like Mona Lisa. It's not the time to creep behind a camera. It's time to be part of this collective, and be proud.

First come Veena Auntie and Salil, who seems to have grown a foot since I last saw him. Squarely a tween and unable to make direct eye contact, he mumbles that he's taking

343

the Red Cross babysitting course so he can start babysitting this summer. "Way to be legit," I say, high-fiving him, and he grins, his teeth now covered in braces.

Young kids and their parents or grandparents arrive, along with Frances Willard and Northwestern kids. They all peer at the installations with genuine interest, looking at my photos and flashing me bright smiles before wandering over to the community crafting table.

A few auntie-uncles trickle in, and I give them my best bear hugs—I admit it's pretty cool to have family friends who show up, comfortable in their skin (i.e., as loud as ever), still saying things like "Wonderful that you're continuing this sweet hobby, betiya, good for you! But still planning on medicine, na?"

And then . . . a suggestion of color, a bit of bowed light. Like a print submerged, the subject takes form, emerging into slow, unmistakable focus. The moment he appears with crystal clarity, a wrecking ball slams into my chest.

Oliver.

A woman and her teenage daughter stand before me, asking how I choose my subjects and what kind of camera I use. I attempt to focus, lacing my suddenly trembling fingers together before me.

"She used to love taking pictures," the woman's saying. I glimpse Oliver making his way over from the other side of the gallery, stopping at installations. "But she's dropped that old pastime." We lock eyes as an electrical surge powers through me.

"I'm always telling her, 'Honey, get your camera and just snap whatever tickles you.'"

He's wearing a gray beret and a suit vest with jeans—strange new accessories. Did he shop for those things himself?

The woman places a confessional hand on my arm. "Ever since she was in a car accident, she's been—between you and me—depressed."

"Mom!"

"What, honey?" The woman turns to her daughter. "There's no shame in being in a car wreck, for goodness' sakes."

"Sorry," the teen says to me, her face burning in a way I recognize. "Like you want to know all that."

"No, no, it's okay. Photography kind of, well—saved me." My words tumble forth in a low, breathy rush. "I went through some stuff last year, and the art helped me work through the . . . pain." I flick a look at Oliver, now at the next installation over, peering at a canvas thick with impasto.

"Oh, I'm sorry to hear that, dear," the mother says to me before addressing her daughter. "See, honey? Even this young lady has had her share of troubles, and photography, she says . . ."

I manage to slip the girl my card, telling her to contact me if she ever has questions, as the room does a seasick dip; the mother-daughter duo floats away, leaving me, unbelievably, face to face with the single person who has dominated my thoughts for almost two years.

"Hey," he says softly.

"Hi." I inhale slowly, breathing in his new patchouli scent. I blink. Here he is, centered in my frame, edges blurred.

He clears his throat. "So I know it looks like I'm stalking you . . ."

I try to smile, though it feels more like a grimace.

"But I do follow what's happening in local galleries, and

you really deserve this," he says, gesturing toward my photographs. His eyes land on the sepia-toned profile of himself, the one visible eye carefully, artfully burned through with a match. "What? It appears I am famous." He leans down to examine the piece, then glances up with an unreadable expression. "Love how you used this technique."

"Thanks," I say simply, my cheeks on fire.

"I'm back in town for the summer," he says, looking straight into my eyes. My heart leaps in response—muscle memory, maybe?

"Hmm. How was your first year?" I swipe at my forehead with my sleeve. Someone a few exhibits over squeals; two women embrace as though they haven't seen each other in a century.

"Amazing. I love it there."

I feel a pang; he loves a place that doesn't include me.

"And how's your sister?" I ask, recovering. "Her baby must be almost a year old now." My voice is tinny in my ears.

"Yeah. Nadine. That kid's a handful. But also awesome." He shifts, sticks a hand in his pocket. "Hey, um. Want to maybe meet me after—for coffee?"

It'd be easy to forgive and forget, to slip and ride his wave. I take a deep, cleansing Spirit of Life breath.

"I can't."

His jaw clenches. "Uh . . . okay."

"I'm—good now, Oliver," I say.

"I wanted to say I'm sorry."

"I'm sorry, too." I step to the side, opening a space for some gallerygoers to get through, only to see with a start that it's a group of my college friends, waiting to greet me.

"I still—" he starts.

"We tried and couldn't make it work," I say breathlessly. "And now there's been all this time and too much has happened." I swallow hard.

"Can we please just talk in private somewhere?" He glances around before looking at me, pleading. "I promise I won't flip out."

I feel a gathering energy, knowing my friends are here. I'm still sweating, but I almost smile as I see Ethan and Aditya making faces and bunny ears behind Oliver's head.

"I'm different now," I say.

"Please. We need to talk." He takes a step closer to me.

"My friends are coming to my parents' place for dinner after the show." Despite everything, there's the old instinct to move closer. *What even?*

"So how about tomorrow?"

I think about tomorrow, how it's pitched toward three open months of sultry summer nights . . . and the sense of powerlessness that comes with being with Oliver. "Um . . ."

"Look, just think about it. I'll be out back, right after the show." He gestures toward the eastern windows of the gallery. "Our old meeting spot."

"Ra-Ra!" Jaiden steps between Oliver and me. He's dark-skinned and handsome and over six feet tall; everyone is entranced by him, especially women. He bends over and hugs me hard, lifting me off the ground. "You art goddess! Marry me!"

I laugh in spite of myself. When he sets me down, Cara steps in, hissing in my ear: "What. Is. Happening . . . ?"

Cara and I have spent countless hours discussing Oliver. Every quality, every remark and action has come under scrutiny amid the low-grade depression I suffered in the aftermath of everything. The grieving, the crushing guilt, the darkness, the weight like a heavy blanket you have no will to move out from under, Lewis Capaldi's "Someone You Loved" playing on repeat . . . Cara eventually took me to a university counselor, Mrs. Behl, who over several months helped me process Aajoba's death, Oliver, even Nilesh. . . . She taught me tools to temper and release the pain, like placing consuming thoughts in a mental box before setting it to "sail" upon Lake Michigan. Exercises I once would have found hokey, but now . . .

I give her a crumpled smile. She hands me her water bottle, then turns to Oliver, her glossy black hair swinging. "I'm Cara."

"Hey, how ya doin'? Oliver," he says, grasping her hand.

I chug Cara's water, then hear myself making introductions, while murmurs of 'Hey' and ' 'Sup man?' come from these new dear friends of mine who intuitively know how to show that I'm rocking my life without him.

"We're so proud of our girl," Jaiden says, giving me a sideways hug. The others draw in close, a united front. Oliver holds his beret in his hands; his hair is shorn close along his neck and above his ears, a long flop of it slicked straight back on top. The angles and planes of him are sharper than I remember. He looks good. He glances across the room, but it seems to be at nothing.

"Um," he says as the band's young saxophonist bursts into a solo. "So maybe I'll see you out back after?" I hesitate. "Just think about it," he says, his eyes flat.

I nod, and he half waves to my friends, heading straight for the door.

Several new people have gathered at my exhibit, some glancing around expectantly, seeking the artist. I turn to my friends, hold my arms open for a group hug: "You guys . . ." I'm suddenly choked up.

"We'll wait for you on the beach," says Laina, tugging on a lock of my hair. "And then a Bollywood film at your house tonight, Uma's choice," she says, winking. Inspired by Cara's childhood love for K-dramas, my new friends are obsessed with Bollywood, and to Ma's huge surprise, I've become a quiet convert: the films remind me of my family and India— a delectable comfort stew. "You know you don't have to meet him," she murmurs, touching my cheekbone with her fist.

I step over to my exhibit and smile, introducing my-self to the newcomers. Above their shoulders and through the leaded glass, I glimpse a shadowed figure slipping away toward the beach, out of sight.

A woman with crinkly blue eyes and curly hair leans in. "What inspires you?"

———

I clear some empty cups and plates off the side table in my corner of the gallery before making my way toward Ashwini, the curator and organizer.

"Very thought-provoking pieces you've created there," she says, covering cheese and crackers with foil. "I got a lot of inquiries into *Dawnings*, Rani. You should be proud." She smiles kindly. "I know you're busy being premed, but I hope you submit work for our next gathering."

"I will," I tell her. "Thanks so much, Ashwini."

My heart pounds as I make my way around back along the stone path. I pass the lighthouse and waterfall pond, and now have the full view of the grassy yard behind the Harley Clarke Mansion—our old meeting place. Why did I accept meeting here in this den of infinite memories? I scan the secluded park, wondering if he'll stand me up. . . .

But there he is.

Sitting and facing the lake, his arm outstretched along the back of the bench, he waits. I twist my rings; suddenly, I'm not sure I should do this. A text comes in. Cara.

OMFG! Who invited him??
Are you gonna meet him?

Yes

Ok. Want me to lurk/attack O if necessary?

Plz no

Btw our golden retrievers want to play on the beach. Come here when you're done?

I smile. We call our guy friends "our golden retrievers" because they're unreasonably happy and always want to play.

I lean up against a massive tree trunk and text back:

350

She writes:

You do. But NO REMINISCING, FFS

I close my eyes and breathe in the scent of lilac and freshly cut grass. Summer will soon be in full force. I observe Oliver sitting at the end of the bench, taking in the scenery. A watch on his arm glints in the low light—it's new, too. I inhale deeply and stride across the grassy yard enclosed by a small forest of gigantic trees.

As I approach, he turns, and I watch his features remake themselves in recognition and relief.

"Hey. Rani." He shifts. "Thanks for meeting. Wasn't sure you'd be able to tear yourself away from that formidable posse of yours." He smiles, and my insides lurch.

"Yeah—they're pretty great," I say, recovering. "And also a tad . . . protective?"

"I can see that."

We stare at each other a moment, my heart racing. Maybe this was a bad idea.

The giant oaks sway, creaking softly.

"I'm sorry about your grandfather," he says.

A seagull cries in the distance. "Yeah. Thanks." We gaze out at the water, silence stretching between us. "I—um. How's your mom? And Kathy?"

"How much time do you have?" He sighs quietly. "Honestly, they're still kicking. Motherhood looks good on Kathy,

351

at least. She and the baby, Nadine, have this, like, spiritual connection."

"I can totally see her being a great mom."

"Yeah. Hey, speaking of great: excellent work in there. Ambitious stuff. Not that I'm surprised."

"Ambition: my superpower." I shrug, and he laughs. "What are *you* working on now?"

"Lately I've been mulling over the concept of memory," he says.

"Oh" is all I hear myself say.

"Yeah." He shifts, facing me. "So, memory is selective, right? Every person's remembrance, even of a shared experience, differs majorly." His hands move as he talks. "It's all based in perspective, a narrative we tell ourselves. Personal spin."

"Limitless subject, really." We're making small talk about art, as if things were normal.

"Indeed. I just started exploring the idea using decoupage."

"I love decoupage."

"Yeah. Not a far cry from that first art project we did together at Noyes, right?"

I smile but say nothing. No reminiscing . . .

"So," he says, "I've been tapping into my own memories. . . . I mean, our relationship alone could fuel me artistically for the rest of my life." He looks at me playfully, but I see a shadow in his eyes.

I hold his gaze but stay silent.

"I, for example, remember *everything* between us," he says. "Just as it was."

"So the rest of us remember with our own personal spin . . . but you, O Great One, remember . . . The Truth?"

He laughs, the rasp of his voice jogging my memories. "I really am an asshole that way." We watch the water, a million thoughts racing through my mind. "Do you still think about us?"

I keep my eyes on the distant horizon, unable to answer.

"Because I—well, I do. And—" He falters. "Maybe we could be—friends again? Spend a little time together."

I stare at his hand on the bench between us, remembering everything in a blinding flash, the feverish nights together. How our connection at one time felt rare and brilliant. How exalted and revered he could make me feel.

"Spend a little time together . . . ," I repeat.

"Yeah."

"You mean while you're in town for the summer?"

"Well, no. I mean, for however long . . . you want to."

"However long I want to," I echo. I pick up a stick and rub its pointed end into a patch of dirt where the grass is worn away.

"Rani. I'm sorry. I know I made some mistakes. I can't rewind time. But maybe we could get to know each other again. Our new and improved versions." He scoots close, his body facing mine. He reaches out as if to touch the side of my face but stops just short.

"You were great," I sigh, scratching deeper into the dirt with the point of my stick. "Sometimes."

He bursts out laughing. "Fair enough."

I smile. "And I appreciate that you never—rushed me. Or

made me feel like I had to—*do*—anything. Well, except that one time—"

He laughs again. This time, I don't smile.

"I liked—what we had. Before everything." I look him in the eye. "I loved you. Trusted you."

"You *know* we'd still be together if it weren't for your freaking parents," he says.

The wind whips now with ferocity, leaves rustling so loudly, I'm not sure I heard him right.

"You've actually never met my parents," I say carefully. "And what happened between us wasn't about them."

"Are you on crack? It had *everything* to do with your parents."

I toss the stick and take a long chug from Cara's water bottle. I remember this side of Oliver—his righteousness, the sudden indignation. How his mouth could curl into a sneer without warning.

I inhale. I know what to say. I've said it in the mirror countless times, alone in my dorm room. I've muttered it to myself those long walks through campus. I've drifted off to sleep, dreaming that one day, I'd have the chance to say these words to Oliver. The gulls caw louder, as though fighting to be heard over the crushing waves.

"When we first met, you had the power to make me feel—amazing," I say. "Like I was funny. Smart. Sexy. Like I had artistic vision and talent."

"You do. You are all of those things."

"You made me feel like what we had was an original. Like I was seen."

He holds my gaze.

I take another deep, ragged breath. "There was so much

354

about you that I loved. That drove me crazy. In the very best ways."

I watch the rims of his eyes moisten, shining in the moonlight.

I hesitate. "But my . . . Indianness, I guess you could call it—didn't define me like you wanted, and instead of taking cues from me, you'd force things in ways that felt appropriating. Fetishizing. Disrespectful."

"None of that's accurate, Rani."

"And when you didn't get what you needed, you'd disparage me, my family, even aspects of my culture, the one you supposedly wanted to be a part of."

"I never did understand why you were weird about your Indianness with me. And I was frustrated with the way you let your parents run your life."

His words hang in the air between us. "Oliver. There are things you'll never truly understand because as a white male, there are obstacles and realities you'll never have to face. And you didn't *want* to understand. I don't know if you ever acknowledged it, but the mural was an act of aggression, and a huge . . . betrayal."

"Look, I should've shown you the mural beforehand, but a part of me wanted to . . . get your attention. Maybe even hurt you for not letting me into your life. I know that's fucked up and you deserved better. We both deserved better."

I watch the distant water. If Kate were here, she'd call Oliver out on his male privilege, on the way he just took only partial responsibility for his transgressions. . . .

He moves closer. "Rani. Think about this."

I close my eyes. Each time he utters my name is a riot in

my heart. "We can't just pick up again, now that you're home and have some time on your hands."

"I just want to spend some time talking."

I swallow. "I've had to work hard to—get you out of my system." Going back to Oliver would undo everything I've fought so hard to regain. . . .

"Seriously," he says, "this would be a new and im-proved me."

"I want to feel empowered by love, not trapped by it," I say finally.

"That's what I want, too."

"But I don't think I can have that with you."

"Rani. Listen. Artists consult me all the time on issues of racial and feminist messaging in art. . . . I'm viewed as a *pro-gressive*, and you know that. We can make this work."

I'm silent.

"Please. I still love you," he says.

Something surges inside me, steadies me. I turn to him. "Love . . . doesn't belittle," I say carefully. "It's not supposed to make you feel broken, empty, addicted, and self-conscious. Or question your sense of self. We can't . . . *romanticize* the kind of love that essentially just hurts, Oliver. The kind that's gaslighting or objectifying, despite your best intentions." I stare into his strange, familiar eyes, and I'm startled to see a flash of surrender there.

I trace the moonstone of Shalini's ring, its silver bezel strong and smooth.

He sighs. "Rani, just tell me you'll think about it."

I nod.

"Um. Can I walk you back?" he asks.

"No, I'll stay here a minute. Thanks, though."

"Are you sure?"

"Yeah, really. My friends—they're right there," I say, gesturing to the beach. Dark silhouettes dance by the shoreline.

He smiles sadly. "You need a minute and I could use a decade." He squints out at the water. "I miss you."

My throat swells again, tears threatening. I will not get sucked into the deep, guilt-inducing, destructive dream of him. I glance away, not trusting my voice.

He stretches his leg out long, roots around in his pocket, and produces a rumpled square of paper. He hands it to me. "Here's my new number. I wrote it down since I figured your phone would probably be dead." I grin despite myself.

He looks straight into my eyes for full heart-stopping impact. "I want you to know you—you were everything to me," he says.

And then he's on his feet, striding toward the parking lot. I consider calling out to him, but instead, I'm silent and still as a statue amid the creaking trees and whipping wind. A car starts, then purrs through the lot, away toward Sheridan.

He's gone.

I shake, recovering from being close to him, his scent, his skin. His voice, deep and resonant, telling me the very thing I questioned all year: *You were everything to me.*

We spun our dreams through the trick of the lens, seeking refuge in each other as need and greed took us out. *I can't get close enough.* Longing and obsession composed the dark portrait of our complicated fantasy, yet for a while, it felt like sustenance.

Oliver.

Despite this fresh pain, there's a jagged light of clarity: Oliver encouraged my art. Art that connected me to Aajoba, to India. Art that led my parents and community to see that academics isn't everything. Art that helped me process sorrow, embrace a new identity, a new life . . .

I'd sought freedom in Oliver, but stumbled instead into a series of traps—some that maybe I unwittingly set myself.

I know the kind of love that feels like freedom exists. I've seen it between Aaji and Aajoba, between Kate and Henry. It glows in my own parents' bond. It's there between Cara and her hometown girlfriend, Tonya, whose eyes shine with such joy when they're together that it almost hurts to see.

Maybe the kind of love that's fused with pain is compatible with our biology, making us resilient. Maybe loving someone deeply—even if it leaves you to bleed—inoculates and strengthens you, so that when you stumble upon great love, you'll recognize it. And hold it close.

I'm sorry, Oliver.

With Oliver's scrap in my hand, I drift to the edge of the grassy lookout.

Breathless, I gaze south at Chicago's lights twinkling on the night water as waves pound the breakwater one by one. *It's all right . . . it's all right*, they murmur in their rhythms. Welled-up tears slide down my cheeks, the trees and the violet starry sky my silent witnesses.

I loved and was loved deeply. I was once someone's everything, and that's something.

I stare at the scrap covered in Oliver's unmistakable scrawl. Deliberately, I fold it in half, then in half again, lining up the edges the way Aajoba taught me years ago when we sent dozens of white paper boats sailing into the flooding monsoon streets. As Oliver's number disappears inside the crisp folds of this tiny new boat, a text dings in.

WHERE ARE YOU? GET YOUR ASS DOWN HERE OR WE WILL STORM YOU GUYS IN AN UTTERLY EMBARRASSING FASHION THAT YOU WILL BOTH ETERNALLY REGRET.

I laugh, flicking away a tear. Cara loves all caps. I tap a text back.

I'M COMING FFS

And then I see it—a grassy, overgrown trail at the base of the stone steps, snaking out to the open shoreline. How had I never noticed it before? I slip down the steps and follow it through the dunes and out to the wide beach before hopping onto the breakwater's rusty plank. A few strides down and I find myself gazing into the dark swirl of Lake Michigan, crouched low. Arm outstretched, I set my tiny paper boat out to sail, and watch it get swept by the current toward the endless inky horizon, diving in the distance like a friendly dolphin, a mermaid . . .

Goodbye, Oliver. . . .

And then my legs know what to do, striding down the plank toward the shore, dropping to land and picking up speed as I cross the wide, sandy beach, toward my friends who are there, running, laughing, calling my name.

AUTHOR'S NOTE

When we reject the single story, when we realize
that there is never a single story about any place,
we regain a kind of paradise.

—CHIMAMANDA NGOZI ADICHIE

Once, while visiting from India, my grandmother knit me a patchwork blanket. Amid the heat of summer and by the breeze of a fan, she told family stories, producing one woolly patch after another. I learned that the summer my grandfather was stationed in Aurangabad, India, the family moved into what ended up being an honest-to-goodness haunted house, complete with doors slamming out of nowhere and the mysterious wailing of babies at night. I learned about the fluffy white dog my mother once doted on, and how she always shared her dessert with her little brother after he'd gobbled his up first. As colorful stories trickled forth about various relatives, intricate stitch patterns fell off my grandmother's needles like magic. While she grafted the swatches together, I couldn't help but think that these family stories, set oceans away, held a secret message: they revealed a history that, until then, had been loose, disconnected, hazy.

I thought a lot about that blanket as I wrote this story,

and the ways love, family, friendship, and culture are woven through us—along with the betrayals we endure. I hoped to show how our struggle to hold on to ourselves in the face of others' ideals can lead to a special kind of empowerment—once we discover what "ourselves" really means.

Though no scene in this fictional work mirrors true-life events, its themes are ones I closely relate to. Born and raised in the suburbs of Chicago, and despite living amid many kind and thoughtful people, I still found myself confronting microaggressions, stereotyping, and a lurking sense of invisibility as a brown girl in America. Writing this book helped me see the ways we shield our culture from jeers and sneers, resist dehumanizing cultural and gender-based stereotypes, and protect our traditions from being plundered for their cool, steal-worthy aspects—sometimes all in the same week. I wrote this story to help me better understand this widespread, exhausting, messy phenomenon—and how we might rise above it.

Through my process of research and writing, I learned the ways our identities are shaped by sexuality, race, and cultural expectations. I became intrigued by the duality of growing up across cultures, and how longing for acceptance might impact our best judgment when it comes to love. And as I wrote, my mind was with you, my readers, who may know a thing or two firsthand about Rani's world; I hoped this story would help you feel both seen and understood.

And for those readers who haven't experienced the kind of discrimination Rani does, I hope this story inspires you to speak out in solidarity with those struggling to be accepted and valued, as Kate does for Rani, or the way Tonio and Rani try to do for one another. I hope it sparks conversations about the fact that racism and stereotyping occur in places we might expect, but also, surprisingly and painfully, from sources we don't—like our closest friendships and relationships. I hope it serves as a reminder that when someone you love hurts you (maybe even unintentionally, or because they are in pain themselves), the world is filled with people who do listen, who respect boundaries—cultural or otherwise—and who love back with the dignity and humanity each one of us deserves.

American Betiya is about family, friendship, and firsts. It's about freedom and traditions, cultural awareness and cultural carelessness, artistic expression and betrayal. It's about loving and living, losing and finding. And about rediscovering our stories, our songs, ourselves.

I still have that patchwork blanket my grandmother knit for me all those years ago, and now that she's gone, I cherish it more than ever. Every knitted patch varies in color and texture, woven tight with the truths of my heritage and lending me strength when I need it. I wish you the discovery of your own truths as you speak up and speak out, the patchwork of who you choose to be, keeping you warm along the way.

With love,
Anuradha

ACKNOWLEDGMENTS

"Thank you" does not begin to express what I feel for all the dedicated people who helped make *American Betiya* a reality. First and foremost, I'd like to thank my editor, Katherine Harrison, who was so attuned to what I needed to say with this story, and whose wise and thoughtful suggestions revealed a deep sensitivity toward my culture and issues of racial identity. Thank you, Katherine, for instinctively knowing all the insightful ways to bring out this story's shine. It's an absolute privilege working with you.

I so appreciate SCBWI for those early days of encouragement and education and, years later, for honoring *American Betiya* with the nationwide Emerging Voices Award. Thanks to Martin and Sue Schmitt for helping realize the dreams of writers from diverse backgrounds, and to the talented Kim Turrisi, who guided me as I made my choice to sign with my wonderful agent, Alex Slater. Thank you, Alex, for always encouraging me to write into the heart of my truths and obsessions, and for your passion and advocacy for my work. I am so grateful to you.

Many thanks to the incredibly gifted team at Alfred A. Knopf, Penguin Random House, including Gianna Lakenauth, Artie Bennett, Alison Kolani, Renée Cafiero, Amy Schroeder,

Nancee Adams, Joy Simpkins, Jake Eldred, Larsson McSwain, Angela Carlino, Orli Moscowitz, Louis Milgrom, Kristopher Kam, and my entire marketing and publicity team. I am grateful for your tireless dedication to the making of this book, and honored to have gotten to work with such brilliant people.

My heartfelt thanks go to my rock-star writing group, Lauren Fox, Liam Callanan, Jon Olson, Christina Clancy, and Aims McGuinness, and my kick-ass critique partner, Liza Wiemer, for workshopping this story with so much care and believing in me even when I didn't. Thanks also to Elana K. Arnold, Padma Venkatraman, Akemi Dawn Bowman, Kathleen Glasgow, Gae Polisner, Nandini Bajpai, Namrata Tripathi, Hal DeLong, and Preeti Chhibber for their early reads, encouragement, and astute feedback.

Thank you to Saqiba Suleman, whose breathtaking art on my cover is a true honor.

My appreciation goes to Jill Schnaiberg, Erin Loughlin, Rachel Baum, Svapna Sabnis, Bela Roongta, Laj Waghray, Nirmal Raja, Cheryl Sawdy, Madhavi Morankar, my 21ders debut family, class of 2k21 books, the Desi KidLit community, and #TeamSlater for their support throughout this journey.

Immense thanks to Daniel Goldin and the rest of the phenomenal staff at Boswell Books, along with all bookshops, librarians, booksellers, and book bloggers, for their enthusiasm in promoting authors and the celebration of stories. Thanks also to my students and friends at Lake Bluff School for cheering me on, and to all teachers everywhere, who, with joy and creativity, magically turn little people into lifelong readers. And speaking of magic, I'd like to send out sincere thanks to *my* readers; I'm so thrilled that this story made its way to you.

To Aaron Mack for giving me permission to base Saul's epic film on your and Brian Craft's genius creation, *Sex for Your Soul*, a film that obviously left its indelible mark on *my* soul. Thank you for the inspiration.

And to my parents, Neela and Sudhakar, with love and admiration: thank you for the many ways you teach and inspire me. Thanks to my sister, Anjali, for her endless support, and my superhero brother-in-law, Chad, for his web skills and for knowing just when to remind me that this book won't write itself. Thanks also to Ma and Pa, Suneela, Mihir, Daven, Ashwin, Naveen, Riaan, and the Chandvadkar, Deshmukh, Rajurkar, and Natu families for their love.

Deep appreciation to Ajay and Avi, for the joy you bring. Watching you become the generous, thoughtful people that you are has been one of the greatest gifts of my life. I love you.

And finally, my profound gratitude goes to Piyush, for raising this book baby with me. Your love is at the heart of it all.